Somebody to Love

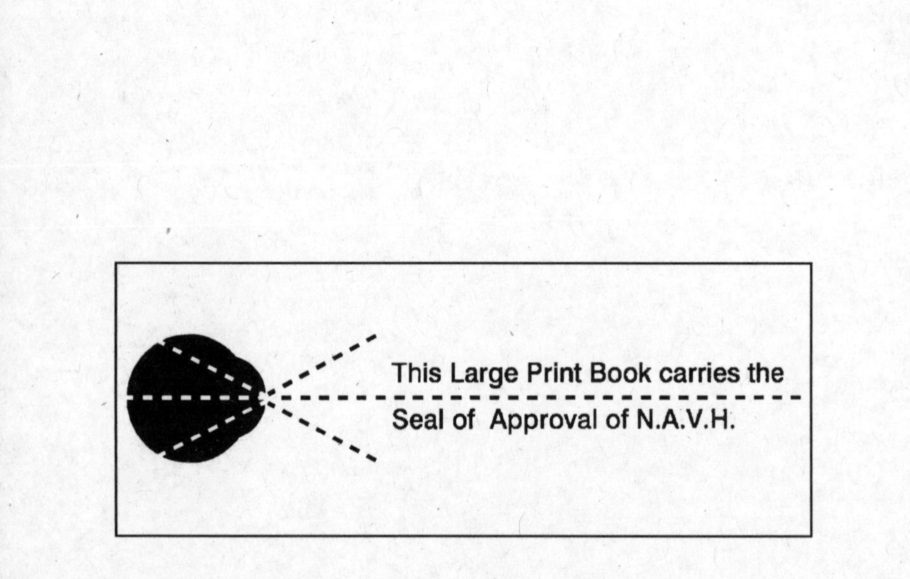
This Large Print Book carries the
Seal of Approval of N.A.V.H.

Somebody to Love

Lori Wilde

THORNDIKE PRESS
A part of Gale, Cengage Learning

Detroit • New York • San Francisco • New Haven, Conn • Waterville, Maine • London

GALE
CENGAGE Learning

Thorndike Press® Large Print Romance.
The text of this Large Print edition is unabridged.
Other aspects of the book may vary from the original edition.
Set in 16 pt. Plantin.

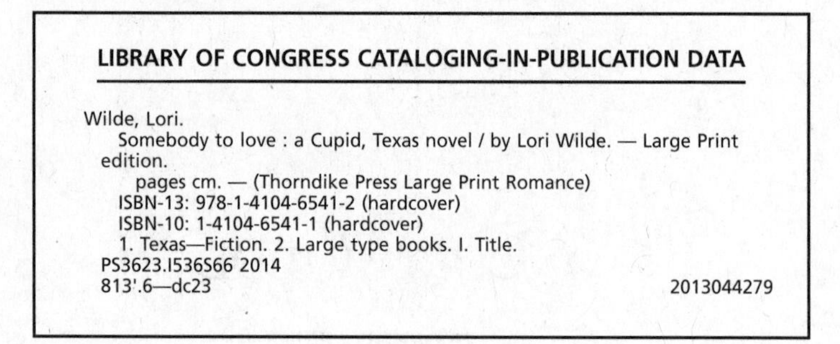
LIBRARY OF CONGRESS CATALOGING-IN-PUBLICATION DATA

Wilde, Lori.
Somebody to love : a Cupid, Texas novel / by Lori Wilde. — Large Print edition.
pages cm. — (Thorndike Press Large Print Romance)
ISBN-13: 978-1-4104-6541-2 (hardcover)
ISBN-10: 1-4104-6541-1 (hardcover)
1. Texas—Fiction. 2. Large type books. I. Title.
PS3623.I536S66 2014
813'.6—dc23 2013044279

Published in 2014 by arrangement with Avon Books, an imprint of HarperCollins Publishers

Printed in the United States of America
1 2 3 4 5 6 7 18 17 16 15 14

To Gayle and Ron Harris, owners of Books and Crannies in Terrell, the best little bookstore in Texas! Your warmth and hospitality made me feel right at home. You two are an unsung treasure, and your own romance is the stuff of legends.

Prologue

Archaeology: The scientific study of
material evidence to find out about
human cultures of the past.

Dear Cupid,

I've gone and ruined everything by falling in love with my best friend. Now, not only have I lost my lover, I've lost the one person in the world that I could tell anything to. But that's not the half of it. I thought I was doing a good thing by searching for something meaningful. People accused me of being frivolous and shallow, so I was determined to earn a little respect, prove I could commit, dig deep, find my roots, and discover who and what I am. Guess what? I did and that's what started all the trouble. The things I have uncovered could destroy people I love. I'm at my wits' end. I don't know how much longer I can hang on. Help!

Spontaneous to a Fault

Zoey McCleary quivered atop Widow's Peak on private land, directly across from Mount Livermore, the very spot where her parents had died more than twenty years earlier in an airplane crash that had also severely wounded her older sister, Natalie, while she had come out of the accident without a scrape.

Not so lucky now, huh, McCleary. Looks like you've used up the last of your nine lives.

In her hand she crushed the crumpled letter she'd written to Cupid the previous evening. Last night, she thought she'd smacked rock bottom. Now she fully understood how much farther she had to fall.

She stared down the sixty-five hundred feet to the town of Cupid, Texas, nestled in the cradle of the Davis Mountains. It was the only home she'd ever known. The town had been named after an impressive seven-foot stalagmite found in the local caverns that bore an uncanny resemblance to the Roman god of love. Local legend had it that if you wrote a letter, begging for divine intervention, Cupid would grant your wish. Her family on the Greenwood-Fant side was steeped neck deep in the lore, the lot of them avid beseechers of Cupid's goodwill.

It was total romantic bullshit and she knew it. Writing that letter spoke to precisely how desperate she was. Forgone conclusion — when a girl turned to a mythological cherub for Hail Mary help, she was seriously screwed.

However, it was the other side of the family that had driven her up the mountain, McClearys and their dark, ancestral secret.

Her pulse beat a hot stampede across her eardrums; she was exposed and vulnerable, stiff with fear, tension strained muscles, sweat slicked skin, nicks and scratches oozed blood, lungs flapped with the excruciating pain of trying to draw in air after a dead run up the mountain.

Heat from the setting summer sun warmed her cheeks. Desert wind whipped through the Davis Mountains, blowing sandy topsoil over her face. She licked her dry lips, tasted grit. On three sides of her yawned sheer drop-off. Overhead, a dozen buzzards circled.

Waiting.

Something tickled her cheek, feather-soft and startling as the sweet sensation of an unexpected midnight kiss. She gasped and brushed at her face, her work-roughened fingertips scratching her skin, and for one crazy moment she thought, *Jericho.*

But of course it wasn't Jericho. It was merely the caress of a passing cloud. Her impulsiveness had driven her here before she'd had a chance to tell him she loved him as more than just a friend, and now she would never have that chance.

She put her palm to her lips, kissed it, whispered, "Jericho," and blew the kiss into the gathering mist. "I'll love you throughout all eternity."

From behind her, she heard her pursuers crashing through the aspen and madrone trees, cursing black ugly threats. They were coming for her. This was it, the end of the trail, the end of the world, the end of *her,* and nowhere left to go but down.

The thundering footsteps were nearer now, closing in. Soon, her trackers would emerge from the forest and join her on the skinned, igneous peak.

Her heart took flight, faster than a hummingbird and thudding with jumpy brutality. Panic shuddered her bones. She could not stop trembling no matter how hard she willed it.

Teeth chattered. Knees wobbled. Nostrils flared.

Don't just stand there. Do something! Do something!

But what?

There was only one solution, only one clear way out.

Zoey gathered her courage, took her last deep breath, and jumped.

Chapter 1

Flake: To remove a stone fragment
from a core or tool.

Six weeks earlier . . .

The mewling was so soft that Zoey almost didn't hear it. She had just slung her backpack onto the passenger seat of the Cupid's Rest Bed-and-Breakfast van parked in the student lot at Sul Ross University, anthropology and archaeology textbooks spilling out, and stuck the keys into the ignition when something caused her to stop, cock her head, and listen.

"Mew."

Faint. Helpless.

She plastered a shaky hand to her chest. Holy freak-out. Was there a kitty hiding inside the engine? If she had started the van . . . Zoey gulped against that grisly scenario, popped the hood latch, unbuckled her seat belt, and got out. Raising the hood, she peered into the engine. No cat. That was good, right?

"Mew."

She muscled closer, angling her neck to get a good look at nooks and crannies hidden amid hoses and gears and whatnot. "C'mon little sucker, where are you?"

"Mew."

Hmm. Sounded like it could be coming from underneath the van. Zoey bent over to take a look, her brown-sugar colored ponytail flopping down over her head and brushing the ground. She spied a tiny kitten with bluish-white body fur and a slate gray face, curled up tight against the back tire. A blue-point Siamese.

"Ooh, look at you, pretty baby. Where did you come from, little guy? Or gal, whatevs."

The kitten narrowed its eyes as if to say, *I'll never tell the likes of you my secrets.*

"Kitty, kitty, kitty." She moved to the rear of the van, crouched down, and rubbed her fingertips together as if she had a tasty treat she was willing to share. "You gotta come out from under there so I can go home."

The trembling Siamese boldly met her stare. It might be scared, but it was scrappy. Gently, she moved to close her hand around the kitten, but it sprinted to the back tire on the opposite side of the van.

She tracked around to the other side and got down on her hands and knees. "Hey there. Still me. I didn't go anywhere. Here's the deal, I can't go anywhere and risk squashing you, so it would really benefit us both if you'd let me help you."

The kitten darted back to the other tire.

"Not buying it, huh?" She sighed, got up, and returned to the other side. This time, she lay on her belly against the warm asphalt and walked two fingers toward the woebegone creature. "Look, I get that you're all stealth ninja kitty and everything, kudos on the mad sprinting skills by the way, but I gotta go."

"Rrrowww." Fur bristling, the kitten arched its back, sent her a get-the-hell-away-from-me-*bee*otch-or-you'll-be-sorry-you-didn't-make-out-your-will hiss and swatted a warning paw.

"Seriously, I can't be late again for the luncheon meeting of volunteers who answer the lonely hearts letters written to Cupid. I'm already skating the razor's edge with that bunch over my habitual tardiness and yes, while it is sorta hypocritical of me to give advice to the brokenhearted when I myself have never actually been in love, somebody's got to answer those letters and you don't look as if you've got a mind to do it for me. And even if you were willing, there's the whole no opposable thumbs issue. Sorry if that hurts your feelings, just stating the facts."

The kitten's fur settled back into place and he or she canted its head as if trying to figure what she was yammering about. It was so darned cute and the talking did seem to help.

"If I'm not really qualified to answer the letters and I can't seem to show up on time, why don't I just quit? Good question, Egbert. You don't mind if I call you Egbert, do you? Unless it's Egbertlina. Is it Egbertlina? I can't really tell from here if you're a boy or a girl, but to answer your question, it's this whole family obligation thing. We — just to clarify, that's me and my sister, Natalie — are descended from Millie Greenwood, the woman who started this whole letter-writing mess when she wrote a letter to Cupid asking him to help her snare her true love, John Fant and it worked stupendously. He dumped Elizabeth Nielson at the altar for Millie, who was just a poor housemaid. It's all terribly romantic."

Her sister, Natalie was enamored of that legend, but to Zoey, it was all a bunch of blah, blah about long-dead people. Then again, if she were being honest, jealousy could have something to do with her lack of interest. Unlike her sister, *she* wasn't the oldest daughter of the oldest daughter of the oldest daughter of Millie Greenwood. She had no real stake in keeping the fairy tale alive.

As she spoke, Zoey slowly inched her hand closer to the Siamese.

The kitten's hair flared again.

Zoey backed off.

She fumbled in the pocket of her blue jean shorts for her cell phone, and flicked it on to check the time. Twenty minutes to twelve. No way was she going to make it to the meeting on time, especially since she still had to drive the thirty miles from Alpine to Cupid.

Every Monday, Wednesday, and Friday from noon to one-thirty, the volunteers met to answer letters from the lovelorn written to Cupid. The letter-writing tradition had started in the 1930s after the Depression hit and the town had a desperate need of extra income and did anything they could to encourage tourism. Grandmother Rose had spearheaded the campaign, gathering some of the local women to answer the overwhelming number of letters that people left at the base of the Cupid stalagmite inside the Cupid Caverns. At first, the replies to the letters were left on a bulletin board posted outside the caverns, but that became unwieldy, and in the 1940s someone had the idea of doing away with the bulletin board and instead printing the letters and "Cupid's" reply in a free weekly newspaper that was paid for, and distributed by, local businesses. Great marketing ploy, but somebody had to answer all those freaking letters.

Should she call her sister and say she was going to be late or roll the dice and see if she could get there in the nick of time if she drove hell-bent for leather?

If you get another speeding ticket, they'll cancel your insurance.

Dammit. She ducked her head under the van again. "I don't mean to scare you, kiddo, but this standoff isn't working for me. Something's gotta give, so if you want to spit and hiss, have at it."

The kitten arched its spine, flattened its ears, took her suggestion, and hissed long and loud.

Blowing out her breath, she got serious with kitty. "No more pussyfooting around. You cannot stay under the van. This is non-negotiable."

The Siamese slapped her hand with amazingly sharp little claws, managed to make contact with her index finger and draw blood.

"Ouch." She popped her finger into her mouth. "Anyone ever tell you that you're a vicious little cuss?"

"Hey there, Zoe-Eyes," oozed a deep, masculine voice.

Only one person called her that. She jumped to her feet, spun around, and came face to face with six-foot-two-inches of lean, raven-haired he-man.

Zoey grinned from ear-to-ear at the sight of her very best friend in the whole wide world. "Jericho Hezekiah Chance!"

He held out his arms and she flew across the asphalt to throw herself into them, his familiar scent enveloping her in his hearty hug. But while his scent might have been familiar, there was something decidedly different. His muscles were leaner, harder, and his eyes darker, warier. And the way he held her not the easy camaraderie of old, all loose-limbed and casual. Now there was a tightness about him that set her heart knocking against her chest. What the hell?

She tilted her chin up

He smiled down at her.

"How did you know it was me?" she asked, surprised her voice came out stunted and breathless.

"I'd recognize that cute fanny anywhere."

Her skin tingled electrically. Whenever he said things like that, her naughty thoughts went to . . . well . . . places where they had no business going. Their relationship was strictly platonic, always had been, always would be, but sometimes she couldn't help wondering if he wanted more from her and that made her want more from him and wanting more was perilous territory.

Zoey pulled back. "It was the Cupid's Rest van. That's how you knew it was me, not my fanny." Ugh, why had she repeated the word "fanny"? She put a hand to her backside. *Stop calling attention to it!* She dropped her arm, forced a laugh.

His smile turned wicked. "Uh-huh. That's it. The van."

What did that smile mean? Was he flirting with her? Once upon a time, she thought so, but then she'd pulled a bonehead move and kissed him and he'd been horrified, and things had been weird between them for months afterward. She was not going to make that mistake again.

Put away the second-guessing. He's your friend. That's it. Too bad, since Jericho was endlessly hot. If he wasn't her best friend . . . But he was, wasn't he? *Forget it.* With her palm, she shaded her eyes from the sun.

He possessed skin the color of a walnut hull, and normally, he sported a five o'clock shadow, but today he was freshly shaven and had on a gray business suit with somber blue tie. She couldn't ever recall seeing him in a suit before. Why was her cowboy archaeologist in a suit and tie? His cheekbones were razor-sharp and his nose had a slight bump at the bridge that, along with his dark eyebrows, gave him a hawkish appearance. At first glance, no one pegged him for a science nerd, but he spent as much time indoors analyzing, cataloging, and teaching as he did outdoors digging up artifacts.

"You should wear sunglasses," he said. "Protect your eyes."

"You're not wearing them."

He patted the front pocket of his suit jacket. "Took them off when I spied you. Had to get an unobstructed view. You're a sight for sore eyes."

She wrinkled her nose. "Is something wrong?"

"What makes you ask that?"

"You can't hide anything from me. I know you too well. Something's up."

He paused. "Mallory and I broke up."

Oh goody. Okay, that was tacky. "I'm so sorry to hear that. You guys were so good together, two peas in a pod — introspective, quiet, and cerebral."

"That was part of the problem. We were too much alike."

"What happened?" She held up a stop-sign palm. "No wait, save that story. We'll go out drinking. Wednesday is half-price beer night at Chantilly's. You can tell me all about it then."

"That's okay. I don't need a shoulder to cry on. It was a long time coming."

"So what are you doing here dressed like a banker?" She plucked a fine piece of lint off his lapel.

A sudden stillness settled over him that was both patient and predatory, the same darkly fascinating threat as a Big Bend mountain lion methodically stalking prey. What was this? Something was decidedly different. There was a hard-edged steeliness to him that hadn't been there before. He'd left Cupid not much more than a boy, but he'd returned a fully developed man. Unnerved, she dropped her arms and stepped back.

"I've got a one o'clock job interview at the Center for Big Bend Studies."

"You're way early."

"I know. I was nervous. Didn't want to be late."

"Is this for the position Dr. Keen vacated?"

"It is."

"You scoundrel!" Playfully, she swatted his shoulder. "Why didn't you tell me you were applying?"

"I didn't want to jinx it. Besides, I wanted to surprise you."

She beamed up at him. "Best surprise I've had all week."

"Wish me luck. I understand there's been over thirty applicants."

"Pfft. With your credentials the competition doesn't stand a chance."

"It's not as cut and dried as all that." He swept his dark gaze over the length of her body.

A strange shiver started at the bottom of her spine, but she managed to suppress it, clapping her hands more to get back on keel than anything else. When in doubt, rah, rah, rah always worked. "I'm so excited. Will you be living in Alpine or coming home to Cupid?"

"One step at a time. I have to get hired first."

"Oh." She laced her fingers together, did a little jig. "This is so wonderful. Wait, I just thought of something. If you get the job, you'll be my instructor for this summer's field school. Dibs on teacher's pet."

"You're taking the field school for certain?"

"I will if I can coax Walker into loosening the purse strings on my trust. I've sort of overspent my budget the last few months."

"Fair warning. If I get hired, I'm not cutting you any slack just because we're friends. I'm a tough instructor."

She waved away his threat. "We're going to have so much fun."

"And work very hard."

"Hard can be fun," she teased.

Jericho's face reddened and he tugged at his collar. Ha! She'd embarrassed him. That's what he got for making the fanny comment, but now she was feeling off kilter too.

"Let's not get ahead of ourselves. There's a lot of ifs first. If I get the job and if Walker gives you the money for tuition, we can worry about the rest after that."

"It's gonna happen. Mark my word," she said.

Jericho's chuckle was deep and inviting. "I love your self-confidence, Zoe-Eyes."

Love.

Why did that word seem to stand out from the others? And why was she feeling warm and squishy inside because of it? Nothing wrong with loving your best friend, right? There were all kinds of love. For instance, she loved Urban Decay waterproof mascara, Chee-tos — the puffy kind, Aunt Sandra's to-die-for banana pudding, skinny-dipping in Lake Cupid on a hot summer evening, and lying on the hood of a car staring up at the darkest night sky in the entire US of A, and making wishes when a star streaked flaming bright. Never mind that more often than not, she cast her wish as a single question.

When is my soul mate going to show up?

"And I'm so happy you're here," she chattered, pushing past her feelings. She learned a long time ago that the best way to deal with melancholy was to keep her mind, and body, busy. "Do you realize how long it's been since we've seen each other in person?"

Jericho put a palm to the back of his neck. "It's been three years since I moved to Utah for my PhD in anthropology."

"That's right." She playfully swatted his shoulder. "You're a doctor now. We must definitely celebrate. Chantilly's tonight. Be there seven-thirtyish and put on your best dancing boots. We're gonna do some serious boot scootin'. I haven't had a decent dance partner since you abandoned me."

Jericho smiled, shook his head. "Damn,

I've missed you."

"Me too. Missed you, that is, not me. How could I miss me?"

"That mind of yours runs a hundred and fifty miles an hour."

"Ya think?" She winked.

"I know so. Chantilly's tonight. It's a date."

Date.

She knew he didn't mean it that way. Why was she thinking like this? She and Jericho were just friends, but c'mon, who could deny the man filled out a pair of pants in the most drool-worthy way?

His hand rested on her shoulder. "It is good to see you again, pal."

Zoey's lips went cold. Pal. Buddy. Amigo. Friend. A guy who wanted to sleep with a girl did not call her "pal."

Jericho leaned over and lightly kissed her cheek, a platonic peck. Brotherly. Clearly, nothing had changed for him in three years. Fine. Good. She'd use that as a damper to douse the tiny flame that flickered in her heart. The feeling would pass. It always did. What she needed was a new boyfriend. Maybe she'd find one tonight at Chantilly's.

"I better get to that interview."

"Good luck!" She wriggled her fingers and turned back to the van, her heart thudding strangely. She was about to get in when she remembered about the kitten. Maybe she'd gotten lucky and it had taken off when she'd been talking to Jericho.

This time, so that her rump wouldn't be in the air, she crouched and ducked her head underneath the van. The Siamese was curled up asleep. Aha. Gotcha now. She reached around to pick it up and the kitten leaped as if she'd touched it with a live wire and darted to the opposite side of the van.

"Not again." She groaned.

"What's wrong?"

Zoey jumped, whacking her head against the undercarriage. "Ow!"

"I'm sorry, I didn't mean to startle you," Jericho apologized. "When I saw you on the ground, part of me said to just let it go, it is Zoey after all, but the curious part of me that knows whatever you do is never boring, had to come over and see what was up."

She rubbed the top of her head, glanced up at him. "You're too sly. You should wear a bell or something."

"Probably my Native American blood. Hunter DNA."

"Yeah, all one sixteenth of it." She got to her feet.

"One sixteenth Comanche," he said.

"Strong genes. Stamps the bloodline forever."

"I've heard this brag before."

"So you have. Are you going to tell me what you're doing?"

"Catfishing," she replied.

Jericho rolled his eyes upward and addressed the sky. "I had to ask."

"As it turns out I'm really lousy at it."

"*It* being . . . ?"

"Stubborn kitten doesn't want to be rescued."

"Ah," he said. "I'm finally on board the Zoey thought-train. It's been so long since we've talked in person that I've gotten out of the rhythm. Let's see if I can help."

How many times had he helped her out of a jam? Two dozen at least, probably three if she thought about it long enough. *Ya think by now you should be able to handle your own problems.* You'd think, but she scooted over to make room for him.

Jericho crouched beside her, his scent getting all tangled up with the smell of asphalt and kitten. His shoulder brushed against hers and she caught her breath.

The kitten stared at them, eyes wide, muscles bunched.

"The poor thing must think we're ganging up on him. I'll go to the other side of the van," she said, hopping up quick. Whew. Gotta put some distance between her and those broad shoulders. Once on the other side, she dropped down on her knees again and settled in to watch him.

Jericho made a low, soothing sound in the back of his throat, but he did not touch the Siamese.

The curious kitten cocked its head.

"That's right little guy, come out, come out. We won't hurt you."

He spoke soft and slow and as if by magic, the kitten crept forward. After a few minutes, he put his hand down and the little Siamese came over to nibble on his pinky finger and then, finally, curled up in his palm and started purring.

"I'll be damned," Zoey muttered. "You missed your calling. You should have been a cat whisperer."

With the kitten cradled against his chest, Jericho got to his feet. She hustled around the van to join him once more. "Is it a boy or a girl?"

Jericho checked. "Boy. You wanna hold him?"

"Yes."

He transferred the cat over to her.

"Hey, there, Egbert," she crooned. The kitten looked up at her with sleepy eyes. It was still purring. Happy now. Apparently they'd just gotten off on the wrong foot.

"Egbert?"

"I named him already. Eggy for short."

"That's dangerous."

"How so?"

"When you start naming animals they have a tendency to become your pet."

"If I can't find his owner maybe I will keep him."

Jericho put a palm over his mouth, amusement deepening his chocolate eyes to coffee.

"Are you laughing at me?"

"Nope." He nodded.

"Liar. You *are* laughing at me."

He dropped his hand to show that he wasn't smiling, but he had his lips pressed together so tightly she knew it was all he could do to keep from bursting out in a belly laugh.

"What is so funny?" She frowned. Normally, she loved making him laugh, but it was the principle of the thing.

"Nothing."

"You don't think I can own a cat?"

"No one owns a cat. They own you."

"Fine, you don't think I can take care of a cat."

"I never said that."

"You looked both entertained and skeptical. Like it's the most outrageous idea you ever heard of."

"Have you ever owned a pet?"

"Sure. Lots."

"Name one."

"Um . . . I had a hamster once, or maybe it was a gerbil."

"What was its name?"

She crinkled her nose. "I can't recall."

"Apparently he was quite beloved."

"Sarcasm, cheap shot for the uninspired."

Jericho chuckled. "God, I've missed you. Repartee is not the same in e-mail."

"Why do you think I keep trying to get you on Twitter? It's *the* medium for one-liners. Junie Mae's on it," she said, referring to his stepgrandmother. "She's the Twitter Queen."

"You're the one who excels at one-liners."

"True." She tapped her chin. "Your e-mails do tend to run along the lines of *War and Peace,* the unabridged."

"So whatever happened to the hamster?"

"Got out of its cage and ran away."

He dipped his head, arched one eyebrow, and slowly shook his head.

"What? It happens."

"I seemed to remember you also had goldfish. What happened to them?"

"They died."

He held out his palms. "You're proving my case."

"They're goldfish. How long do they last? A couple of weeks tops."

"Mine lived for twelve years."

"Show-off."

"Simply stating my case."

"Which is that I couldn't possibly be a responsible pet owner?"

"Trying to establish a precedent."

"Natalie and I had a dog once."

"And who took care of it?"

"Natalie, but that's beside the point."

"Is it?"

"Jeez, Jericho, whose side are you on?"

"Egbert's."

"You seriously don't think I can take care of a cat?"

"Zoey, you can do anything you can set your mind to. I believe that one hundred percent."

"But . . . ?"

"Some people just aren't meant to be pet owners. There's nothing wrong with that."

"Wow, way to stomp on a girl's feelings."

"It's just that you have so many interests. You're always on the go, never at home. A pet requires a lot of time and attention."

He was right. She did have trouble sitting

still, but that didn't mean she couldn't own a cat. The deal was, she never really had much of a reason to stay home.

"He might belong to someone," Jericho said. "So the point could be moot."

"I'll take him to a vet," she said. "See if he's been chipped, and I'll put up notices, post on a few social media sites."

"Are you sure you don't want me to take charge of him?"

Earlier, he'd sort of bruised her ego, but now she was just plain irritated. She sniffed. "I can do this, besides you have an interview."

"I meant after the interview. Just offering to let you off the hook."

She looked at the kitten, who was staring at her with such a trusting expression that her stomach flopped over. She could be a cat owner. Why not? "Thanks for the offer, Jericho, but I'm in this hook, line, and sinker."

And she might have darn well believed it too, if he hadn't laughed.

Chapter 2

Culture: Common beliefs and practices of a group of people.

Mind churning, Jericho walked across campus to Ferguson Hall for his interview.

The last thing he wanted was to hurt Zoey's feelings. She was the very best friend he'd ever had, bar none. Never mind that she was four years younger and an extremely attractive woman. When he was with Zoey he felt comfortable, relaxed, and accepted in a way he'd never felt with any romantic partner. She was the one woman he could tell anything to without fear of being judged.

He treasured their friendship. Put it right up there with archaeological digs, Fort Worth barbecue, Hank Williams music, and his favorite worn-out pair of handmade cowboy boots. Scratch that. Their friendship topped all those things, even the digs.

Which was precisely why he had kept

things strictly platonic all these years, even though there had been times when it had taken all the strength — and cold showers — he could muster not to take her to bed.

For instance, the time she'd kissed him.

Jericho rubbed a palm across his mouth. It had been Zoey's twenty-first birthday and right after he'd earned his master's degree and been accepted into the PhD program at the University of Utah. They'd been celebrating and had just left Chantilly's. Over the course of the evening, Zoey had discovered a shooter drink called Firecracker that was made from Goldschlager cinnamon schnapps, tequila, and Rumple Minze, and when she drank it, the girl turned into a Roman candle.

He'd walked her home along the lakeside path that led from the marina bar to the Cupid's Rest B&B where she lived with her sister, his palm pressed against her back as he guided her, fearful that she'd slip and take a header into the water.

Suddenly, she stopped, tipped back her head, and howled at the full moon. "Woohoo! I'm finally twenty-one!"

"Okay, Wolf woman, let's concentrate on getting home in one piece," he said.

"I'd rather concentrate on this."

"What?"

"This." She flung her arms around his neck and pressed her cinnamon-flavored lips against his.

Puzzlingly blindsided and feeling loose from a couple of Firecrackers himself, for one millisecond he'd almost kissed her back. Lord knew he wanted to, but he was driving to Utah the next day and Zoey was a few stages past tipsy. He simply couldn't take advantage of the situation, but most of all, he feared kissing her would set off a raging forest fire of desire that could not be contained.

And nothing terrified Jericho more than losing control.

So he forced himself to stand there, absorbing the heat of her sweet lips but not responding, until finally, slowly, she untangled her arms from around his neck and stepped back to look at him with those big, green doe eyes.

"Well," she said briskly. "That didn't turn out the way I'd imagined."

He told her then he didn't want to do anything to harm their friendship. She agreed. The next morning, wearing sunglasses and drinking Red Bull, she came to see him off. When he casually mentioned something about what had happened the previous night, she pretended she didn't remember anything about it and they left things like that.

It was the last time they'd seen each other in person, and while things had been a bit awkward for a little while, to his relief, the kiss hadn't changed anything between them. They e-mailed, texted, kept up with each other on social media sites, and did face-time phone calls.

Once in a while, in the dark of a lonely night, desire would get the better of him and he'd kick around the idea of saying, *Screw it, let the chips fall where they may,* and telling her how he felt, but something always got in the way of deepening their relationship.

In that regard, they had the worst timing in the world. When they were teenagers the four-year age difference had been too great. Then when Zoey was old enough, Jericho had a steady girlfriend. Whenever he was free, inevitably she was hooked up with someone. Realistically, if they were meant to be anything more than friends, wouldn't the timing have been right at some point?

He'd imagined that with three years and a thousand miles between them, those lurking embers might have finally been extinguished, but one look at Zoey's sweet little tush waggling in the air as she tried to coax the kitten from underneath the van and his body had hardened. He knew he was in trouble. Leaving him face-to-face with the real reason he would never make a move on her.

Zoey was like a bright jungle parrot — free-spirited, vibrant, quicksilver, and curious. He'd watched the revolving door of men come and go through her life, and he was the only constant. He knew it was because he didn't push her for anything more than friendship. Whenever a guy started talking long-term commitment, Zoey got itchy feet and invariably showed him the door. People and things that were out of reach fascinated her, but once she got what she wanted, she quickly lost interest. He couldn't bear it if she lost interest in him. By holding himself apart, he kept her close.

Twisted reasoning, maybe, but losing her was what he ultimately feared most, and who said fear was logical?

There was only one solution, only one way to keep from getting left in Zoey's dust. Erect a few walls. Keep his hands to himself. Protect his heart. Protect them both. Because you couldn't cage a bright bird like Zoey; she soared only when she was free.

He stopped, took out his phone, and sent

her a quick text message. *Sorry. Can't make it tonight. Something's come up.*

It wasn't a lie. Something *had* come up. Something he feared he could no longer control.

Outside Ferguson Hall he took a minute to straighten his tie, run a hand through his hair, and practice a smile. Was it a mistake coming back here after all?

It was the wrong time to be worrying about that. He didn't have to take the job if it was offered.

If.

Operative word. His bank account was lower than a snake's belly after graduate school, but at least he'd gotten through it without school loans, and that was saying something. If he got the job he wasn't in much of a position to refuse it.

He had to wait for a few minutes, but then the director, Dr. Sinton, came out to shake his hand. The older man had a jaunty step and the perpetual tan of a tennis lover. His salt and pepper hair was academically long and he sported a soul patch on his chin. "Good to see you again, Jericho, come on into my office."

Although his smile was cheery, something in the man's voice dropped acid pellets into Jericho's gut. He eased down on the edge of the chair Dr. Sinton waved at before taking his own seat behind the desk.

They made small talk first and the director told him about the position and the summer field school. Finally, Dr. Sinton picked up the curriculum vitae Jericho had e-mailed to him Monday and looked over it. "You've the best credentials of anyone who has applied for the job."

Jericho already knew that.

"Because you did some of your undergraduate course work at Sul Ross and served as an intern here at the center, that gives you another leg up." Dr. Sinton tapped his desk with an index finger, pounding out a slow, steady beat.

He knew that too.

"And hell, I'm just going to say it. I like you, Jericho."

He knew that as well.

"But . . . ."

Yep, here it came.

"You've got the stink of that mess at the University of Utah on you, son."

"It was a personal matter that leached into the professional arena when it shouldn't have," Jericho said. "I regret that."

"I'm all for giving a man a chance," Dr. Sinton said. "But I've got a stack of qualified applicants and a board that prefers to walk the path of least resistance. I can't make you any promises."

"I don't expect any favors, sir. I just asked to be judged on my professional merits."

"As you are well aware, academic politics just doesn't work that way."

Jericho nodded. "Is this an outright rejection?"

"No, no. I'm going to bat for you with the board. I'm simply preparing you for the reality of what you're up against."

"I appreciate your candor."

Dr. Sinton stood up. Jericho followed suit. "The board meets on Friday morning. You'll have our answer by noon."

"Thank you."

Dr. Sinton reached across the desk to shake his hand. "On future applications, feel free to put down my name. I'll give you a good reference."

Was that code for you-don't-stand-a-chance-in-hell-of-getting-this-job? If he couldn't get a job on hometown turf, where *could* he get one?

"I appreciate that." He headed for the door.

"Jericho?"

He stopped, turned back.

"You'll get past this. Don't beat yourself up too hard. We've all been there in one way or another."

Yeah, maybe so, but I bet you never slugged your dean.

"I despair that Zoey is ever going to grow up. She turns twenty-four in two months and she still can't manage to show up on time."

At the sound of her name, Zoey screeched to a halt in the hallway of the Cupid Community Center outside the open door leading to the room where the love letter volunteers gathered. It was Natalie's voice.

Way to stab your only sibling in the back, sis.

The kitten squirmed inside the backpack that she carried in front of her. Zoey stuck her hand through the open zipper to stroke Eggy's fur. He popped his head out and licked the back of her hand with his rough little tongue.

Aww. She was already incautiously in love with the little guy. Bad idea to get too attached too soon, he probably belonged to someone.

"Zoey's still young. Some of us are late bloomers." Aunt Sandra's voice drifted out into the corridor.

"I read where chronic tardiness is a control mechanism," added Aunt Carol Ann. If anyone knew about control mechanisms it was she.

"Control mechanism? How is tardiness a control mechanism?" Natalie asked. "To me it shows a clear lack of control."

"No, no," Carol Ann said. "You misunderstand. Zoey's tardiness isn't about her self-control. Subconsciously, she does it to control *us.*"

Zoey bit her bottom lip. *What a load of hockey pucks and for that matter, a bit narcissistic on Carol Ann's part.*

"We gotta face the fact that Zoey is probably never going to change," said Great-Aunt Delia. "And simply love her for who she is, just as we forgive you, Carol Ann, for sometimes being a tight ass."

Zoey snickered. That was sweet. She wanted to kiss Great-Aunt Delia's wrinkled cheek.

Natalie's sigh was audible, even from where Zoey was standing. "I just wished she could commit to something. Most people could have gotten two undergraduate degrees in the amount of time it's taking her to get one."

"Be fair. She has stuck with archaeology for over a year now," Junie Mae Prufrock contributed. Junie Mae ran the LaDeDa Day Spa and Hair Salon next door to Natalie's B&B. She was the only one of the eight regular members of the volunteers that Zoey wasn't related to and she was also Jericho's stepgrandmother. "That's an improvement."

"Yes, but I've been braced for that to come to an end," Natalie said. "She is finishing up all the courses she can take at Sul Ross and I have a feeling she only went into archaeology to impress Jericho. If she's serious she's going to have to transfer out of the area to finish her degree. I'm wondering if maybe that is why she's dragging her feet. Fear of leaving her plushly feathered nest and not being able to make it on her own."

Zoey puffed out her cheeks with air. That wasn't the reason. Was it?

"*Malheureusement,* I suppose it's our fault," came the dulcet tones of Mignon Martin, a distant cousin by marriage. While Mignon spoke impeccable English, she still punctuated her sentences with French words. She'd been born and raised in Loire, France. She and her husband, Michael, ran Mon Amour, one of three local vineyards. "Zoey was only two when your parents died and we pampered her." She pronounced her name *Zoo-ee.*

"Plus, she's the youngest of all you girls,

spoiling her was our pleasure," Great-Aunt Delia pointed out.

"It's true," Natalie said. "We've never demanded anything of her."

"It was easy to let her slide," Sandra added. "She has such a sunny personality and she's never down in the dumps."

Zoey shifted the backpack to the crook of her arm. Well, maybe not never, but true enough she rarely battled bouts of the blues.

"She's too impulsive," Carol Ann said.

"Spontaneous to a fault," Sandra agreed.

"That's the main thing that trips her up in life," Carol Ann continued. "We should have made her stick with a few things. How many activities was she involved in as a kid?"

"Ballet, softball, soccer, Girl Scouts, volleyball, golf, track, choir, science camp, piano lessons, drum lessons, saxophone. You name it, Zoey tried it." That was from Junie Mae. "None of which she stuck with for more than a couple of weeks."

What was this? Kick-Zoey-in-the-teeth-for-no-good-reason day? This was where eavesdropping got you, finding out things you really didn't want to hear. She should stroll right in there, head held high, and act like they had not been bashing her nine ways to Sunday.

Natalie cleared her throat. "We're blaming ourselves for the way Zoey has turned out.

We might have influenced her behavior, yes, but at some point she has to assume responsibility for her actions."

"Maybe we should hold an intervention," Sandra said. "You know, like they do for alcoholics and drug addicts and gamblers."

Say what? Zoey felt sick to her stomach. She shouldn't have stopped for that Taco Bell burrito. *Uh-huh, go ahead and convince yourself it's the burrito and not the fact your family is dissing you for being an impulsive slacker.*

"Do you think she might have attention deficit disorder or something?" Junie Mae asked.

"I've always thought so," Carol Ann said. "But she made straight A's in school so they never had her tested for it."

"She's dead good at puzzles," Sandra said. "She can take one overview glance and see where pieces belong and solve them lickety-split. She's a sharp girl, even if she's restless."

"Zoey's issue is more impulse control than anything else," Natalie said. "She can't seem to stop herself from acting on whatever random thought pops into her head."

Mignon clucked her tongue. "*Dommage,* she can't seem to live up to her potential."

Zoey blinked against the sudden moisture

clinging to her lashes. Damn, she must have gotten something in her eye.

At that moment, the door to the ladies' restroom opened and her first cousin Melody exited, pushing a sweep of thick, golden blond hair from her forehead. She dressed simply but elegantly, in pressed khaki capri pants, a black scoop neck T-shirt, strappy black sandals, and a gold cuff bracelet on her wrist.

Melody, who was the oldest of Carol Ann's three children and her only daughter, was a Madison Avenue advertising executive home on vacation. She was substituting on the volunteer committee for their cousin Lace, the curator of the Cupid Botanical Gardens, who was on her honeymoon in Costa Rica with her new husband, ex-quarterback for the Dallas Cowboys, Pierce Hollister.

Growing up, Melody had been Zoey's role model. The one who got away and made good in the big city. But Zoey's interest in archaeology had gradually sapped her cravings for city life. While she did like fashion and makeup and going to parties and those kinds of things, she was at heart a simple country girl. She'd rather dig in the dirt than go shopping — most of the time, anyway.

"Hey cuz, what are you doing lurking out here?"

"Just heading in." Zoey forced a bright smile and followed her cousin into the room.

The women gathered around the oblong table spread with stacks of love letters, turned to look at her, and for the first time, she didn't see their familiar faces, but instead saw them through the dispassionate lens of a detached observer — noticing, listening, honing her new anthropological skills.

It was the little things that spoke loudest: Mignon's vintage Pelikan fountain pen with the gold nib illustrating her flair for both the romantic and the finer things in life. The gentle way Natalie rested a protective hand on her belly, already madly in love with the baby boy who wouldn't be born for another four months. Carol Ann's flawlessly ironed crisp white blouse, refined gray pencil skirt, and black boots polished to a reflective shine. The neon yellow tennis balls cut to fit the bottom of Great-Aunt Delia's aluminum walker so she could push it across the floor instead of having to lift the walker with each step. Junie Mae's blond hair teased so high that if she were to dye it blue she could pass for Marge Simpson. The easygoing dark freckles dotting Sandra's caramel-colored nose and the intricate stitching of Melody's stylish designer handbag. Each detail told her something about them.

What would an anthropologist deduce about *her* clothes, hairstyles, and possessions? Did she really want to know?

"What on earth is that moving around in your backpack?" Carol Ann asked.

Eggy popped his head out.

"A kitten?" Natalie said in that I-know-best, big-sister tone of hers. "Do *not* tell me you've adopted a kitten."

"Okay." Zoey took Eggy out of the backpack and plunked down at the table with him in her lap. "I won't tell you."

The Siamese curled up into a ball and started purring. She didn't have to tell how she and Eggy had gotten off to a rocky start. Things were copacetic between them now.

"Zoey, really." Her sister shook her head.

"What?" Okay, so maybe her nose was out of joint over the conversation she'd overheard. "Why can't I adopt a cat?"

The women sitting around the table exchanged glances. The looks on their faces said, *Maybe this is a prime time for that intervention.*

"Honey," Sandra said. "Are you sure it's a good idea?"

"What's the big deal? So I'm adopting a cat." She shrugged. "People do it all the time."

"A pet is a big responsibility." Junie Mae fondled her blow-dryer earrings.

Zoey looked around the table. First Jericho and now her family and friends? Sheesh. Was that how people truly saw her? As flighty and incompetent? She thought of herself as bubbly and outgoing. "You guys don't think I can take care of a cat."

"It's not that," Mignon placated, her numerous bracelets jangling when she waved her hand. "You're just so busy."

"Let's not pussyfoot around this," Great-Aunt Delia said. "You're too unreliable for a pet. They need to be fed and taken to the vet and cleaned up after."

"I can do that." Zoey stroked the kitten's fur.

"You don't have the best track record when it comes to long-term commitment," Melody chimed in.

"First time for everything," Zoey said blithely against the sting of their criticism.

"What's the longest time you've kept a boyfriend?" Melody prodded. "Four months?"

"Twenty years."

Melody's perfectly arched eyebrows shot

up. “Who is that?”

“Jericho.”

“Oh him.” Melody waved a hand. “He’s just a friend. That doesn’t count.”

“Why not?”

“It takes a lot more to maintain a romantic relationship than a friendship.” Melody picked up a Cupid letter from the stack in the middle of the table. “Should we get back to work?”

The older women exchanged glances again.

“Miss Melody,” Junie Mae said stiffly. “Friendships take just as much TLC as romantic relationships.”

Melody’s mouth dropped open, but before she could retaliate, bare knuckles rapped against the open door.

“Good afternoon, ladies!” Walker McCleary boomed.

Walker was Zoey and Natalie’s father’s first cousin and patriarch of the Cupid McClearys. He wore his salt and pepper hair parted straight down the middle, round wire-frame glasses, and a bristly mustache. Cookie duster, he called it. He was built like a rain barrel, round and stout, and wore colorful suspenders to keep his pants up. He looked quite a bit like Teddy Roosevelt. Today, he sported hunter green suspenders over a sage-colored Oxford shirt with white cuffs and collars, and his white pharmacist lab coat was thrown over the ensemble.

How cool was that? Just when she wanted to speak to Walker about money for the summer field school, he appeared.

Everyone greeted him with hearty hellos.

Zoey pushed back her chair, the metal legs scraping loudly against the tile floor because she moved so fast, and she almost hopped to her feet, but a pair of tiny claws dug into her skin. Oops, that was right, she had a cat in her lap. She was a pet owner now — well, maybe, if Eggy didn't belong to someone else — and she had to be more careful.

"What brings you to our little klatch, Walker?" Carol Ann asked.

Walker's eyes were bright and his face flushed. He shifted his weight from foot to foot. For a big man, he was entertainingly nimble. He paused for a moment, swept his gaze around the room. "Exciting news."

"Well?" Great-Aunt Delia said. "Spit it out, man. Some of us are living on borrowed time."

Walker rubbed his palms together like he was trying to start a fire. "My book about August McCleary has hit the *New York Times* best-seller list!"

Everyone clapped and cheered.

Walker raised a silencing palm, his grin spreading opossum-eating big. "But that's not the best part."

The other women all leaned forward in their chairs.

"Universal Studios wants to option *A Time to Heal.* It's going to be a movie!"

That brought them all to their feet. Congratulating him effusively, they shook his hand, pounded him on the back, and asked a hundred questions. How much money would he get? Would they film any of the scenes in Cupid? What actor would play August McCleary? That last question had them off and running.

"I think they should cast Sam Elliot." Junie Mae sighed. "What a voice."

"George Clooney." Carol Ann swooned.

"Vincent Cassel." Mignon smiled.

"Denzel Washington," Sandra opined.

"He's African American," Carol Ann pointed out.

"So?" Sandra sank her hands on her hips. "Denzel's got the acting chops to pull it off."

Everyone nodded over that. Denzel could pull off just about anything.

"Sean Connery," Great-Aunt Delia suggested.

"He's Scottish," Natalie said. "The McClearys are Irish."

"And he's far too old," Melody insisted. "All those actors you guys are naming are too old. August was only thirty-nine when he compounded the medication that stopped the Spanish flu in its track here in the Trans-Pecos. Colin Farrell is perfect for the job."

"He *is* Irish," Natalie conceded.

Carol Ann nodded. "And quite handsome."

"Not to mention a very good actor," Junie Mae added.

"Clearly you ladies don't understand anything about moviemaking," Walker said, as if he knew everything there was to know about the art. "Less than ten percent of movies that are optioned actually end up getting made."

Everyone looked crestfallen over that news.

"Well," Natalie said. "You did make the *New York Times* list. That's something."

That stirred another mob of questions.

Zoey tucked Eggy into the crook of her arm. Since Walker was walking on air, it was the perfect time to hit him up for money. "Cousin Walker," she called over the noise, and waved her hand like she was signaling an airplane in for landing.

"Wait, wait." Walker raised stop-sign

palms. "All the details will be discussed at my private party tonight at Chantilly's. Open bar."

That brought more cheering and applause.

"Woot!" Zoey exclaimed. "But there's something important I have to ask you, it's not about your book or the movie —"

Hold up, Miss Spontaneous-to-a-Fault. Is this really the right time and way to ask? Why not save it for the party after Walker has a few drinks in him and you've got Jericho as backup? C'mon, prove to yourself, if not to everyone else, that you can control your impulsiveness.

"What is it, Zoey?" Walker asked.

Proudly, she held her tongue, and instead of bugging him about paying for her field school, she asked, "May I bring a friend?"

CHAPTER 3

Flint: A hard, brittle stone, usually a type of chalk or limestone that can be flaked in any direction and easily shaped.

"I wish people would quit fawning over Walker and give someone else a chance at him." Zoey tossed a peanut into the air and with an upturned face, caught it smoothly in her open mouth.

Jericho and Zoey were sitting side by side at the bar. They'd been there for thirty minutes, waiting for the crowd to thin. Chantilly's was packed to the rafters and Walker McCleary, proprietor of McCleary's Pharmacy and newly minted author of *A Time to Heal,* the biography of pioneer pharmacist August McCleary, stood by the buffet table surrounded by his adoring community.

Whenever Jericho thought about Zoey's illustrious family, both branches of which had founded and formed this town, he couldn't help feeling intimidated by how deep her roots ran. The kicker was she didn't seem to appreciate the power of her heritage. Family ties meant a lot to Jericho, probably because he had so few.

On the long buffet table sat a white sheet cake baked in the shape of an apothecary's mortar and pestle with royal blue icing that spelled out: "Congratulations Walker." Even though Walker's book was hardcover, someone had put "Paperback Writer" on the jukebox.

The walls were made of Texas limestone, and the floor was stained cement. The owner of the bar, gristle-bearded Jasper Grass, who looked like an 1860s prospect miner, was behind the counter, twisting caps off beer bottles as fast as people lined up to ask for them. Nothing much had changed here in the three years Jericho had been away.

Against his better judgment, he had shown up for the party after Zoey had called and begged him to come. He had a tough time denying her anything, and truth be told, he didn't want to be alone tonight, not after that bumpy job interview.

Zoey swiveled a hundred and eighty degrees on her barstool while simultaneously tossing another peanut into the air, and snagging it in mid-whirl.

He shook his head. "Amazing talent."

"Cultivated by years of misspent youth," she chirped zealously.

But he detected a wistful note in her tone. What was that about?

"Hey, watch what I can do with a cherry stem." She finished the revolution, fished a maraschino cherry from her cherry martini, and popped it into her mouth. Her jaw worked for a quick minute, and then she proudly stuck out her tongue to show him the woody cherry stem tied into a neat knot. "Ta-da."

Cherry juice clung to her lips, but she didn't seem to care, and that was okay by him. She folded the tangled cherry stem into a cocktail napkin. In the golden glow of the neon beer signs, she looked like a naughty celestial nymph. A hot ripple started in the pit of his stomach and undulated downward in serpentine waves. Clenching his jaw, he picked up his drink and glanced away from her adroit pink tongue.

She inclined her head toward Walker and his congregation. "Maybe we should just go over and muscle everyone out of the way."

"Patience," he said.

"You know that is not my strong suit."

"All the more reason to cultivate it. A good archaeologist is infinitely patient." He slid her a sidelong glance. Her whole-wheat colored hair was drawn up in a casual, girl-next-door ponytail that, in spite of its messy innocence, made her look wildly sexy. When had she gotten so damn beautiful?

"That's why you're a brilliant archaeologist. You've got the patience of . . . of . . ." She snapped her fingers. "Who was that Bible guy?"

"Job."

She shook her head. "Not him. Job was kinda whiny. 'Why me, God,' and all that. I'm talking about the dude who worked for his would-be father-in-law for seven years to marry the woman he loved and the guy pulled a bait and switch and made him marry the older, ugly daughter first and then he had to work for the guy for seven more years before he got to marry the one he really wanted."

"That's a twisted version of the chain of events, but you mean Jacob."

"Yeah. That's the one." She shook her index finger at him. "You've got the patience of Jacob. I mean besides all that waiting, once he finally snagged Rachel he had to put up with two wives. Can you imagine that honey-do list? 'Hey, Jake, you brought camel dung in on your sandals, clean up your mess.' Or, 'We're having date cake for dinner, shimmy up that date palm and get us a bushel,' or 'I don't care if you visited *her* tent last night, it's *my* turn for a little pinch and tickle.' " She paused for a breath. "How come in polygamous cultures it's always one guy and gobs of women and not one woman and gobs of guys? Maybe because guys wrote down the history, ya think?"

He smiled. Whiplash chatter. That was his Zoey. The woman possessed a brain so nimble that few could fully keep up with her sharp — and granted occasionally nonsensical — mental acumen, but he could. "Pinch and tickle?"

She nudged him lightly in the ribs with her elbow, lowered her eyelashes, and winked. "You know what I mean."

His pulse skipped. Was she flirting with him? *Quick, deflect, deflect.*

"How's the kitten?" he asked, surprised to hear his voice come out hoarse and scratchy.

"*A*-dorable. I bought Eggy a bed and a scratching post and a litter box that I put in my bathroom. I had no idea kittens slept so much."

"He'll be more active at night. Cats are

nocturnal."

"Oh good. I am so not a morning person."

"Tell me about it," Jericho said. "Remember that time at astronomy camp when you hid in the closet because you didn't want to get up for eight o'clock classes and the entire camp went on a crazed manhunt searching for you?"

Her eyes met his. "And a crackerjack detective of a camp counselor found me sound asleep and totally safe."

"I wasn't a crackerjack detective. I just knew you better than anyone else," he said.

She touched his shoulder. "Do you remember the year I jumped off Telescope Cliff into Tranquility Pool?"

Jericho scowled. "How could I forget? You gave me a heart attack. That was damn reckless of you, Zoey."

"You're still pissed off about it?" Her laugh sounded a little shaky.

"What if the water hadn't been deep enough? You would have broken your neck. Spent your life in a wheelchair or worse." He tightened his grip on the long-necked beer bottle in his hand. At fourteen, she'd been a sassy little pistol, all bravado and no common sense. Honestly, on that score, not much had changed.

"I wouldn't have broken my neck," she

said confidently.

"Don't be glib. You're not immune to the laws of physics. If you don't know for sure the depth of the water, diving off a cliff into a pool is a damn foolhardy thing to do." He glowered.

She drummed her fingers against the polished wood of the bar. "I've heard this lecture before."

"I might have spoken the words, but I don't think you heard them."

Her eyes widened. "Dude, chillax. What are you getting so worked up about? It was ten years ago."

Why? Because he'd been responsible for her, and for one horrifying moment, he thought she'd killed her fool self on his watch. He'd never been so scared in his life as at the moment he dove into the water after her, leaving the other campers in his charge standing at the top of Telescope Cliff, gaping in shock and awe.

Even now, the memory had his heart rate kicking up. He'd stared down that cliff to where she'd dropped into the pool. She hadn't come up and she hadn't come up and she hadn't come up. He'd been forced to throw caution to the wind and jump in too, desperately searching the water, guilt and fear gnawing him up inside, until finally, he came up for air and spied her sitting on the bank soaking wet and laughing at him.

Fury, born from expelled adrenaline and stark terror, had taken over. He'd slogged through the water, snatched her up by the hand, and marched her straight back to the camp, immune to her apologies and cajoling. He'd turned her over to his supervisor and said if they didn't kick Zoey out of camp, he was resigning, but her pedigree was the double threat of Fant and McCleary, the two richest families in Cupid. She stayed put and the camp manager had talked him out of quitting, but he insisted on being transferred to a younger group of campers. He simply couldn't stand by and watch her do reckless things that put her life in jeopardy.

Zoey rubbed his upper arm. "Just to let you know, I planned the whole thing. I sneaked down to Tranquility Pool the night before to find out how deep it was so I could dive off during our hike to impress you and the other kids."

Jericho stared at her. Was it true? Or was she just saying that now in retrospect? "You never told me that."

"I didn't tell you because you were so busy yelling at me that I couldn't get a word in edgewise, and besides, everyone was so awed by my daring that telling you would have shot my cool reputation."

He snorted. "Since when have you not been able to get a word in?"

"That day. You were like a pot of scalding water boiling over."

"As I had every right to be. You were under my supervision. I tried my best to keep you safe, but how was I to know you'd take a crazy impulsive leap off a cliff? It was damn random. Who could anticipate that?"

"I might be impulsive, but I'm not stupid. The risks I take are calculated."

He canted his head, eyed her for a long moment without saying anything. He didn't believe that for a moment.

She notched her chin up, blinked, but held her ground. "It's true."

"What about the time you borrowed your Aunt Carol Ann's car without permission before you had a license and went off joyriding to Marfa?"

"I went there to see you, I might add, and the road from here to Marfa is long, lonely, and straight as a ribbon. If I'd run off the road the worst thing I would have hit was a cactus. I weighed the odds."

"Something could have hit *you,* like a pronghorn or a mule deer."

"But one didn't, did it?"

Jericho shook his head. "If I had a dollar for every time you scared the living hell out of me —"

"You worry too much." She patted his cheek. "And you're too young to be such a fussbudget, but I will give you that I was kind of a hellion when I was a teenager."

He arched an eyebrow. "Kind of?"

"Okay, I *was* a hellion, but I outgrew it." She grinned and swatted his shoulder. "Stop looking so dubious."

Her touch sent a trail of sparks shooting along his nerve endings. Taken aback, Jericho leaned away from her and picked at the Budweiser label wrapped around his beer bottle.

"So what happened with Mallory?" Zoey reached across him for the bowl of peanuts on the bar; her breasts lightly grazed his forearm.

The bright sparks burst into rolling flames. Jericho froze. While she was leaning forward, her cute little purple shirt pulled up, creating a gap of bare skin between the shirt's hem and the waistband of her low-rise jeans, exposing the whale-tail of her purple thong panty. He gulped. What was going on here? He wasn't going to lie. Yes, he'd been attracted to Zoey in the past, but nothing to this extent.

"Well?" She settled cluelessly back down on her barstool and the thong disappeared. Thankfully. Sadly.

Knocked senseless by what he'd seen, Jericho grunted. "Huh?"

"Mallory."

"I don't want to talk about it." *I'd rather sit here and watch you.*

"Oh no, no, no." She waggled a finger. "You're not getting out of this. It's non-negotiable. Break-ups must be dissected."

He grunted. "What for?"

"So you can put the past behind you."

"Mallory is so far in my rearview mirror, I'd have to drive around the world to run over her."

"Ouch! Do I detect some bitterness?"

"None at all."

She narrowed her eyes at him.

He held up his right palm like he was swearing on a Bible in a court of law. "I promise. It's all fine."

"Hmm." She rubbed her chin pensively. "When exactly did you guys break up?"

"Just before Christmas break."

She sank her hands on her hips, inclined her head at him. "Almost six months ago! Why didn't you tell me before now?"

He shrugged. Why? He didn't really know.

She sniffed. "I thought we were best friends."

"We are."

"And yet you keep something this big from me?"

"It wasn't *that* big."

"Breakups are always big news. Remember that for future reference. You and Mallory went together for over two years. What happened?"

"Graduate level anthropology."

"Huh?"

He studied her face. God, she had gorgeous eyes, a plump mouth, and round, guileless cheeks. *Stop staring.* "I was the teaching assistant for fundamentals of evolutionary ecology and Mallory needed the class for her core curriculum and the course wasn't being offered again until the following fall. If she didn't take it that semester it would throw off her graduation date."

"And?"

"I should have asked for another class. I knew better, but I didn't listen to that voice of reason." Much like now, when every shred of common sense he possessed was hollering at him to stop thinking about purple thong panties and move away from her, but instead, he actually leaned closer.

"Well, it's not like she started dating you to get a good grade or anything. You guys were already living together and you were the TA, not the actual professor. Not such a major abuse in the grand scheme of things."

"Even so, it's ethically questionable to date a student, whether TA or full-fledged professor."

She made a steeple with her fingertips. "I'm assuming being Mallory's teacher must have led to problems in the bedroom."

He winced and took another swallow of beer. "You might say that."

"That."

He chuckled. "You're trying to cheer me up."

"You'd do the same for me."

"I would."

"So what was between you? Power struggle? Or were you too soft on her?"

He met her gaze. "On the contrary, I gave her a D."

"In bed?" She grinned. The imp. "Or in class?"

"I don't rate lovers on an alphabetical scale."

She leaned toward him, smelling of cherries, and Zoeyness — how he'd missed that scent — and lowered her voice. "What scale *do* you rate them on?"

"I don't rate my lovers at all. Do you?"

"You mean other than small, medium, and large?" she quipped.

"Whew," he said. "I'm out of practice. You make me feel like I've just run around in circles at a dead sprint."

She laughed. "Hurry and ketchup, tomato. I've missed this something fierce."

Me too. "It's impossible to keep up with you."

She looked pleased at that. "I'm guessing Mallory was plenty miffed when she got the D."

"It shouldn't have come as a surprise. Her work was subpar and she'd had all semester to improve. I warned her. She said I was being too hard on her."

"Were you?"

"Maybe," he admitted. "But I couldn't very well allow her to skate by just because she was living with me."

"Not even for the sake of your relationship?"

"No."

"Hmm." Zoey took the last cherry from her martini and popped it into her mouth. A dribble of juice stained her lips red.

He had an overwhelming urge to scoot closer and kiss the sweet glistening droplet away, but he forced himself to stay rooted on the stool. *You gotta stop this.* "Hmm what?"

"I'm just thinking that you must not have loved her if you couldn't at least give her a C minus. That way she would have passed. With a D, she would have to take the course over."

"You would have me compromise my standards?"

"C'mon, for love you have to give a little."

That's the thing. He wasn't sure he'd ever loved Mallory. To be quite honest, he wasn't even sure what love was. "You don't have to feel sorry for her. She appealed the grade to the professor, and since we were living together it turned into this big thing, so even though he conceded she'd done D level work, I was called on the carpet for not making him aware of our relationship and he adjusted her grade to a C. Of course, that was all before I found out *why* she'd done D level work."

"I feel a cliché coming on."

"Yep." He took another sip of beer. "She was boffing the dean of the English department behind my back."

"Oh foul! How come it was bad form for you to date a student but not for the dean?"

"She wasn't a student in his department."

"Still, completely uncool." Zoey knotted

up one of her small fists. "Good thing she's not here right now. I'd be tempted to let her have it."

"Violence is not the way to solve anything. Learned that the hard way after I decked the dean when I found him in our bed with Mallory, wearing my favorite cowboy hat."

"Wait a minute, who was wearing your favorite cowboy hat, Mallory or the dude."

"The dude, but he was wearing it on his Johnson."

"Eww. Low class."

"Definitely."

"What did you do with the cowboy hat?"

"What do you think? I burned it."

"What happened with the dude?"

"He initially filed assault charges and it turned into a thing and I was almost suspended over it, but Mallory talked him into dropping the charges and smoothed things over."

"How nice of her."

"Wasn't it? Except archaeology is a small world and everyone knows everyone. The incident could very well affect my chances of getting this job."

"Well, that blows."

"Big chunks."

"Do ya think —" Zoey slapped a palm over her mouth.

"What?"

"Nothing."

"It's something or you wouldn't have said it," he prodded her.

She pursed her lips, slid them from one side of her face to the other like she was trying her best not to blurt what was on her mind.

"Go ahead, spit it out. I can take it."

"Could it be . . . umm . . . maybe, just maybe, you *wanted* her to break up with you. If that's true, failing her was a pretty passive-aggressive move, but if it was subconscious, you might not even realize that's why you did it."

He hardened his jaw. "I gave her a D because that's what she earned."

"Would you have given her a higher grade if she had been your soul mate?"

"Zoey, there's no such thing as soul mates."

"Ah." She nodded. "I know what the deal is."

"Enlighten me." He picked up a cocktail napkin, and mopped the condensation off his beer bottle.

"You haven't felt *it* yet."

"It what?"

"The melding of minds that happens when you meet your better half."

He snorted. "You've been living in Cupid too long."

"Hey, Natalie wasn't a big believer in soul mates either until she met Dade. Look at them over there." She nodded toward a corner table.

Zoey's pregnant older sister sat with her husband, Dade Vega, who was a former Navy SEAL. He and his buddy Red Daggett ran a security business, and their biggest customer was a Canadian firm that had purchased and reopened the old Fant silver mine in a nearby county. Zoey had told him all about Dade and Red in their e-mails and phone calls, but he'd never met the men in person before tonight. Natalie and Dade stared deeply into each other's eyes, as if they were the only two people in the place. They did indeed look very happy, but Jericho was a scientist. He understood that compatibility had more to do with shared values, beliefs, and interests than some romantic notion of soul mates, but Zoey was Zoey and she had her own ideas about love.

"Just because your sister and her husband have a great relationship it doesn't make them soul mates. For instance, you and I get along like hydrogen and oxygen, and we're not soul mates. Explain that."

Her eyelids lowered, but he could see her peeking at him beneath the dark fringe of lashes, and his gut twitched. "You're right. As different as you and I are, we should hate each other. I guess some things are inexplicable."

"Have you?" he asked without even realizing he was going to ask it. "Ever felt this mind meld?"

This time she held his gaze for so long that Jericho forgot to take a breath. "If I had, I'd be like Natalie over there, sucking face with my soul mate."

He exhaled, heavier than he intended.

"Don't resist it, Jericho. Your one true love could be in this bar right this minute." She spun back around so she could survey the entire room.

"You think?" he said, never taking his eyes off her.

"Ooh." She elbowed him in the ribs again. "Check out the blonde at four o'clock. She's new in town. A nurse at Cupid General and I heard she's single, although I don't remember her name. Cheryl or Cherie or Sharla or something."

Why was she trying to fix him up? Was she muddily clueless how he felt about her? Or was it that she did not have similar feelings for him and was trying to hook him up before he could do something really stupid, like tell her what was on his mind?

"Not big on blondes," he mumbled.

She frowned. "Since when? Mallory was blond."

"Exactly." Did she ever wonder *what if* when it came to the two of them taking their friendship to the next obvious level now that they were both single? Of course, they couldn't do it *now.* Not when his career was in limbo. He had nothing to offer her, and Zoey deserved the world on a platter.

"Pish." She waved her wrist like it was made of overcooked spaghetti. "You can't exclude an entire hair color group because you had a rough go-round with one member of said hair color group."

"I'm not really interested in getting involved with anyone right now."

"Why not? If it's been almost six months since you guys broke up — and I'm still mad at you, by the way, for not telling me about it when it happened — time to get back on that Appaloosa."

"I'm not ready," he insisted.

"What about her?" She nodded at a brunette who'd just strolled through the door. A man waved at the woman and she rushed over to kiss him. "Okay, maybe not her."

Jericho swallowed. Christ, why was he

feeling like a shoeless man lost in the Chihuahuan Desert without a canteen? "What about you?"

"What about me?"

"When was the last time you were in a relationship?" he asked as a sudden spurt of fear made him worry that she was already in a relationship and had simply been waiting for the right moment to tell him.

"You wanna pick my next boyfriend for me? Have at it." She swept her gaze over him. "I'm partial to tall, dark, and handsome."

He gulped. *Me. Pick me.* "No one in this place is good enough for you," he said earnestly.

"Aw, aren't you sweet." She leaned forward, giving him an unobstructed view down the front of her shirt.

She wouldn't think "sweet" if she knew what was crashing through his mind. Jericho had to force himself to wrench his gaze off her cleavage. Damn V-neck blouses anyway.

"But seriously, who would you pick out for me?" she prodded.

"Depends on what you're looking for," he said through stiff lips. He hated this game. "Long-term commitment or casual fun?"

Even though she was smiling, there was

something unusually serious in her expression. "If I said 'commitment,' would you believe me?"

His chest tightened. "Not if you're truly serious about a career in archaeology. It's going to take years to get your career off the ground, and marriage would derail you. Are you serious about archaeology, Zoe-Eyes?"

"I'm serious about archaeology. No one believes me, but I am." Her eyes blazed and her hands curled into excited fists.

Her enthusiasm infected him with the heady, but oh-so-nefariously-spontaneous Zoey virus. Whenever he was around her, he felt enlivened the same way he did when a dig yielded a find — fevered, intense, trenchant.

"I picked up my love of it from you," she said. "You're quite irresistible when you talk archaeology."

"I am?"

"Totally. Why do you think I changed my major for the fourth time? Your love of archaeology won me over in spite of everyone telling me it's a hard career to make a living in."

"Not if you're devoted to it."

She winced. "I guess that's another reason everyone discouraged me. Devotion has never been my strong suit."

"But you really want this?"

"I do."

A cowboy sauntered by with a plate of cake. Zoey's gaze followed him. The cowboy paused and winked at her. So much for her undivided attention.

Jericho knotted a fist against his thigh, bit the inside of his cheek. "Not him."

"I just realized something," she said, her attention shifting from the cowboy to the buffet.

"What's that?"

"Walker's cake is half chocolate. C'mon, let's go get some before it's all gone." She hopped off the stool and took off, leaving him little choice but to follow.

CHAPTER 4

Attribute: A characteristic such as color or measurement of length or width.

Eager to have something to do besides think about the way Jericho was affecting her, Zoey had already sliced and plated two pieces of cake — chocolate for her, vanilla for him, by the time he reached the buffet table. The way he'd been looking at her all evening unnerved her. Whenever his gaze lingered on hers, there was a spark in his eyes that she'd never seen before.

Worse, her body responded to his heated looks like a flower to the sun. Her nipples tightened and her skin prickled and a squirmy sensation took root low in her belly. She'd used the excuse of chocolate cake to put some distance between them, at least momentarily, until she could regain her equilibrium.

She couldn't resist glancing adroitly at

him from beneath her lashes. In his faded Wranglers, worn cowboy boots, yoked shirt the color of claret, with the sleeves rolled up to reveal muscle-corded forearms; he looked more cowboy than scientist. No denying it, his eyes were caressing her.

Her pulse sprinted and she felt brilliantly bright and unsettlingly powerful. Was she imagining it or had something monumental shifted in their relationship since his return? But how? And why? More importantly, what did it mean?

His hot gaze gobbled her up and her bones liquefied.

Quickly, she turned, and cake in hand, sailed over to Walker. "You remember Jericho." Zoey nodded toward him as he came to stand beside her. "He just got his PhD in anthropology to go with his master's degree in archaeology."

Walker shook Jericho's hand. "Of course, Craig and Angie Chance's boy. Are you home to stay?"

"Depends. I'm waiting to see if I get hired at the Center for Big Bend Studies," Jericho said.

"You'll get the job. They'd be foolish not to hire homegrown talent." Walker shifted his weight.

"If he gets it, he'll be teaching the field

school this summer." Zoey swallowed a bite of cake and her pride. It was embarrassing having to ask a trustee for money. "You know, that's where archaeology students learn how to conduct digs and I was hoping to take the course, but that means I'll need —"

Walker held up his palm. "Let me just stop you right there, Zoey."

Her stomach sank. He was going to say no. She brightened her smile, widened her eyes, and just kept talking. *Power through.* "I know you weren't going to give me any more money until September, but I won't be able to participate in the field school unless I can come up with two thousand dollars. I really did try to stick to the budget you put me on, but I had some unexpected expenses."

Walker lowered his head and looked over the rim of his glasses at her. "Zoey, there's a reason your grandfather Raymond left me in charge of your trust. You're irresponsible with money."

"But this is for my education."

"Do you want me to break it down for you exactly how much money you've blown on college? You've changed your major four times, and now archaeology? Do you know how impractical that degree is? It's little more than interesting cocktail party conversation starter." Walker shifted his gaze to Jericho. "No offense to you intended. You're a different story. You have your doctorate and you're a dedicated scholar, you will be successful at this career, but we all know Zoey is never going to do anything with it. She's a dabbler. She needs to settle down, take hold, get a regular job or get married and start having babies. She's wasted enough time and money in school, delaying growing up."

That same horrible feeling of worthlessness and shame that she'd felt when she stood outside the door of the community center hit her squarely in the solar plexus. *Ooph.* She set down the cake, put a hand to her stomach.

"I have to disagree with you there, Dr. McCleary," Jericho interjected. "Yes, Zoey has tried a few different career tracks to see which ones fit, but you have to appreciate that she's young and has a vibrant mind. I really do believe she's found her niche and she'll finish her degree and give archaeology her all." His eyes were bright and sharp, as if he truly believed what he was saying.

Zoey's heart fluttered. Ahh, he was taking up for her. How sweet. Jericho was her hero.

He stepped closer, put a hand to her back,

whispered against her ear, "Don't back down."

His warm breath sent a sweet shiver sliding down her spine. Briefly, she closed her eyes. *Gotta stop feeling this way. It's not smart.*

Walker studied Jericho speculatively. "You think I should throw good money after bad?"

"I'm saying give her a chance to prove herself."

Walker folded his arms over his chest. "She's had numerous chances."

"She deserves one more." Jericho held Walker's stare.

"Please," Zoey wheedled, surprised to realize how much she wanted this.

Walker rubbed his mustache with a thumb and index finger.

Zoey batted her eyes and linked her arm through Walker's. Okay, yes, maybe it was manipulative, but charm rarely failed her. "I can't begin to tell you how much this means to me."

"As much as that mini-bike you just had to have?" Walker's tone went flat.

Her face heated. Rubbing her jaw, she winced. Walker bought the mini-bike for her thirteenth birthday, most likely because her relatives on the Fant side of the family had refused to do so. She'd smashed the banana yellow Bonanza into a mesquite tree after her boy cousins had challenged her to a race. She'd seen the tree coming and tried to veer out of the way, but her cousins had her hemmed in. She could have jumped off. She should have jumped off. Every cell in her body had screamed at her to jump off, but she'd been determined she could keep up with the boys. She'd broken her jaw during the accident and her teeth had been wired shut for weeks, which had been the worst thing of all for a motor mouth.

"Why didn't you jump off?" the doctor asked. "You wouldn't have been injured this badly if you'd bailed out."

After that incident, she vowed to always follow her instincts. Now look where following her instincts had gotten her. Everyone believing she was a noncommittal flake who couldn't stick with anything. Well, she was determined to prove them all wrong. If Walker wouldn't give her the money, she'd find some other way to get it.

"All right," Walker relented. "Because of Jericho's belief in you, I'll give you the money —"

"Woot!" Zoey exclaimed, and threw her arms around his neck. "Thank you, Walker, thank you so much!"

"But wait," he said. "Calm down."

That was always hard for her to do. She stepped back, took a deep breath. "Trying."

"There's a big stipulation, so I want you to think long and hard before you agree."

"Wh . . ." She cleared her throat, straightened her spine. "What is it?"

"You have to stay with this dig, no flaking out and quitting when you get bored. Prove to me that you can settle on something and stick with it or —"

"I can do it," she interrupted. "I *want* to do it."

"That's never stopped you from losing interest before. In fact, you're not even letting me finish my sentence."

"Okay, I'll shut up." She plastered a palm over her mouth.

"If you take the money and don't finish the dig, then I'm cutting off your trust."

"Completely? As in —"

"Turning it all over to charity."

"Forever?"

"That's what I'm saying."

Zoey's eyes grew wide. Alarm ripped through her. "You have the power to do that?"

"Not only do I have the power, but I can and I will. It's written in the trust agreement. Make up your mind once and for all. Finish the dig or you're completely broke."

■ ■ ■ ■

Cupid's Rest Bed-and-Breakfast was on the opposite side of Lake Cupid from Chantilly's Marina Bar and less than half a mile away. The night was warm and the stars were out, the moon nothing more than a sly *Mona Lisa* smile halfway up the sky.

Hypnotized, Jericho watched her skip down the steps ahead of him, following the well-worn walking path that skirted the lake. The potent feelings he'd been trying to squash all evening swelled inside him like a living animal, clawing and fighting against his self-control. No matter how objective he tried to be, he was still a man, vulnerable to the allure of an attractive woman, just like any other guy. Of course, he'd lusted after women before, but nothing like this, nothing so primal, so basically male. He wanted Zoey and he wanted her this *second.*

If another man had chosen this unlucky moment to approach her, he wouldn't have hesitated to toss him into the lake. What was happening to him? Where was this coming from? Why the growling Neanderthal impulses? How had he been able to simply be friends with her all these years, but now he didn't have a friendly thought in his brain? Not when it came to Zoey.

"Be careful in the dark," he called, but his warning came too late.

Her heel must have snagged on something because unexpectedly she spun, stumbled, and if he hadn't taken two long-legged strides to catch up to her, she would have fallen.

His arm went around her. She let out a gasp.

"Gotcha," he said softly, and righted her so that she was facing him.

In spite of almost having fallen, she looked supple and graceful with the wind rippling the silky material of her blouse and her soft, wide mouth pursed so fetchingly. Her light brown hair tumbling about her shoulders, her inquisitive eyes simultaneously quick and easygoing. Her pupils dilated and she darted out that sweet pink tongue to lick her lips shiny.

Christ, she looked like a pinup.

Mere inches separated them. His hand was on her elbow. Their chests were almost touching, her breasts rising and falling at a staggering pace.

"You okay?" he asked. Somehow both his hands were now resting on her shoulders. She gulped so forcefully that he could see the muscles in her throat work. What a long, lovely neck. His mouth burned to taste it.

"Uh-huh," she whispered.

"You've got to learn to slow down and take your time," he murmured, and lowered his eyelids. "Unless you've got a fire to put out."

"Maybe I do." Her gaze fixed on his lips, before flicking up to lock onto his. "Have a fire to put out, that is."

How quickly he'd gotten in over his head. He should have known better than to quip with a master. He wondered how other men defended themselves against her quick wit. They probably were so busy drooling over her and calculating the odds of getting her into bed that they didn't even bother. His stomach clenched.

"Do you remember this spot?" she asked.

How could he forget? It was where they'd stood the time she'd kissed him. They were finally going to talk about this? Should he admit that he did remember, or deny it? What was the best course of action? Uncertain, he nodded, barely.

"Wasn't that stupid of me?" She laughed low and gruff. "Kissing you like that. What was I thinking?"

"Neither one of us was doing much thinking that night." He grunted. "We'd been celebrating your birthday."

"You had your head on straight. Nothing new there." She laughed again, but her eyes were solemn. "I was the fool, believing that if we kissed that it would change things between us. Pretty lame, huh?"

"Zoey," he murmured, his entire body tightening. She had been trying to change things between them? He never knew that. He'd just thought she was intoxicated . . . and utterly *intoxicating.* Much like now.

She whacked her forehead with the heel of her palm. "I should have known it was going to be like kissing my brother."

Like kissing her brother? Whap! Kick to the ego.

Involuntarily, he curled his hands into fists. Here he'd been playing these romantic fantasies over in his head and Zoey was cutting him off at the knees. A brotherly kiss, huh? That's not how he remembered it.

Maybe she recalled it that way because he hadn't kissed her back. Hell, now he wished that he *had* kissed her back. What if he was to kiss her right now and wipe all that brotherly nonsense right out of her head? What would she say to that?

He lowered his head, his gaze hooked on that luscious, cherry-stem-tying little mouth. He was going to damn well do it. He was going to kiss her and rock her world.

"Ooh, look." She pushed back from him and pointed up at a bright meteor streaking all the way across. "Shooting star."

Relief and disappointment mixed inside him, and turned to a mess of complicated emotional goo. He wanted to kiss her, but he was also glad she moved before he'd pulled the trigger. He wasn't sure he wanted to make that irrevocable step, at least not yet.

"Make a wish," she insisted.

"I'm a scientist. I don't believe in wishes."

"C'mon, be unrealistic for once, make an exception."

"Wishing on a body of matter falling into the earth's atmosphere is not going to make my wish come true."

"What is your wish?" she whispered.

"If I told you, it wouldn't come true."

"I thought you didn't believe."

"I don't."

"That's too bad," she said with a casual shrug, but her tone was heartbreakingly sad.

"What's that?"

"You're missing out on a lot of fun and wonder."

He stared at her, torn between the urge to explore her fun-filled wonder world and the deep-seated fear that if he did so, it would be his world that got upended, not hers.

She reached up a trembling finger and started to run it down his cheek, but he shackled her wrist with his hand, stopping her in mid-stroke.

"Don't." The word came out far more abrupt than he intended. If she touched him, he'd come undone.

Her eyes rounded and she sucked in an audible deep breath. She stared at his fingers manacling her hand and then she did something that had him sucking in his own breath.

Zoey sank against him, dropped her cheek to his shoulder, and sighed softly. "How do you manage it?"

"Manage what?" he croaked, the feel of her against him more extraordinary than a rare archaeological find.

"To smell so clean at the end of the day. Like spray starch and soap."

"Took a shower," he said. "After you called and told me to come."

Come.

Unfortunate word choice under the circumstances, especially since the word echoed out over the lake — *come, come, come.*

He gulped.

She lifted her head from his shoulder, met his eyes and with an enigmatic grin, rose up on her toes to plant a kiss on his cheek.

Jericho turned to stone. Literally. Every muscle — and he did mean every single one — hardened.

Her warm breath raised gooseflesh on the back of his neck and the scent of cherries teased his nose. He turned his head and stared straight into her eyes. All he'd have to do was lean forward just the tiniest bit and their mouths would be touching.

Hold on to your self-control.

But what man in his right mind could resist this? Resist her?

Don't do something you'll live to regret.

He went to fist his hands and that's when he realized he still had hold of her wrist. His fingers sprang apart, releasing her.

"Look," she said.

"What?" He blinked, still addled from the lingering imprint of her lips on his cheek.

She pointed at the sky as a meteor streaked by. "Last chance to make your dream come true."

I wish, I wish, I wish I had the courage to tell Jericho how I really felt.

That's what Zoey wished for as she'd watched the star blaze across the sky. She lay in bed staring up at the ceiling, elbows bent to the sides, the back of her head cradled in her upturned palms, Eggy curled up sleeping in the center of her chest. His purring vibrations comforted her.

Why had she told Jericho that kissing him had been like kissing her brother? Why? Because she was scared. What if she'd admitted the truth that on that long-ago night, the simple brushing of their lips had rocked her world? Her skin tingled at the memory and she shuddered.

Eggy raised his head.

"Yeah, I'm nuts, but it's okay. Go back to sleep." She reached out to scratch the kitten behind his ears.

Eggy climbed higher and nestled under her chin. His purring vibrated her throat. She giggled. How fun he was. What had kept her from getting a pet before now?

Oh yeah, she'd been afraid a pet would curtail her freedom. Ha! She'd had Eggy for only one day and already her life felt lavishly enriched. Except there was the issue of what to do with the kitten when she went off to field school.

Hmm. She'd have to figure that out.

Tomorrow she had so much to do. Take Eggy to the vet to make sure he was healthy. Post messages about finding him. Study for final exams. And Jericho? What was she going to do about her growing feelings for him? Placing her tongue against the roof of her mouth, she rolled over, displacing Eggy. She tucked her knees to her chest and the kitten took the narrow space in between.

"I can't tell Jericho how I really feel," she whispered to the Siamese. "He could end up being my instructor, and after that cautionary tale about him and Mallory, well, that was a downer. Besides, what if he doesn't feel the same way? If I come right out and say the words and he doesn't feel the same way, will our friendship survive?"

Eggy mewed.

"You're right. I should keep my mouth shut. At least until I find out if he's going to get the teaching job. Thanks so much. You're the best sounding board."

Okay, it was decided. Lips zipped. Maybe when she told him the truth later on, he wouldn't hold that kiss-like-a-brother comment against her. That is, if she ever dared tell him at all.

"Eggy," she whispered. "What in the heck is going on with us?"

CHAPTER 5

Cultural dating: The process of comparing objects archaeologists find with information they already have.

Jericho's stepgrandmother Junie Mae insisted that he stay with her until he heard back from Dr. Sinton about whether he got the job. While he wanted to spend time with her, he hesitated because she lived right next door to Zoey. Once upon a time, that would have been a plus, but now? After what passed between them at Chantilly's, being near her was swiftly becoming a liability.

In the end, he hadn't been able to resist, even though staying at a motel in Alpine would have been far more prudent. With nothing to do but wait to hear from Dr. Sinton and knowing he'd go nuts without something to keep him occupied, he repaired things around the house and in his stepgrandmother's beauty salon — unstuck a drawer, replaced an electrical outlet, and painted the living room. By Friday, he'd already blown through all the chores Junie Mae dreamed up for him.

As for Zoey, he'd seen little of her since the night of Walker's party, and he couldn't shake the feeling she was avoiding him. While part of him was relieved, an equal part of him was disturbed by her absence. He knew she was studying for her final exams, but yesterday she'd turned him down when he'd ask her if she wanted to grab dinner.

Was Zoey upset with him for some reason he knew nothing about? Should he force the issue to see if something *was* up? Nah. Let it ride. She couldn't stay off by herself for long. It wasn't in her nature.

But even Natalie commented on her sister's suddenly overly industrious behavior when she peered over the backyard fence at Jericho on Friday morning. He was mending a cement crack in Junie Mae's turtle pond to keep from pacing a hole in the floor as he waited on the call from Dr. Sinton.

"Is Zoey trying to prove some kind of point?" Natalie asked him. "Normally, she's quite happy to skate by with B's. Now she seems hell-bent on getting a 4.0."

"Walker did issue her a challenge," he

pointed out.

"That's never worked on her before."

Jericho shrugged as if he hadn't been asking himself these same questions. "Maybe this time she's truly inspired to turn over a new leaf."

Natalie looked skeptical, but didn't say anything else about it. "How are your parents?"

"Good."

"Are they still in China?"

He nodded. "They love it there. Their mission work gives them a true sense of purpose. I have to admire that."

"They must be really proud of you getting your doctorate."

"They are." Too bad his parents hadn't been able to leave their missionary work in China to see him graduate.

Why should this degree be any different?

He shook his head. No feeling sorry for himself. He was a lucky man and he'd made peace with his parents' career choices a long time ago. Although when he was a little kid he'd had trouble understanding why those poor children in China were more important to them than he was. It wasn't until years later that he'd learned the great risks his parents had taken as underground activists in a country that had banned Christian missionaries. They could have been imprisoned or worse. To take him with them could have endangered his life.

"Give them my best when you speak to them again," Natalie said.

"Thank you, I will."

Natalie went back inside the B&B and Jericho returned to his work on the pond.

After his folks went to Asia, leaving him with his grandpa Prufrock and Junie Mae, he'd felt displaced, homesick, and lonely, until someone told him — he couldn't remember who it was now — that China was on the opposite side of the world from Cupid and that if you dug a deep tunnel straight down through the earth you'd come out there.

He'd been eight years old that summer, a quiet only child with a too-big vocabulary for his age. Grandpa Prufrock and Junie Mae had tried their best, but with Grandpa at work and Junie Mae running her hair salon out of the front of the house, for the large part of the day he hadn't had anyone to talk to. After rambling around for two days, Jericho decided he was going to dig that hole to China and find his folks. He made the mistake of tackling the project in the noonday heat, and after a few minutes, sweat was streaming down his back and his head hurt from the brightness of the sun, but he kept on digging, desperate to be reunited with his mom and dad.

"Whatcha doin'?"

The sound of a kid's voice caused him to stop and glance over his shoulder to see a pigtailed girl, in short pink coveralls, straddling the cedar fence.

"Digging a hole," he'd mumbled.

"Canna help?"

Part of him wanted to tell her to buzz off, she was little more than a baby, after all, but the lonely part of him shrugged. "I don't mind."

She climbed down the fence and came over. She smelled like oranges and she had moss green eyes that seemed to take up most of her face. "Whatcha name?"

"Jericho."

She wrinkled a tiny button nose dotted with freckles, tested out his name on her tongue. "Jerry-ee-co."

"Jericho," he corrected.

"I'm Zoey."

"Hi."

"How old are you?" she asked.

"Eight."

She held up four fingers. "I'm this many."

Wow, she was just a baby. He should tell her to go away. He didn't need a little kid underfoot.

"Whatcha doin' here?" She waved at the house.

"I live here now," he said gloomily.

Her wide eyes grew even wider and she grinned like that was the best news she'd ever heard. "Goody."

"Why do you say that?"

"I love makin' new friends."

Jericho scowled. "We're not friends."

"Sure we are," she said blithely. "Where is you mommy and daddy?"

"They went to China."

"Where dat?"

"On the opposite side of the world."

"Whadda they go there for?"

"To help kids."

"How come they didn't take you wid 'em?"

He shrugged, trying to pretend he didn't care, but his stomach hurt. "I dunno."

She pondered that a moment, then said very matter-of-factly, "My mommy and daddy are dead, but I don't 'member them."

That intrigued him. "How'd they die?"

"Big old plane crash. I was in the crash too, but I don't 'member that neither. My big sista Natty got hurted in the crash too. She didn't die but now she walks funny." Zoey limped around the yard to demonstrate.

"That's sad."

"Yeah, but don't tell her I tole you. She don't like to talk 'bout it."

Jericho nodded.

Zoey sank her hands on her hips, and studied his handiwork. "So ya diggin' a hole."

"Yep."

"What for?"

"To get to China."

"To find your mommy and daddy?"

"Yep."

"Canna help ya dig?"

He didn't much like the idea of her going to China with him. She might be company along the way, but what would he do with her when he got there? He shook his head. "Only got one shovel."

"Oh, don't worry 'bout that. My gram's got plenty o' shovels."

Jericho examined the hole. He wasn't making much progress. Might as well let her help for a while and then later he'd tell her she couldn't come with him all the way to China.

They dug for three days, finding all kinds of artifacts; arrowheads, a cigar box with the bones of some small animal in it — that particularly fascinated Zoey and she made up stories about what the animal was and who'd buried it — three marbles, a plastic microwave dinner plate, two pennies, and a live scorpion that almost stung Zoey. When Junie Mae finally spied the huge crater in the back of the yard, she made them quit digging, but from that experience the seed of Jericho's love for archaeology was planted.

He lived next door to the McClearys for the next four years until Grandpa Prufrock had gotten sick. His parents came home during that time, but he was shocked to realize he barely knew them. Six months later, they parked him with an aunt in Marfa and returned to the Orient.

That's where they were today. Gansu Province this time. Crusaders. Now and forever. For better or worse, it's who they were.

He glanced at his watch. Ten minutes past twelve. Dr. Sinton said that he'd let him know of the board's decision before noon. Just to check and make sure he hadn't missed a call, he pulled his cell phone from his pocket and turned it on. No missed calls. No text messages. Ah damn.

Disappointment lodged in his belly. Well, that was that. Apparently he didn't get the job. Now what?

Feeling numb, he cleaned the cement off the trowel and put away the supplies. That took a few more minutes and still no phone call.

Let go of hope. There's no point torturing yourself. Accept what is and start making other plans.

"Hey there." A soft, feminine voice broke through his reverie.

He turned to see Zoey coming through the backyard gate. She wore a short red flared skirt, cute matching sandals that showcased exceptional legs, and a red and white striped tank top. He broke into a smile because she always made him smile even in the face of bad news, but then he noticed she was biting her bottom lip and her big green eyes were misty.

Immediately, he strode toward her, his protective instincts raising the hairs on his arms. "What is it? What's wrong?"

She clamped her lips together, shook her head.

Alarm lit him up. "Zoey?"

"Eggy's gone," she whimpered.

Aw hell. He'd been scared something like this was going to happen. Take one defenseless kitten, mix with one well-meaning but ditzy young woman, and you had a recipe for an accident waiting to happen.

He slid his arms around her. "I'm so sorry, Zoe-Eyes. How'd he die?"

Zoey glowered, planted both palms against his chest, and shoved him backward. "Get off."

Jericho stumbled. "Whoa, what is it?"

She folded her arms over her chest. "You thought I killed Eggy."

"I didn't say that."

Her green eyes flared to the color of jade and she shifted her hands to her hips, arms akimbo. "You assumed he was dead."

"You said Eggy was gone. It's not an illogical assumption."

"Because I'm such an airhead I can't even keep a kitten alive," she said flatly.

"You're putting words in my mouth."

"He's not dead. I did not kill him." She managed to look both forlorn and irritated at the same time.

Jericho's heart contracted. Damn, he'd hurt her feelings again. "I jumped to conclusions. My bad."

"Eggy's owner reclaimed him. A woman and her seven-year-old daughter had come to visit her older son at Sul Ross and somehow the kitten got out of their car. They didn't notice that Eggy was missing until they got all the way home to San Antonio. The son saw my posts in the campus newsletter and called me. I just dropped Eggy off at his dorm room. If he hadn't seen the post when he did, they would have never known what happened to the kitten. This is his last semester at Sul Ross and he just finishing up his finals. He's leaving Alpine for good next week."

"Aw, you were within days of keeping Eggy. I'm sorry."

She forced a smile, but her bottom lip trembled.

He reached out again and drew her into his arms. "I know it hurts right now, but in the big scheme of things it's probably for the best."

"Because I couldn't possibly take care of a cat. I know, I know, you and my family have made that abundantly clear."

"No," he said softly, and brushed a strand of hair from her forehead. "Because you've got a four-week commitment to field school coming up and you simply don't have the time for a new kitten."

A single tear slid down her cheek.

"Ah, damn, sweetheart, it's gonna be okay." He held her close, felt the steady beating of her heart against his chest.

"I don't know why I'm crying." She sniffled. "I'm not the least bit sentimental."

He smiled, but didn't contradict her.

"I mean it's just a kitten, right?"

"Right."

She buried her face in his shirt. "Oh Jericho, I got so attached to Eggy. When that kitten looked me in the eyes it was like he knew exactly what I was thinking, and his fur was so soft and his sweet little purr both put me to sleep at night and woke me up in the morning."

He rubbed a circle over her back with his palm. "It will be all right. You'll get another cat at a more convenient time."

"I honestly didn't expect losing him would hurt this much. I only had him for a few days."

"Love can change your life in an instant," he murmured.

She pulled back slightly and looked up into his face. Tears dusted her lashes and she looked so darn sad, her eyes yanked at his heartstrings. He gave her a wry smile, cupped her cheek with his palm.

He never intended on kissing her, but in that moment it seemed as inevitable as breathing. His hand moved from her cheek to her chin and he tipped her head back even farther without even considering that he was about to make a big mistake. He simply lowered his head and claimed her mouth.

A soft little sigh escaped her lips while she simultaneously slipped her arms around his waist.

He had kissed his fair share of women over the years. Some of those kisses had been pleasant, some sweet, some romantic, some thrilling, some wild, some breath-stealingly passionate, but none of them had ever been like this one — pleasant, sweet, romantic, thrilling, wild, *and* breath-stealingly passionate, all rolled into one. For years he'd dreamed about kissing her like this and the reality far exceeded his expectations. This kiss reached down, took hold of something deep within Jericho, and squeezed all resistance out of him.

She tasted of summer, camaraderie, and childhood memories — homemade vanilla ice cream, campfire s'mores, ice-cold watermelon. She smelled of moon glow, whispers, and midnight shadows — fresh, familiar, yet strangely exotic. She made him think of secret trysts, heartfelt hopes, creaky back-porch swings, quilted pallets in the dewy grass, and a sky full of falling stars.

Finally, reluctantly, the need for air forced him to break the kiss. Transported. He'd been exuberantly transported into another time and place. An incredible place that combined past, present, and future into one big tangle of perfect. He peered down into those big eyes staring up at him so full of life, drew in a deep breath, and felt his soul — yes, he was just going to say it no matter how unscientific the term — snap back into his body with an edgy click.

Home.

He was home. It didn't matter that he hadn't gotten the job. This was where he wanted to be.

A sublime expression crossed her face, topped by an enigmatic smile. She laughed, low and gentle, and stepped from the circle of his embrace, but she stopped there. Didn't turn and flee. Twin pink splotches colored the apples of her cheeks and her eyes darkened, going from briny olive to a richer, mossy green.

Jericho's fingers itched to pull her back into his arms, kiss her again, harder, longer, fiercer. C'mon, who the hell was he trying to kid? He wanted to do a whole lot more than kiss her, but the rational part of his brain that had come temporarily unhinged regained a tiny foothold. *Don't. Just don't.*

Her breathing matched his own — hot, short, and quick. Her pupils dilated. Her nostrils quivered.

"Don't you dare tell me that was the least bit brotherly."

"No." She gasped. "Not brotherly, not cousinly, not even best-friendly. That kiss was . . . *whew.*" She fanned herself. "An inventive way to comfort a friend in need. For a minute there I forgot all about Eggy."

"Me too," he rasped, because he didn't know what else to say.

"Thanks for cheering me up."

Was that all she thought it was? His gut lurched. Jericho speared his hand through his hair. Why had he crossed that line? He knew better. What had happened to his self-control? "Zoey, I . . ."

"Uh-huh."

"I'm sorry. That was inexcusable."

"I don't know about that." She fingered her lips. "I found it pretty impressive."

"Not the kiss," he clarified. "The kiss was a chart-topper. I'm talking about my behavior."

"Hey." She shrugged casually, but he could see tension tighten the muscles in her neck. "Don't worry about it. We all get carried away sometimes."

Not me. That's what he found so disturbing — his loss of control. He stared at her and it was all he could do not to yank her back into his arms and do it all over again.

She put a hand to her mouth. "What?"

"I'm just wondering where do we go from here?"

"Nowhere," she said firmly, but lowered her head and cast him a sideways glance. Brown-sugar curls escaped from the clip at the back of her head, falling in carefree, silky waves that had him thinking about caramel swirls. God, she was beautiful, magnetic. All he wanted was to taste those lips a second time.

He gulped. *Easy. Easy. You've got to stop thinking like this.*

Zoey started walking backward toward the door, toe to heel.

"Don't go," he said, although it sounded like someone else spoke the words.

She stopped halfway to the door, hovered with one foot off the ground like a fawn too scared to move in the face of danger.

"We're not going to let a little kiss get in the way of our friendship, are we?" he asked, giving voice to his greatest fear.

"No." She laughed too loudly. "Of course not."

"Then don't run off."

She put her foot on the ground but still looked as if she could turn and sprint away at any second. She reached up to take the clip from her hair, sending her pert breasts rising higher with the motion, and the remainder of the soft strands fell to her shoulders in voluminous waves.

The kiss had caused his body to harden in the obvious places. Thing was, he was still hard; add to that surging breasts and tumbling hair and he was in serious trouble. He moved over to a lawn chair, sat down hard, and crossed his legs, unable to do much thinking against the hot rush of blood pounding through him, and prayed she hadn't noticed the very obvious signs of his arousal.

He motioned to the lawn chair. "Have a seat."

Awkwardly, she came to perch on the edge of the chair, rested her palms on the seat either side of her legs, ready to quickly propel herself up from the chair if circumstances demanded it.

A hesitant smile plucked at the corners of her mouth. "We're good, honestly. We don't need to talk about it. What's one little kiss among friends? We've kissed before. It was no big deal." She shrugged again.

The motion drew his attention to those smooth shoulders barely covered by the spaghetti straps of her candy cane tank top. He ached to trace his tongue over one of those shoulders, and track hungry kisses to the hollow of her throat to feel the throbbing of that fluttering blue pulse. Barely aware that he was doing it, Jericho gripped the lawn chair's armrests. He had to get himself in hand. *Now.*

She ran the tip of her tongue over her lips.

Did she have any notion what she was doing to him? Yeah, she probably did. The woman knew how to flirt, no doubt about it, but there was much more to her than met the eye. Yes, she knew how to have a good time, but there was substance to her that she'd never had to dig deep to unearth. Was it bat-shit crazy of him to want to help her find herself?

The prospect both enticed and scared the hell out of him. Never once in his professional life had he felt this off balance. Not even when he punched the dean that Mallory was sleeping with. But he sure felt off balance now, his equilibrium shot. Not because he didn't know what he wanted, but precisely because he did.

Warning! Dangerous territory.

He wished he hadn't kissed her. Now he knew exactly what he'd been missing. If kissing her was that phenomenal, what on God's green earth would making love to her feel like?

CHAPTER 6

Area of Potential Effects: The geographic area within which an undertaking may cause changes in the character or use of historic properties.

They sat staring at each other for what seemed like half a century. Zoey's pulse was pounding so loudly she couldn't hear her own thoughts. She pushed up off the lawn chair, tried to sound as casual as she could. "That it?"

A trickle of sweat slid down the side of his face. He stood too. "Yeah."

Jericho had kissed her, completely and thoroughly. The way she'd always dreamed he would kiss her. When his lips met hers, she closed her eyes, melted against him, heard the lid to the music box of her daydreams pop open and the playlist of her secret fantasies spill out like the soundtrack from *My Best Friend's Wedding* — "Wishing and Hoping," "The Way You Look Tonight," "I Say a Little Prayer." She'd wanted to do cartwheels and somersaults and back flips and she definitely wanted to kiss him again and again and again.

So why did she have a desperate, clawing need to flee? Why? Because she ached to get off by herself and assess what had just happened. Everything between them had irrevocably shifted and she couldn't fully process that fallout. Not when he was standing and staring at her as if he'd never seen her before.

Self-consciously, she put a hand to her cheek.

Jericho's cell phone rang.

They both jumped.

Without taking his eyes off her, Jericho peeled the phone from his back pocket, and placed it to his ear. "Hello."

Perfect time to bow out before her heart beat right out of her chest. Zoey pivoted and was on her way out the gate when he said, "Yes sir, Dr. Sinton."

She stopped, turned back. Had he gotten the job?

His face gave nothing away. "I understand."

She crossed her fingers. *Please let him get it.* If he didn't get the job, he'd leave Cupid.

"Yes sir. Thank you. I appreciate it." He hung up.

"Well?" She breathed, her hands clasped.

At last, he grinned. "I got the job."

"That's wonderful!" She moved to hug him, but he put up a palm.

"But I'm on probation and there's a big stipulation."

"What's that?" she asked.

"Under no circumstances am I to get romantically involved with a student. If I do, it's my job."

"Oh," she said, just as it fully dawned on her. Jericho was now her instructor and for the foreseeable future, an intimate relationship between them was strictly forbidden. "So, hey, Teach. Look at you."

"This means we can't . . . that what just occurred between us can*not* be repeated."

"Yeah." She nodded. "I got that."

"We should talk about this."

"It's okay." She shrugged and tried to appear unaffected. "We're cool."

"You might be," he said tightly, "but I'm not. I just kissed my best friend and the thoughts I'm having about her are anything but friendly." His words, the way his hot eyes were gobbling her up, sent a sweet, dark shiver through her.

"Jericho, I —"

"Don't pretend you're not having the same reaction." His gaze shifted from her face to her breasts where her traitorous nipples were beaded up so hard and tight they were poking through her bra and straining against the material of her snug-fitting, Lycra-blend tank top.

Briefly, she closed her eyes, willed her saucy nipples to settle down and cooperate. "Hands off. I get it. I can hang."

"Are you sure?" He took a step toward her as if testing her resolve and it was all she could do not to back up.

"Positive," she affirmed.

"We'll be in close proximity on this dig. Living in tents onsite for four weeks."

She put a finger in the air. "But with weekends off."

"Still, that's a lot of time together."

"With a whole dig team of people around," she reminded him.

"That's a damn good thing."

Her eyes met his. "Why is that?"

"Because I'm not sure I could keep my hands off you if we were alone."

"Oh, Jericho." She gulped. "What are you saying?"

His eyes darkened and his upper lip pulled back. "I want you so badly I can taste it."

She gulped. Her knees were shaking. "Me too."

"But we cannot act on this."

"No," she whispered.

"I have a job to do and you have a course to complete."

"Yes."

"Can you handle it?"

She notched her chin up. "I can if you can. It's only four weeks. We can resist anything for four weeks, right?"

"Right," he said, but he didn't sound the least bit convinced.

"So." She was ready to stop talking about it. "Dr. Jericho Chance, project archaeologist for the Center for Big Bend Studies. Fancy."

"Hasn't fully sunk in yet."

"I knew you would get it."

"Yes, but the position has got strings attached. Considering how I'm feeling about you, maybe I should turn the job down."

"Don't you dare! I'll only be your student for the length of the dig school. After that, since Sul Ross doesn't offer an undergraduate degree in archaeology, I'll transfer to another college."

"Yes, but that's assuming we can control ourselves."

She dropped his gaze. Did they have to

keep belaboring the point? She understood. He'd given her a boot-knocking, breath-stealing, mind-blowing, best-friends-make-the-best-kind-of-lovers kiss, and now they couldn't do anything about it. Duly noted, cataloged and filed under "Oh My Sleepless Nights."

Trying for light and casual, but making sure to keep her arms folded over her recalcitrant breasts, she changed the subject. "So, project director, where is our field school dig going to be held?"

Jericho ran a hand through his hair. "During my interview, Dr. Sinton told me it's a toss-up between Gilliland Canyon in Big Bend, Nature Conservancy's Independence Creek Preserve in Terrell County, or Triangle Mount in Jeff Davis."

"Triangle Mount? We're talking home sweet home! Are we hoping to put to rest the rumors that Triangle Mount is really a North American pyramid?"

Triangle Mount was on private land owned by the August McCleary Foundation.

On the heels of rather unscientific claims that some flatiron mountains in Bosnia were actually ancient pyramids, there had been much speculation that Triangle Mount was a pyramid as well. Truly, the tetrahedron-shaped mountain did resemble what an Egyptian pyramid would look like covered with West Texas soil and scrub brush. Lately, various conspiracy theorists, UFO aficionados, fans of the Marfa Lights mystery, adventure seekers, and bored teens had taken to trespassing on McCleary Foundation land to confirm the crackpot theory. The foundation board members, increasingly frustrated by the invasion, had discussed hiring security to keep trespassers off the land.

"It's bollocks, of course," Jericho said. "The theory is something that serious archaeologists dismiss out of hand and because of limited funding won't even waste time on debunking, but all scholars must guard against both complacency and a sense of superiority. There's always that rare exception to explore. Besides, it would make a great field school project. There are a lot of Native American artifacts in these mountains and no one has ever excavated that particular area before, and if we lay to rest the myth, we can stop the problem they're having with trespassers."

"You gotta admit that it *is* a perfect triangle. Easy to see where the rumors come from and why people are fascinated by the notion of pyramids in West Texas."

"Don't get too worked up. Triangle Mount is the dark horse. Director Sinton is leaning toward Gilliland Canyon."

"What determines which dig site we'll choose?"

"Funding, for one thing. For another, we need permission. It's easier to gain access to government land. In the past, the McCleary Foundation has been resistant to granting admittance. The center has asked, and been refused, several times."

She cocked her head. "You know, I might be able to twist arms where the center has failed. The chairman of the board, Marcus Winz-Smith, is a distant McCleary cousin, and timely enough, the semiannual board meeting is next week, I can go see him in person."

Jericho scratched his chin, his blunt-cut nails rasped appealingly against his stubble. Not five minutes ago that stubble was nicely abrading her face. "You do have a talent for twisting arms, but honestly, I don't know if Triangle Mount is the best project for us."

"Hey, I've got nothing to lose. In fact, I'll even ask if the foundation will consider chipping in to help fund the dig."

"Let's not push our luck."

"Why not? All they can say is no and we

won't be any worse off than we were before."

"It's up to you." He shrugged.

"Consider it done." She snapped her fingers. "Triangle Mount, here we come."

"Why does excavating Triangle Mount mean so much to you?" he asked.

Her chin notched up. "For one thing, it's part of my family history. For another thing, I've always had a feeling that there was something special under that mountain. I know it doesn't make any sense from a logical, scientific point of view, but no one ever accused me of being logical." She laughed. "The flatiron has captured my imagination and won't leave me alone."

"And that's it?"

"Well," she said. "There is the fact if we get permission to excavate Triangle Mount, it will be a feather in your cap and earn brownie points for you with Dr. Sinton."

"Don't stick your neck out for me."

"But isn't that what best friends are for?"

Jericho looked at her with such hot longing, that Zoey had to wonder if they even *were* best friends anymore. With that kiss, had they crossed an invisible line from which there was no going back?

On Thursday afternoon, almost a week since

Jericho had kissed her, Zoey was on her way to the August McCleary Foundation's semiannual board meeting. She was leaving nothing to chance. She smiled at her pun. Honestly, she'd leave everything to chance — Jericho Chance, that is — if she could, but Jericho was in a precarious position as a brand-new instructor for the field school and on probation to boot. He couldn't go around rocking boats, but she sure could. It was one of the things she did best.

Then again, he'd done some hellacious boat rocking in Junie Mae's backyard last week. She sighed dreamily and touched her lips. Too bad. Too darn bad that they had to put this thing between them in cold storage for a few more weeks. Then again, if she could keep him at arm's length while they worked side by side, it would be clear proof she could control her impulses. Right?

Ah, but can you?

There was the rub.

What did she want more? Jericho or her trust fund?

Hold out for a few weeks and you don't have to choose.

Her distant cousin and chairman of the foundation board, Marcus Winz-Smith, was also CEO of a boutique pharmaceutical company headquartered in Austin. While

Cousin Walker had taken the helm of the string of Trans-Pecos pharmacies started by Great-Great-Uncle August before they'd been bought out by a big corporation in the 1980s — except for the flagship store in Cupid that Cousin Walker still ran — Marcus's side of the family had inherited the original formula that August used to heal those stricken with the Spanish flu in 1918.

Marcus made some alterations and adjustments and invented Flugon, a medication administered to patients at the first signs of flu symptoms in order to lessen the severity of the virus. Under Winz-Smith's expert management, Flugon was rapidly becoming a worldwide go-to antiviral of choice.

The foundation's offices were on the top floor of a converted old Victorian. The bottom floor housed the Cupid Museum, which was filled with dusty old history that had never much interested Zoey before, in spite of the fact that eighty percent of the history in it was related to her family on one side or the other.

A cowbell clanked when she walked through the door and the old floorboards creaked beneath her feet. The board meeting was scheduled for two and it was ten minutes until the hour. She hoped to intercept Winz-Smith before he ducked upstairs.

The thin woman behind the welcome counter, Tabitha Crispin, was a sometimes member of the Letters to Cupid volunteers. She sported a gray poodle-perm and bright red rectangular reading glasses perched on the end of her sharp, long nose. When Zoey was a kid, she thought Tabitha was a witch, what with the name and the nose and her tendency to dress in black. Someone must have told Tabitha to brighten up for the tourists, because today she wore gray and she was busy dipping strawberries into a bowl of sugar, holding them by the green stem and nibbling on them like a rabbit.

Tabitha greeted her with a hearty hello that belied her generally dour appearance.

"Morning." Zoey nodded.

"Didja come to see August's formulary we just put on display?" Tabitha waved toward a glass case in the middle of the musty-smelling room. "Granted it's dull as dirt, but with Walker's biography about your great-great-uncle August hitting the *New York Times* best-seller list and that Universal Studios deal in the offing, there's been a lot of interest in seeing the formulary. Amazing how all this time Cupid has been sitting on this bit of history just waiting for your cousin Walker to write about it."

"Uh-huh." Zoey wandered over to the

case where the leather-bound journal was displayed on a stand and opened in the middle to the empirical formula that was the genesis of Flugon.

The entry was dated June 6, 1914, in a spidery scrawl, four years before the catastrophic Spanish flu seized the world in a death grip. Zoey squinted. The chemical formula was all mathy and complicated, a diagram of atoms and the molecules that made up the compound.

Totally boring, except for an odd little drawing in the top corner of the page that consisted of two side-by-side triangles; the one on the right was slightly taller and there was a small dot just below the peak of that triangle. In between the triangles, at the base level was a narrow oval — almost the shape of an almond — and directly above the oval was arciform that resembled an eyebrow arched over an eye. The whole thing made her think of a deconstructed Eye of Providence. She loved puzzles, and the drawing intrigued her.

"What's this doodle above the molecular formula?" she asked Tabitha.

"Just that. A doodle. August was a big doodler. Book is filled with 'em. I'm surprised you don't know that. You're a McCleary, after all. You should know your family history," Tabitha chided.

Yeah, yeah, she got that a lot.

"Have you ever investigated the McCleary family tree? Fascinating stuff, your ancestry. Didja know we have traced it to the first McCleary who ever set foot in the Trans-Pecos back in the eighteenth century?"

"Nah." Zoey shrugged. "I'm not much of a history buff."

"Those who don't know history are doomed to repeat it," Tabitha said. "That's a quote from Edmund Burke."

"Whoever that is," she mumbled.

Tabitha pulled a book from underneath the counter and flipped it open. "Did you know that Marcus is a popular McCleary name? There have been four since the first McClearys came to Jeff Davis County."

Zoey forced herself not to yawn. "Uh-huh."

"It's a beautiful name. If you ever have a son, you might consider using it. There's something very comforting about tradition. I'm jealous you have such a long pedigree on both sides of your family. You don't know how lucky you are. My family is very small. My Tommy and I never had any children of our own, although we had a lot of fun trying." Tabitha winked. "If you get what I mean."

Eeew. She did not need the image of Tabitha having sex burned into her brain.

"Look at all the great family names you have to choose from for your children." Tabitha started reading off names on a list of long-departed McClearys from the book. "Zachariah, Jeb, Edward, Gerald, and of course the four Marcuses. Or if you have girls you can choose from Claudia, Christina, Clarissa, Charlotte, Catherine."

Zoey covered a yawn with her palm.

"Hmm," Tabitha mused. "They really had a thing for C names when it came to females. Do you think it was because they liked alliteration? Catherine McCleary has a nice ring to it, don't you think? Although the girls would have lost the alliteration when they married and back then women never kept their maiden names. Makes you wonder why the family didn't do the C thing with the boys instead. If I would have had a son I always thought I might have named him Chaucer."

Looks like Tabitha's imaginary kid had dodged a daily beating. Wow. Hanging out in the museum by herself all day with nothing to do but dust old books and read yellowed musty tomes about long dead folks must have gone to the old girl's head.

Zoey cast an eye toward the door. Tabitha

might be curator of the Cupid Museum, but she was also gatekeeper to the foundation offices. There was a chain draped across the stairs that led up to the second floor. She couldn't really vault over the chain and lay in wait for Winz-Smith. That held no finesse, and besides, Tabitha wouldn't go for it. She took her duties seriously.

Best course of action? When in doubt, charm, charm, charm.

"I can't believe how spotless you keep this place," Zoey said. "Must be difficult with tourists traipsing in sand and getting fingerprints all over the display cases."

Tabitha reached underneath the counter for a bottle of Windex and a polishing rag. "My secret weapon."

"You deserve a raise."

"We survive on donations," she said. "Minimum wage works for me. I have a nice Halliburton pension from my Tommy, God rest his soul. I do this mostly to get out of the house."

"Listen, Mrs. Crispin —"

"You've known me long enough to call me Tabby."

Zoey sauntered over to the counter. Oh this was good, first-name basis. "Tabby." She lowered her voice to a conspiratorial tone. "Is there any way I can speak to Mr.

Winz-Smith before the meeting starts?"

"Oh my, no." Tabitha pressed a hand to her chest. "He's on a very tight time schedule. He flies in on his private jet for the meetings and flies right out again. He's a very important man."

Damn! Why hadn't she thought about ambushing Winz-Smith at the Cupid Airport? Maybe because she had a mental block about the airport since that's where her parents had flown out of the day they were killed.

"I wouldn't take up much of his time. We could walk and talk."

Tabitha narrowed her eyes to slits, and in the light slanting through the blinds, she looked exactly like a storybook witch. "I have strict instructions to keep people away from him. You know how some folks are about drug company executives. Think they're all evil because they make money off sick people."

"But he's my cousin."

"Very distantly. Have you ever spoken to him?"

"No, but I saw him once at a family reunion when I was a kid. I think it was him anyway."

"Might as well be a stranger. You want to speak to him, you have to request a meeting through the proper channels just like anybody else."

Male voices spoke from behind the house. Was it Winz-Smith coming in through the rear entrance?

"Don't even think about it," Tabby warned.

Zoey assessed the older woman. She could outrun her, no doubt about it, and at least get in a handshake and a quick plea to Winz-Smith before Tabby booted her out of the museum.

"I keep a Taser under the counter," Tabby threatened. "Wanna see it?"

Zoey raised both palms. "I'm good."

Two men came into the museum through the back door. One was close to six-foot-five and built like a shipping pod. He had on a suit that bulged at the seams and he still wore dark sunglasses indoors. He might as well walk around with a red neon sign above his head that flashed "Bodyguard."

The second man was fortysomething and the prettiest guy she'd ever seen. He was Rob Lowe and Pierce Brosnan rolled into one — lush dark hair, piercing blue eyes, perfectly symmetrical features. His suit was tailored to fit his sleek, toned body. His nails were manicured, his hair freshly clipped, and his clean-shaven face was as smooth as the proverbial baby's behind. He was the sort of man who'd make the majority of women swoon and drool. Once upon a time, Zoey would have been one of those women, but now all she could do was compare him to Jericho and he came up seriously lacking — why go for soft and pretty when you could have ruggedly masculine?

Just thinking about Jericho sent a sweet shiver through her.

"Good afternoon, Mrs. Crispin," the pretty man said.

Tabby blushed like a schoolgirl. "Hello, Mr. Winz-Smith. I have a fresh pot of coffee brewed. Your favorite dark French roast."

Marcus Winz-Smith cast a glance at the big fellow, who nodded and walked off, ostensibly to fetch a cup of coffee for his boss. From the pocket of Winz-Smith's suit jacket protruded a rolled up copy of the *American Journal of Botany.* The very same issue her cousin Lace's article had appeared in. Talk about serendipity. What a great way to introduce herself to Cousin Marcus.

Tabby caught Zoey's eye and was jerking her head toward the front door, but Zoey ignored her and instead blurted to Winz-Smith, "Have you read the article on the Golden Flame agave?"

Both of Winz-Smith's eyebrows went up

and he pulled the magazine from his pocket. "You read the *American Journal of Botany*?"

"Only because my cousin Lace wrote the article," she admitted. "Usually, I'm more of a *Cosmo* girl."

He laughed. "Fascinating article. Your cousin has a brilliant mind and she seems thoroughly convinced that the Golden Flame agave is not only real, but has not gone extinct."

Zoey knew more about hanging drywall than she did botany, but she wasn't about to waste a great opportunity. She stuck out her hand, moved toward Winz-Smith, and prayed Tabby wouldn't make good — or bad, depending on how you looked at it — on her innuendo that she'd use the stun gun if Zoey approached Winz-Smith. Hey, impulsivity sometimes paid off. You never knew until you tried.

"Hi," she said brightly. "I'm Zoey McCleary and we're cousins too. Something like first cousins four times removed, I think, or maybe it's second cousins three times removed. I don't really understand how all that cousin stuff works."

"Ah," he said, taking her hand and holding it a little too long, while his gaze captured hers. "We meet at last."

"You've heard of me?" That came out a

little too high and breathy. She cleared her throat.

"The irrepressible beneficiary of Raymond McCleary's trust that our cousin Walker administers?" He chuckled. "Walker speaks of you often."

"I bet he didn't use the word 'irrepressible.' "

"No, indeed." Winz-Smith stroked his chin. "I believe Walker's exact words were 'wild child.' "

Et tu, Walker? Yeah, well, she was on the road to fixing that. "Not all that wild," she denied.

Winz-Smith smiled big, showing a row of stark white teeth.

Dude, seriously, you gotta cool it with the whitening strips. Nobody needs a mouthful of Chiclets.

His gaze strolled over her, sliding from her neck to her boobs right on down to her hips, making her wish she had on an overcoat. Oh, ick! They were related. Normally, she had no compunctions about using her sex appeal to wrap men around her little finger, but he was making her uncomfortable.

She took a deep breath and launched into her spiel about why excavating Triangle Mount was a good idea.

Tabby's head came up and her spine stiffened. "Oh no, you don't, missy." She charged over, arms flapping as if Zoey was a pesky crow diving into a cornfield, one hand wrapped around the Taser.

Winz-Smith slapped the older woman with one of his stunning smiles, stopping her dead in her tracks. "It's fine, Tabby. I find my dear cousin quite entertaining and I can't believe I'm just now making her acquaintance."

Mr. Bodyguard returned with the cup of coffee and now there were other board members coming through the back entrance. Walker was on the board too and she wanted to get this out before he showed up, just in case he decided to put the brakes on the project.

"It's because you don't live around here," Zoey said.

"More's the pity." He looked at her in a decidedly uncousinly manner.

She gulped. "So about excavating Triangle Mount . . ."

"How does this benefit me?" he asked.

"Think of it like this." She forced herself to shoot him a beguiling smile and immediately felt the urge for a scalding shower. "If you give us permission to excavate the place, it will be a hedge against those trespassers —"

"How's that?"

"They're not going to come around with people up there. We'll have everything roped off around the site, and once we prove that Triangle Mount isn't a pyramid, that will lay the whole issue to rest and the looky-loos will be onto a new mystery."

"But what if you find out it *is* a pyramid?"

"Then you can turn it into a whole thing and charge admission."

"The lands are a nature preserve. The idea is to keep it pristine. Hence the preserve part."

"We're only interested in Triangle Mount. Nothing else on the foundation's vast acreage," she said. "We promise not to disturb anything else."

"Hmm." Winz-Smith looked pensive.

"Anyway, that's my pitch. I hope you'll give it serious consideration." She nibbled her bottom lip and shifted from foot to foot.

For the longest time, he said nothing.

"Well?" She caught her breath, held it.

"You can relax, Zoey," Winz-Smith said. "Dr. Chance has already made your case. Although it takes a majority vote of the board members to make it official, I'm in your corner."

"Jericho talked to you?"

"Indeed," he said. "He met my plane at the airport."

"And you just let me blab?"

"Just wanted to see if you were as invested in the project as Dr. Chance is."

"Oh, I am, I am."

"Then if you'll allow us to get down to business . . ." He waved at the staircase.

"Oh yes, right." Zoey grinned, thanked Mr. Winz-Smith for his time and Tabby for not Tasering her, and left the museum feeling pleased as Punchinello.

Well, well, well, so Jericho could be just a little bit impulsive himself. If she could rub off on him, surely a bit of his cautiousness would rub off on her. Unfortunately, that thought caused her mind to hop to a wholly different kind of rubbing.

CHAPTER 7

Excavation: Digging up artifacts and features from an archaeological site in order to analyze and predict past human behavior.

With Winz-Smith's backing, the board readily approved their request to allow the field school access to August McCleary's nature refuge and to fund the dig. Zoey learned later the only dissenting vote had been Walker's. But Winz-Smith had one nonnegotiable condition. Excavation was restricted exclusively to Triangle Mount. If they violated that rule, not only would they face immediate eviction, but also the Center for Big Bend Studies would have to pay back the money the foundation spent on the dig. A contract to that effect had been drawn up and signed.

Zoey broke the news to the love letter volunteers that she wasn't going to be able to answer letters for the committee for the next month and that Tabitha Crispin had agreed to fill in for her. She could tell they were skeptical she'd last the entire month, even with Walker's stipulation. Let 'em scoff. She'd prove herself.

Under Jericho's supervision, she and the other thirteen students who comprised the dig team spent the ensuing three weeks preparing for excavation. There were nine guys to the six girls. Zoey was amused to learn that setting up fieldwork often took as long as the dig itself. They collected as much documentation as they could find from old maps, to soil surveys, to land records. Jericho had the students test their technical abilities with aerial photography, satellite imagery, and geographic information systems. After that, they moved onto gathering the equipment they would need — shovels, trowels, coring tools, augers, colorful flagging tape, machetes, copies of maps for everyone on the team, measuring tapes, rulers, compasses, waterproof markers, plastic bags, magnifying glasses, graph paper, clipboards, GPS units, tablet computers, first aid kits, insect repellent, sunblock.

They conducted surface and subsurface investigations, shovel testing, and core probing. Their efforts at a judgmental sampling — which meant they looked for places to dig where they thought archaeological sites might be — were somewhat hampered by Winz-Smith's insistence they restrict their search strictly to Triangle Mount, but combined with probabilistic sampling, meaning they used math to give them a more objective guess, they located a promising spot.

The recording process seemed endless. Jericho's mantra was "record everything" and he reminded them of it about five hundred times a day. They took photographs, filled out forms, and organized their research and wrote up a dig plan. Zoey forced herself to embrace the "boring" parts. After all, she was determined to prove to herself that she had the grit to stick to this.

Jericho was a stickler for both safety and field ethics. He insisted on a safety plan in case of accidents and safety rules to circumvent them. He held an archaeology day for the community to generate local support for the project and designated a day when the public could come help them dig, after running it past Winz-Smith first.

Finally, they made arrangements for earthmoving equipment and operators to come in to break ground and lastly, set up the eight tents where they would be living during the duration of field school, the end of which would culminate just before the Fourth of July weekend. They'd bunk two to a tent. Zoey's roommate was Catrina Bello, a foreign exchange student from Portugal, who had a flawless command of English. She was as beautiful as her name; model tall with Angelina Jolie lips and a way of shrugging that made Zoey feel distinctly dismissed. But hey, she could get along with anyone.

At six A.M., on the morning of June 8, the dig began in earnest.

Zoey started out full of enthusiasm. She hadn't been a cheerleader her junior year of high school for nothing, never mind that she'd quit the activity halfway through the school year to take up track and field, and that lasted only a few weeks before she decided to play the saxophone, until it turned out she wasn't the least bit musically inclined, but no more of that nonsense. She loved archaeology and she was sticking with it.

Besides, it was fun when the guys took their shirts off in the arid heat. Especially Jericho. The last time she'd seen him shirtless they'd been teenagers, and he'd certainly filled out nicely since then.

His strong neck blended into powerful shoulders and muscle-packed chest that set her mouth instantly watering. When he strained at his work, gripping a shovel with his big hands, mammoth biceps bunched tight. A uniform dusting of dark hair highlighted his pecs before trailing down to rippled abs as tight as a trampoline. Naughtily, she allowed her gaze to stray to his crotch, where his jeans stretched taut.

She dipped the brim of her pink straw cowgirl hat down over her eyes so she could watch him surreptitiously without being caught ogling. Such a shame that he was off limits. The things she wanted to do to that man!

If that cautionary tale he'd told her about his disastrous, line-crossing teacher/student relationship with Mallory wasn't enough to thwart her, the thought of getting him fired certainly did. Plus there was the whole screwing up their friendship thing to consider. As delicious as his washboard abs and squirm-inducing biceps were, a few moments of sinful pleasure would not be worth the price.

What if getting intimate strengthened your connection instead?

That provocative question had been circling her head from the moment she'd seen him again in the Sul Ross parking lot, and it had spurred her decision to stick with archaeology. She needed to know that she had the stuff to make a big commitment and stick to it.

By the third day of shoveling and troweling and peeling back layers of strata and screening soil when they still had not found a thing, Zoey's zest was waning faster than beer at a frat house kegger. As she lay on her uncomfortable cot that night, exhausted to the bone and listening to Catrina snore — beautiful she might be, but the girl could give a buzz saw a run for its money — she couldn't help thinking that if she quit the field school, Jericho would no longer be her instructor. That would open the door for something more to develop between them, but then Walker's threat to cut off her trust fund entirely put a stop to those thoughts. She'd waited for Jericho for twenty years, what were a few more weeks?

"I'm no quitter," she announced out loud, hoping that if she said it enough she'd start to believe it.

Catrina sat up on her cot. "What?"

"Nothing, never mind. Go back to sleep."

On Thursday, the fourth day of the dig, Jericho left the dig site for a faculty meeting at the university. The second his pickup truck disappeared from view, the nine male students clustered around Catrina, offering to help her shift sand. Frustrated with both the fruitless dig and the Catrina worshipping and with no shirtless Jericho to hold her interest, Zoey climbed from the excavation site, wiped the sweat from her brow, and wandered over to the ice chest for something to drink.

She stood gulping down the water and looking out over at Widow's Peak, which was a good two thousand feet taller than Triangle Mount's forty-five-hundred-foot elevation. In the flat desert terrain that stretched between the two mountains was a small, oval-shaped lake that shimmered an enticing blue. It wasn't far away, maybe a mile off, and while Winz-Smith had forbidden them to excavate anywhere but Triangle Mount, he hadn't said they couldn't go swimming in the lake.

The cool waters called to her. *Come take a dip.*

Zoey glanced over at her fellow students. They were either busy digging or bird-dogging Catrina. No one noticed when she picked up her backpack and slipped off.

Thirty minutes later, she was doing the backstroke in her underwear, savoring the refreshing swim and the stark, natural beauty of her surroundings. She could see why past McClearys had set aside this land for a nature preserve. Unless an airplane happened to fly over, it was easy to imagine she'd stepped into a time machine and gone back two hundred years.

She wished Jericho were here with her. He knew so much about history. She'd love to hear him talk about what life had been like those days. Although she could just hear him tell her, *You wouldn't like it, Zoe-Eyes. No cell phones. No iPads. No texting. No Twitter.*

Maybe she would have liked it, though. That is, if Jericho could go back in time with her.

She floated, allowing her mind to wander. From this vantage point, she had a clear view of the top of Widow's Peak and pictured her and Jericho building a log cabin together. It was probably harder than it looked, but Jericho was handy that way. Honestly, the man seemed to know something about almost everything. Speaking of Jericho, she better get back before he returned and caught her goofing off.

After she got out of the lake, shimmied back into her clothes, and tucked her wet hair up underneath her cowgirl hat — it would dry in nothing flat in the desert heat — for the first time she noticed two earthen mounds a few yards from the water. The mounds were covered with scrub brush and cactus and other inhospitable vegetation. Before she started taking archaeology courses she would never have looked at a mound of earth and thought, *There's something underneath there,* but that's exactly what she thought now. A prickly sensation that was strangely akin to a static electric shock lit up her nerve ends and then settled with a hard jolt in the pit of her stomach.

She pulled a copy of the area maps from her backpack and studied them to see if the mounds had already been recorded. Nothing. Hmm, could there have been a settlement here at one time? What if she found a village that no one had ever heard of? Her pulse skipped a beat.

Her enthusiasm that had worn away came charging back stronger than ever. This was why she'd become interested in archaeology. The heady thrill of discovery. With trembling fingers, she took the collapsible shovel she kept stowed in her backpack and went over to the larger of the two mounds. Remembering everything Jericho had taught her, she started to dig.

■ ■ ■ ■

"Where's Zoey?" Jericho asked when he returned to the dig site to find her missing.

The students blinked and glanced around.

"She was just here," said Avery Slocum.

Avery was a bit older than the other students and was working on his master's at Texas A&M. He'd joined their field school as a volunteer. Because he had the most experience, Jericho made him second in command and they were sharing a tent. Avery had hot eyes for Catrina and she seemed interested in him as well. Jericho had warned the younger man about the perils of getting intimately involved with a fellow student on a dig, but his words of caution fell on lust-deafened ears. Since Avery was neither an employee of, nor a student at, Sul Ross, Jericho didn't have much authority to forbid him to strike up a romance with Catrina, plus he felt like a hypocrite doing so. Every time Jericho looked at Zoey he was on the verge of breaking a dozen rules himself. They were all adults here. As long as Avery and Catrina's budding relationship didn't interfere with the work, he'd stay out of their business.

As for himself, well, he was *not* going to do anything about his deepening feelings for Zoey, at least not until the dig was over. Too much was at stake for them both.

But where was she?

Shaking his head, Jericho scanned the site. There really wasn't anywhere to disappear to in the immediate vicinity. Maybe the relentless sun had given her a headache and she'd gone to lie down in her tent. He pivoted and headed down the incline to check her tent, when from the corner of his eye, he caught movement on the valley floor between the two mountains and near the small lake.

He stopped and narrowed his eyes. Something — or someone — was down there. He stalked to his pickup truck parked at the bottom of Triangle Mount, pulled a pair of binoculars from the glove compartment, returned to his vantage point, and focused in on the movement.

Yep. It was Zoey. What the hell was she doing down there? He narrowed his eyes, looked again. Digging. She was digging. Right where Winz-Smith's contract had expressly forbidden them to dig.

Swearing under his breath, he started to reach for his cell phone to call her and chew her out, but then remembered cell service out here was nonexistent.

"What's up?" Avery came to stand at his elbow.

"Slight problem, nothing to worry about. Stay here and supervise the dig. I'll be back in a bit." He thrust the binoculars at Avery, who promptly peered through them.

"What's she doing down there?"

"That," Jericho threw over his shoulder as he headed toward the lake, "is the million-dollar question, and knowing Zoey, it's got a screwball answer."

Zoey was so absorbed in her digging and the artifacts she was unearthing that she didn't hear or see a thing until a pair of cowboy boots planted themselves in front of her.

Uh-oh. Busted.

Pulse thumping, she slowly raised her head, taking in the tips of those dusty boots to the frayed hem of faded Wranglers to the longhorn belt buckle that crowned his zipper — she stopped there a minute to admire the package — then moved on up to sinewy arms folded tightly over a chest so honed she could see the definition of muscles through his white cotton shirt.

Finally, she tipped her head all the way back and grinned nervously up at Jericho's thundercloud face.

"Hi!" she chirped, and tried her best to look adorable.

"Care to explain yourself?" he asked in a spookily soft voice.

Zoey gulped. "I'm digging."

"I can see that. What I want to know is *why* are you digging?"

She dialed her grin up a notch. "I'm an archaeologist. We dig. That's what we do."

He sank his hands on his hips, did not crack a smile. "Your extreme cuteness is not going to get you out of trouble."

"No?"

He shook his head.

She measured off an inch with her thumb and index finger. "Not even a little bit?"

"Zoey, I'm just trying to do my job here. I didn't think it would be that hard for you to follow the rules. Not when there's so much at stake for us both."

She pressed a hand to her belly. "I didn't mean to cause trouble —"

"You never do." His scowl deepened.

Her heart tripped over itself. The last time he looked this mad at her was that time at summer camp when she'd jumped off the cliff into a pool. She hadn't even stopped to consider what she was doing. Just jumped in with both feet like always.

"Are you *trying* to ruin this dig?"

"No, no, quite the opposite. In fact, I'm making the dig. Look at this." She made a move to stand, but she'd been squatting for so long that when she tried to get up, her head spun.

He put out a hand and she grabbed onto it and he tugged her to her feet. Her head was still reeling. He slid his arm around her waist. "You okay?"

His body heat intensified the noonday heat. Simultaneously, she wanted to press closer — burn out, flare out, flame out in a blaze of glory — and save herself by pulling as far away from him as she could get.

"Fine," she whispered hoarsely and took a step back.

"Here." He reached in his backpack, drew out a bottle of Gatorade, and pressed it into her palm. "Drink."

It wasn't until she'd downed the entire bottle that she realized how dehydrated she'd become and noticed that she had numerous scratches criss-crossed up and down her hands and arms. Her clothes were already dry, her hair too. How long had she been digging?

Jericho took the empty bottle from her and tucked it back into his pack. "Feeling better?"

"Yes." She put her palms to her lower spine and stretched out the kinks.

His gaze strayed to the ground and the dirt-covered artifacts she'd piled up. "This isn't proper procedure. Not to mention it's a clear violation of the contract we signed with the foundation."

Sheepishly, she ducked her head. "I know, I know. I didn't mean to start digging. I came down here for a swim and then I saw these two mounds. My intention was merely to take a soil sample, but in the first scoop of sand, I found this." With the toe of her hiking boot, she touched the blue and white crockery shard she'd unearthed. "I got so excited I kept digging and couldn't stop because I just kept finding stuff."

Arms draped over his thigh, Jericho crouched beside the artifacts she'd collected and examined her discoveries — the broken crockery, a piece of metal that could have been the tip of a knife blade, the sole of an old boot, the bones of some small animal, and another object about the size of a half dollar, but was more irregular in shape, and so encrusted with dirt and mineral deposits they couldn't tell what it was.

"How old do you think this stuff is?" she asked.

"These items are obviously historic, so if

Triangle Mount is a prehistoric pyramid, this settlement is not related to it. My guess? Two hundred years, give or take."

"That was back when Apaches, Comanches, and Kiowa roamed the Trans-Pecos and at least a good fifty years before Cupid was founded."

"Yes."

"But here's the really exciting thing." She touched his shoulder, and immediately her fingers tingled. "This settlement isn't on any map."

He stood up, looking as disconcerted as she felt. Was it because she'd touched him or because of her find?

She fumbled for the maps, passed them to him. "And I've never heard anyone talk about a settlement being out here. Perhaps I've stumbled across something that no one knows about."

Jericho unfolded the maps and she leaned across him for a better look. The simple smell of man and land tangled up in her nose, and for a second, she got dizzy again.

"Indeed," he said, fire lighting up his voice.

"It's not what we were looking for, but I think this is even better," she went on. "The settlement could very well have been a Cupid precursor."

"Let's not get ahead of ourselves," he cautioned. "The reason it's not on any map might be because it was nothing more than a passing encampment or a single family dwelling."

"Look at the size of these two mounds." She waved a hand. "It's more than that and you know it. Your cautious side just won't allow you to take that leap."

"Not yet. Not until we have more evidence."

She clapped her hands. "I can't wait to get the crew over here and get started."

The light in Jericho's eyes died. "You know we cannot excavate here. It's out of the question."

"You're going to walk away from a find?"

Jericho pulled a palm down his mouth. He looked so torn. "We can't do this. We have to walk away."

"I'm a McCleary. This is McCleary land."

"You're not the legal owner."

"Have you ever heard the expression that it's easier to get forgiveness than permission?"

"And have you ever heard of a legally binding contract? We signed one, remember?"

"Damn. I knew you were going to say that."

"Because I'm right."

"How about this? We could do a little research first, see if we can find anything that will tell us what this settlement was and then approach Winz-Smith and ask for permission to dig here. We don't have to tell him I already found something. Just that I took a swim and spied the mounds and suspected they might be a settlement."

Jericho put a hand to the nape of his neck, eyed the artifacts she'd already uncovered. "We've already got a dig under way."

"And we've unearthed absolutely nothing."

"So far. It's only been four days."

"But what if we don't find anything at all on Triangle Mount?"

"The point of the field school is to teach students the proper way to conduct a dig, and all the August McCleary Foundation wants is for us to debunk the pyramid myth. It's good enough for those purposes."

"Aren't you the least bit curious about who these people were and what happened to them?" she wheedled.

"Of course I am. Archaeologists live for surprises like this."

"Well then?"

He was shaking his head, but when his eyes met hers, she knew she'd gotten her foot in the crack of the door. "I guess there wouldn't be any harm in doing some leg-work. If we can find something that indicates a settlement, we can go into a meeting with Winz-Smith armed with research.

"Woo-hoo!" Zoey hollered, swept off her cowgirl hat, tossed it in the air, and jumped into his arms.

Jericho caught her. What else could he do when she'd hurled herself at him like a cannonball? Let her fall?

Her legs enfolded around his waist, his arms wrapped around her. She stared into his eyes. He stared right back. Her scent tangled up in his nose, lit a fire deep inside him. She was impossible to ignore and already he was getting hard.

Get out while you still can!

Their timing had always been off. For the longest time, she'd simply been too young for him, then when she'd come of age, he was moving to Utah. It seemed that whenever one of them was unattached, the other was in a relationship.

Hey, you're both finally unattached at the same time and the age difference is moot at this point.

But if the risk of mucking up their friendship wasn't enough to stop him, something else hung over his head. He was now officially her instructor and this was his dream job, the position he'd spent his life working toward.

More bad timing.

Plus he'd already made the mistake of getting mixed up with one of his students, and look how that had turned out. His affair with Mallory had come close to imploding both of their careers. He wasn't about to make that mistake again.

He untangled her arms from around his neck, set her on the ground, and clenched his jaw to fight off the raging attraction.

"One thing for sure, we can't keep doing this," he said.

"Doing what?" she asked so innocently that he realized she had absolutely no idea how much she affected him.

"Being alone together. Spontaneous jumping into each other's arms."

Zoey hooted. "You've never once jumped into my arms."

"For obvious reasons. I'd crush you."

A mischievous smile lit her lips. "I used to jump into your arms all the time, remember? It was never a problem."

Jericho ducked his head. "Yeah, um . . . that was before."

"Before what?"

Before one look from you sent me into testosterone overload. "Things changed."

"Oh," she said, her expression half jovial, half sad. "Maybe if we just give it some time they'll change back the way they were."

But I don't want things to change back the way they were.

He liked feeling this way about his best friend, except it scared him too, on so many levels. Zoey's mind was mercurial and it changed as quickly as wind direction. Did he really want to risk getting caught in an updraft? Sometimes being cautious was annoying. While it served him well as a scientist, it also held him back, keeping him from enjoying the moment because he was too busy worrying about tomorrow. But in this case, extreme caution was a virtue.

"C'mon," he said. "Let's get out of here."

She bent to pick up the artifacts she'd unearthed. Her total lack of protocol set his teeth on edge. *She's new at this. Cut her some slack.* "What are you doing?"

"Taking them with us."

"We can't take them with us."

"So we're just going to leave them here?"

Since they weren't allowed to excavate here, they should just leave the artifacts, but neither could Jericho bear the thought of leaving them lying exposed on the ground, out in the elements. He supposed they could bury them where she'd found them, but that didn't sit well with his sense of order either.

"Why can't we take them with us?"

"That's looting."

"Not if we bring them back. We could take them, clean them up, and examine them —"

"No. We have to put them back where you found them."

"Aw, man."

"You caused it."

"And you're not cutting me one inch of slack." She stuffed her hands into her pockets.

"Sometimes, Zoey, you simply have to follow the rules."

"You're right," she said. "I'll put it back."

He helped her return the artifacts into the ground, but he didn't admit to her how much it killed him to do so. "We'll do some research," he reassured her. "I promise you that, and then we can approach Winz-Smith about extending the dig to include these mounds."

"When can we do that?"

"We've got our official site to work on right now, this will have to wait."

"But we haven't found anything over there

and right here is this juicy mound of artifacts."

He had to give her that. "Okay, tomorrow morning you and I will drive into Cupid and do a little research. If we find nothing, it's over. Got it?"

"Got it."

"You'll let it lie?"

"I will."

"Not a peep to our crew."

"Lips zipped."

"I hope I don't live to regret this," he mumbled as he followed her bouncy butt back to Triangle Mount.

CHAPTER 8

Evolution: The gradual process by which living organisms develop over time.

"Get out."

That night, Zoey blinked awake in the darkened tent she shared with Catrina. "Huh?"

"Get out." Catrina prodded her in the ribs with her bare foot.

She propped herself up on her elbows on the thin narrow cot, mussed hair falling into her eyes, and peered past Catrina to the man standing behind her. Avery Slocum.

Avery held up a hand. "Hey, Zoey."

"What is this?"

"Avery and I need some privacy."

"And I need a good night's sleep. We have to get up at first light."

"This is urgent," Catrina insisted.

"Use Avery's tent."

"You know he's rooming with Dr.

Chance."

"Seriously? Can't you two wait until the dig is over?"

"No. Dig sex is the appeal. We don't want to have a relationship, just a hot hookup. Now get out."

Zoey rolled over onto her side, punched her pillow. "Go find somewhere else to have your bonkathon."

"We're doing you the courtesy of throwing you out," Catrina said, "but if you'd really rather stay for the show, okay by —"

Zoey threw back the covers and hopped to her feet, shuffled around for her slippers. "I'm going. I'm gone. I'm out of here."

Avery chortled.

The next thing she knew she was standing outside the tent with her pillow in one hand, a light blanket in the other, looking up at a rash of stars. Great. Now what? She supposed she could go climb in Jericho's pickup parked at the bottom of Triangle Mount, but that meant walking through the brambles and rocks in the dark. Not to mention running into snakes and night creatures while dressed in her pajamas and house shoes.

Of course, since Avery was in her tent, that meant Jericho had a vacancy in his. Could she just tiptoe in there and see if she could slide onto Avery's cot without waking Jericho?

The night air was nippy and smelled of charcoal from the barbecue where the group had grilled meats and vegetables for dinner. She wrapped the blanket around her, and cast a sidelong glance at Jericho's tent. What if she tried it and he woke up while she was in the process and assumed she'd come to see him? She blew out her breath. Couldn't have that. Maybe she could just wait the couple out. How long could it take?

From inside the tent behind her came noises of heavy-duty lovemaking. From the sound of things, apparently it could take a long time. Whatever. She didn't want to stay here and listen to this. She scurried over to Jericho's tent, paused outside the closed flap.

"Jericho," she whispered.

Somewhere in the distance a coyote howled.

She lifted the flap, whispered louder, "Jericho."

"Zoey?" His deep voice wrapped around her in the chilly night air, warming her instantly.

She slipped into his tent. He sat up on his cot, his head brushing the top of the tent. He was a tall man, forcefully lean, and in the green glow from the digital clock on the small camp table, she could see that his chest was bare. Did he sleep in the nude? Or did he have on BVDs beneath the blanket covering his waist? The scandalous question teased her.

Shadows honed his high cheekbones to sharp ridges as prominent and compelling as Triangle Mount. Darkness hooded his eyes, giving him the appearance of a stranger. How was it she could know him so well, and yet in this moment, still feel as if they'd just met? She had an overwhelming urge to move toward him, put her finger to his lips, and trace them. She battled every womanly urge inside her not to do just that.

Acting glibber than she felt, Zoey plunked down on the edge of the empty cot across from him.

His eyes darkened with an emotion she couldn't read. "What is it?"

"Catrina and Avery are hooking up in my tent and since I have no desire to either be part of a threesome or a voyeur, here I am." She held her arms out wide and then realized belatededly she was not wearing a bra and her nipples were beaded up tight. She grabbed her pillow, clutched it to her chest.

"Zoey," he said hoarsely. "You have to go."

"I won't be any trouble. I don't snore. At least I don't think I do. No one ever told me I snore. Catrina, on the other hand, could wake the dead with her snoring," she rattled. When she got nervous she had a tendency to babble. "We're talking coffins flying open emptying out vampires, zombies walking the earth, whole ball of wax."

"You can't stay in here." His tone gentled. "People will talk."

"I know. So, um . . . then could you just go tell Avery to return to his tent so I can have mine back?"

"They are adults. I can't tell them how to run their sex lives."

"And yet, you can't have sex with whom-ever you want."

"That's different. I'm the instructor and I'm on probation."

They stared at each other.

She'd forgotten how handsome he was. Or maybe she'd never fully appreciated his good looks before. He was her buddy, after all, you didn't think about your buddy in those terms, right? But she was noticing and thinking and appreciating right now.

He curled his hands into fists and swal-lowed so hard that his Adam's apple bobbed. "You've got to go."

"But where?"

"You're right." He shook his head. "That's thoughtless of me. *I* have to go. You can stay here and I'll clear out." He swung his legs over the side of his cot and stood up to reach for his pants. He wasn't going commando, wore traditional tidy whites, but even in the darkness there was no missing his arousal.

Jericho had a serious boner.

Over her?

She did some gulping of her own and dropped her gaze as Jericho pulled up his jeans. Now, she was staring at his long bare toes. Damn! Even the man's toes were sexy. She fell back on the cot, covered her head with the pillow. She heard the slither of a zipper, the cling of a belt buckle, felt her face heat. No one would ever accuse her of being shy, but she couldn't help wondering if this was how a virgin felt on her wedding night — scared, excited, nervous, anticipatory, sick to her stomach.

"Zoey?"

"Uh-huh?" It came out muffled against the goose-down pillow.

"Are you okay?"

"Fine," she lied. She could feel him standing over her and her pulse skipped like a jump rope. An old playground rhyme went through her head. *Cinderella, dressed in yel-*

low, went upstairs to kiss her fellow. Did kids even jump rope these days?

"Try to get some rest."

She flung off the pillow, looked up at him. "Where will you go?"

"To sleep in the back of my pickup."

"I feel guilty throwing you out of your own tent."

"It's not your fault. I'll have a talk with Avery in the morning and tell him that he and Catrina need to find another spot for their midnight rendezvous."

"Thanks," she said. Why was it so hard to catch her breath?

He stood looking at her, and not moving.

"I really don't see why you have to go," she said. "Everyone already knows we're best friends. That's no secret. And it's also no secret that Avery has been bird-dogging Catrina. We'll just explain what happened."

He shook his head. "Considering my situation, that's playing with fire."

"Really, I'm sure I could convince everyone —"

"That's not the real problem," he interrupted.

"What is?" The words slipped thinly across her lips.

He lowered his eyes, swept his gaze over her. "You know."

"I do?"

"You. Me. Alone. Midnight. Not a safe combination."

"How . . ." She was finally able to haul in a deep breath. "Why . . ."

"Did this happen?" he finished for her.

She stared up at him, nodded mutely.

"I have no idea. It came out of nowhere."

She was at a distinct disadvantage, on her back, on the cot, Jericho looming above her.

"I'm gonna go," he said.

"Good idea," she croaked.

It wasn't fair of her to throw him out of his own tent, but she didn't know what else to do. A minnow of sadness swam in her stomach, small but troublesome. Once upon a time, she'd felt so comfortable around him. Now, since that kiss, everything was awkward and fraught with hidden meaning. Was she losing her best friend all because of a little sexual attraction?

A little?

His eyes gleamed wolfishly. She'd never seen Jericho like this. It both turned her on and scared her.

"I feel like —" He chuffed out air, stabbed his hand through his hair.

"What?" she prompted softly, remembering a time when he held nothing back, told her everything, and she did the same with him. But now? Things were different.

He shook his head, stepped back. "Never mind."

She sat up, and regained a bit of equilibrium. "Go ahead. You can say it."

He pulled a palm down his face. "It's just that . . ."

"What?"

"Now don't get your feelings hurt."

"Who me? The water-off-a-duck's-back girl? C'mon, you know I can handle it."

He sighed, sank down on his cot directly across from her. "Zoey, whenever I'm around you, I feel like I'm losing my mind."

She made him crazy. Was that good or bad?

"I was looking so forward to coming home and seeing you again and now this — *thing* has ruined what we had." He scowled.

Okay, bad news. The way he said "thing" made it sound like being attracted to her was the worst thing on earth. The minnow mushroomed into a shark and she put a palm to her queasy stomach.

Jericho reached for his shirt, slipped it on and started buttoning it over his Herculean chest. Her heart hammered headily.

"Every time I look at you I remember that damn kiss. I can't stop thinking about what it would be like to —" He shook his head more forcefully this time. "Never mind."

The belly shark spawned babies, multiplied, a whole school of predators eating her up from the inside. "What?" she whispered.

His eyes met hers, dark and dangerous. What had happened to the slightly nerdy boy-next-door she'd known for twenty years? "Do I really have to spell it out for you, Zoey?"

She raised a shaky hand to her throat. "Can we . . . er . . . can you make this feeling go away?"

"What do you think I've been trying to do for the past few weeks? I've been keeping my distance as much as I can. I knew being together at the dig was going to be tough, I just didn't understand exactly how difficult it was going to be."

"If that's the case then why did you kiss me?"

"I kissed you before I got the job, remember."

"Even so, if you're feeling this tortured about it . . ."

"I don't know." He fished his work boots from underneath the cot and shoved his feet into them. "That's the crazy part. You've got this pull on me that I can't seem to break no matter how much I want to."

He didn't want to be attracted to her? Her nose felt stuffy. She wrinkled it. "Sounds like an addiction."

"I've never been addicted to anything so I can't speak about that, but if this is how addicts feel, heaven help the poor bastards."

Wow. Exactly how many woman-eating sharks could a girl hold in her stomach until they killed her? He could have kicked her in the head and it would have hurt less, but she wasn't about to let him know exactly how much his words stung. *Don that alligator skin, pronto.*

"I don't mean to be blunt, just laying it on the table." He looked as mournful as she felt.

"Do you want me to quit the dig?" she murmured, crossing her fingers and gritting her teeth, aching for him to say yes, even if it meant losing her trust fund. *Quitter.* All right, truth? She honestly wanted him to say no, but could a girl's arms actually hurt from keeping someone at arm's length, because her biceps were already trembling.

The same dilemma warred on his face. He had to be thinking about the mistake he'd made with Mallory and how it had caused problems with his career. "I've got to have some air. I'll see you in the morning."

Then just like that, he tucked his blanket under his arm and walked out of the tent, leaving Zoey feeling sorely disappointed.

Jericho's insides were twisted up like overgrown tree roots — entwined, snarled, constricted. He turned over on his side on the hard truck bed, drew the baize blanket to his shoulder. It smelled of lime rich soil, cool metal, and the slightly camphor scent of benzoin. Every time he tried to close his eyes he saw Zoey's face, a dear face he knew so well. A face he could look at for a hundred years and never get tired of seeing.

He groaned. Ah shit. He was in one hell of a pickle. What was wrong with him? He was a sensible man, famous for being practical and down-to-earth. How was it that he kept thinking colossally irrational thoughts about his best friend?

It would be a hell of a lot easier if he could just tell her to quit the dig. Come right out and say, "Go." Considering her history, archaeology was just another of her passing fancies. Nothing stuck with Zoey for long, that's simply the way she was, and it was the primary reason these feelings scared him so damn much, but he could not be responsible for her losing her trust fund.

He was the opposite. When he latched on

to something, he internalized, made it part of who he was. What a recipe for disaster. Him latching on, her passing through.

Then again, he was usually pretty good about resisting temptation. He was a scientist after all, who knew how to lead with his brain and tuck his emotions away, but sometimes, even the most dedicated of scientists had cravings that no amount of logic could cure or explain.

That's where he was. Stuck on the conflicting horns of want and need. He wanted Zoey, but needed to stay away from her. Ultimately, when it came down to the battle of logic versus desire, logic usually lost.

And that's what disturbed him most of all.

The following morning Zoey was determined to act like nothing was different between her and Jericho. Putting a happy face on rocky situations had gotten her this far in life, and she wasn't about to abandon that philosophy now. She whistled while she took her turn making breakfast for the camp — burritos with scrambled eggs, salsa, and sausage. One of the other campers, Piper Patrolla, a shy, petite brunette who wore thick-lensed, lavender-framed glasses and a purple pith helmet, came over to help her.

Piper was from Marfa, and like Zoey, this was her first field school experience. She didn't talk much but she was always scribbling in a black and white composition notebook. Every time Zoey looked at her, she thought, *Harriet the Spy.*

She and Piper worked in companionable silence until Catrina stumbled out of their tent and strolled over to the coffeepot. Piper tucked her notebook under her arm, stuck a pen behind her ear, and slunk off the minute Catrina appeared.

"Are you always this freaking Mary Poppins in the morning?" Catrina groused.

"Always." Zoey beamed. "Even after I've been kicked out of my own tent."

Catrina gave her one of those sly gilded looks of hers that could have meant just about anything, lifted her coffee mug to her lips, and took a long sip. "Don't pretend you didn't take full advantage of it."

"What are you talking about?"

"Admit it. Avery and I did you a favor."

"In what way?" Play dumb. That was the way to go.

"Boom-chika-bow-wow." Catrina winked.

"Is that how you see it?" Zoey poured half a jar of Pace picante sauce over the egg and sausage mixture, and stirred it with a spatula as the rest of the dig team emerged from their tents, but no Jericho. He'd never come back to his tent, and when she'd gone to check on him, he had not been in the back of his pickup. "Because that's not how it is."

"You and Dr. Chance are obviously hot for each other. A blind person can see it."

Zoey put a hand to her cheek. Was it that evident? "We're just longtime friends."

Catrina snorted. "Even after last night?"

Especially after last night. "Are you trying to say that you and Avery arranged your little tryst out of the concern for my love life?"

Catrina laughed. "It was worth a shot."

Zoey put the pan of food on the camp table, stood up, and dusted her hand on the seat of her jeans. "I would appreciate it if you and Avery would find another place for your late night hookups."

Avery came out of her tent, scratching his bare chest. Catrina stared at him and licked her lips.

"And dude," Zoey yelled at him, "put a shirt on. Believe it or not there's some among us that don't want to see your naked junk."

Avery met Catrina's eyes. "What's wrong with her?"

"She didn't get any last night."

"You owe me ten bucks," Avery said. "Told you Chance is one controlled cat."

"May I speak to you in private, Avery?" Jericho's deep voice made everyone jump as he appeared from behind the copse of mesquite trees to the west of their camp.

Instantly, Zoey's pulse started pounding. "Breakfast is ready," she announced at large as she watched Avery and Jericho walk away together.

The rest of the group converged on the breakfast she'd made. She took a burrito for herself and sat down at the table with the crew. One of the guys, a gangly second-year student named Braden, who possessed carrot red hair, exceptionally knobby knees, and eyes the color of a glacier, was busily trying to work a nail puzzle. He'd been at the same puzzle all week. Zoey thought he and Piper would make a cute couple if either one of them would look up from what they were doing long enough to have a conversation with each other.

"Da-*amn,*" Braden exclaimed. "This thing is impossible."

To distract herself from thoughts of Jericho, Zoey stuck out her palm. "Let me see it."

Snorting his disgust, Braden dropped the puzzle into her palm.

She had it solved in under a minute.

Braden blinked. "How'd you do that?"

"I have a knack for puzzles."

"You must have done this one before. No one can do a puzzle that quick."

"I can. Got any more puzzles?"

"Yes," Braden said, disappeared into his tent and returned with a horseshoe puzzle.

Zoey solved that one in less than fifteen seconds.

"Da-*amn,* woman. You are good."

"Told ya."

"So are you like a genius or something?"

"Not at all. I'm just good at seeing patterns in things." She finished her burrito and went to help Piper scrub the dishes. She was elbow-deep in suds when she heard footsteps behind her.

"You ready?"

She turned to find Jericho standing there. "Ready for what?"

"Research."

"Huh?"

"I promised you that we'd research those artifacts you found. See if we can locate any information about a settlement having been where those mounds are."

"Oh yeah," she said, yesterday's enthusiasm long gone after the way he'd treated her last night.

He stepped closer. "You okay?"

"Fine," she lied. Just looking at him made her simultaneously hot and cold. "How about you?"

"Good. Great. Fantastic. You sleep well?"

"Like an infant. You?"

"Couldn't have slept better if I'd popped an Ambien."

Oh, clearly she was not the only liar. The dark circles under his eyes said he hadn't slept a wink. "Well, I couldn't have slept better if I'd had sex all night," she bragged.

"Me either. In fact, who sleeps when they have sex all night?"

"Good thing we didn't have sex all night. Ya know" — she shrugged casually, desperate to belie the fierce thudding of her heart — "since we slept so well."

"Good thing," he echoed.

"Sleep is way better than sex." *Just shut the freaking hell up, Zoey.* "Sex is so overrated."

"Uh-huh." A smile plucking the corners of Jericho's mouth said, *Not if you're doing it with me.* "I'm going to wait for you in the truck. Come on down when you're ready."

Chapter 9

Obsidian dating: When obsidian is exposed by flaking, a physical change takes place as water is taken into the material's structure, which occurs at a slow, constant rate.

The ride into Cupid was excruciatingly quiet. Zoey sat as far on her side of the truck as she could get. Jericho drummed his fingers on the steering wheel. They both stared straight ahead. After ten minutes of cruising down the long, straight desert road, she couldn't take the silence any longer.

"Mind if we have some tunes?" she asked.

He waved a hand at the satellite radio. "Be my guest."

She knew he liked alternative rock, so she switched it to one of those stations. Savage Garden was playing "Truly, Madly, Deeply." The duo sang about standing on a mountain with someone they loved. Ulp. Zoey punched buttons. Get away from the mushy love stuff, ASAP. She'd try some classic rock. Queen. "You're My Best Friend." Ack! Punch. Punch. Peter Gabriel. "In Your Eyes." What was this? Love song morning? Forget what Jericho liked. She'd pick something she liked. Upbeat and cheery. Good old bubblegum pop. Toy-Box. "Best Friend." Seriously? C'mon. She shut off the radio.

"Couldn't find anything you like?"

On the contrary, she'd found something she liked very much. Him. That was the problem. "Not in the mood for music after all."

"I've got some archaeology lectures on mp3. Do you want to listen to that?"

"Um, yeah. Sounds good."

Jericho loaded up a lecture. The speaker spoke in a boring monotone. Wonderful. There was nothing sexual or stimulating about that.

She slid him a sidelong glance. What a profile! Those intriguing angles and lines of him. She'd studied that profile countless times over the years, but in an odd way, she'd never actually *seen* it until now. Never realized how his Native American heritage so majestically carved his bone structure. It was an exquisite profile. Brave and true.

Honorable. Kingly. He possessed thick, black hair that could have given a young Elvis Presley a run for his money. Hair that made a woman ache to plunge her fingers through it.

Her stomach fluttered, last night's scary minnow-sharks turned to light-winged butterflies. What was he thinking? Was he concentrating on the lecture, or was he, as she was, shackled with deep desire and forbidden thoughts of sex, sex, sex?

A flick of the tongue, a lick of the lips, the sweet remembrances of that fine backyard kiss. Torture. She had to stop torturing herself like this. But alas, she could not. Every breath she took filled her lungs with smells of him — sand and leather and sun, and underneath, the rich musk of man.

His hands squeezed the steering wheel, the muscles in his wrists and forearms tightly bunched. She wallowed in the sight of those forearms spread with dark hairs, blue cotton shirt rolled up to the elbows, leather Fossil watchband strapped to his right wrist. A hot heaviness settled low in her abdomen, a heated anchor of raw hunger. What was happening here? Why was it happening? What had changed between them? Three years and more than a thousand miles? Was that enough to tip a solid friendship on its axis? Turn it into something far more sensual?

Apparently so.

Was there any way to put things back the way they used to be? If so, she wished someone would give her a road map, because she'd steered way off course and couldn't find her way back.

She couldn't remember a time when she hadn't known him. He was as much a fixture in her life as her sister, Natalie. He'd always just been there, consistent as the Davis Mountains standing guard over the Chihuahuan Desert. If something were to drive him from her life, she didn't think she could bear the loss.

"How's your parents," she asked, to distract herself.

He smiled, shook his head. "The same. They'll never change. Which is good, I suppose. The world needs more Craigs and Angies."

"Maybe so, but the Craigs and Angies shouldn't have children," she said.

He turned his head to look at her. "Why do you say that?"

"Look at how they treated you."

"If they hadn't had a kid, I wouldn't be here."

She folded her arms over her chest. "I'm

still mad at them for the way they abandoned you."

"They don't see it like that. To them, they were protecting me."

"Hey, here's a thought, stay home and take care of your own kid before you start sprinting off to help orphans in other countries."

"They believe their work is a calling."

"What do you believe?" she asked.

"I believe it's not my place to judge them."

"Wow, obviously I'm not as enlightened as you because I judge them plenty for the way they dumped you on relatives."

"Why the strong feelings suddenly? You've never said anything about this before."

She shrugged. "I've been thinking a lot lately about our childhoods."

"Me too," he said softly. "Two parentless kids cobbling together their own makeshift family."

That's what was so weird about this thing. Growing up, they'd been almost like siblings, and then along the way they'd morphed into best friends, and now things between them were changing again.

Was it a natural evolution or were they simply drawn to each other because they currently had a vacuum in their respective love lives? She was at a career crossroads as well, and Jericho seemed to hold the key. He was shedding the skin of his tattered relationship with Mallory and truly starting his professional career. Was this attraction nothing more than need-fulfillment on both their parts? Could they trust their feelings? Should they?

"We were a couple of lonely kids with big imaginations," she murmured. "We thought we could dig through the earth to China."

"You saved me, you know," he said, his voice husky.

"What do you mean?"

"I was pretty wounded, but I didn't know how to show it or ask for what I needed from my grandpa and Junie Mae. Digging that hole with you . . . well, it made a tough time bearable."

A hard lump clumped up her throat. "Glad I could help." She tried for glib, but it came out stupidly sentimental.

Jericho extended his right hand and rested it on the console between them, palm up.

Zoey caught her breath. Did he want her to take his hand? She sneaked another glance at him. His eyes drilled the road, his expression unreadable.

Unable to resist what was clearly an invitation, shakily she laid her hand on top of his. He closed his fingers around hers, interlacing them. She stared down at their joined hands — his large, hers tiny in comparison — and her mouth went dry.

She remembered other times they'd held hands — when he'd guided her through the Cupid Caverns after she confessed she was afraid of the dark. The time they decided to climb up the roof of the B&B for a better vantage point from which to watch the Fourth of July fireworks being shot off at Cupid Lake and she'd slipped and he'd reached down his hand to catch her before she fell. At his grandpa Prufrock's funeral, when he'd been unable to cry, his eyes dry and red-rimmed, she'd reached out to take his hand and he had not shaken her off.

But none of those instances had ever felt like this. Then he'd either been rescuing her or she'd been comforting him. This was . . . well . . . she did not know what this was, but it was neither rescue nor comfort.

He squeezed her fingers.

She squeezed back.

And if they hadn't pulled up in front of the Cupid Museum, Zoey couldn't help feeling they might have gone on holding hands forever.

"We have no record of any settlement ever having existed in the valley between Triangle

Mount and Widow's Peak," said the docent at the Trans-Pecos Historical Society in Alpine three hours later. The petite woman carefully unrolled a yellowed map of the area. "This is the oldest map we have on record. It's from 1803 and well before either Fort Davis or Fort Stockton was built. As you can see, there's nothing at the location you're interested in." She pointed out the area. "But that doesn't mean there wasn't some kind of settlement in there before 1803 or even a later settlement that was so short-lived that it never made it onto a map."

Jericho shook his head. This was the third confirmation that the mounds Zoey had started excavating had never been recognized as a settlement. Tabitha Crispin at the Cupid Museum had told them the same thing, as well as the research librarian at Sul Ross. Three strikes and they were out.

"Thank you for your time," he told the woman.

"No problem. Feel free to give us a call if you have any more questions. I think it's quite exciting that you're excavating Triangle Mount. There's been such an air of mystery about it for years," the docent said.

He ushered Zoey toward the door and it was all he could do not to put a possessive palm to the small of her back. In fact, to keep from doing it, he stuck his right hand into his pocket and used his left hand to push the door lever. He was already regretting offering his hand to her in the pickup on the drive from the dig site. He couldn't say why he'd done it, but he wasn't about to compound the problem.

They stepped out into sunlight so bright that they both whipped out their sunglasses simultaneously and slipped them on.

"I'm sorry I wasted your time," she said, her disappointment palpable. "We lost a whole day researching when we could have been digging."

"Nothing is lost," he said. "The team is still digging and this is part of the process. You follow leads and sometimes it's a dead end."

"But it's not a dead end, Jericho. I found those artifacts. There is something under those mounds whether the settlement was ever recorded or not."

"You know we can't act on those finds. If we do so without permission, the school will be held liable, I'll lose my job and Walker could cut off your funds, not to mention it will ruin the field school for the other students. Without some kind of proof there was a settlement beneath those mounds, we have nothing to twist Winz-Smith's arms with."

"I know." She sighed. "I wished I never started digging there in the first place. We might as well head back."

"Don't give up so quickly. You do have a tendency to quit when the going gets tough."

"Yeah, according to my family, it's my fatal flaw."

"I wouldn't say fatal." He chuckled. "You just need a little dose of stick-to-itiveness."

"Meaning?" She flashed him a hopeful look. She looked too cute in that pink straw cowgirl hat and denim shorts. It was all he could do to keep from ogling her gorgeous legs. Okay, so he couldn't keep from it. He ogled. Big-time.

"I've got an ace up my sleeve," he said. "It's not as good as official documentation, but it's something."

"What's that?"

"Oral history."

She arched her eyebrows. "From whom?"

"Let's grab some lunch first and I'll tell you my plan." He didn't bother asking what she wanted to eat. He knew her favorite casual dining place in Alpine. A cozy mom-and-pop joint.

"Yummm," she said, practically breathing

the sound as they pulled up at the Sandwich Hut. "You remembered."

"Of course I remembered. If this place was an airline we'd have maxed out frequent flier miles, as many times as we've eaten here." But back then they'd only been friends, going Dutch. Now they were . . . what? Professor and student, his stern left brain provided, but that's *not* what his frisky right brain was thinking.

He did his level damnedest not to stare at her butt as she sauntered through the entrance ahead of him, and failed spectacularly. When she spun around to ask him if he wanted to split the Big Bend, the restaurant's premier sandwich, she caught him in mid-ogle.

Face heating, he quickly glanced away.

"I saw that," she teased.

Chagrined, he decided to just go with it. "Hey, it's not my fault you have the sexiest fanny this side of the Pecos."

"Why, thank you for the compliment."

The owner and his wife, Max and Molly Marino, spied Jericho and came over to welcome him home, and they insisted on giving him and Zoey complimentary beers. He wasn't much for drinking during the middle of the day, but hey, maybe it would help him unwind a little. He'd been tight as a top ever since he'd come home and discovered his feelings for Zoey had warped into something he did not fully understand. He'd missed her, that was for damn sure.

"You two look so cute together," Molly said. "How come you're just friends?"

Zoey stroked her chin and gave him a sideways look. She was going to let him field that question.

Jericho shifted his weight, met Zoey's eyes. "She's way too much woman for me. She'd wear me out in a New York minute."

"Hey, shoot for the stars, I always say." Max slung an arm around his wife's shoulder. "If I hadn't been cocky about my chances, I wouldn't ever have landed a gem like my Molly."

"What if I come up short?" Jericho asked, because he really wanted to know the answer. What would happen if he made a serious move on Zoey — after the dig was over, of course — and he simply could not keep up with her? The woman was lightning — quick and hot. He was more like hinky-punk — lingering and cool.

"At least you would have had a great time failing." Max chuckled.

Molly whispered something to Zoey, who burst out laughing.

"Take it from a sandwich man," Max told

him. "You two are more compatible than you might think. Do you have any idea how many couples can't split a Big Bend because they don't like the same things?"

"My husband is convinced that sandwich compatibility leads to compatibility in the bedroom," Molly said. "And I tend to agree."

Amid the good-natured ribbing, Jericho led Zoey to a vacant table at the back of the restaurant. "What did Molly say to you?"

Zoey grinned impishly. "You sure you really want to know?"

"Will I be embarrassed?"

"Probably. She said if the size of your hands are any indication I would be in for a treat."

Jericho whirled his head around to stare at the matronly Molly, who waved from behind the checkout counter. "Molly said that?"

"Um-hmm and from the size of Max's hands, she knows what she's talking about." Zoey was trying to get his goat. What would she say if he turned the tables on her?

"You're just dying to find out if the old myth is true, aren't you? That the size of a man's hands translates into the size of his . . . er . . . other appendages." He splayed his palm in the middle of the table.

Her gaze fixed on his hand and her eyes widened. "Does it in your case?"

"There are some things," he drawled, "that need to be experienced firsthand."

Her face turned the color of ripe cherries and she ducked her head just as a server slid their sandwich and beers in front of them. Zoey plucked up the beer and took a long gulp. "Ah," she declared. "I was so thirsty."

"You're just trying to change the subject."

"Absolutely!"

This was fun. Usually, Zoey was the outrageous one.

"I'm digging in," she announced, picked up her half of the Big Bend, and sank her teeth into the toasted baguette stuffed with smoked turkey, roasted buffalo beef sliced wafer thin, crisp slices of candied bacon, fried egg and Colby Jack cheese. Not the healthiest sandwich in the world, but for the occasional splurge, it was decadently delicious. Just like the sexy woman in front of him.

Jericho shook off the thought. He admired the way she went at everything with total gusto. Even the way she'd dug up those artifacts the day before. Yes, her impulsiveness had put them in a tough spot, but she'd figured out something was under those mounds, and for a novice archaeologist, that was pretty impressive. He hated that they wouldn't be able to dig there, but maybe all was not lost. They did have one last hope.

"So," she said, wiping the juice from her mouth with a napkin. "Where are we going from here?"

He took a swallow of ice-cold beer. It went down easy. "Think about it. Where are you most likely to obtain an oral history?"

"From someone who knows the topic."

"And who is that?"

She wrinkled her nose in the cute little way of hers. "A history buff?"

"Not necessarily."

"Someone who is old enough to know a lot of history?"

"Exactly. The older the better, and where might we find someone like that?"

She beamed. "Oh, I know where you're going with this. We need a local informant. Are you impressed that I know the lingo?"

"Zoey, you never cease to impress me."

Her face pinked with delight, and her delight delighted him. "Are we headed to the nursing home to talk to your maternal great-grandmother? Isn't she the oldest living person in Cupid?"

"At a hundred and two, she is," he said, "and she spent her entire life in Jeff Davis

County. The only problem is that sometimes she's lucid and sometimes she's not. Hopefully, we'll catch her on a good day."

"If that's the case can we trust her oral history?" Zoey caught her bottom lip between her teeth.

"Oral histories are always prejudiced by point of view and memory, but when you don't have anything else to support your theories, they're a starting point, and you'd be surprised at how helpful they can be, even if they're not completely accurate or objective. If we can get something out of my great-grandmother, it might be enough to take to Winz-Smith and ask for his permission to dig the mounds."

"Well, what are we waiting for?"

Her wildfire enthusiasm lit him up inside. While he loved his work, it had been a long time since he'd seen archaeology through beginner's eyes and she made him remember the pure excitement of discovery. Or was the adrenaline surging through him much more complicated than that? One thing was for sure, whenever he was around her he felt more alive. Always had, probably always would. Leaving one big question.

What was he going to do about it?

CHAPTER 10

Traditions: Customs or beliefs passed down from adults to children.

"Granny Helen," Jericho called to the wizened woman crumpled in a wheelchair by the window. Zoey trailed behind him feeling out of place.

Granny Helen was tiny, birdlike. Her face was wreathed in wrinkles, her hands gnarled with arthritis. She narrowed dark brown eyes cloudy with cataracts and then broke into a toothless smile. Her high patrician cheekbones spoke to her Comanche ancestry. "Joe?"

Zoey winced. Joe was Jericho's grandfather, Helen's only son, and he'd been dead for more than fifteen years.

"No Granny, I'm Jericho, your great-grandson," he corrected gently, took the chair beside her, and reached for her hand.

"Angie's boy?"

"That's right."

"Where's Joe? He doesn't come see me anymore." Her eyes misted and her bottom lip trembled. "Why doesn't he come see me anymore?"

Jericho patted his great-grandmother's arm. "How have you been?"

"Who's that?" Granny Helen peered around him at Zoey.

"That's my friend, Zoey McCleary. You've met her before. When we were kids."

Granny Helen assessed her with a hard eye. "She's no friend."

Unsettled, Zoey shifted her weight and wrapped her arms around herself. This did not appear to be one of the elderly woman's good days.

"Sure she is. I've known her most of my life."

"You can't fool me, boy. I see the way you're looking at her. You don't look at a friend that way."

Jericho's eyes met hers. Zap! A hot spark sprang from him to her. Zoey dropped his gaze. Things were quickly getting sticky between them.

"Listen, Granny, we wanted to ask you about when you were a girl."

"You shouldn't make a lover out of a friend." Granny fretted, her gaze focusing on a red bird that had come to perch on the outside of the window. "It won't work."

Zoey's pulse quickened.

"Why not?" Jericho ventured.

Granny Helen plucked at the hem of her floral blouse. "They tried it and look what happened."

"Who is that?"

"Little Wolf and Clarissa."

Sadness tugged the corners of Jericho's mouth downward and he blew out a long breath.

"Who are Little Wolf and Clarissa?" Zoey asked.

Jericho shook his head. "It's a fairy tale she used to tell me as a kid."

"Have some respect, boy," Granny Helen scolded, her voice growing stronger. "Little Wolf and Clarissa were as real as you and me."

"Yes, ma'am," he placated.

"Girl." Granny Helen pointed a knotty finger at Zoey. "Get me my cigar box."

"Where is it?" Zoey glanced around the room.

"In the closet."

Dutifully, Zoey went to the wardrobe and searched around until she found a well-worn Aurelia Biltmore cigar box on the top shelf underneath a stack of folded nightgowns, and brought it back to her.

The elderly woman settled the box into her lap and opened it up. She took out old black and white photographs of long-dead relatives, a jar of baby teeth, a half-finished cross-stitch project, clippings of newspaper articles about various historical events in Cupid, one of which was how Zoey's great-great-uncle August McCleary saved the Trans-Pecos from the Spanish flu with his medicinal concoction. It was that article that spurred Cousin Walker to do research and write August's biography.

From the bottom of the box Granny Helen dug out a Native American beaded medallion. She placed the medallion in Jericho's palm. The beadwork depicted a bright yellow flame on a background of dark green.

"What is this?" Jericho asked.

"Your heritage. Passed down from my full-blood mama and her mama before that. Take it."

"I didn't know Comanches did much beadwork."

"Our family was special," she said proudly.

"In what way?"

"Keepers of the Flame."

Jericho looked unconvinced. "How come you never told me about this before?"

"I forgot about it. Until now. Until I saw her." She pointed at Zoey. "That's why you have to stay away from her. She's one of them."

"One of who?"

Her eyelids flickered and she looked momentarily confused. "Where's Joe?"

"Granny," Jericho said gently. "Grandpa Joe passed away."

Her eyes widened, her bottom lip trembled, and a single tear slid down her cheek. "Gone. It's all gone. Everything gone."

"I'm not gone. I'm here," Jericho said.

She shook her head. "Don't get old, son. You lose everything."

Jericho smoothed her hair, spoke soothing noises.

Zoey's heart wrenched for the poor woman. She moved to kneel in front of Granny Helen. "Could you tell me the story of Little Wolf and Clarissa? I've never heard it."

That perked her up. She raised her head, wiped away the tear. "You never heard about Little Wolf and Clarissa?"

"No."

Jericho gave her a grateful smile and silently mouthed, *Thank you.*

Granny Helen set the cigar box on the

window ledge, and the red bird flew away. She smoothed wrinkles from her floral cotton skirt, and for the first time since they'd come into the room, she seemed completely clearheaded. "Little Wolf was a handsome Comanche boy. As handsome as that one when he was little." She smiled at Jericho.

"He is handsome, isn't he?"

"Watch it. He's not for you," Granny Helen snapped. "You're too much like Clarissa."

Zoey rocked back on her heels. What could she say to that?

"I know you're a good girl," Granny Helen's voice softened. "I can see it in your eyes, but being good does not change the facts. You two don't belong together."

Granny's words caught her with an uppercut. Her stomach churned and she wished she hadn't eaten that Big Bend sandwich. *Don't freak, she's just an elderly woman whose mind isn't what it used to be. Don't take what she says to heart.*

"Granny," Jericho said, gently but sternly. "Zoey is my best friend."

"Just be sure you keep it that way. Otherwise, there's nothing but trouble."

Alarm tightened her throat. "You were telling us about Little Wolf," Zoey prodded, hoping to get her back on topic.

"Was I? Oh yes. One day Little Wolf went to gather water at a crystal-clear lake," Granny Helen went on. "He slipped on a wet rock and fell in. The water was over his head and Little Wolf couldn't swim."

"He went to gather water all by himself?" Zoey asked.

"The men were off on a hunting party and the women were tending the camp. All the other children were either too small to go off on their own, or old enough to go hunting with the braves. As he was going down for the third time, Little Wolf knew he was about to die and prayed to the Great Spirit to save him."

Granny Helen paused a long moment, stared blankly over Zoey's head as if she'd forgotten the story or was seeing something from a long-ago past.

Zoey couldn't stand the suspense any longer. "Was he saved?"

Granny Helen blinked and continued. "Just when that boy thought he'd breathed his last, someone grabbed him by the hair and pulled him out of the deep."

Riveted by the story, Zoey asked, "Who saved him?"

"As Little Wolf lay on the ground gasping for air, he looked up into the face of a blond-haired, blue-eyed angel. She was Clarissa, the young daughter of a pioneer settler."

"That must have been dramatic," Zoey breathed. "Praying to be rescued and at the last moment a pretty girl saves you."

"Make no mistake. Pretty as she was, Clarissa was Little Wolf's enemy. Her people had invaded the land of his people, but they were children and they didn't care about stuff like that. They became fast friends even though they knew their families would not approve." Granny Helen's voice took on a dreamy quality.

"Ooh conflict, the heart of any juicy story." Zoey looked at Jericho, who was studying her with a pensive expression.

"By the light of the moon, Little Wolf and Clarissa would slip off at night to play with each other," Granny Helen went on.

Zoey gulped. "I can see where this is about to go horribly wrong."

Granny Helen nodded. "One night, Clarissa's father caught her frolicking with Little Wolf and forbade her to ever see him again."

"Whew," Zoey said. "At least it wasn't worse."

"They didn't see each other for many moons. Missionaries came to the land and built schools and attempted to convert the Native Americans to their religion. Little Wolf's tribe was peaceful people and they allowed him to go to school. He was very happy to find out that Clarissa also went to the same school and they resumed their friendship as best they could under the stern glares of the priests."

"But they were just friends, right?"

"For the time being." Granny Helen looked from Jericho to Zoey and back again. "They were still children after all, but their bodies were already starting to change."

"Oh dear," Zoey murmured.

"One day they foolishly shared a kiss and they were caught by one of the priests. Little Wolf was cast out of the school and Clarissa's parents no longer allowed her to leave the settlement. By this time, they were desperately in love and being apart only fanned the flames of their longing." Granny Helen paused to take a long, deep breath. Clearly, so much talking was taking a toll on her.

"It's okay," Jericho said. "You don't have to go on. Do you want us to help you to bed?"

Granny Helen glowered at him. "I'm fine, Joe. Just need to rest a minute."

Concern knit Jericho's brow. Was it because she'd called him by his grandfather's name again? But he didn't correct her.

She rested a frail hand on Zoey's shoulder. "So the friends-turned-lovebirds were separated again."

Zoey couldn't resist sliding another glance Jericho's way, and his dark eyes burned hers. What was going on inside his head?

A knock sounded on the open door and a nurse came into the room. "You've got visitors, Helen. How nice."

"This is my son Joe and his new wife Junie Mae," Granny Helen said.

The nurse smiled and shook a white medicine cup that rattled with pills. "Time for your afternoon meds."

"What happened with Little Wolf and Clarissa?" Zoey asked, anxious to hear the rest of the story.

Granny Helen blinked at her. "Who?"

"You were telling us the romance of Little Wolf and Clarissa."

The elderly woman looked over at Jericho. "Who is she, Joe? And what's she talking about?"

"It's all right." Jericho leaned down to kiss her cheek. "Don't worry about it."

"You know." Granny Helen sighed. "Maybe I will go back to bed."

"I'll help her back," the nurse said.

"We'll let you rest now, Granny." Jericho patted her hand.

The tender care he took with his great-grandmother touched Zoey's heart. He was a good man. She'd always known it, but now? She couldn't explain these tangled emotions surging inside her, but nothing had ever felt so right.

"Wow." Zoey blew out her breath as they walked out of the nursing home. "That must have been hard for you when she mistook you for your grandfather."

"Breaks my heart," he said, "but she's been like that ever since I've known her. I don't know how much of what she says is truth or fiction."

"She seemed pretty clear when she was telling about Little Wolf and Clarissa."

"Probably because it's a love story. She used to be a matchmaker, you know. When she was young."

"Really?"

"Yep."

"Does she have Alzheimer's?"

"No. It's some other form of senility."

"We didn't even get to ask her if she knew anything about a settlement. I got her sidetracked with that story."

"I'm glad you did. I hated having to tell her Grandpa Joe was dead and I feel guilty for not coming home to see her these past three years. Junie Mae looks in on her, but I should have come home."

Zoey linked her arm through his, rested her head on his shoulder. "Stop beating yourself up. You had to finish your degree, and you were so good with her."

"So were you."

"Do you know the rest of the Little Wolf and Clarissa story?"

"Not really." he said. "Although I think I recall that it ends tragically."

"Oh no. I was afraid of that."

"Makes me wish I'd listened to her stories more closely when I was little. She had so many of them and she'd just ramble on. A little boy's attention span can only take so much of that."

"Too bad your grandfather is gone too. He might have been able to shed some light on her stories."

"Taking oral histories is often fascinating, but it can also be emotionally wrenching," he said. "Like today."

"What do you make of that medallion she gave you?"

"For all I know she bought it at a craft fair years ago." He walked around to the passenger side of his pickup with her, paused to unlock the door.

"We've got to let this thing about the settlement go, don't we?"

He nodded. "Looks like it."

"Too bad."

Jericho was standing so close to her she could smell the peppery scent of his cologne. His lips were so near that if she went up on tiptoes and leaned forward just a little bit, they would be kissing.

A shiver ran through her. All this time she believed in the Cupid legend that falling in love would be like a lightning strike. That just one look and you would instantly know. The ingrained belief had kept her searching for a stranger, for that split-second knowledge of *he's the one.* She'd never once considered that love could sneak up on you in devious increments.

Before she could fully process that realization, Jericho's phone rang. He opened the door with one hand and nodded for her to slide on in, while taking his cell from his pocket with the other hand.

"Hello?" He listened for a moment, his face breaking into a grin. "Leave it right where you found it. We're on our way."

"What is?" she asked as he severed the call.

"We've got to get back to the dig. They've found something."

■ ■ ■ ■

Jericho knelt over the excavated unit floor dug in ten-centimeter levels to a depth of sixty centimeters. The unit floor was a light-colored natural stratum underneath a cultural stratum packed with white shells and darker soil. Avery had made sure to segregate the soils of the different strata and he'd left the artifact in situ as the team had found it. In the time it had taken Jericho and Zoey to get back, Avery had also measured, drawn, photographed, and laboriously recorded everything exactly as it lay.

He praised Avery for his control and called the rest of the students over to start troweling away the rest of the stratum around the artifact, leaving it on a pedestal of dirt. Zoey bagged the fresh soil for later processing. Once everything had been properly processed and recorded, Jericho was ready to unearth the artifact.

"What is it?" Avery breathed.

Jericho carefully extracted it, and that familiar old magic swept over him. God, he loved this job.

The artifact had a head made of sharp-edged stone lashed to a wooden handle through a hole burned into the center.

Leather thongs had been looped through the hole and used to secure the stone to the handle. On the shaft of the wood there appeared to be carvings encrusted with soil. He wouldn't be able to make out what the carvings were until he cleaned up the artifacts. His heartbeat quickened.

"Looks to be a tomahawk," he said. "Probably around two hundred years old."

"So it's not anything from an ancient pyramid builder." Avery sounded disappointed.

"No, but it's a grand find. Great job, team." He glanced over to see Zoey staring at the artifact, her face enrapt.

They were crouching side by side and he couldn't believe he was sharing this with her, and his heart suddenly seemed too big to fit in his chest.

A lock of hair had fallen across her face and he didn't even stop to think, just reached out his big tanned hand and tucked it behind her soft, delicate ear so she could get a better look at the artifact.

She sucked in her breath, but did not move a muscle.

Aware that every eye in the dig site was latched on to them and there were whispers going on behind palms, Jericho steeped her in archaeological terminology. In the hushed tones of foreplay, he described Native American rituals, customs, traditions, and cultural beliefs. Although he'd never been exceptionally adept at seduction, without provocation his voice lowered and his tone deepened, with the intention of drawing her — and only her — into his narrative. All the while, he was slowly sliding his hand down her arm.

She never uttered a sound, only glanced from his hand to his face with a stiff expression on her lips. Was she horrified? Hell, he certainly was. What had come over him? They were not alone. He was feeding the flames of their attraction faster than if he'd chunked balsa wood on to a campfire.

He should move his hand away, but couldn't seem to make himself do it. So to keep up appearances, he maintained a blank expression, kept talking about artifacts and history and details of their discovery, but inwardly he was alarmingly aware of his thundering pulse. He remembered how she'd been his first archaeology assistant back there in his grandfather's backyard. How she'd looked at him then as she was looking at him now. Like he was crazy, but dammit, she wanted in on the adventure anyway. Now, as she had then, she made him feel as if it were just the two of them, wrapped in a conspiratorial cocoon, against the world.

Heat swamped his body and he was getting short of breath and he felt as if he'd just done wind sprints up the Sul Ross bleachers, and still he could not stop touching her. To cover his tracks, he took the artifact and placed it in her palm, making it seem as if that's what he'd been intending all along.

Her eyes met his and a huge grin lit up her face. "That is the most awesome thing I've ever seen."

"And we're just getting started," he said, but he was not talking about the tomahawk.

"You didn't think we'd find anything, did you?" she asked.

"Not really," he admitted, still breathless and wondering if she'd seen through him. "This is beyond my wildest expectations."

He stood, his joints aching from crouching so long, and he was startled to see the sun was kissing the horizon. They'd been at this for hours. He was about to suggest they bring in the battery-powered lamps and keep digging when he remembered that it was Friday evening and the students had the weekend free.

"Let's put away the tools and then you're excused for the weekend," he said. "Go out, let off some steam, and come back at seven A.M. on Monday morning relaxed and ready to get back to work."

Hyped up, and chattering at warp speed, students began gathering up the gear and stowing everything appropriately.

Zoey came up to him as he bagged the tomahawk. "You're going to take the tomahawk back to the archaeology lab at Sul Ross tonight so you can clean it and take a closer look, aren't you?"

He grinned. "You know me too well. I can't resist."

"Well, I intend on being with you when you do it."

He was dopily pleased to hear her say that. He wanted her with him. They covered the dig site with plastic, and on their way out, they closed and padlocked the entrance gate.

And Jericho couldn't help thinking this was the best day he'd had in a very long time.

Chapter 11

Magnetic dating: A method of dating that compares the magnetism in an object with changes in the earth's magnetic field over time.

They stopped for fast food at a drive-through and ate in the pickup on the way to Alpine. "We'll eat healthier tomorrow," he promised.

To most people, drive-through fast food wouldn't have been romantic, but to Zoey, consumed by the thrill of success and the fire in Jericho's voice as he talked about their find and how excited he was that she'd been there to discover it with him, this was better than a fancy dinner at a five-star restaurant. *This* was passion.

And so were the feelings pushing hotly through her veins.

They arrived at the lab and Jericho turned on the overhead fluorescent light to review a room of long wide tables, high-intensity lamps, plenty of shelving, a big sink with a sand trap, cleaning tools, various containers, and other supplies. A radio rested on a tall metal file cabinet, and Jericho went over to turn it on.

"Music helps you concentrate," she declared.

"You know me too well."

"I remember you blasting Stone Temple Pilots when you studied."

He examined the tomahawk thoroughly under a magnifying glass. "Look." He breathed. "There's what appears to be a strand of dark hair wedged against a small crack in the wood. Hand me an evidence bag, will you?"

She passed him a bag and he put the collected strand in the baggie and carefully wrote on the label where he'd found it. Then he took the tomahawk to the cleaning sink and filled a plastic tub with water. Zoey came to stand beside him to observe the process.

"Don't wash finds directly in the sink," he cautioned. "Mud can instantly clog the drain. Hand me one of those toothbrushes, please." He nodded at a cup full of soft-bristled toothbrushes beside the sink.

She got the toothbrush for him and he

gently scrubbed the stone hatchet part of the tomahawk under the water so that he didn't splash mud everywhere, while at the same time taking care to keep the wooden handle out of the water.

"Wood is perishable, so we don't want to submerse it," he said. "I'll dry brush it with a fine paintbrush. You have to be very careful when cleaning or you can end up losing information or damaging the artifacts."

"We learned that in class," she said, "but until you're hands-on it doesn't fully register."

He put the tomahawk on a drying rack, went to the computer, and started inputting information about the artifact. When the tomahawk was dry, he took it over to a table, spread butcher paper down underneath a high-intensity lamp, and sat down to clean the handle with a fine paintbrush.

"What can I do to help?" she asked.

"Get the e-reader out of my pack and open up the book on Native American cultures of the Southwest. There's a chapter in there on symbolism."

"Will do." She retrieved the e-reader, found the book and chapter, and sat in the chair beside him, fascinated as he painstakingly whisked away the dirt to reveal the first carving on the handle.

It was amazing how gentle his big hands were, how carefully he held the fragile artifact. She liked that his clothes were dusty and his collar was askew and his hair was mussed. She admired his intensity, his dedication to detail, and his devotion to his craft. It turned her on. She crossed her legs and willed the feeling away, but, alas, it did not work.

Sitting there beside him, Zoey was pulled like warm taffy in two directions. Part of her wanted to run before she did something irrevocably reckless, another part of her — the essential Zoey part of her — longed to fling herself into his arms, tell him she was quitting the field school, and beg him to make love to her. Instant gratification over longterm gain. Wasn't that always her modus operandi?

All she had to do was hold out three more weeks. Why did it feel so impossible?

He had most of the dirt worked off the first etching. "Could you pass me the magnifying glass so I can see it more clearly?"

She passed the magnifying glass to him like a scrub nurse seamlessly feeding a scalpel to a surgeon. "What is it an etching of?"

"A Native American brave." Jericho gave the magnifying glass back to her so she could have a look for herself.

She put the glass to her eyes. "He looks very young, practically a boy. After hearing your granny's story today, it makes me think of Little Wolf. Could this tomahawk have belonged to the young brave whose likeness is etched here? You know, sort of like signing it with his likeness?"

"Possibly. It could also be telling a story. It wasn't uncommon for Native Americans to depict their myths and legends through carvings. Although the nomadic tribes in the Southwest were less likely to do so."

"Fascinating."

"Would you like to clean off the next carving?" he asked, and handed her the paintbrush.

"You trust me not to screw it up?"

"Zoe-Eyes, there's not a person on this earth I trust more than you."

Her pulse skipped. *Don't get mushy.* "Which might not be saying a lot since you're kinda suspicious by nature," she teased.

"Actually, it says everything."

Their gazes met. Her heart chugged like a sumo wrestler climbing Mount Everest. Okay, not a sexy image, but that's exactly what she needed, something unattractive to chase off these crazy, uncontrollable romantic thoughts.

"Here," he said, and scooted her chair closer to his. "Get directly under the light."

"If I get any closer I'm going to have to start taking off clothes. It's hot in here," she quipped, and immediately regretted it when his eyelids lowered and he gave her a look that was pure sensual heat.

"Archaeologists have to acclimate themselves to all kinds of changes in temperature," he murmured.

She gulped. "I'm beginning to realize that."

He picked up the magnifying glass, held it above the tomahawk handle for her to look through as she worked.

Get to work. Right.

She forced herself to glance away from him and focus on the artifact. Carefully, mostly because he trusted her and she feared letting him down, Zoey brushed away the dirt from the second etching, small piles of soil accumulating on the butcher paper as she worked.

Jericho was leaning over her shoulder, his head almost touching hers, his breath feathering the fine hairs at her temple. If she swiveled her neck, their lips would be touching.

Concentrate.

The radio played softly in the background and she focused on the sound, testing out Jericho's theory. He was right. Music helped sweep you into the work.

It took patience, something she normally did not possess a big supply of, but to her surprise she quickly became enthralled with the delicacy of the unveiling. A curve here, an angle there; it was fun to watch the etching appear. When she reached a stubborn chunk of dirt that refused to yield, Jericho passed her a sharpened bamboo skewer.

"Use this to pick off the stubborn dirt," he said.

She put down the paintbrush and picked up the bamboo skewer to do as he directed. "I never realized it before, but archaeologists are destruction artists. Reverse sculptors. We take away to reveal what once was, with new information about the past being our art."

"Which is why we must take supreme care to preserve what we can," he said. "It's a delicate balance, undermining the old in order to serve the new, without disturbing what was precious about the old in the first place."

"That's quite poetic and insightful."

"We are telling the story of human history, after all."

"Archaeology is such a noble profession. I can't figure out why it took me so long to find it." On the radio, Linkin Park was singing, "Somewhere I Belong." She shivered against the snarl of emotions pushing against her chest.

"Cold?"

"Uh-huh." She wasn't about to admit she was feeling oddly melancholy.

"I thought you were hot," he said.

"Guess I acclimated." She finished digging out the clod of dirt, put down the skewer, picked up the paintbrush and went back to whisking. The engraving emerged and she could finally make out what it was. "It's a young woman. This is getting romantic. Boy meets girl. I wonder how many other designs are etched into the handle?"

"Only one way to find out. Keep going."

"Don't you want to work on it some more?"

He shook his head. "I'm having more fun watching you. This is your first find. Go to it."

"Well, it's not technically my first find. I did find those artifacts in those mounds by the lake."

Jericho laid a finger against his lips. "Shh. Those finds did not happen."

"We found those things in Junie Mae's

backyard."

"Okay, it's your first official find."

She grinned and started in again. A few minutes later, they were looking at the etching of a lynx. "What does a lynx symbolize?"

He consulted the book on his e-reader. "Keeper of the secrets or guardian. It could also be listener or guide."

"Hmm, what if the young brave and maiden were having a secret affair?" She met his gaze.

"A taboo romance they had to hide," he murmured.

"A multicultural romance when that wasn't cool."

"The conflict."

"The angst."

"The star-crossed love."

"Hey." She waved the paintbrush. "That's very romantic. I'm rubbing off on you."

He didn't respond to her comment, but his eyes glittered with an enigmatic light. "Keep going."

They were midway down the handle now and Zoey got busy exposing the next totem. "Ooh," she breathed a few minutes later. "It's a scorpion. That feels ominous."

"The scorpion has been known to represent strength, transformation, passion, and chaos," he read.

"Boy. Girl. Secrets. Passion. Chaos. Sounds like falling in love with the wrong person to me."

"This story reminds me more and more of Little Wolf and Clarissa."

"Me too." Zoey rubbed her palms together. "Imagine if this tomahawk once belonged to Little Wolf."

"That's a big stretch. You're getting carried away. Not only is that leap farfetched, it's unscientific," Jericho cautioned.

"I wasn't going to write a treatise about it for an anthropological journal. I was just having fun playing *what if?*"

"Just making sure you know the difference between science and fantasy."

"You could use a little more fantasy in your life, Mr. By-the-Book."

"You think so?" His lips tipped up sardonically and in that moment he looked so arrogantly male that her womb twinged and twitched.

"I know so." Overcome by the startling sensation, she nodded, widened her eyes. It was odd, feeling these hot feelings and having to play it cool. "All work and no play makes Jericho a dull boy."

"So I'm dull now, am I?" He leaned in, his hard angular mouth far too close to hers.

Her breath slipped shallowly over her parted teeth. Why couldn't she stop looking at his lips? "Well, maybe not dull . . ."

"Are we going to finish this?"

For one startling second she thought he meant the kiss that seemed to be on the verge of happening, and then it occurred to her that he was talking about cleaning off the tomahawk. Her tongue was glued to the roof of her mouth, and it took a moment to dislodge it so that she could answer. "Sure."

Her hand trembled slightly as she picked up the paintbrush once more. This time she exposed a desert frog.

Jericho consulted the e-reader once more. "The frog has numerous meanings. Rebirth or cleansing, hidden beauty, peace, adaptability, medicine, poor character judgment, and power.

"Multipurpose totem. Maybe it's meant to have several meanings in the context of the story, ya think?"

"You're at the bottom of the handle. There looks to be only one carving left."

"It's like that last present on Christmas morning. No matter how enticing it looks, you don't want to open it because you know when you do, Christmas is officially over. You want to savor it."

"As I recall, you always tore through your

Christmas presents with rapid gusto," he said.

"I didn't say I could ever resist opening that last package as soon as I got to it. I merely said I *wanted* to savor it, not that I ever accomplished my goal."

He grinned.

"What are you smiling at?"

"You."

Feeling oddly shy, Zoey put a hand to her cheek. This wasn't like her. She didn't have a shy bone in her body. "What about me?"

"Do you realize you've been sitting in one spot for hours? I never thought you had it in you to sit still for so long, butterfly. You're not the same girl who ripped through the Christmas presents."

"What time is it?" She shifted her gaze to the clock. "Holy crap, it's one A.M."

"Is there a problem? You've always been a night owl."

"Yes, but that's when I'm out dancing." She pushed back her chair, got to her feet, stretched out her spine.

Jericho stood too. "Which is why I'm very impressed."

"I'm so amped up over this find, honestly, I don't think I could sleep a wink."

"Me either. I can't begin to tell you how special this is for me, being here with you on your first dig, on our home turf. It's —"

"Like kismet," she whispered.

Their gazes were manacled. Jericho's eyes darkened.

"Zoey."

"Uh-huh."

"I think it was a really bad idea for us to have ended up here alone."

"Probably." She lifted her chin. "We were so caught up in the mystery of the find that we didn't fully think this through."

"It is heady stuff."

"We could leave now," she said. "Get out of here before it's too late."

"We could do that."

"We should do that."

"Or . . ." He slid over to turn up the volume on the radio. It was Bonnie Raitt singing, "Something to Talk About." He held out his hand to her. "We could dance. Celebrate our find."

Foolishly, she tempted fate and put her hand into his. Jericho pulled her into his arms and two-stepped her around the lab. They stared into each other's eyes, lost in the moment, knowing they were playing with fire but unable to stop themselves. If he had kissed her then, she would have pulled him down on top of her and made love to him right there on the floor.

"How is it that Bonnie Raitt is on the same station as Linkin Park?" she asked.

"It's on my mp3 playlist."

"You put a song about best friends becoming lovers on your playlist?"

"Looks like."

"When did you make this playlist?"

"Before I left Utah."

"So before you even saw me again you were thinking . . ."

"Yeah," he said huskily, and spun her until she was laughing and dizzy, drunk with the joy and the dangerousness of the moment.

"So we're doing this."

"Not officially. Not yet. Not until the dig is over."

"I think the cow already got out of the barn on that one."

Jericho groaned, let go of her, stepped away, snapped off the music. "How did I get here again? Having a relationship with one of my students."

"It's not the same thing, you know."

"What's not?"

"You and me. You can't compare this to what happened with Mallory."

"No?"

"No, and if you can't see that, you're a very myopic scientist. You and me are solid."

"How can you be so sure?"

"We make a good team."

"We always did."

"See, you know it too."

He canted his head. "You've been thinking about this awhile."

"Since that night I kissed you outside Chantilly's on my twenty-first birthday. I just tried to ignore it."

"So did I."

"The big question is what took us so long to get together?"

"My fears."

"What are your fears?"

"That I could never satisfy you for long. That you'll grow bored and leave me for something or someone more exciting."

"Jericho, you have me endlessly intrigued."

"Is that only because you can't have me?"

She stepped closer, laughed. "Oh, I could have you."

He closed the gap. "You think so?"

"I know so," she murmured. "What I don't know is how much longer I can hold out for you. All I want to do is quit the dig so I can be with you."

"And you'd lose your trust fund and let yourself down in the process. We can hold out."

"Not when I'm having naughty thoughts I shouldn't be having." She lightly touched his arm.

He curled his hands into tight fists. "You're not the only one."

"Seeing you in action today." She shook her head. "Wow. You are sexier than Indiana Jones."

"Not a real person."

"Okay, you're sexier than Harrison Ford."

"I better be. He's a senior citizen. Maybe we should just go to bed." His face flushed. "No, no, wait, I didn't mean that the way it sounded. We shouldn't go to bed. Not with each other, I mean. We should sleep in our respective beds. You go home. I'll return to the dig site."

"Because going to bed with me would be the very worst thing in the world?"

"I could lose my job."

"Not if I quit."

"We're going around in circles."

"Trying to find a way out."

"There's not one. All we have to do is wait. We've waited all these years. A few more weeks are nothing."

Her chest heaved. "I'm so hot for you I can't stand it."

"You've got to stop talking like that."

"What? Speaking the truth."

"Yep. Lie to me, baby."

"I don't want you," she said. "Not one

tiny little bit. When I look at you my blood does not boil. My heart does not race. My nipples do not get hard. My stomach does not jump around like water on a sizzling iron skillet. I —"

But she got no further as Jericho's mouth clamped down on hers. Instantly, she melted against him, taking his greedy tongue deep into her mouth. *Uh-oh, should you be doing this?* whispered a voice in the back of her head, but her body shouted louder, drowning out the common sense she'd been trying too hard to cultivate. She would quit the dig. Everyone expected her to quit anyway. Why not live down to their low expectations of her? Somehow, she'd manage. She'd get a job and put herself through archaeology school. People did it all the time. She could too. Her fingers went crazy, plucking at the buttons of his shirt, desperate to get it off him, to see that bare chest, to run her tongue over him, lick salt from his skin.

His hands roamed over her body, down her waist, to her hips and around to her butt, grabbing hold and pulling her up tight against him. She was drowning in a pool of unmitigated pleasure.

You need to quit before you sleep with Jericho, otherwise he could lose his job.

She groaned and tried to fight the passion surfing through her in scalding hot waves. Wrenching her lips from his, she stepped back, gasping for air.

And her entire body ached.

His hands spanned her waist and the next thing she knew, he'd lifted her up and settled her onto her back on one of the long folding tables.

Dizzy, dazed, she tried to protest, but she could not form a coherent word. He leaned over her, his mouth covering hers while his hands worked at the snap of her pants. Was this really happening? Were they about to make love? Her heart crashed around in her chest like a bumper car bouncing off the rails. *I quit. I surrender. I give up. Take me, I'm yours.*

His fingers inched her zipper down.

Oh God, oh God, it was really happening. Finally. Finally.

Next, he stripped both her pants and panties to her ankles, then planted his mouth on her navel and kissed a trail all the way down to —

Her eyes rolled back in her head and she stopped breathing. She was sinking quickly. No hope of regaining her equilibrium now. Over and out. Gone, baby, gone. Leaping without looking at a damn thing. His tongue, oh his beautiful tongue, was doing things she had no idea tongues could do. Her best friend was becoming the best lover she'd ever had.

"Jericho," she whispered. Or thought she whispered. She still wasn't sure her mouth was working. Maybe she didn't say it. Maybe his name was seared so deeply into her brain it just felt like she was saying it over and over. *Jericho, Jericho, Jericho.*

Either way, he didn't answer her.

His hands slid under her butt, cradled her tenderly, and nudged her legs farther apart. He let out a low-throated growl of masculine appreciation. "Gorgeous," he crooned.

She had her eyes squeezed so tightly closed that yellow streaks of lightning flashed across the backs of her lids. Good thing she was lying down or she might have passed right out.

Whoa, hold on. No passing out now. Not when he's just now getting to the juicy part.

"Please," she whimpered. "Please."

His tongue toyed with her, devastated her. He pushed her higher and higher, his hands manacled around her waist, his mouth taking complete and utter possession of her. She belonged to him, one hundred percent.

Then his tongue did this mind-blowing maneuver that left her gasping for air and clutching desperately at his hair, tugging and mewling. She arched against his mouth and he took her to a place she had never been before. A place filled with stars and moonbeams and raw delicious pleasure. She shuddered and writhed and cried. He owned her. She was his adoring slave. If he asked her to crawl on her hands and knees on burning coals, she would have happily complied.

For one long incredible moment she hung on the flight of exaltation, free and silent and buoyant as parasailing, adrift on a blind current of rippling sensation.

And then she burst. A pop. An implosion. The ripples turned to crashing waves, crested high, then, bit by bit, ebbed away.

She was vaguely aware of hands tugging her pants up, zipping up the zipper, snapping the snap. Arms went underneath her, lifted her to her feet. At long last she opened her eyes and looked into his dear, familiar face.

Jericho put a gentle hand on her shoulder. His touch was an electrical switch, lighting up every nerve ending in a domino effect, spreading throughout her body like the power in a city coming on after a long blackout. She hummed and surged and glowed. She'd never felt anything like it, knew that she never would again with any other man.

The sensation was so overwhelming; so incredibly mind-boggling after the avalanche of things she'd already felt. Zoey sagged helplessly against him, grateful for the arm he slipped around her waist. He hooked a finger under her chin, tilted her face up to meet his gaze.

Jericho smiled softly and her heart flipped. Oh God, she was in so much trouble here. If he did not love her back the way she loved him, it would destroy her.

"I'm going to kiss you one more time," he said. "And then that's it until the field school is over. We'll make sure never to be alone again until then. Got it?"

She nodded even as she wanted to whimper *no.* He was right. And for this very moment all that mattered was his mouth on hers and his fingers threading through her hair and his luminous eyes staring at her like she was the greatest find he'd ever unearthed.

He took his time, kissing her thoroughly, slowly. She could taste the heat of his need, but he held himself in restraint, no rushing, no grabbing, just patient and precise. His hands were considerate too, not grabby and kneading roughly like a lot of guys would do, but caressing, cherishing. When the time came to go all the way, he would be the most considerate of lovers — a rugged man with callus-roughened fingers who even so had possessed a treasure trove of foreplay techniques. She could tell from the way he flicked his tongue over her palate at the same time his fingers lightly stroked a sensitive spot behind her ear, tickling an erogenous zone that made her moan.

He drew her close and held her then, simply held her in the circle of those corded arms of his, sturdy as oaks. He rested his chin on the top of her head. She pressed her ear against his chest, heard the strong, hard thumping of his heart.

It was such a beautiful moment that she never wanted it to end. His scent filled her nose. His husky breathing soothed her ears. She could have stood there until the end of time if the sound of footsteps on the sidewalk outside the door hadn't simultaneously jerked both their heads up.

"Dr. Chance," a voice called out. "Are you in there?"

"It's Director Sinton!" she whispered, completely freaked out. "What are we going to do?"

"Closet!" he exclaimed, and dragged her into it.

CHAPTER 12

Preserve: To keep safe and protect from injury, harm, or destruction.

Wishing he could kick his own ass for losing control, Jericho shut the closet door on Zoey and belatedly realized that if Dr. Sinton discovered her hiding in the closet it would look far more suspicious than if he'd simply found them in the room together. Dammit! Whenever he was around her, he simply could not think straight. They might not have fully consummated their relationship, but what he'd just done to her definitely qualified as crossing a line. Out of breath, he stepped away from the closet just as Dr. Sinton walked into the room.

"What are you doing here so late?" Dr. Sinton blinked, his hair messy, a sheet crease on his cheek. He wore pajamas with a robe thrown over them.

"Working."

"It's almost two in the morning." Dr. Sinton's gaze honed in on Jericho's chest and that's when he realized his shirt was unbuttoned halfway.

He shrugged. He could still taste Zoey on his tongue and it rattled him to the bone. "I got hot." *No lie there.* "What are you doing up at this hour, Director?"

"I live across the street from the college. I got up to get a glass of water and saw the light was on over here. I thought maybe some pranksters were up to no good."

"No sir, just me."

"Where are your students?"

"They have the weekend off."

"Oh, right."

From the corner of his eyes, Jericho spied Zoey's purse behind the door. Aw shit. "I'm here analyzing a find we made at the dig site. It's fascinating. Let me show you." He moved to stand in front of her purse, and gestured toward the table where there were two chairs pulled out indicating a pair had been sitting at the table.

Dr. Sinton didn't seem to home in on that fact. He pulled a pair of reading glasses from the pocket of his robe and moved toward the table. "What have you got here?"

"Tomahawk."

Dr. Sinton picked up the magnifying glass.

"May I?"

"By all means." Jericho waved, and while Sinton was investigating the tomahawk, he slowly pushed Zoey's purse across the floor toward the desk. There was a good two feet of open floor between the purse and desk. If Sinton glanced up now, he was screwed.

"Upon cursory appraisal it appears to be around two hundred years old, give or take," Sinton said.

"That was my guesstimate as well."

"The Trans-Pecos was brutal territory back in the early 1800s. Didn't really get settled until the later part of that century."

"Uh-huh." He kept pushing the purse. It whispered silkily across the tile, another few inches and he could kick it under the desk and out of sight.

"This is why I was so impressed when you managed to not only wrangle permission out of the August McCleary Foundation for the field school, but to get them to fund the dig. Kudos."

"It wasn't my doing, sir. All the credit belongs to Zoey McCleary. She made it happen with the board of directors." One last thrust and he almost had the purse concealed.

"Family does have its privileges, doesn't it?"

"It does." He kicked the purse under the desk. Whew. Sweat trickled down his brow.

"You are making sure the students toe the line on the conditions the board set forth? No digging anywhere but Triangle Mount."

"Everyone is aware of the edict," he hedged.

Bump.

Jericho froze. Was that Zoey making noises from inside the closet? Dr. Sinton seemed oblivious, so maybe he was hearing things. *Don't look at the closet. Don't look at the closet.* He looked.

Dr. Sinton raised his head, tomahawk in one hand, and magnifying glass in the other to catch Jericho staring at the closet.

Double dammit.

"Something the matter? You seem nervous."

"Not nervous. Just excited. I didn't expect to find much on Triangle Mount. I was so excited, in fact, I couldn't wait to finish excavation before bringing the tomahawk back here to examine it."

"And I've interrupted you." Dr. Sinton shook his head. "My apologies. I see there's still another totem left to be revealed on this handle."

"Yes sir."

"Would you mind if I cleaned it?"

Jericho swallowed back a groan. *Leave already!* "Not at all."

Dr. Sinton looked like a little kid who'd just gotten served his favorite flavor of ice cream. He sat down at the table, picked up the paintbrush. "I sure do miss fieldwork."

Poor Zoey was stuck in that dark closet having no idea what was going on out here. His head throbbed. How in the hell had he gotten himself into this situation? *Be cool, or Sinton is going to figure out something is going on.*

"It's a coyote," Dr. Sinton sang out.

Trying to be cool, Jericho sauntered over.

"The coyote is universally a trickster." Dr. Sinton traced a finger over the totem he'd exposed.

"It has other meanings," Jericho said. "Depending on the tribal culture. In fact, the coyote has a wide range of symbolism." He knew because he'd just read it when he and Zoey were going over the tomahawk. "The coyote also may symbolize intelligence, stealth, wisdom, innocence, and folly."

"Sounds contradictory to me."

"Aren't most things in life?"

"You've got a point there. Good grief. It's two-thirty. My wife's going to have a fit." Dr. Sinton got to his feet. "It's easy to get carried away when you're working on a find."

Tell me about it. Jericho walked toward the door, hoping to hurry Dr. Sinton along.

All at once there was a loud sneeze from the closet.

Jericho froze.

The director looked from Jericho's half-unbuttoned shirt to the strap of Zoey's purse sticking out from under the desk to the closet door and back to Jericho again.

Ah shit, this was it. His career over before it ever really started. "Sir, I can explain —"

Dr. Sinton held up a silencing hand. "I was young once. I know the power of the Indiana Jones mystique when it comes to the ladies. How do you think I caught Mrs. Sinton?" He winked. "Just as long as it's not a student in that . . ."

He might as well come clean. Take his medicine. He deserved whatever punishment Dr. Sinton decided to dish out. Maybe the director would take pity on him. He opened his mouth to confess.

"But you wouldn't do that, would you?" Dr. Sinton clamped an iron hand on Jericho's shoulder. "Because you like your job too much to do something that damn dumb. I'm going to go home now. I suggest you let your young woman out of the closet and go to bed yourself."

"I'm so sorry," Zoey said on the drive back to Cupid. "I tried my best not to sneeze, but the harder I tried not to sneeze, the worse it got. I mean you see it in the movies where people try not to sneeze so they don't get caught but you never think that if you were actually in a situation where you needed to keep quiet that you'll suddenly have to sneeze —"

"You're prattling," Jericho pointed out.

"I know, but it's only because I'm so sorry. I came within inches of ruining your career. If Dr. Sinton hadn't been terrified of finding a naked woman in the closet and he'd come to investigate the sneezing . . ." She made a choking noise and a slicing motion across her throat.

"It's not your fault. It's dusty in the closet. There are rocks and soil samples in there. I should have owned up to the whole thing."

"No, no. I'm glad you didn't and if you had, I would have told Dr. Sinton I'd already quit the dig."

"It doesn't matter now. We got away with it, but it brings home the fact that we have to stay away from each other, Zoey. We cannot be alone together for the next three weeks. Even this is dangerous."

"We haven't done anything. Nothing's happened."

"You call what we did nothing?"

"Okay, *something* happened, but we didn't cross a line. No line was crossed."

"I'm not sure Dr. Sinton would agree with that." He pulled up in front of the Cupid's Rest. All the lights were off inside.

He parked out front and walked her to the door. The town was asleep. Crickets chirped. Somewhere in the distance a dog barked. The streetlights were on, but they were hidden by shadows from the bushes flanking the sidewalk.

"One more kiss for the road?" she asked when they reached the front door.

"Don't push your luck," he growled, but then pulled her against his chest for a punishing kiss before turning and sprinting back to the truck, leaving Zoey standing on the porch, fingering her lips and sighing dreamily.

Back in his tent on Triangle Mount, Jericho listened to the lonely call of coyotes and thought about the events of the day, from their exciting find, to kissing Zoey, to getting caught by Dr. Sinton. He was ashamed of his behavior. He should have more self-control, and yet, no matter how much he might wish it had not happened, he couldn't regret it.

So he'd stupidly done it again on her front porch. Kissed her fierce and brazen, a take-no-prisoners attack that had sent her backing against the door and clacked their teeth together so loudly that for one horrifying moment, he feared he'd broken her tooth.

But she'd laughed and lashed her arms around his neck and pulled his head down, extending the kiss until they were both recklessly breathless. She was so warm and soft and willing, smelling of watermelon shampoo and sand and woman.

His body throbbed painfully. It had been months since he'd been with a woman and abstinence was taking its toll, especially after what he'd done to her in the lab. He did not know how he'd kept himself from doing more. And not just any woman would do. Zoey was the one he craved and he couldn't seem to stop himself from yearning for her no matter how hard he tried. He wanted her with a need that shook him to his very core.

This was so unlike him, the inability to delay gratification; normally he was a patient man with practiced self-control. He was *proud* of the fact he'd been able to keep at bay the drooling cave dweller that was hiding inside every man.

How had the change come about, this shift from best friend to longed-for lover? How did he stop this insatiable thirst? He was so afraid he would not be able to keep his hands-off promise.

A rat of a thought scurried through his brain. He could resign his job. Tell Dr. Sinton that he could not uphold the conditions of his probationary employment. If he was no longer Zoey's instructor, he could have her, nothing to stand in the way. His greedy body turned happily stony at the prospect.

But that was short-term thinking. This was his dream job. He wanted to work in the Trans-Pecos, always had, and it wasn't as if archaeology jobs grew on trees. It might be months or even years before he found one as appealing as this one. He could do this. He could hold on to his control.

Three weeks. Only three weeks.

Except, as sexy as Zoey was and as badly as he wanted her, Jericho was not so sure he could do it.

The dig resumed at seven o'clock on Monday morning. Jericho had brought pictures of the tomahawk back from the lab for the other students to see. Everyone tried their hand at interpreting the symbols and what they meant. They were so fired up to find more artifacts that by noon they'd troweled down the unit floor another ten-centimeter layer of strata.

Today, Zoey was on screening duty, which meant she was shifting through the excavated soil searching for smaller artifacts and ecofacts (plant and animal remains.) Even careful troweling missed tons of minuscule finds, so screening was an absolute necessity. Her arms were already exhausted from shaking the dry screen and she had to dump it between each session to get out roots and pebbles and live bugs.

She tried her best to keep from watching Jericho, and he was avoiding her as well. When their gazes did accidentally meet, they both instantly glanced away. But as the heat wore on and the shirts started coming off, she told herself she would not look, but when Jericho passed by, stripped bare to the waist, his sleek olive-skinned body dewy with sweat, Zoey's eyes bugged right out of her head.

He was a beaut, no doubt about it. The noonday sun glistened over his broad shoulders and brawn biceps, caressed his hard angles, and highlighted the impressive definition of his obliques. Her bedazzled eyes tracked his easy, loose-limbed movements, her neck swiveling as he strode past, seemingly oblivious to her gape-mouthed stare. She gathered in the sight of his smooth expanse of tanned back gleaming like polished stone and chiseled in clean lines of rippling muscles and sharp-edged bone. He could have been a warrior chieftain, sprung from history's earth.

Her stomach squeezed and a familiar fever pumped through her blood, strumming with yearning desire.

I want. She tasted it all so acutely — the bittersweet ache of longing.

Unable to bear her misery a second longer, she mumbled to no one in particular, "I'm taking my lunch break," and headed off down the mountain toward the camp.

A few minutes later she made herself a sandwich and plunked down on a camp chair underneath the shade of an umbrella beside Catrina.

"Something is amiss," Catrina observed.

"I don't know what you mean," Zoey said, taking a long drink of cold bottled water.

"You and Jericho were thick as thieves and now you aren't even speaking to each other."

"We were not thick as thieves."

"Did you have a lovers' quarrel?" She purred the R in lover, making the word sound smoky and suggestive.

"We are not lovers. We've just known each other a long time."

"Mm-huh. I do not believe you."

"Believe whatever you want."

"Maybe you are not lovers yet, but you will be."

"We won't," she said firmly.

"I see the way he looks at you. Like you are candle wax and he is a flame." Catrina unfurled her long, caramel-colored legs.

"Very poetic, seriously, you should study literature instead of archaeology. It doesn't really seem like your thing."

"Just know that you are fooling no one." Catrina finished off her sandwich, put the paper wrappings in the recycling bin, and strolled back toward the dig site. "Oh and by the way, I am tired of digging. I will take over your job on the dry screen."

Zoey's mouth went dry and her sandwich got stuck halfway. She had to gulp more water to get it down. Were she and Jericho really that obvious? In the wee hours of Saturday morning, they'd had a very close call with Dr. Sinton, but their luck was not going to hold. She really was going to have to quit the dig. There wasn't any other way. They'd already slipped too far.

With an ache in her stomach, she followed

Catrina's swaying backside. She climbed down into the unit with a couple of the other team members, picked up the trowel that Catrina had left behind, and went to work.

After a few minutes, she got into the Zen of digging. It could be quite peaceful, this steady careful scraping of dirt, peeling back the earth in search of secrets and it calmed her in a way no other activity ever had. She liked being outdoors. Liked feeling sweat drip down her back. Liked how strong and capable her hands had become, even if her fingernails were broken and ragged. It proved she'd put in a hard day of good old-fashioned labor. Her stomach settled and her anxiety over Catrina's goading flowed out of her.

In fact, she was so zoned out that for a second, it didn't register when her trowel came into contact with something besides soil. The material resisted, stretched. She stopped, put down her trowel, pushed her cowgirl hat back on her head, and leaned in for a closer look. It appeared to be a corner of a tanned animal hide.

"Je—" she almost called him by his first name, but stopped herself in the nick of time. "Dr. Chance, I've found something."

Immediately, everyone stopped what they

were doing and came near, but left a path for Jericho to thread over to where Zoey was kneeling. He crouched beside her. So close. Instantly, her body responded.

"What have you found?"

She showed him the tiny corner of hide poking up from the dirt.

He sucked in a deep breath, crouched to examine it more closely, and then looked over at her. "It's your find. Go ahead and excavate it."

"I'm afraid I won't do it right," she admitted.

"You're perfectly capable. I'm right here."

Following every protocol to the letter, Zoey slowly, cautiously removed the dirt from around the hide, and as the soil fell away, she saw that her find was much larger than she originally suspected and it wasn't flat, but rolled up like a rawhide map.

"Did Native Americans do yoga?" She giggled.

"It looks as if it could be a medicine bundle," Jericho observed.

"What's that?" Piper asked, and pushed her glasses up on her short nose.

"The bundle is a container to protect items they used in healing and religious ceremonies," Jericho explained.

"Da-*amn,* this is the coolest dig ever,"

carrot-topped Braden said. "A tomahawk and a medicine bundle. Kick ass."

It took another hour of diligent extraction to get the find recorded, photographed and documented. Eager to see it, everyone crowded around, but the artifact looked like nothing more than rolled up dirty animal skin.

"We bag it and tag it and take it back to the lab," Jericho said.

"Can we do it today?" Avery asked. "We missed out on the tomahawk."

"There might be more artifacts to be found here." Jericho swept his hand over the area. "And it's almost an hour drive to the lab."

"We could set up a field lab in one of the tents," she suggested. "Just for a place to take a look at the medicine bundle."

"That's a good idea." Jericho nodded. "Why don't you take charge of that?"

Yeah, sure, she could do that.

Taking Catrina and Piper with her, she returned to base camp to transform the tent she and Catrina shared into a field lab, temporarily removing the cots and moving in one of the folding tables they normally used to prep and serve food on. Thirty minutes later, the rest of the group joined them at camp to examine the medicine bundle.

It was four in the afternoon as the entire team of fifteen, including Jericho, ringed the table in the center of the tent. He passed out vinyl gloves to everyone.

"Before we get started, I want to make something absolutely clear," he said.

Everyone gave him their full attention.

"No one talks about this. When the time comes, we'll do a press release and have a town hall meeting to discuss the find. In the meantime, no one says a word to anyone about what we've discovered here. We don't want looky-loos descending upon us en masse. That means nothing gets out on social media. If anyone leaks anything, you're off the team immediately. Got it?"

"Yes," they replied in unison.

"Now that we have that out of the way, let's get to it." He moved to stand at the center of the table, students parting to let him pass. Zoey thrilled to his authority. She wasn't accustomed to seeing his commanding side. It was kinda hot.

"Medicine bundles were sacred to the Native Americans," he said. "There were personal medicine bundles that were used for religious purposes and protection, shaman bundles primarily used for healing, and tribal bundles that were for the entire tribes. These were mostly religious in nature, although they could also be used for healing as well, especially in the case where an infection was sweeping through the tribe. Although the people who made and used this medicine bundle are long gone, we want to respect the sacredness of their cultural beliefs and handle the bundle with care and reverence."

He raised his head, looked around the table at everyone, and slowly untied the leather thong binding that held the medicine bundle closed.

"Should we say a prayer or something?" Avery asked.

"It's creepy." Catrina shuddered and Avery slipped an arm around her waist. She rested her dark head on his shoulder.

Zoey felt jealous. She wished Jericho could put his arm around her, but he was on the opposite side of the table, his gaze intent on what he was doing. The pulse at the hollow of his throat bounded. He was excited. So was she. But more from watching him get excited over the artifact than because of the artifact itself.

"Feels like a séance." Piper pushed her glasses up on the end of her nose and leaned in for a closer look. "Do you think we could call up a spirit if we held hands and chanted?"

"There are no such things as spirits," Braden said.

"Don't be so small-minded," Piper retorted. "There are more things in heaven and earth than science can explain."

"Respect, people," Jericho said. "Let's keep the chatter to a minimum and focus on our job. Who's got the camera?"

"I do." Braden held up a pocket camera.

"Who's recording?"

"Me." Piper had her notebook open.

Gingerly, Jericho unfolded the bundle and revealed what one might expect inside a medicine bundle. Botanicals like seeds, pinecones, grass, and dried crushed flower petals. Animal remains, teeth, hair, feathers, and bones. Rocks, arrowheads, limestone, crystals. But it was what was beaded into the center of the hide itself that stopped Zoey's breathing.

It was the same symbol of a yellow flame on a dark green background as the medallion Granny Helen had given Jericho.

The Keepers of the Flame.

She jerked her eyes upward, collided hard into Jericho's gaze, and saw that he was just as stunned as she.

Chapter 13

Myths and legends: Stories passed down through generations, about heroic individuals, spectacular events, or powerful gods. Myths represent a culture's beliefs and explain its customs; while some are fictional, others may be based on real persons or events.

Jericho stared down at the symbol beaded into the leather hide of the medicine bundle as a strange sensation of déjà vu moved through him. The hairs on the nape of his neck lifted. What in the hell was this?

The other students hadn't noticed the change in him. They were busy examining the contents of the medicine bundle, but Zoey knew. How had the same symbol on the beaded medallion Granny Helen had given him ended up on the animal hide Zoey had found buried below the surface of Triangle Mount? This was no link to ancient pyramid builders, but it was an unnerving find all the same.

At least for him.

Outside, the wind kicked up, sending eddies of dirt and debris spattering against the tent and whistling around the entrance flap.

Catrina let out a little squeal, and curled her face against Avery's chest.

Some of the others looked nervous too, but not Zoey. Her eyes were bright, inquisitive. "Spooky," she teased. "Do you think the gods want their medicine bundle back?"

Piper stepped closer to Braden, who put a tentative arm around her shoulder. She did not shrug him off.

"Kidding," Zoey said.

"It is not funny." Catrina lifted her chin. "What if we have disturbed a burial ground?"

"There's no evidence that's the case," Jericho said. "Shake off the heebie-jeebies. It's just the wind. We're scientists here. Let's act like it. There're no ghosts, no spirits, no angry gods seeking revenge."

"But isn't that disrespecting the religion of whoever owned this bundle?" Zoey asked. "Obviously, they believed in the power of the medicine bundle and if we're going to respect their culture, shouldn't we approach it with the appropriate sense of reverence whether we share their beliefs or not?"

She made a strong point, and hell, truth be known, he admired her for calling him on it, and honestly, he was a little unnerved himself by the medallion that matched the one Granny Helen had given him.

"You're right," he said. "I don't mean to disrespect anyone's beliefs and we are going to handle this artifact with the utmost care, as we do with any find. But what I don't want is for students to start scaring themselves with flights of fantasy."

Everyone shook off their worries at that, and laughed at their susceptibility. Meticulously, they went through the medicine bundle, cataloging, photographing, and making notes of their find. Jericho tried to focus on what they were doing but his mind was muddled by the beaded Golden Flame on a dark green background and the sight of Zoey across the table from him.

She moved with such simple, compact ease, so competent and smooth, like she'd been doing this all her life. She was a natural, and that surprised him. Never in his wildest imagination would he have believed she could slip so easily into the precision chores. He watched her small hands as she measured and calibrated, stored seeds and crushed dry petals into glass cylinders, stoppered them with a cork and wrote in Sharpie where, when, and how they were removed from the medicine bundle.

Long shadows slanted across the tent. The sun was almost gone. Where had the time vanished?

Some of the students had started drifting away — Braden to start a campfire, Avery and Catrina to cook dinner for the crew, Piper to input data into the computer, others to go to the bathroom or get something to drink. At one point, it was just he and Zoey at the table processing the artifact. Her hair was piled up on the top of her head with a clip, soft tendrils falling free and drifting down her shoulders. Her bottom lip was drawn up between her teeth as she worked. Her skin was creamy as highfat ice cream, her cheeks rosy from a long day in the sun in spite of the sunblock he'd watched her slather on that morning. Her V-neck T-shirt clung to her breasts, and when she leaned forward, she unknowingly gave him a great view of her cleavage.

God, she was gorgeous.

"We should take this to Lace," she said. Her eyes met his and a stone hot bolt of mental electricity shot from her to him.

"What?" He blinked, mesmerized by her

beauty and dull-witted from it at the same time.

"The botanicals," she explained. "We should take them to my cousin Lace. She'll know what they are. In fact, we should take the entire bundle to her. She's got a lab of her own."

It was a sound proposition. Zoey's cousin, Dr. Lace Bettingfield Hollister, was a botanist who oversaw the Cupid Botanical Gardens and had actually turned down a chance to work for the Smithsonian. She knew more about plants than anyone in the Trans-Pecos.

But he knew he couldn't risk being alone with Zoey, not even for the drive into Cupid. If he got in close quarters with her again, with no one else around, this time he would not be satisfied with kisses.

"We could take the whole crew with us," she said, reading his thoughts.

It unnerved him, how she knew him so well, and how she managed to stay one step ahead of him. "Or we could ask Lace to come here."

"Cell reception up here is lousy, but sometimes I can get a text through when I can't make a call. Let me see if I can send her a text message." Zoey pulled out her phone and started texting.

A couple of minutes later, her cell phone dinged.

Zoey read the missive, grinned. "Her appetite has been whetted. She's on her way with equipment in tow."

"That's good."

They worked in silence for several minutes while various team members drifted in and out of the field lab. At one point, Zoey raised her head and looked around and Jericho couldn't resist doing the same. For the moment, they were alone in the tent.

"So what do you make of this?" With a gloved hand she tapped the beaded medallion sewn into the center of the hide. "In the context of what your great-grandmother gave you?"

"Evidently, the design of the medallion is authentic to the Native Americans who once stayed on Triangle Mount. We can't assume anything more than that," he said levelly, ignoring the quickening of his pulse.

"You don't think there is any possibility that you could indeed be descended from the people who made this medicine bundle?"

"That's an unsubstantiated leap. We have no idea where Granny Helen got that medallion. She's full of stories and her mind is quite mixed up. And besides, if I was descended from this tribe, don't you think someone in my family would have mentioned it before now?"

Zoey shrugged. "Maybe Granny Helen was the only one in your family who knew."

"And maybe she heard the story from someone else and appropriated it as her own. The mind plays tricks, Zoey. Every good scientist must take care not to fall prey to confirmation bias or wishful thinking. We have to resist the natural human instinct to seek confirmation for what we believe is the truth. Our perception colors everything, but we can't allow it to pass for scientific proof."

"Okay," she said. "This is the hard part of being a scientist, questioning my own eyes and ears and thoughts."

"Difficult maybe, but essential if you hope to get at the truth."

"I'm trying, I'm trying."

The tent flap opened. "The botanist is here," Avery announced, and led Zoey's cousin inside.

Dr. Lace Bettingfield, recently married to former pro-football star Pierce Hollister, ducked her head under the low opening as she entered, carrying a microscope case in one hand, another hard-sided plastic case in the other. She wore her chin-length raven hair swept back off her forehead, black-framed spectacles perched on the end of her elegant nose and a sapphire wedding ring that matched the color of her intelligent blue eyes. She possessed creamy skin in spite of the fact she spent much time outdoors, and a Rubenesque figure. She looked like a scholarly, voluptuous Snow White. While she was quite beautiful, she had nothing on her cousin, at least not to Jericho's way of thinking.

Zoey moved to clear off the end of their worktable so Lace would have a place to set up her equipment.

With Lace's arrival, the students came back inside the tent to watch the proceedings, bringing with them the smoky mesquite smell of the campfire, crowding the small space to its limit.

Lace stopped in mid-step, stared at the tanned hide stretched out over the table. All the contents had been removed, cataloged, labeled, and stored, leaving only the skin, with the beaded medallion sewn into it. She audibly sucked in her breath. "Omigosh."

"What is it?" Zoey canted her head.

Lace clutched her cousin's arm. "I scarcely dare to hope."

"Is it a significant find?"

"If it's what I think it is, unbelievably so. Gloves." Lace stuck out a hand to Jericho.

He plucked two vinyl gloves from the box and passed them to her. She slipped on the gloves, bent over to examine the hide, her fingers strumming over the beads of the medallion like it was a rosary.

It touched something inside Jericho when he saw that Lace's hand was trembling. She was seriously *moved* by their discovery. For some reason, her reaction made him nervous.

"Magnifying glass." Lace stuck out her hand.

Jericho settled a magnifying glass in her upturned palm. A flick of her wrist and she turned it around, focused it on the intricate beadwork and leaned so close he thought she was going to bump her nose up against it.

A long moment passed where no one spoke. It was an eerie silence, and strangely still after the windstorm they'd experienced earlier that evening.

A visible shudder ran through Lace's body. "It is!"

"What? What?" Zoey asked.

"The Golden Flame agave," Lace whispered with the reverential tones of a priest conducting midnight Mass on Christmas Eve.

"What's that?" Jericho asked.

"Lace's equivalent of Bigfoot," Zoey supplied. "A mythological plant no one but her seems to believe still existed, if indeed it ever did."

"It did," Lace said firmly. "And this helps back up my theory." She straightened, pinned Jericho with a serious stare. "Zoey said you found botanicals in the medicine bag."

He nodded and motioned for Catrina to retrieve the botanicals they'd found inside the hide. Lace unsnapped the latches on her cases and set up her microscope. Zoey brought her a folding camp chair. Looking quite queenly, Lace sat down, used tweezers to extract a small bit of the dried crushed petals they'd found, put them on a slide, and clipped it into place underneath the microscope lens.

The scent of roasting meat wafted into the tent. Jericho's stomach growled and he realized he hadn't eaten a thing since breakfast, but he wasn't about to leave now. Zoey inched over to stand by him while they waited for Lace's assessment. He could feel the heat from her warm little body, and it was all he could do not to touch her.

After what felt like an eternity, Lace raised her head from the microscope. A beatific smile crossed her face and she looked as if her consciousness had reached a whole new level and she'd been transported to utopian Shangri-la. She made a small I've-discovered-a-cure-for-the-world's-ills sound that was half chuff, half laugh. "It's from the flower of an agave plant I've never seen before."

"And you know all there is about agaves," Zoey said.

"It's my life work." Her eyes shone like polished marble, bright and slick. "I'm completely convinced it's from the Golden Flame, and here's why." She launched into a complicated botanical hypothesis that left them all blinking. Clearly, the woman was a brilliant scientist.

Zoey flattened her hand and soared it over her head. "Whoosh, zoom. You left me in the dust with that explanation."

"You might have to bottom line it for us," Jericho said. "We're not botanical archaeologists."

"Oops." Lace pressed three fingers to her mouth. "Sorry. I tend to get carried away. Let's start with the basic myth and legend of the Golden Flame agave."

"A story." Zoey sighed happily. "Oh goody. Much easier to process than those Latin names you sling around."

"The prevailing myth of the Golden Flame

agave centers on the assertion that the extraction made from steeping crushed petals has healing properties capable of curing orthomyxoviridae."

"Zoom." Zoey repeated the over-her-head gesture. "Still too lofty, cuz."

"Gotcha," Lace said. "Rumor has it that a shot of tea made from the flower of the Golden Flame agave will kick the flu's ass."

"Why didn't you just say so?" Zoey grinned in her irrepressible way. "See? How hard was that to speak regular-people-ese?"

"Hey," Avery said. "Is this the same plant that they make tequila from?"

"No, you're referring to *Agave tequilana,*" Lace said. "But this cactus would be in the same family. It is the process of procuring the desired liquid that is different."

"So *Agave golden flameiana,*" Zoey said. "Has a nice ring to it."

"Sounds like steak. Kinda makes you hungry, huh?" Piper rubbed her stomach.

"That's not how botanical naming —" Lace stopped herself, waved both hands back and forth. "Never mind."

"Let's stop interrupting Dr. Bettingfield," Jericho said. He was getting anxious to find out just what all this meant, especially since he had an identical Golden Flame medallion in his pocket.

"Like Bigfoot, as my cousin was so quick to compare this to, there's been lots of speculation about the Golden Flame but no real proof. Many agaves are century plants, but the name is a misnomer. Most of them live only ten to thirty years."

"Still," Catrina mused. "That is a long time for a plant."

"While this is a generalization — I don't want to zoom over Zoey's head again." Lace paused to grin. "Century plants bloom only once just before they die."

"So they go out in a flame of glory." Braden nodded.

"Exactly. There are a lot of romantic myths around these plants, which is what makes most botanists so skeptical that the Golden Flame is real. Although there are some who believe it once existed but is now extinct. I think they're all wrong."

"What's your hypothesis?" Jericho asked her.

Lace rummaged in her case, pulled out a copy of the *American Journal of Botany,* flipped it open to an article she'd authored, and passed it to Jericho. The title was: "Plant of the Century — A Case for the Existence of the Golden Flame Agave in the Davis Mountain Range." "I believe the Golden Flame is a true century plant that blooms only once every hundred years and that the flowers from the plant, when brewed into a tea, are indeed a strong antiviral."

Jericho skimmed the article. "Interesting premise."

"I wonder if Cousin Walker came across this while researching August McCleary's biography," Zoey supplied.

"I can't speak for your cousin, but this very well could be how your great-great-uncle August saved the Trans-Pecos from the Spanish flu. Fifty million people died of it worldwide, but only a rare few died of it here."

"That's what makes Walker's book on August so compelling." Zoey tapped her chin with an index finger. "The near-miraculous healings."

"Yes. How did August manage to do what no other physician was able to do and stomp it out? It's my contention, Zoey, that your great-great-uncle August got his hands on the Golden Flame when it was in bloom, dried the petals, compounded them, and then later used them to cure the Spanish flu."

"How did he know about the Golden Flame?"

Lace shrugged. "I can't speak to that."

"Is there anything in his formulary about it?" Zoey asked.

Lace shook her head. "It's not in his formula for the flu remedy, but if he was trying to keep the active ingredient proprietary, he simply might not have recorded it as part of the recipe. Or perhaps he kept a second, secret formulary no one else knew about."

"If he used it in 1918 that means the Golden Flame could be close to blooming again," Zoey mused. "Right?"

"It does. His recorded formula is dated 1914, four years before the Spanish flu bludgeoned the country. He was already a well-known apothecary in the area, and the plant probably doesn't bloom every hundred years on the dot. It could be ninety-six years or a hundred and two. Botany is changeable and adaptive."

"You've really thought this through," Jericho said.

"I've been doing research on this for seven years. In fact, this article is part of my doctorate thesis and I've found soil and climate analysis to support my theory. Turn the page." Lace motioned with her index finger, toggling it like she was flipping a page.

"What?" Jericho looked up.

"I drew an illustration of what I believe the Golden Flame looks like when in full bloom," Lace said. "It's on the next page."

Jericho flipped the page and there it was. A drawing of a plant that looked eerily similar to the beaded design on the medallions, both the one in his pocket and the one sewn into the medicine bundle hide. He felt as if an invisible hand grabbed him by the throat, held him in the grip of a magnetic force.

"The Golden Flame *is* a very rare plant, on the verge of extinction. From my calculations about the plant's characteristics, the soil, altitude, and climate, I believe the Davis Mountains are the only place that it grows. Not only that, but I've narrowed this agave's natural habitat specifically to the mountainous terrain of the August McCleary Foundation nature preserve. I say as much in the article." Lace nodded at the magazine in his hand.

"So the plant has either got to be here on Triangle Mount or on Widow's Peak? Those are the only two mountains on foundation land." Zoey mused.

"Yes, and because Widow's Peak is at a higher altitude, I tend to think it most likely grows there."

"Even though we found botanicals of the

Golden Flame here on Triangle Mount?" Jericho interjected.

Lace shrugged. "It's an evolving theory."

Zoey shook her head. "Brainiac. I have no idea how you figured all that out."

"I factored in the cellular structure of a comparative agave species to —"

"Zoom!" Zoey said before her cousin could start spouting Latin names.

"Sorry. Occupational hazard," Lace apologized. "Back to the story. The most compelling legend I stumbled across in my research was about the Keepers of the Flame."

Zoey swiveled her head to look at him. Their gazes met and her eyes widened. Slowly, she inched her foot over and rested it against his. No one else would have noticed, but she was letting him know she was right there with him.

A strong yearning came over him, so stark and pure it burned his chest. He wanted her. Not just in his bed. Not just for a few nights. Not just as a friend. He wanted her as his woman. Forever. The intensity of his yearning tasted bright and sharp, bittersweet and brilliant.

"Who are the Keepers of the Flame?" Zoey asked. Her voice cut clear and certain through the tension thick inside the tent.

"The Keepers of the Flame were born of

Comanche blood," Lace said. "But they were different. Special. Mystics, you might say. Unlike the rest of the Comanche tribes who were nomadic warriors, this small group was stationary in the Davis Mountains and peaceful. They were great healers and kept 'medicine' for their brethren who came to them when they were sick, wounded, or needed spiritual guidance."

"Is this factual history?" Jericho asked. "Or legend?"

"Until now, until this . . ." She swept her hand at the medicine bundle. "It was nothing except a fanciful story. There had never been any definitive evidence that this small sect was real. But your find changes *everything.* This is proof that the Keepers of the Flame existed and so did the Golden Flame agave. This is monumental, Jericho. A find of a lifetime."

"And on your first real job as a professor!" Zoey marveled.

A murmur went through the students as it fully sank in what they were all a part of.

The importance of the find was not lost on Jericho. This discovery would shape his entire career and the rest of his life and the lives and careers of the students under his tutelage. If he had any lingering thoughts of sacrificing everything for a night in Zoey's arms, it all flew out the window. He simply could not make love to her. He could not cross that line. Not now. Not yet. He *had* to hold himself at bay. Too much was at stake for both of them.

Zoey went up on tiptoes and whispered in his ear. "Just think," she said. "You're descended from these people."

And for the first time since Granny Helen told her strange story, he believed it was a real possibility.

"Now comes the important question for you guys," Lace said.

"What's that?" Jericho and Zoey asked in unison.

"What happened to the Keepers of the Flame? Obviously, they must have died out. How, until now, did they disappear without a trace?"

Chapter 14

Context: The physical setting, location, and cultural association of artifacts and features within an archaeological site.

A scream woke Zoey in the middle of the night.

After Lace departed, the group had converted the tent back to sleeping quarters, eaten dinner, and sat around the campfire until midnight discussing the ramifications of their find and Lace's hypothesis about the Golden Flame agave.

Zoey had sat across the fire from Jericho, watching his shadowy face in the flickering firelight. He revealed none of his emotions to the group. No one else knew about the medallion Granny Helen had given him, and apparently, he was determined to keep it that way. It was all she could do not to pull him aside and ask him how he was feeling. She didn't have that right. Not here.

Not yet. So she'd wistfully gone to bed and fallen into a fitful sleep peppered with dreams of bloodshed and murder.

The second scream told her that the sound did not come from her nightmare.

Instantly, she bolted up, flung back the covers and stumbled to her feet. "Catrina," she whispered. "Did you hear that?"

No answer.

She glanced over at her roommate's cot. Empty. Was Catrina the one doing the screaming?

Heart pumping, she jammed her feet into her slippers and raced out into the darkness. Other team members had gathered, holding flashlights and staring at one another, tousle-haired and wide-eyed, but Catrina was not among them.

"What's happening?" Jericho demanded, emerging from his tent ahead of Avery. He had pulled on jeans and thrown on a shirt, but he'd neither yet snapped his Levi's nor buttoned up his Western shirt.

Damn her, she couldn't help staring and drooling. Completely inappropriate given the circumstances, but there you had it. When had she ever been appropriate?

A third scream ripped down the mountain, echoed out into the thick darkness, raising the hairs on her neck.

"The dig site." Jericho took the lead, charging up the mountain, the group — in various states of dress — trailing after him.

They were halfway to the dig site when Catrina came stumbling toward them in the darkness, jabbering frantically in Portuguese and trembling all over, her eyes rolling wildly in her head.

Jericho grabbed her by the shoulders. "What is it? What's wrong?"

"Fa . . . fa . . . fantasma," she stammered. *"Ghost."*

Everyone huddled around her. Jericho gathered her in his arms and she buried her sobbing face against his chest.

Uneasiness rippled through Zoey. Not because she believed in ghosts, but something about this did not feel right.

"Where did you see this apparition?" Jericho quizzed her.

From the shelter of his arms, Catrina shook her head, extended a slender index finger, and pointed toward the dig site.

"Try to calm down," Jericho soothed. "You're all right. You're safe."

A knuckle of jealousy doubled up inside Zoey and punched against her chest wall. It bothered her that Jericho was comforting Catrina. It was nice of him and all that, but she couldn't help feeling that Catrina was making this up for attention.

Avery rubbed Catrina's shoulder. "Shh, shh. It's okay."

Finally, Jericho eased her away from him and Zoey breathed a little easier. Still, Catrina was a sly one. Zoey didn't trust her any farther than she could throw her. "Can you tell me exactly what you saw?" he asked.

"A dark man dressed in a black hat and long black duster," she said. "Standing in the middle of the dig right where Zoey found the medicine bundle. He had no face." She shuddered again.

A few people audibly sucked in their breaths. The breeze ruffled hair, sent students crossing their arms and drawing clothing more tightly around them. It was summer, yes, but nights in the desert mountain could turn surprisingly cool, and Zoey suspected that some of the shivering had as much to do with Catrina's unnerving story as it did the night air.

"El hombre vestido de negro," Piper murmured. "Did you see an unusual light as well?"

El hombre vestido de negro was a Pecos legend about a faceless spirit who roamed graveyards and cemeteries in a foredoomed quest for salvation. It was rumored that anyone he touched was forever marked by the terrifying experience. Mysteriously moving lights followed in his wake, and some believed *el hombre vestido de negro* was the cause of the infamous Marfa Lights.

"Sim," Catrina replied in Portuguese. "Yes. Green glowing lights around him."

"Sure it wasn't fireflies?" Zoey asked.

"*El hombre vestido de negro* is a *bulto,* a walking shadow. A *bulto* must pay for the evil deeds he committed in life. In death, he must right wrongs, fulfill the unfulfilled purpose, pay that unpaid debt, seek out that special something or someone." Piper went on. The girl was a regular Grolier's.

"Where'd you get that from?" Braden asked.

"*Castle Gap and the Pecos Frontier* by Patrick Dearen," Piper said. "Wanna borrow it when I get done?"

Zoey eyed Catrina, who had linked her arms through Jericho's, and wondered if she'd gotten a peek at Piper's book. "Looks like you're pretty special to the man in black, Catrina. What wrong did you do?"

"That's silliness," Catrina said sharply. "There is no reason a ghost would want me."

"Well," Avery said. "You *are* pretty hot. Do ghosts get boners?"

The women groaned at that.

"What were you doing at the dig site in the middle of the night?" Jericho asked sharply.

Catrina shrugged. "I couldn't sleep."

Jericho frowned. "So you took a walk in the dark alone knowing there are coyotes, javelinas, rattlesnakes, and mountain lions out there?"

"I did not think about that." Catrina lifted a haughty chin.

"Well, think about it from now on. Everyone, back to bed. We have to be up at dawn." Jericho herded everyone toward the camp.

Zoey fell into step beside him. They allowed the others to get several feet ahead of them. "I don't believe Catrina, do you?"

"No," he said. "I don't, but for the life of me, I can't figure out why she'd lie."

The next morning everyone was sluggish and bleary-eyed from interrupted sleep.

There wasn't much talking during breakfast or when Jericho laid out the dig plans for the day. They'd found a tomahawk and a medicine bundle; he was fully confident that they were going to find evidence of an entire civilization. He debated when to tell Dr. Sinton about the find and decided to wait and see if they unearthed anything new today before sharing the news with the director.

Zoey was subdued this morning, not her usual chipper self. It was all he could do to keep himself from cornering and asking her what was wrong. He couldn't help thinking she was right that Catrina was up to something, but he had no idea what that was. Simply a bid for attention perhaps? Or was she trying to sabotage the dig in some way? To what end?

He wished he could talk to Zoey about it, ask her opinion, but whenever he got around her, his hands seemed to have a mind of their own. And whenever he so much as looked at her, his dick hardened. She drove him crazy at every turn and that was without even trying.

She was ahead of him on the path up to Triangle Mount, carrying supplies and walking beside Piper. He let his gaze slide over her shapely body, felt a sharp ache stab him low and permanent. When he finally had a chance to make love to her he was going to spend hours at it. Doing his best to drive her completely out of her mind with lust for him. He was determined to do whatever it took to prove to her that he could keep her satisfied for a lifetime.

If she had been alone, he would have hurried to catch up with her. It was good she wasn't alone or he might have done something or said something that he should not. His mind was not on his work. He was daydreaming, caught up in the fantasy of what she tasted like in her most feminine spot and precisely how he was going to show her what she meant to him. And because of that, it came as a shock when just as they neared the dig site, Braden came running toward him.

"Dr. Chance! Dr. Chance! Come quick. The ladder rungs collapsed on Avery and he fell into the pit floor where someone had left out a bunch of tools and an ice pick impaled him through the foot!"

It was ironic that the dig safety officer was the one to get hurt. Avery was in charge of making sure the equipment was put away each night, and as they carried him back down the mountain on a litter, he swore he'd made sure everything had been stowed the previous evening. If that were true, how had chisels and picks, trowels and shovels come to be strewn across the floor of the pit?

"I made sure everything was put up, Dr. Chance." Avery winced against the pain. "No doubt."

At his adamant declaration, Zoey shot Catrina a look. The other woman had been out and about in the middle of the night, and Zoey hadn't been able to shake the feeling that she had been up to something underhanded.

Someone said, half jokingly, but half serious, "Maybe it was *el hombre vestido de negro.*"

When they reached camp, they got another surprise in the form of a Cupid patrol officer who had driven up to deliver a message to Braden that his father had had a heart attack and been rushed to a hospital in El Paso.

"What's going on?" someone mumbled.

"It's a curse," someone else said.

"Freaky-deaky," supplied a third student.

Jericho asked the officer to drive a distraught Braden into Cupid where he could arrange transportation home to be with his family. Afterward, Jericho turned to the remaining students. "In light of the latest turn of events, I think we better call it a day. You're all excused. Come back tomorrow with a clear head and remember, keep quiet about what's going on up here. We don't want to compromise our dig."

Everyone nodded in agreement.

"Zoey," he asked. "Can you go with me to

take Avery to the hospital?"

"Absolutely," she said.

Jericho used his shoulder to get underneath Avery's arm and lever him up on his good leg. Avery grunted and bit down hard on his bottom lip. He was pale and sweaty. The ice pick was sticking all the way through the middle of his injured foot. Zoey went over and braced her shoulder underneath Avery's other arm.

"Catrina?" Avery asked. "Will you come too?"

Catrina backed up, pressed a hand to her stomach. "I hate hospitals. I'll see you when you get out." She turned and scurried after the other students, who were taking the university van back to Alpine.

Avery looked like he was about to cry. "Ah, hell, why am I disappointed? I knew she wasn't the kind of woman you could count on in a pinch."

"It's okay," Zoey said, and reached up to squeeze the hand that was draped over her shoulder. "We're here. You're going to be all right."

"Catrina is an impulsive free spirit up for anything, which makes her great in the sack, but you can't count on her for anything," Avery bemoaned as they carefully guided him into the extended cab portion of Jericho's pickup.

Zoey glanced over at Jericho, who was on the other side of the truck, helping Avery angle himself across the seat while keeping his injured leg as still as possible.

He raised his gaze and she could see it as clearly spelled out on his face as if it had been carved there. *Zoey is an impulsive free spirit who is up for anything. Is she the kind of woman I can count on when the going gets tough?*

She glowered at him. "You've known me for twenty years. Do you really have to ask that?"

"What?" Jericho blinked. "I didn't say anything."

"You don't have to," she muttered as she climbed into the passenger seat. "I can read your mind, so watch yourself."

He laughed low and soft.

Two hours later, they'd gotten Avery admitted into Cupid General Hospital, where he was taken to surgery to have the ice pick removed from his foot and then sent to the recovery unit, where he was currently sleeping off the anesthesia. Jericho had called Avery's parents and told them what was going on, and they'd shown up a few minutes ago to see after their son. He'd also called Dr. Sinton to catch him up on the events of the past two days. Throughout the whole thing, he was calm, cool, and collected, just as Jericho always was, so it surprised her when after he'd hung up from his conversation, his shoulders slumped and he leaned his head back against the wall in the corridor outside the recovery waiting room and looked completely exhausted.

She moved to put a hand on his shoulder. "Are you okay?"

"The whole dig is falling apart," he mumbled.

"It's not."

"Um, are you not paying attention? Catrina saw a ghost." He held up one finger. "Avery got an ice pick through his foot." He held up a second finger. "And Braden's father had a heart attack." Up went finger number three. "All in the course of twenty-four hours."

"Yes, Avery got hurt and Braden's father had a heart attack, but those things have nothing to do with you. You're doing a wonderful job. We made a significant discovery."

"The significance of which you and I haven't even been able to talk about yet."

"Because we resolved to stay away from each other as much as possible."

"That's not working worth a damn anyway. Here we are alone again and it's all I can do from yanking you into my arms and kissing you silly." He blew out his breath, dragged a palm down his face. "There's something else you don't know."

The concerned look in his eyes sent goose bumps spreading up her arm. "What is it?"

"While I was helping get Avery out of the pit, I noticed that the rungs on the ladder had been filed down so that they would break. It wasn't any damn ghost that did that."

Zoey gasped. "Are you saying one of the other students did it? That he or she purposely filed down the rungs so they'd give way and strewn tools around so someone would fall and get hurt?"

"I don't know what I'm saying. I'm just telling you what I observed."

"That's heavy duty, but sort of random. I mean what were the odds that even if the ladder broke that someone would fall on a sharp tool?"

"I'm not even sure the filed down rungs relate to the tools being left out. Could just be coincidence."

"Maybe Catrina did see someone in the dig last night."

"Big question, why was she really out there to begin with?" he asked.

"You wanna go to Chantilly's? Get a beer? Discuss?"

"I have a better idea," he said. "Let's grab a six-pack, and go back to Triangle Mount. I hate leaving the place unguarded since we've made those finds. I know I told everyone they couldn't talk about it, but you know human nature. Someone is bound to talk and the last thing we need is a bunch of people snooping around up there."

"Maybe one of the students already did talk about it and that's why someone was snooping around the dig," she said.

"But why file down the ladder rungs?"

"Make it look like angry spirits?"

"To what end?"

Zoey shrugged. "To scare us off."

"Again, why?"

"I dunno. I'm not Sherlock Holmes."

"This feels more like a Scooby-Doo mystery to me."

She smiled. "In the Scooby-Doo mysteries it's always the caretaker who done it."

"Does the nature preserve have a caretaker?"

She wrinkled her nose. "I have no idea, but I could check."

"That was a joke."

"I know."

"So about that six-pack . . ."

"Umm," she hedged. "I don't know if going back up there with just the two of us is a smart idea. I thought we agreed that we weren't supposed to be alone together."

He looked at her. "We're not. We shouldn't, but dammit, Zoey, I've missed talking to you. I *need* to talk to you. Without you to talk to I feel like half my brain has been removed."

His words warmed her from the inside out. She reached out to touch his cheek. "I feel the same way."

He clenched his jaw. "We're treading on dangerous ground."

"We are," she said. "Which is why I think we should go see your granny Helen again instead of being alone with each other."

He narrowed his eyes. "What for?"

"You're not curious to hear more about the Keepers of the Flame?"

He blew out his breath. "Yeah, well I don't think I've fully processed the fact that my great-granny was in possession of the same medallion we found on a two-hundred-year-old artifact."

"Is that because you could very well be descended from the Keepers of the Flame?"

"It's damn eerie."

"That's why I think we should go see her again."

"What if she's no more lucid than she was the last time?" He doffed his cowboy hat, pierced his fingers through his hair. "Hell, she could be worse than before."

"What have you got to lose?"

"My whole identity of myself?"

"No way. I've never met anyone more certain of who he is and what he wants out of life than you are. From the time you were eight years old you knew that you wanted to be an archaeologist."

His eyes met hers and his sultry expression telegraphed a clear message. *I want you.*

Her pulse flamed inside her veins. She glanced down the hallway. A kitchen attendant was pushing a large rolling metal meal cart toward the elevator. Quickly, she darted out her tongue to moisten her lips and thought *he's going to kiss me.*

But he did not. He simply stood there staring at her so hard, setting off the triphammer of her pulse.

He reached out with those long, capable fingers and cupped her cheek. "This is killing me, you know."

"Too bad," she said tartly, because if she didn't do something to erect a barrier *she* was going to kiss him and they were in a public place. No telling who might see them. "I'm going to visit your granny. You can come if you want, but I'm not waiting around."

"Oh you're not, huh?" An amused smile plucked at the corners of his mouth.

"Nope." She turned and headed toward the exit, her heart hammering crazily.

"Anyone ever tell you that you're a sassy wench?"

She stopped, turned back. "All the time. You coming or not?"

"Not until you do," he quipped, stalking toward her.

It took her for the full length of a heartbeat to realize what he meant. "Seriously, dude, unless you want me to strip off your clothes and do you right here in the hospital corridor, ya gotta stop talking like that."

He hissed in his breath through clenched teeth, his dark eyes burning with rolling heat. "I don't mean to talk like this, but whenever I'm around you, I can't seem to help myself. Is this what you feel like all the time? Unable to filter every thought that pops into your head?"

She caught her bottom lip up between her teeth. "Yeah, I guess, kinda."

"It's a startling way to live."

"Tell me about it." She laughed. "But you must be rubbing off on me, because I'm having some thoughts right now that are locked in the vault."

He lowered his voice. "Would you tell me your secrets if I had a key?"

You've already got the key, Magic Tongue. "When the dig is over, I promise I will tell you everything."

"We better stop this," he said, practically panting.

"You started it."

"I'm trying to finish it."

"You're not doing a very good job."

"Yeah, I know that."

"So let's take our minds off us and put them where they belong."

"Where's that?"

"Scooby-Doo."

Chapter 15

Migration: Moving from one country,
region, place, or site to another,
for feeding or breeding.

"Jericho," Granny Helen said when they walked into her room. A vase of fresh-cut roses in full bloom sat on her bedside table. She was in the wheelchair again, but today, his great-grandmother looked much more alert and she'd recognized him right away. Positive signs. "And your pretty girlfriend too."

"Zoey," he said. "Her name is Zoey."

"Helloey, Zoey." Granny Helen giggled and her face melted into a gummy smile. "That rhymes."

"You're in a good mood this afternoon," Zoey said.

"I remembered what I had for breakfast. It's always a good day if I remember what I had for breakfast. Oatmeal with cinnamon and raisins, strawberry yogurt, and buttered toast!" She looked as proud of herself as if she'd won the lotto.

"Short-term memory recall is a good thing," Jericho said. Maybe they would be able to get some more information out of her.

He waved Zoey into the chair beside his granny and crouched on the floor in front of her. "Do you remember the other day when we came to see you?"

She shook her head. "No, but Joe came to see me."

"That wasn't Grandpa Joe," he said. "That was me."

"It was?" She squinted at him.

"Yes, and you gave me this." He pulled the beaded medallion from his shirt pocket and showed it to her. "Do you remember?"

"The Keepers of the Flame," she said softly and held out a hand as gnarled as a tree root.

He put the medallion between the knuckles of her fingers and she held it up to her face and repeated, "The Keepers of the Flame."

"We found a similar medallion beaded into the hide of a medicine bundle up on Triangle Mount," he said. "Do you know anything about that?"

"Little Wolf and Clarissa," she said promptly.

"Did Little Wolf live on Triangle Mount?" he asked.

"That's where the Keepers of the Flame lived."

"Was Little Wolf one of the Keepers of the Flame?"

She nodded.

"When we were here before you told us about Little Wolf and Clarissa," Zoey said. "But you didn't finish your story."

Granny Helen rubbed the medallion against her chin. "How far did I get?"

"You told us that they shared at kiss at the mission school and Little Wolf got kicked out and Clarissa's family wouldn't allow her to leave the settlement," Zoey reminded her.

"Oh yes." Granny Helen sighed. "So sad."

They waited, and when she didn't continue, Jericho nudged her a bit. "Did Little Wolf and Clarissa ever see each other again after that?"

"Yes they did. Such a shame."

He and Zoey exchanged glances.

"What happened?" Zoey leaned forward, rested her elbows on her knees and her chin in her upturned palms.

"So much sorrow." The way she said it

was so mournful and low it drilled a chill down Jericho's spine.

"Were Little Wolf and Clarissa real people, or is this just a romantic story?" he ventured.

She raised her head and looked at him with crow-sharp eyes. "They were as real as you and me. Little Wolf and Clarissa pined for each other. That kiss had ignited a deep passion that had grown and flourished from the seed of their friendship. They were deeply loyal to each other. Would *die* for each other." She stopped, hiccupped. "They *did* die for each other."

Zoey flashed him a look that said, *Uh-oh.*

Granny Helen's memory could not be trusted, plus she did have a flair for the dramatic. He could not take what she said to heart and yet he found himself getting drawn into the narrative, her whispery voice full of creaks and hesitation and as soothingly interesting as a soft breeze rattling dried beans in mesquite trees.

"Little Wolf and Clarissa sent each other messages through a homing pigeon that would fly high above Clarissa's settlement by the lake to Little Wolf's home on the mountaintop. Every day they would write to each other about their plans for the day they would finally be old enough to be together."

She paused to catch her breath. Shook her head at the beaded medallion. "Ah, the folly of youth."

Her eyes glazed as if she was staring into her own past and for a minute, Jericho feared she'd slipped into confusion, but she shook herself with a determined movement and extended the beaded medallion to him. It was warm from her hand.

"One day, the pigeon did not come back. Little Wolf tried not to worry. Maybe Clarissa's parents had found out about the letters and stopped her from writing, he thought. Another day passed, and then another. Still no letter."

A nurse had come to stand in the doorway, but she did not interrupt. Just stood with her shoulder against the doorjamb, listening.

"It was the dead of winter and Little Wolf feared the pigeon had died. He desperately wanted to see Clarissa, so in the middle of the night, he slipped down into the settlement, quiet as a shadow, and waited."

Zoey scooted to the end of the chair, her knees tight as springs, her hands clenched into fists.

"The menfolk were on the porch, talking in hushed tones. They looked very sad. As he listened, Little Wolf soon learned a great plague had fallen upon the village and his beloved Clarissa was deathly ill. The white man doctor said there was nothing he could do to save her. But Little Wolf could! His tribe was the Keepers of the Flame. They had great medicine that could heal any plague. He went back to his home and made up a dose of medicine and the next morning, he went back to the settlement to face Clarissa's father." Granny Helen's voice had quickened as she spoke as if to get it all in before the curtain of forgetfulness fell over her again.

Jericho could feel his great-grandmother's urgency but he didn't know how much of it had to do with the mesmerizing tragedy of the story she was telling or the fact she was trying to outtalk the memory loss that was snapping at her heels.

"She's having a very good day," the nurse murmured.

Granny Helen cut the nurse a sharp glare and kept on going. "Clarissa's father immediately took him prisoner, but Little Wolf explained that he was there to save Clarissa's life with a special potion. Her father was suspicious of Little Wolf's offering, but Clarissa's mother begged him to let Little Wolf try to save her. They had nothing to lose. Clarissa was dying. Finally, her father relented. By the time Little Wolf reached Clarissa's side, she was almost gone."

If someone had dropped a pin in the room it would have sounded as loud as a bomb, it was that quiet. Another nurse had come to stand beside the first nurse. "I haven't seen her this lucid in years," she whispered.

"Did he heal her?" Zoey asked. "Did Little Wolf's potion save Clarissa?"

"It did indeed. It was powerful medicine, and combined with the power of Little Wolf's love, Clarissa was healed."

"Oh thank God, I thought she was going to die." Zoey splayed a hand over her mouth.

"Yes, Clarissa was saved, but when her father saw how much Little Wolf loved her and how much she loved him, he was very concerned. He could not allow his daughter to love a savage. He would rather she be dead. That's the way it was back then. Forbidden love. Besides, there was the matter of the medicine that could heal the plague. Clarissa's father wanted that medicine to save his settlement."

"Oh no he didn't," the second nurse exclaimed.

"Oh yes he did." Granny Helen nodded ruefully.

Jericho's anthropologist mind was trying

to piece together how much of this might be true, how much was a wide stretch of myth, legend, and overactive imagination. Over the years such stories invariably gathered momentum, growing more farfetched as each teller of the tale embellished and made it his or her own. He thought of the Greenwood-Fant legend that permeated Cupid, understood it had been blown out of all kinds of proportion, where in order to promote tourism, the town actively encouraged the belief that if you wrote a letter to Cupid asking for his intervention in your love life, that your wish would come true. It was absolute foolishness, but people wanted to believe it, so they did. Maybe it was because at the core of any good fable there was a grain of truth, and in this one, the truth seemed to be that Little Wolf and Clarissa had been childhood friends whose love had bloomed into something bigger and threatened the mores of their time and culture.

He studied Zoey in profile — that pert nose, those loveable cheeks, and that determined little chin. Every time he looked at her, it took his breath away. He felt a sense of complete wonder. Had Little Wolf felt like this the moment he realized that love for his friend had turned into something so overwhelmingly wonderful he could not even fathom the depths of it?

"So they imprisoned Little Wolf," Granny Helen went on. "And the men of the village went to his mountain home and took the medicine from his people by force. They stole the healing plant that rightfully belonged to the Keepers of the Flame and they left behind their sickness. Their plague infected the Keepers of the Flame, and without their medicine, they all died. While the settlers cured their own people with the spoils of their pillage."

"Assholes!" Zoey exclaimed.

"You can say that again," Granny Helen said.

"Assholes."

Granny Helen smiled at Jericho. "I like her."

Jericho grinned at Zoey. "She *is* pretty special."

"You oughta marry her."

He was about to say, *Maybe I just will,* but a panicked expression reddened Zoey's cheeks, and doubt set up in his stomach like cement. He was so much farther down the road to committing to her than she was to him. He could see it in the way her body went rigid and how she shifted her legs away from him. A lump doubled up in his throat, and he gulped it back.

"Clarissa was beside herself with grief over what they'd done to her beloved Little Wolf." Granny Helen stopped to moisten her lips. "When no one was watching Clarissa, she stole the keys to the shackles her father had used to imprison Little Wolf and she sneaked to the shed where he was being held captive."

"She must have been so scared." Zoey pressed a fist to her lips.

Granny looked her squarely in the eyes. "Great love conquers all fear."

"If only it were that easy." Zoey hunched her shoulders inward and peeped at him from the corner of her eye. What was going on in that head of hers?

"Oh, there's nothing easy about it," Granny Helen declared. "Clarissa and Little Wolf ran away together, but the only way out of the valley was up one of the mountains. They could not go to Little Wolf's mountain because the sickness was there. So they had to climb a much higher mountain to get out of the valley."

A third nurse had joined the first two in the doorway. Granny Helen was becoming the attraction of the day.

"When Clarissa's father found both her and Little Wolf gone, he sounded the alarm, and the men of the valley tracked them up the mountain. It was winter, remember, in the blowing cold, and Clarissa was still weak from her illness."

"This is getting worse and worse." Zoey cringed on the edge of her seat.

"Indeed." Granny Helen shook her head. "They made it to the top of the mountain, but Clarissa's father and his men were right behind them. They knew if they were caught they would be separated or worse, that Little Wolf would be killed for daring to run off with her."

The trio of nurses crept closer into the room. Zoey wrung her hands. Even Jericho's muscles tensed as the story stirred his own fight-or-flight response. He was on that mountain. He was Little Wolf and Zoey was Clarissa and damn, why was he being so fanciful? It wasn't the least bit scientific.

"The men were almost upon them. They could hear them crashing through the trees. Clarissa and Little Wolf looked at each other, shared one last kiss, vowed their undying love for each other throughout eternity, held each other's hands, and jumped off the mountain."

"Eeep!" cried Zoey.

"To their deaths?" gasped one of the nurses.

Granny Helen cocked her head. "Well, you don't jump off a mountain to your *life,* now do you?"

Jericho snorted at her irreverence. That and the fact the story was so miserably sad he didn't want to dwell on it. A dismissive snort seemed in order. Now he remembered why he'd forgotten this story Granny Helen had told when he was a kid. It was simply too damn sad. He also understood why this particular tale wasn't more widely circulated in the community. This legend didn't hold the upbeat optimism that was inherent in the Cupid legend. No wonder Millie Greenwood's story, where true love conquered all, had stomped this one out of the local lore.

"The villagers were so guilty and ashamed of what they'd done that they burned down their own settlement and the families scattered to the wind . . ." Granny Helen's voice trailed off.

"That's horrible," said the second nurse. "Just horrible."

"Forgetting your own name ninety percent of the time is what's horrible," Granny Helen said. "At least Little Wolf and Clarissa got to be together."

"But only in death," Zoey protested. "It's so unfair."

Granny shrugged. "Better than never having loved at all. The real moral of the story is that you should take love when and where you can find it because none of us know how long we have left."

Everyone murmured in agreement over that.

Zoey touched Granny Helen's arm. "Thank you for telling us the story."

"Come see me again," she said. "I have a bunch more stories to tell. If my memory holds out."

Jericho stood up, tucked the beaded medallion back into his pocket. "We will, Granny, I promise."

"You're a good boy, Joe," she said, calling him by his grandfather's name and patting her cheek with her curled hand, the clarity already fading from her eyes.

He wished he could have known her when she was young and vibrant. They said their good-byes to Granny Helen. Zoey was unusually quiet as they walked outside.

"That was some story," he said.

Zoey stopped walking. The wind picked up her hair, blew the strands lightly across her face. "Jericho, do you mind if I stay in town for the rest of the day? I'll drive myself back up to Triangle Mount in the morning."

His hopes nosedived. Had Granny Helen's story about best-friends-turned-lovers leaping off a mountain given her second thoughts about deepening their relationship? But their situation was completely different from that of Little Wolf and Clarissa. She had to know that.

He touched her shoulder. "Is something wrong?"

She forced a smile. "I'm fine, really."

"It's just a fable, Zoey. Nothing true about it."

"Except for the beaded medallion we found on the medicine bundle."

"I'm sure there's a logical explanation for that."

"Yes, and the explanation is that you very well could be descended from Little Wolf."

"Little Wolf died, remember? If he indeed ever existed."

"Well, not a direct descendant of Little Wolf, obviously, but from his family lineage."

"According to Granny Helen, all the Keepers of the Flame died in the plague."

"That could be an exaggeration for story sake or maybe your great-grandmother doesn't know for sure. Maybe there were members of the community who were off on a hunting party when all this went down."

"We weren't able to find any documentation about this Keepers of the Flame sect in our research. Not a footnote, not a passing reference, not a whisper."

"We just dug up proof," Zoey said.

"The tomahawk and medicine bundle haven't been fully analyzed. We can't jump to conclusions. We need solid evidence to prove the theory."

"Science over gut instinct, huh?"

"When you're an archaeologist, yes, always."

"I guess that's my lesson for today."

They stood there a moment, looking at each other. Something was going on in that mysterious brain of hers, but damn if he knew what it was.

"Zoe-Eyes, is there anything you want to share with me?"

"Not yet," she said.

"You know you can tell me anything."

"I know . . . it's . . ."

"That story unnerved you."

She nodded.

"Do you want a ride to the B&B?"

"I'm good. I don't mind walking."

It was ninety-five degrees and a two-mile hike to the B&B; why was she turning down a ride? Was she that ready to put some distance between them?

Feeling shut out, but determined not to show that he was hurt, Jericho nodded. "All right. I'm going back to the hospital to check on Avery and then call Braden to see how he and his family are holding up. I'll see you back at camp tomorrow."

"Bye," she said cheerfully and gave him a soft punch on the shoulder like she used to do when they were kids, but he couldn't help feeling it was a desperate attempt to put things back the way they used to be.

The minute Jericho was out of sight, Zoey turned and headed toward the Cupid Museum, which was just a couple of blocks north of the retirement home. She had a gnawing feeling deep in her gut that she couldn't really articulate. The thought was at the back of her mind, heavy as a velvet curtain. A thought she did not want to think. But even so, she knew she had to do this for her peace of mind. She wasn't ready to tell Jericho about it. Not until she confirmed her nagging suspicion.

It was a quarter after two when she arrived at the museum. A few tourists were wandering around the displays. Tabitha was behind the counter, this time dipping apple slices in caramel sauce.

"Hi," Zoey said breathlessly.

"What's going on up at Triangle Mount?" Tabitha asked. "I've heard rumors of *el hombre vestido de negro* sightings and ice pick accidents and heart attacks and cursed Native American artifacts."

"Nothing but gossip." Zoey waved a breezy hand. Clearly someone had disobeyed Jericho's edict to keep lips zipped, but he had anticipated as much. "How are things on the Cupid letter committee?"

"Fine, fine, they miss you."

"Who?"

"The volunteers."

"Really?" That surprised her.

"All they can talk about is how proud they are of you for digging in your heels and sticking with this field school thing."

Well, that was nice to hear.

"Wait, what are you doing here? Why aren't you up on Triangle Mount?"

"Mmm, well . . ." She grasped for an excuse.

Tabitha narrowed her eyes. "Did you quit? Walker's gonna cut off your trust."

"No, no, not at all," Zoey rushed to say. "I've just been thinking about what you said when I was here before."

"What was that?"

"That I should know my family history and that you have the McCleary family tree archived here."

"Sure we do. You do know that the McClearys were in Jeff Davis County long before the Fants, right?"

"No," she said. "I didn't know that. The Fant side loves to say how they were the first family of Cupid."

"Of Cupid, maybe, but there were McClearys in the Trans-Pecos when the Fants were back in Baltimore."

"Could I see that book with the McCleary family tree?" Zoey asked.

"Hang on. I can do you one better." Tabitha popped the last caramel-dipped apple slice in her mouth, chewed industriously. She wiped her fingers on a paper napkin and hopped off her stool. "I'll be back in two shakes of a lamb's tail."

The doorbell tinkled as tourists drifted out. Zoey went over to the showcase in the center of the room that housed Great-Great-Uncle August's formulary. Would the medicine bundle they'd found be on display here one day? The thought raised goose bumps on her arms. She thought of her ancestors both Fant and McCleary and how they'd formed their corner of far southwest Texas. Would Universal Studios actually make a movie of Cousin Walker's book? A thrill rippled underneath the goose bumps at the possibility.

While she waited for Tabitha, she again studied that odd doodle at the corner of the page of August McCleary's medicinal recipe. It reminded her of something she couldn't quite put her finger on. The part of her brain that loved puzzles mentally turned the doodle on its side, and then upside down.

"Here we go," Tabitha said, coming back into the room with a large rolled-up chart in her hand. She unrolled it on the wooden counter, the bangle bracelets at her wrist clanging together as she did so and anchoring the four sides with a stapler, an empty coffee mug, a tape dispenser, and an e-reader. She crooked a finger at Zoey, indicating she should come on the sacred side of the counter, and clicked the chain on a green banker's light that cast a rectangular yellow glow over the McCleary family lineage.

"As you can see here . . ." Tabitha tapped a forefinger against the chart that Zoey noticed had been painted mauve with a slapdash hand. The scent of caramel hung in the air. "Zachariah McCleary came to Jeff Davis County in 1793. If you want to know where Zachariah came from before that, ask your cousin Walker. While researching *A Time to Heal* he did the McCleary genealogy all the way back to Donegal County in Ireland."

"I think I've heard Walker mention that before."

"Have you read Walker's book yet?"

Zoey shook her head.

"For shame! A book by your cousin, about your great-great-uncle, and you haven't read it?" Tabitha clicked her tongue.

"I'm a student. In school. Lots of textbooks to read," Zoey said, reluctant to admit she had so much energy it was difficult for her to sit and read for any length of time.

"Still, it's your duty as a McCleary to read Walker's book."

Zoey hung her head. "I will, I promise, but maybe I could just wait for the movie."

The older woman gave her a stern look. "Don't be lazy. Read the book. Besides, Walker says movie deals are tenuous at best. They can fall through at the drop of a derby."

"Who do you think they should cast to play August?" Zoey asked to lighten things up. "Melody thinks it should be Colin Farrell."

Tabitha wrinkled her brow. "He's got tattoos."

"So?"

"When I was young only thugs had tattoos and your uncle August was not a thug."

Zoey resisted rolling her eyes. "Then who would be your pick?"

"Me?" Tabitha's cheeks pinked. "I'd cast Orlando Bloom."

"Interesting choice. You do know he has tattoos too."

"No!"

"Just saying." Zoey suppressed a grin.

"Well, never mind that. Back to the reason you're here." Tabitha used a finger to trace the branches of the family tree. "Zachariah McCleary married Elspeth Osborn and they had five children, Edward, Gerald, Claudia, Catherine, and —"

Zoey's eyes had already run ahead of Tabitha's tracing mauve fingernail and saw what she'd feared she was going to see as she'd sat in Granny Helen's room listening to the tragic story of star-crossed love gone terribly wrong.

Zachariah McCleary's youngest daughter was named Clarissa.

Chapter 16

Backdirt: The soil excavated from test pits, typically used to refill them once the excavations are terminated.

While Zoey was learning about Clarissa McCleary, Jericho made a disturbing discovery of his own. He arrived at Triangle Mount to find a brand-new black Land Rover parked at the base of the flatiron and a man walking down from their campsite.

From behind sunglasses, he squinted against the sun. Who was that?

Jericho parked beside the Land Rover and got out. The man drew nearer, and he recognized Walker McCleary. Wariness knotted up tight in the lining of his belly. What was the pharmacist-turned-author doing here?

"Ah, the illustrious Dr. Chance," Walker called, and raised a hand in greeting.

With heavy, forceful steps, the older man

trod closer. He was dressed in chinos, a long-sleeved white shirt, black suspenders, and a black and white striped bow tie. Sweat was beaded across his beefy brow. He pulled a handkerchief from his back pocket and mopped his face.

"How's the book business, Dr. McCleary?" Jericho asked smoothly, even though tension tightened his throat.

"Very different." Walker tucked the handkerchief back into his pocket, and came over to rest one booted foot on the bumper of Jericho's truck. "Nothing like pharmaceuticals. Everyone needs drugs at some point in their lives, but books" — he shrugged — "a whole big chunk of the population doesn't even read, or at least not regularly."

"And yet, you made the *New York Times* bestseller list with your first book." Every muscle in his body was wiredrawn. What was Walker doing in their empty camp? "That's pretty impressive, huh?"

Zoey's cousin canted his head. "I'm under no illusion about my writing abilities. I can cobble together decent copy, sure, but it's August McCleary's story that's selling books. He was a fascinating, complicated guy."

"How so?"

"The man had his personal demons. Went

through a couple of divorces back when divorce was rare. Plus he had a penchant for cocaine, which might explain the divorces. Remember, cocaine was legal until 1914. But in spite of his problems, he was also a visionary ahead of his time and he literally saved the Trans-Pecos. If he hadn't come up with the formula that quelled the Spanish flu in our area . . ." Walker shuddered. "Don't even want to think about it."

"He also made the McClearys very wealthy in the process," Jericho said dryly.

A wide grin split Walker's face and he dropped his foot back to the ground. "There is that."

"Looks like he's still making you money."

"Gotta admire the man for that if nothing else."

Jericho stared at the older man and waited. When was he going to explain what he was doing up here alone?

"So . . ." Walker slipped his thumbs underneath his suspenders, his elbows sticking out at his sides. "What's going on with you and Zoey?"

An electric tingle ran over Jericho's nerve endings, and embedded with a jolt into the base of his brain. "Um, what do you mean?"

"I've been hearing things." Walker took a step toward him. "It's why I came up here.

To talk to you about her."

Jericho took off his sunglasses, tucked them into his front shirt pocket, and glowered. "What kind of things?"

"You two have been seen together, looking . . ." Walker narrowed his eyes and did not look away. "Chummy."

"We *are* chums. Have been for a long time."

"And that's all?"

Jericho straightened tall, tipped his cowboy hat down on his brow. "I'm also her instructor."

Walker stroked his chin. "And nothing else?"

"Nothing else." He barely shook his head.

"See." Walker canted his head. "There's one thing I never understood. Why you were nothing more than friends with Zoey. She's a sexy, vibrant young woman and you're four years older. Why *haven't* you made a move on her?"

He set his jaw. "That's not really any of your business."

"That right there." Walker held up a finger. "That's what bothers me. If there's some reason you don't find her attractive, why not just admit it?"

For the longest moment, he did not respond. He didn't know what was going on here and he didn't want to do anything to jeopardize Zoey's trust fund. "Why are you being such a hard-ass with her?"

"It's time someone took a strong hand with her and since it's looking like you're not the man for the job, I stepped up to the plate. She's been spoiled and pampered too long."

"You might be in control of her trust, but you don't really know Zoey at all. She's not spoiled or pampered. She's the hardest-working member of my dig crew. She's just so damn bright that it takes a lot to keep her mentally engaged, which makes her look impulsive and restless to regular people. I can't believe her family does not realize that about her. She's —" He bit off the words, belatedly realizing that the more vehemently he rose to her defense, the more he was undermining his assertion that they were nothing more than friends.

Walker's eyebrows went up. "I know I put the hammer down on Zoey with my ultimatum, but I really would hate to see her lose that trust."

"So lift the restrictions." Jericho jutted out his chin.

"Sorry, no can do."

"Why not?"

"Even if she is as bright as you claim, she's

got to learn sometime that her actions have consequences." Walker stuck his hands in his pockets, and then took them out again. "Besides, I don't back down. Not when I take a stand. Not ever. Backing down shows weakness and I didn't become the head of the McCleary clan by being weak."

"So you came up here to —"

Walker puffed out his chest, stepped closer. "Make sure you didn't cause her to throw away her fortune."

Jericho covered the remaining distance between them, glared down at the older man. "I want nothing except what's best for her."

"Good," Walker said. "Just as long as we understand each other."

"Message received," he muttered through gritted teeth. Just in case his own conscience and his potential job loss wasn't enough, Walker had shown up to underscore how precarious this whole situation with Zoey had become.

"So where is everyone?" Walker waved a hand at the camp behind them.

"Camp's closed."

"How come?"

Doling out as little information as he could get away with, he told Walker about the incident with Avery. In a town as small as Cupid, that was bound to get out anyway.

"How long is the dig closed?"

"Through the weekend."

"So Zoey's not here?"

"Do you see her?"

Walker gave a curt nod. "I'm sorry to hear about the kid who got the ice pick through his foot. Hopefully you won't have any more delays."

Without another word, he turned and got into his Land Rover.

Jericho readjusted his cowboy hat, cocking it back on his head as he watched dust billow up from the Land Rover's departing tires, still unsure what that had really been about and why Walker had been in their camp.

Shaking his head, he walked up the steep grade and into camp. Everything looked to be as they'd left it that morning when they'd taken Avery to the hospital. But the emptiness, the quiet was unnerving. Granted, in the vast expanse of the desert mountain range, silence was nothing out of the ordinary, but after a camp full of chattering students, the sudden hush was startling.

Overhead a hawk cried, the haunting sound raising the hairs on his forearms. *Why did you come back up here?* More importantly, why had he left Zoey and come back up here alone?

Jericho ran a palm over his mouth. Why? Because he did his best thinking in solitude and he had a lot of thinking to do about what was going on between him and Zoey. And given Walker unexpectedly showing up, it turned out to be a good thing he had not brought her with him.

But he still missed her.

Think of something else. It's not like he didn't have other things to worry over. Like the fact that someone might be trying to sabotage the dig, and based on what Granny Helen had told them today, he might very well be descended from the people who'd created the medicine bundle they'd excavated.

Speaking of the medicine bundle, he wanted to have another look at it, this time in private.

Jericho unzipped the flap to the tent he shared with Avery and stepped inside. The air was hot and still. Instant sweat popped up on the nape of his neck. He bent down to reach beneath his cot for the box he'd locked the medicine bundle inside the previous evening.

But the storage box wasn't there.

He straightened, scratched his head. He could have sworn he'd put it under the bed.

Where could he have put it? He swept his gaze around the tidy tent. No sign of the box.

The tightness in his gut that had started when he'd seen the Land Rover intensified, and turned sour. Trying not to panic, he searched the tent. No box.

He raced from the tent, went through the other tents one after the other, flipping cots, tossing belongings the students had left behind, but the box was nowhere to be found.

Son of a bitch. Was that the real reason Walker had come up here? To steal the medicine bundle? He had been acting odd.

But for godsakes, why? Jericho didn't have an answer, but all the students had left the dig at the same time. Although he supposed any one of them except Zoey, Avery, or Braden could have doubled back for the medicine bundle. Still, the pharmacist was number one on the suspect list.

Walker was empty-handed when you spotted him.

Yeah, but that didn't mean he hadn't already stowed the box in the Land Rover and once Jericho caught him, had come up with that excuse about his concern over Jericho's relationship with Zoey.

Blood pumping hotly through his veins,

Jericho stalked back down the hill, headed for his pickup and Cupid. If Walker thought he wasn't going to confront him over this, he had another think coming.

It was five o'clock when Zoey reached Triangle Mount. She'd tried several times to call Jericho to tell him about Clarissa, but when she hadn't been able to get through, she assumed he was on the mountain and decided to drive up.

But when she got to the camp the place was empty.

Well, crap.

Sinking her hands on her hips, she gazed down at the lake. From this vintage point, while she could see a portion of the water, she couldn't see the mounds. But she knew they were there.

Lurking.

Waiting.

The proof of her ugly family history.

Zoey gulped. *Don't do it. Leave well enough alone.* She should, she could, she would let it lie.

So why were there sharks in the pit of her stomach? Why was she picking up a shovel from the equipment tent? Why were her legs headed down the flatiron, not to her vehicle, but to the valley floor?

Turn back. Turn back. You vowed to Jericho you would not return to the mounds.

Which was worse? Being a woman who stayed on the surface, skimming breezily through life without ever digging deep, or a woman who broke promises?

You're being impulsive again. Think this through.

She had a mile to think about it, a walk across the dry desert dirt, the evening sun burning against the back of her head. Maybe she could blame it on the sun. It had baked her brain. But that was putting blame on something other than herself. She was the one who stuck the spade in the earth, who carefully extracted artifacts, recorded them in a notebook, and bagged them up. She alone.

While she had learned a lot about archaeology over the course of the last few weeks, there was something she apparently had not learned how to do. Control her impulses. Hadn't that been the point of joining the dig in the first place? To prove she could stick with something and not go off on tangents?

But wasn't that exactly what she *was* doing? Committing to finding out the truth about Clarissa and Little Wolf. The question was would her newfound stick-to-itiveness prove to be her ultimate downfall?

At the same time Zoey was digging up artifacts, Jericho stalked into McCleary Pharmacy ready to breathe fire and roast Walker's hide on a spit.

Zoey's cousin was behind the counter waiting on a woman sitting in a motorized scooter. "Make sure to take these with food," he said, slipping a bottle of pills into a white paper bag and stapling it shut along with a product information sheet.

"Be with you in just a minute." Walker smiled at him.

Jericho curled his hands into fists while he waited for the woman in the scooter to motor away. When she'd gone, he stepped up and planted both fists on the counter. "Where is it?"

Walker stared at Jericho's clenched fist, looked up, blinked. "Where is what?"

"Don't play dumb."

"I can't answer that question when I don't know what you're talking about."

"The medicine bundle. Give it back right now and I won't tell anyone you pilfered it."

"What medicine bundle?"

"In the locked box under the cot in my tent. That's the real reason you were up at the camp. Not to warn me off deepening my relationship with Zoey."

The blank expression on Walker's face said it all. The man had no idea what he was talking about.

Doubt doused the good head of steam he'd worked up on the drive into Cupid and he pushed back from the counter.

Walker's caterpillar eyebrows crawled up on his forehead. "You found a medicine bundle at your dig site and someone stole it from you? How did that happen?"

Jericho glanced around to see people in line behind him. "Forget I said anything and please keep this under your hat."

"Do you think Zoey might have —"

"No!"

"She is impulsive. Maybe she wanted to —"

"No."

"Not realizing that —"

"Zoey did not take the bundle," Jericho said through gritted teeth.

"How do you know?"

"Because I was with her all morning.

"As nothing more than a friend?"

So they were back to that? "Zoey is not a thief."

"I'm sure she was just borrowing it."

"Zoey did not take it and I can't believe

you think so badly of her."

"And I can't believe a man who is nothing more than her friend is looking at me like he wants to punch my face in."

"She didn't do it," he said flatly, and strode from the store.

Once out on the street, he stood on the corner for a long moment, not certain what to do or where to go next.

Dammit. If Walker had not taken the medicine bundle, then who in the hell had?

Two hours after excavating the artifacts a second time and unable to calm down, Zoey paced in her bedroom at the B&B. She'd sneaked in the back way to avoid everyone, although Pearl, the Cupid's Rest cook, had caught her, but she'd bribed the cantankerous older woman into secrecy with a twenty-dollar bill. She wasn't trying to be sneaky; she just didn't want Natalie grilling her about why she was at home and not at the dig site. If her sister started prodding, Zoey feared she'd spill the beans about everything. Keeping her mouth shut had never been one of her strong suits.

Using the tools of the trade and the techniques that Jericho had taught her, she cleared off her dressing table and painstakingly processed the artifacts — broken crockery, the metal tip of a knife blade, the sole of a dried-up boot, small animal bones, and what had originally looked like a half-dollar-sized item encrusted with so much dirt she hadn't been able to recognize it until she'd washed away the grime.

The minute she'd removed the item from the basin of water, she'd known her discovery was going to cause a major shit storm in the community. For there, on her desk, was the terrible confirmation she'd prayed *not* to find.

An old metal button emblazoned with the McCleary family crest.

The horrible realization washed over her again in ugly waves. Granny Helen's fairy tale wasn't simply a fanciful story. Clarissa had existed. Little Wolf had been real, and the twin mounds were remnants of the settlement the McClearys had burned out to hide the traces of their crimes.

And Lace's hypothesis that the Golden Flame agave had not only existed but possessed powerful healing properties was looking more and more like a sure thing. She didn't know how, but she was certain that the potion Zachariah McCleary and his clan had stolen from the Keepers of the Flame in the early 1800s was the same active ingredient that her great-great-uncle August had used in his formula to cure the Spanish flu in 1918.

It was too much. She could not wrap her head around this.

The smell of the evening meal drifted upstairs to her, but she wasn't hungry. In fact, she wondered if she'd ever be able to eat again, knowing what she now knew. Seeing her suspicions confirmed turned her world upside down.

She, Zoey McCleary, was descended from those terrible ancestors who'd stolen the healing medicine and chased Clarissa and Little Wolf up the mountain to their deaths over greed, pettiness, and bigotry.

And Jericho, the man she loved with all her heart and soul, very well could be descended from Little Wolf's clan. What would he say when he knew about the poisonous blood that flowed through her veins?

Hey, ancient history. He's not going to hold your ancestry against you. There's a bigger question here. What's he going to say about you digging up those mounds when you promised you would not go back there?

She placed one hand to her roiling stomach, the other to her mouth. It was all she could do not to throw up.

How could she ever tell him the truth? He

would be so disappointed in her.

A brackish taste filled her mouth. Why oh why had she dug these damnable things back up again?

She flopped down on the bed and stared up at the ceiling, and then burst out laughing at the irony of her situation. Just a few shorts weeks ago she'd made a vow to stick with the field school, to prove she could dig down deep and find something substantial inside her, and she'd done just that.

Only to have it blow up in her face.

If she came out with the truth, then her sister, Natalie, who put so much stock in the family bloodline, would be shattered.

Omigosh!

She sat back up again. When word got out about how August McCleary had cured the flu it very well could sink Cousin Walker's movie deal. August couldn't be lauded as a heroic healer if his medicine had come at the expense of Native Americans' lives. Had Walker known the truth all along and helped cover up history? How many McClearys knew the dirty family secret?

Walker had to know. Tabitha said he'd done extensive family genealogy while researching his book. Still, this was subterranean stuff. She wouldn't have known anything about it if not for Granny Helen's story. Maybe Walker really didn't have a clue. She hoped he didn't know.

Which left her with a huge dilemma. Go public and cause a major kerfuffle for her hometown and family, or keep the awful secret.

It was too much pressure. She couldn't harm her family, but neither could she, in good conscience, continue with the dig when she knew the truth. It would be impossible for her to work side by side with Jericho and not tell him what she'd discovered. And he was such a straight arrow, if he knew what she'd done, he'd insist on telling Dr. Sinton.

Well, you could do what you always do when the going gets tough. Give up.

The solution felt comfortable. Just walk away. She could blow off her promise to herself and break the pact she'd made with her cousin. Yes, Walker would cut off her trust, but all right, she could accept that if it protected the people she loved.

Her family would tease her for dropping out and Natalie would be disappointed. Oh well, at least she would know the real reason she quit wasn't due to a lack of stick-to-itiveness. In fact, if she'd stuck to it a little less, she would never have put two and two together, dug up those artifacts, and figured any of this out.

There was another, more positive reason to quit. A big reason that tipped everything in favor of letting dead relatives lie and dark secrets stay buried.

Jericho.

If she quit the dig she could finally be with him, consummate their combustive attraction, and become his lover. But of course that meant she could never tell him why she'd quit. He could never know that she'd gone behind his back and excavated the mounds a second time.

Do it. Just do it. Make it happen. Don't look back. It's the best solution. Never mind that you'll look like a flake. It's what everyone expects of you anyway. Go ahead and prove them right. People love to be right.

Taking a deep breath, Zoey reached for her laptop computer and started writing an official letter to Dr. Sinton telling him that she was resigning from the field school.

Chapter 17

Diffusion: The transmission of ideas
or materials from culture to culture,
or from one area to another.

Unseeingly, Jericho poked the campfire. Only the snap and crackle of burning logs punctuated the eerie silence. The moon grinned down at him, a wide clown mouth, orange and fat. His mind was deeply troubled. After he returned to the camp following his conversation with Walker, he'd fully examined the ladder Avery had fallen down, and he had not been mistaken, the rungs *had* been filed down.

Not only that but four students had texted or called to quit the dig school. With Braden and Avery out of the picture, that left only nine on the team. Add to that the missing medicine bundle and he felt like a monumental failure. His first job and the students were fleeing as if they were in Exodus.

Someone had not only sabotaged their camp, but looted their archaeological find. The only things that remained from the medicine bundle were the botanicals Lace had taken with her.

Who could have done this and why? While there was a security guard posted at the entrance to foundation land, and they'd put up a fence at the bottom of Triangle Mount, there were many places where someone could enter the property. For the life of him, he could not cipher out who had the means, motive, and opportunity to stir mischief. His greatest hope was that it was a student pulling a prank on him, but he knew in his heart that was not the case.

He reached to grab another beer from the cooler beside him — hey, might as well get stinking drunk, huh — when he heard rustling in the bushes. Probably nothing more nefarious than an armadillo, but wild animals that could harm a man filled these mountains — javelinas, bobcats, coyotes, mountain lions. He picked up the stick he'd been using to poke the fire and got to his feet.

Somewhere down mountain a twig broke in the darkness. Had one of his students returned early? Relief rushed through him at the idea, and it was only then that he realized how tense he was.

"Who's there?" he called.

More rustling.

He stood up. "Hello?"

His words echoed back at him in the still darkness — *hello, hello, hello.*

Could it be the man in black that Catrina had seen the previous night? Someone had filed down the rungs on that ladder and it most certainly was not a ghost. His muscles coiled tight.

"Identify yourself," he commanded, cocking the stick like it was a baseball bat.

Someone stepped from the shadows. "Jericho, it's me."

At the sound of her dear voice, a helpless grin broke across his face. "Zoe-Eyes, what are you doing here?"

"I had to see you. I couldn't bear the thought of you up here by yourself."

"Why did you walk up in the dark?"

"I have a flashlight. I just turned it off when I got close so I could surprise you." She stepped into the light from the campfire, her normally ebullient face somber.

He covered the ground between them. "Are you all right? What's wrong?"

"Who says anything is wrong?" She laughed, but it was an uneasy sound, and she did not meet his gaze.

He cupped her chin in his palm, tilted her head up, and forced her to look at him. The wistful expression in her eyes hit with the impact of a freight train. "I know my best friend."

"You should talk. You've got that moody-broody look on your face that you get when things aren't going according to plan. What's up?"

He noticed how she neatly sidestepped his question with one of her own, but he let it go — for now. He pulled a palm down his face. "Someone stole the medicine bundle."

"What?" she gasped. "No!"

"I wish it weren't true."

She held up a stop-sign palm. "Wait, back up. Tell me everything."

He told her about finding Walker on Triangle Mount, then discovering the missing locked box, his trip back into town to confront Walker.

"Okay, it wasn't Walker. So who else could have taken it and why would they?"

"I've been asking myself those questions repeatedly and come up with nothing."

Zoey narrowed her eyes. "What about Catrina? There is something I don't trust about her."

"We can't willy-nilly point fingers. She left with the others in the university's van and the metal locker was still under my bed then. I saw it just before we left with Avery." He smacked his forehead with the heel of his hand. "Why didn't I take it with us?"

"We had an emergency. None of us were thinking clearly."

"The theft had to have happened when we were all away from camp. I could kick my own ass for not taking it with us. I still haven't told Dr. Sinton about it yet. Trying to find the right way to approach it."

She ran a hand over his shoulder that aroused him more than comforted him. "Stop beating yourself up. Your priority was Avery as it should have been. Dr. Sinton will understand that."

"This whole thing is falling apart. Four students quit today."

Zoey made a face and held up five fingers.

He frowned. "What do you mean?"

"Five students."

Someone else quit?"

"Yes."

"Who?"

"Me."

"Zoey!" His jaw unhinged and a deep-seated disappointment flooded his bloodstream. "You didn't."

She gave a little shrug like it meant nothing, but he did not miss the regret in her eyes. "I sent Dr. Sinton an e-mail telling him that I was withdrawing from the program, effective immediately."

"For godsakes why?"

"So we could be together," she said. "I couldn't stand one second longer not being with you."

"Aww, Zoey, no, no."

"Don't be upset, this is a good thing."

"Good for whom?"

"You. Me. Both of us."

"How's that? I've run off five students and you're going to lose your trust fund."

"I'm happy about it." She leaned into him, her gaze firmly hugging his now. "Honest."

"Walker is not going to have any compunctions about cutting off your money. He made that perfectly clear to me this afternoon."

"I've been giving this a lot of thought and I believe it's actually a good thing. Having the trust has spoiled me, kept me from growing up. I'm ready to make my own way in the world."

"I hate to think you did this all for me."

"Who better?" She breathed and went up on tiptoes to twine her arms around his neck.

"You're playing with fire, sweetheart."

"I know. That's the point." She pursed her

lips, closed her eyes. Her chest rose and fell, her breasts pushing rhythmically against the buttons of her blouse.

Damn, he was just a man. A man who could not resist the temptation of this beautiful creature who just also happened to be his best friend.

That stopped him cold.

"Zoey," he murmured. "Are you *sure* this is what you want?"

She opened her eyes, sighed. "This isn't going the way I planned."

"How did you plan it?"

"That I'd come up here, tell you I wanted to get naked with you, you'd scoop me into your arms and carry me to bed and make love to me until I had a dozen orgasms."

"A dozen?" He chuckled.

"Don't laugh."

"Why a dozen?"

"Going for a personal best."

That astounded him. "In one night?"

"I'm very orgasmic." She shrugged. "It's not a bad thing. Well, unless you happen to be sleeping in the room next to me and the walls are thin."

"You never told me that before."

"We weren't potential lovers before."

"I don't know if I can live up to your expectations."

"Hey, if what happened in the lab was any indication of your prowess, I imagine you'll easily blow past that cool dozen." She ran a finger over his beard stubble.

Jericho shivered. "We're getting sidetracked here. We were talking about retracting your resignation."

"It's a done deal. I've made up my mind. I've already sent the e-mail. Too late to back down now."

"You could always call Dr. Sinton and tell him you sent it in a rash moment. He would probably understand. You can still take it all back." Why was he lobbying for her reinstatement when she was obviously so eager to quit and his body wanted nothing more than to sink into hers and try to break that dozen-orgasms-in-a-night record?

"Don't you see, Jericho? That's just it. I didn't send the e-mail rashly. I've been thinking about it ever since that night at the lab. I want *you* and no one else but *you.*"

He swallowed, and then spoke his greatest fear, the thing that had kept him from taking their relationship to the next level long before now. "What if . . ." He blew out his breath. "What if this thing blows up in our faces?"

"You gotta take a risk sometime, cautious Mr. Scientist. We have a better chance of working out than most."

"Is that right?"

"Yes, we have a solid foundation on which to build."

"Where'd you hear that?"

She waved a hand. "I dunno. Some dating Web site or other."

"So now we're listening to advice from Match.com?"

"It's sound advice, who cares where it's from?"

"I care about ruining our friendship."

"What if it doesn't ruin our friendship? What if it just makes things that much better?"

They both fell silent. In a far-off tree, an owl hooted, a second later, its mate called back.

"I get it," she said.

"What's that?"

"The real reason you're afraid."

"This sounds interesting. Enlighten me."

"You're afraid that I'm too fickle for the long term. For instance, I can't even stick with a four-week dig."

"I never said that." He gently kissed her forehead. "It's just that losing you as my best friend would be the worst thing that ever happened to me."

"We will *always* be best friends, no matter

what," she said staunchly.

It was such an easy thing to promise, but Jericho knew that life was a lot more complicated than that.

"We make a pact. Pinky swear." She grinned at him and held out her pinky finger.

God, the woman was irresistible. He crooked his little finger around hers.

"Jericho Hezekiah Chance, do you solemnly swear that no matter whatever happens between us, we will forever and always be best friends?"

"I do." *I do.* Serious words, and he meant them.

"And I, Zoey Nichole McCleary, do solemnly swear that through all ups and downs, ins and outs . . ." She winked mischievously. "That I will be your best friend until I take my dying breath, no matter what happens."

"Ahh, Zoe-Eyes." His voice came out raspy. She was the best damn thing that had ever happened to him. Bar none.

"Now we seal it with a kiss." She put her lips to his and that was all it took.

Jericho was a goner. Blistering desire burned through him, forest-fire fast. "You sure picked a bad spot to spring this on me, darlin'. Our first time should be in a nice, soft bed. You deserve candlelight and lavender-scented pillows and soft mood music."

"Pfft on that. I'm an adventuresome kind of girl and you're a dig rat. This is the perfect place for our first time."

"Those cots are mighty narrow and —" He put her away from him momentarily.

"What is it?"

"Sleeping bag. I've got a sleeping bag. We can put it in the bed of the truck, sky full of stars. It'll work."

"Gosh, that means we've got to wait for you to find the sleeping —"

He reached one arm around her waist, drew her up tight against his side, leaned down, and gave her a hard, thorough kiss, tasted her sweet flavor and moist heart. She froze for a heartbeat and then kissed him back as fiercely as he'd kissed her. He broke it off abruptly. Left her wanting more. "There. That oughta hold you for five minutes."

"O-*kay.*" She laughed and fingered her lips. "I get it."

"Not yet, you don't, but you will," he promised.

Exactly five minutes later, they were in the back of his truck, the sleeping bag unzipped and spread out over the pickup bed. The air smelled of wood smoke and piñon pine. Overhead a million stars twinkled.

They were on their knees facing each other.

Their gazes struck, sparked.

His hand trembled with excitement as he reached out to stroke her face. Her feminine scent teased his nostrils. His muscles tensed, and sweat rolled down his neck.

Her pupils widened. She flicked out her tongue to moisten her lips. Their quick, shallow breathing mirrored each other.

The knowledge that they were about to have sex in the back of his truck blew Jericho's mind. His most cherished fantasy was about to come true. The look in her eyes told him Zoey was just as turned on as he. But it didn't matter where they were. They could have been on the moon. They could have been on the space shuttle. He was aware of nothing except her.

He had to have her right now or go mad.

Jericho had never felt a thrill quite like this. Not when he unearthed artifacts. Not when he traipsed foreign lands. Not when they'd found the medicine bundle.

What a grand adventure! And it was all the doing of his red-hot best friend.

The blood pumping hotly through his veins shoved him into action. He pulled off her boots, and by the time he was finished, she was already unzipping the fly of her jeans and fumbling at the buckle of her brown leather belt. He grabbed the waistband of her jeans and she lifted her hips as he shucked them off along with her yellow polka dot boy shorts.

He smiled. Whimsical. Just like his Zoey.

When her pants were off, she lay back against the sleeping bag clothed only in the yellow polka dot bra and an unbuttoned blue checked blouse. He splayed a palm across the tautness of her flat belly, just above the beautiful triangle of brown sugar hair at her pubis.

He gazed into her eyes, looking, really looking at her. What delicate skin! What fine bone structure. Being next to her refined features and her petite body, he felt like an oversized oaf. She was cut from silk, he from rough-hewn hemp. She was so small and he was so big, and it occurred to him that he could hurt her.

"No fair," she pouted.

He stared, mesmerized by her beauty. "What's not fair?"

"I'm naked and you're not." She sat up to splay a hand over his chest. "I need to see your body, Jericho."

He wrestled off his shirt, and once freed

from it, flung it over the side of the pickup into the darkness.

"Let me help," she said, her competent hands going to the snap of his jeans. Her soft touch set him on fire.

In record time, he shucked off his boots and his pants, but kept his underwear on at the last minute, suddenly feeling quite shy in front of her. This was his best friend, after all.

Her gaze zeroed in on his erection, straining hard against his boxer briefs.

"Come here." She patted a spot beside her.

He obeyed, settled next to her on the sleeping bag.

Out across the mountain they could hear night sounds — the call of night birds, the rustling of small animals in the scrub brush, the distant yips of coyotes, the muted crackle of the dwindling campfire.

He was usually pretty good at foreplay. He was a guy who knew how to take his time and he did precision work. But for the first time since he could remember, he was at a loss for what to do next. With Zoey, he didn't know where to begin.

"Zoe-Eyes." His voice came out so tight and hard he scarcely recognized it. "This is weird."

"Just kiss me, Jericho. There's no need to overthink it."

That sweet invitation was all it took. He closed his lips over hers. The kiss was heated but tentative, exploring. He touched her belly as he slipped his tongue between her teeth.

She opened her mouth wider and then slowly spread her legs.

Ah, she tasted of cinnamon mints and red-hot passion. She slipped her tongue between his teeth. Their tongues danced. At first, she was the instigator, stealing his breath, numbing his mind, but quickly Jericho took over, letting her know that while he was giving in to her games, he was still in control.

He ran his hand lower, cupped it lightly over her feminine mound, touching the soft crinkle of brown hair, and then he just kept his hand resting there without moving while he teased her tongue with his.

After a few minutes, as their kissing grew more urgent, he slowly stroked that curly hair, moving his fingers downward in lazy circles until he reached the warm, moist folds of her sex. She was damp with desire, but he wanted her soaking wet and begging for release.

"Mmm," she murmured, and shifted against his hand. "That feels good."

He slipped his index finger into her.

She sucked in a gasp of air and her eyes widened with pleasure. He liked seeing what he was doing to her written on her face. The taste of escalating desire spilled into his mouth, raw and peppery as garlic and cayenne. He couldn't stop looking at her. Her eyes shone with pleasure.

"I want to touch you too," she said. "Take off your underwear."

He came out of it, kicking his briefs off across the bed of the truck and then nestling down beside her once more.

Her long brown hair swung loose across her shoulders as she propped herself up on her elbows so she could look at him.

"Sandwich Hut Molly was right," she said, eyeing him in the moonlight. "The size of a man's hand does match his other parts."

He laughed out loud.

With one smooth palm, she reached down to cup his balls in her hand. Startled, he yelped. It felt so dangerously good that Jericho thought he was going to lose it right there. He bit down on his lip to hold back the groan rising in his throat. Closing his eyes, he battled the urge to come.

Gently, she tickled him. Her caress injected a whole new set of rules into their game. His mind spun. What was she up to?

Her audaciousness stirred him. She was a much more complicated woman than he'd ever guessed, and he'd known her twenty years. The wanton expression in her eyes slammed his libido into fifth gear.

Slowly she licked her lips, murmured, "Mmm."

Hormones, blaring like a trumpet, shot straight to his groin. The circuitry of his brain fired cannonballs of hungry electrical impulses to his nerves, his muscles, his every cell in his body.

"Whoa there, missy," he said. "You better just back off that for now."

Truth was, he was hard as cement, and it took every ouch of concentration he had in him not to come. He tightened his stomach muscles and went back to kiss her, stroking her, his fingers strumming over her kitten-soft skin.

He thought of all the romantic things he would normally say to a woman he was having sex with, but now everything he could think of sounded trite and insignificant. There were no right words to tell her how he felt. This was monumental. He wished he knew what to say to her, but he just didn't. All the usual teasing and camaraderie between them had turned into something richer, deeper, and much more complex.

So he just told the truth. "I'm so lucky to be here with you."

"Me too." Her smile heated him like the desert sun kissing the mountaintops good morning, and melted the lump blocking his throat.

His cock throbbed, wanting to be inside her. But in that moment, Jericho realized what he had to do if he wanted to have any chance of satisfying her. He was going to give her the pleasure she deserved and take himself out of the equation. Just as he'd done that night in the lab.

He unhooked her bra, pushed it — along with the blue shirt — off her slender shoulders. Then he dipped his head and took one pert pink nipple into his mouth and sucked lightly, while his hand strayed back to that heavenly triangle between her firm thighs. He slipped a finger inside her again and she was wetter than before.

"Jericho." She breathed his name on a sigh. She ran her fingers through his hair, down his face to his throat.

Her touch was light but he felt it all the way to the tip of his erect shaft. Blood drained from his head, ran down to fill his aching cock. It took every ounce of strength of will he possessed not to jam himself inside her on the spot.

He spent more time at her nipples, teasing and licking, sucking and gently nipping until she was moaning soft as a humming top. Her chest heaved as she struggled to suck in air and her fingers knotted in his hair. He inched from her breasts to her sternum, planting hot kisses on down to her navel.

The lower he went, the faster and shallower her breathing grew, every muscle tightening in response to his mouth.

"Wait," she gasped, when he was almost at his destination.

"What is it?" he whispered.

She made a happy noise, and for a moment, he just had to rock back on his heels and look at her naked body from the top of her head to the rose pink folds of her swollen sex.

The expression in her eyes was languid, sultry as she watched him watching her. She was ready.

The night had gone completely silent. It was as if no world existed beyond their circle of two.

Jericho settled between her legs and lowered his head. Softly, he blew his warm breath against her tender membranes and gently edged her knees farther apart with his shoulders. He couldn't wait to taste her again. He'd dreamed of this nightly since the first time he'd done it to her.

He pressed his mouth to her sweet inner lips. He heard her sharp intake of breath, felt her thighs quiver.

She tasted so sweet! Fresh and womanly. He loved the intimacy of exploring her most precious place with his tongue and lips. Her every thought was translated in her movements and he read her with his tongue. A slight shift in her hips and he corrected, moving right or left, up or down until he had her purring like a sports car engine.

He loved whisking her away on a sea of sensation. She was so responsive to everything he did. She tossed her head from side to side, restless and begging for more.

Gently, he suckled her veiled hood. He ached to be inside her. To feel her pulse around him. He wanted to join her, to fly to the stars with her, but he would not. This was all about her. This was his best friend. He could not be selfish. He wanted to share everything with her. For now and forever.

Sensing that she was edging toward ecstasy, Jericho adroitly strummed his tongue across her straining hood.

The orgasm teased her, elusive but near. He could feel it inside her. A quivering tuning fork. A dam waiting to burst. Pressing . . . pressing . . . pressing. Closer and closer. Lifting, soaring, ready to converge.

"That's it, sweetheart," he cooed. "Yes, yes."

Zoey let out a strangled cry, and tensed in his arms. He felt her muscles contract against his tongue. Her body glistened with perspiration.

He moved up, wrapped his arms around her, and they lay there in the bed of the truck, sweating, shuddering, panting for breath.

"Wow," she said.

"One down, eleven to go."

Her throaty laugh stirred a hundred different emotions inside him. He longed to linger, to cradle her in his arms, kiss her face, brush her hair from her eyes, tell her how absolutely wonderful she was. But before he could, she sat up, hair tousled, mouth grinning, and pushed him back against the bed of the truck.

With a wicked laugh, she said, "Not yet. Now it's your turn."

CHAPTER 18

Direct impacts: Influences that would directly affect a site.

Before she had a chance to make a move, Jericho pulled her into his arms and kissed her solidly. No hesitation. And from the looks of it no regrets. She stared into his eyes and he into hers, and she felt the same hot, sparkly charge of sensation she felt every time he kissed her.

No, that wasn't entirely true. *This* kiss was hotter than ever and she was so thrilled to be held in his arms, to have his palms cupped against her cheeks, to simply be taking this leap from friends to lovers with *him,* that she wanted to holler her joy from the mountaintop.

Finally, he ended the kiss and she nuzzled his neck, wishing she could push her body straight into his, but he wasn't satisfied with that for long and quickly kissed her again.

Blood rushed through her body, heady, dizzying, and in nothing flat she was edgy and trembling.

"I could get seriously used to this," he murmured.

"Me too, but back to that other thing . . ."

"What other thing?"

"Giving as good as I got." She kissed the hollow of his throat, his pulse warm and bounding beneath her lips.

"You don't have to do that."

She canted her head at him. "I *want* to do it."

A masculine groan escaped his lips.

She was determined to pay him in kind for the sweet thing he'd already done for her. Twice. He was the most unselfish man she'd ever known. His altruism deserved a big reward. Oh, plus she had to tell him that she was totally kidding about the dozen orgasms thing.

Zoey wrapped her hand around his steely shaft and let out a soft sigh. "Impressive."

"Just wait," he said, his silky tone both promise and threat.

"Don't get smart." She wagged a finger. "Right now, your fate is in *my* hands."

She stroked her hand over him. Strange how he could be both hard as marble, and at the same time, have skin soft as velvet.

She cupped his balls, and that pulled a ragged growl from his throat.

When she went on her hands and knees, leaned over, and slowly took him into her mouth, he groaned again, louder and longer. He threaded his fingers through her hair, drew her head downward, guiding her to where he wanted her to go. She did not mind his direction, and greedily twined her tongue over his impressive length.

"Zoey, you are so freaking hot," he exclaimed.

She smiled against him. He tasted salty, manly. She peeped up at him. He was gazing down at her as if she'd slid straight down from heaven on a rainbow.

He spread his fingers lower, cupping the back of her head in his big palm. He rocked his hips, but gently, holding back. She stretched her mouth wider, folded her lips around her teeth, putting firm pressure against his shaft as she moved her head up and down at the same time she curled her tongue around the head of him.

"Wh-what are you doing?" he gasped breathlessly.

"Driving you crazy."

"Honey, I'm already insane with desire for you."

She shifted, stroking his shaft with one

hand while her tongue did a dance over his head, flicking and twisting and making him groan all over again.

"Wonderful as this is, I gotta be inside you, Zoe-Eyes. I want to feel myself buried deep inside you."

Gently, he put his arms around her waist and moved her aside as he fumbled for his jeans in the dark, finally found them and pulled out a square foil packet.

"You carry a condom in your pants at all times?"

"Only since that night in the lab. I would have done you then, darlin', but I didn't have a condom and I vowed not to let that happen again."

"Even with a hands-off policy?"

"Hey, I know how tempting you are. Not the strongest man on earth could resist you forever. Besides, much like a Boy Scout, a good archaeologist is always prepared."

"Well, FYI, I started carrying one in my pocket as well, ever since that night, so now we have two. Double your pleasure, double your fun."

"My smart girl," he praised.

Zoey beamed.

He rolled on the condom, and then took her in his arms for an ear-scorching kiss that spun her around and turned her upside down. The other kisses he'd given her had been spectacular, no doubt about it, but this kiss . . .

This kiss crossed some kind of threshold.

There were no words.

Liquid gold couldn't have been prettier or worth more. It was like a kept promise. It was the ultimate summer vacation. It was the longed-for Christmas gift. It was the opposite of overhyped. It was simply the most erotic thing she had ever experienced in the almost twenty-four years she'd spent on earth.

His tongue was sublime, lips nectar of the gods, but what really rocked her world, were the feelings his lips and tongue and teeth stirred inside of her.

She heard a humming deep inside her, like the sound of the earth spinning. She felt an electric tingling that raced through every nerve ending in her body. Her nipples tightened. Her skin burned. Her sex soaked instantly and she was dripping for him.

"Zoey," he whispered against her mouth. "You taste so damn good."

Did he feel it too? This wild rush of chemical reaction?

His hand slid up underneath her back and he pulled her closer. His erection was iron against her thigh. Wherever his mouth touched — her cheek, her chin, her forehead, and her eyelids — she burned.

The wonderful thing about sleeping with your best friend was that you knew you could trust him. You didn't have to worry about what secrets he might be hiding when you knew him as well as you knew yourself. No fear of betrayal. No worries that he wouldn't call you in the morning. No concerns that he'd speak of it with his guy pals.

Blindly, without purposeful thought, Zoey lightly ran her tongue along the pounding pulse at the juncture of his throat and collarbone. How she loved his salty taste. His rugged skin tightened beneath her mouth.

"Baby girl, baby girl, what you do to me," he groaned. "You gotta stop or I'm going to come right now."

The pressure inside her was so intense she couldn't stand it a minute longer. Zoey tugged at him, whimpered. "I want you, I need you."

"Hey, Zoe-Eyes, slow down," Jericho murmured. "You've got nothing to prove. You're with me, remember?"

"I want you inside of me," she growled. "And I'm tired of waiting. Now. I want you now!"

His eyes darkened. "You want it hard and fast?"

"Yes," Zoey demanded, and then nipped his bottom lip up between her teeth.

"Are you sure?"

"Positive."

"We only get one first time," he murmured.

That made her pause. Could she delay gratification, sacrifice friction for that moment to savor? One look into his eyes and her heart melted. He was right. They could do hard and fast later.

"Sweet," she said. "Give it to me sweet and slow."

"Good choice," he said. "I approve."

He pulled her to his chest and held her close and she listened to the steady strum of his heartbeat. Overjoyed to finally be in his arms the way she'd always secretly dreamed. He traced a lazy pattern over her buttocks with his fingertips. Tingles of anticipation started at the base of her neck, crept across her face, over her scalp, darted along her shoulders, trickled down her arms, and finally shuddered softly up her spine.

Electrified by his touch, she felt like a desert flower joyfully blooming after a rare soaking rain. How had she gone for so long without this? It seemed insanity now that they'd never done this before.

They kissed and kissed and kissed, the joining of their mouths a frenzy of happiness. This was a kiss of boundaries being crossed.

Of old personas being shred.

Of welcoming change with open arms.

They melted into each other. A cloud moved over the sky, blacking out the moon and stars. But they didn't need a light to see. They knew each other so well. They'd been emotionally intimate for years, telling each other things they'd never told anyone else. Now they were simply making it official with their bodies, a physical intimacy that completed their bond. Full circle. United. One.

She uttered a low sound and slipped her arms around his neck. His fingers knotted in her hair, his energy blazing as hot as her own. They were tuned to the same frequency, both vibrating with heightened awareness of each other.

The ridges and swirls in her fingertips traced the landscape of his face as they kissed; absorbing the subtle yet distinct changes in terrain from the high planes of his cheeks to the hollows below. She moved, feeling the shape of his head like a sculptor.

Her fingers traveled over him, memorizing every inch. She ran her hand through his hair and traced her fingers over his beard stubble.

So familiar and yet at the same time so strangely foreign to be here with him in this way.

Transcended. Together they transcended who they once were and were emotionally reborn.

Friends to lovers. Lovers and friends. It did not get any more intimate than this. It was almost more than she could handle. Tears welled up in her eyes and her heart stilled with the wonder of it all.

He kissed her harder, as if sensing her changing mood, pulling her back with him to the passion, to the flame. His tongue sweeping her up in a divine pleasure that no man before him had ever unfurled inside her.

The tender sweetness was almost too much. She understood why he feared this could ruin their friendship. If things did not work out between them she could never again be around him without remembering acutely what she'd lost.

He ran his hot palms up her belly. She moaned softly, encouraging him, riding the winds of desire, reveling in the dervish of sensation.

Tingles of anticipation started at the base of her neck, crept across her face, over her scalp, darted along her shoulders, trickled down her arms, and finally shuddered softly up her spine. She was sitting in his lap, between his spread thighs. Such big, muscular thighs, full of power and promise.

"Ah," he said, and in the darkness, his mouth found the hardening tip of her nipple.

Zoey sucked in her breath at the delicious shock of his warm moistness suckling her tender breast.

He curved one arm around her waist, pulling her closer against him. She sighed as a strange alloy of electricity and chemistry fused with emotions sent a surge of bittersweet pleasure flashing through her.

The blackness surrounded them, encompassed them, and defined them. She could feel his erection prodding against her pelvis. He rubbed his beard-stubbled jaw along her breasts, seeking the other nipple. The sensation sent fresh prickles spiking through her.

He tugged lightly on her nipple and she sank closer to him, pressing her pelvis against his and nuzzling his neck. He laughed and the sound was pure delight. He raised his trembling hand and curved it around her breast. The weight of him felt glorious against her skin.

"Such breasts," he murmured. "Such beautiful, magnificent breasts."

"Thank you. I like them."

He went for her lips again, but she moved too quickly and he ended up kissing the tip of her nose.

They laughed. What might have been awkwardness with someone else was nothing but an understanding chuckle between friends. The cloud passed over and the moon was back, shining a soft glow over their naked bodies.

"Let's try this," he said, and flipped her over onto her back.

"Ah, good old missionary-style, huh?"

"There's a reason it's so popular."

"What's that?"

"Nothing like face-to-face, eye-to-eye." He hovered over her, supporting himself on his elbows, and looked down at her.

She gulped.

"I still can't believe this is happening," he said.

"Finally," she said.

"What took us so long to get here?" he murmured.

"Idiots," she said.

"We both had to be ready. You were too

young before. I worry that even now —"

"No more talking," she said, sandwiched his face between her hands, and kissed him again.

She had to have him inside her or go mad. She ran her hands down the length of his bare back, on down to cup his tight buttocks. So hard!

Gently, he bit one of her nipples. His sharp teeth against her tender skin made her gasp in surprise, but it didn't hurt. In fact, what she felt was the exact opposite of pain. Exalted pleasure.

"Make love to me," she demanded. "Take me now!"

The air was musky with the scent of their desire. He settled himself between her legs and slid his throbbing shaft into her, made a hissing sound in the back of his throat. "You feel so good. So tight and warm."

They made love like crazed things, scratching and grappling, banging against the side of the truck — writhing and pumping and arching their sweat-slick bodies. There was no control. They gave vent to heated moans and deep-throated yelps. Zoey wrapped her legs tight around Jericho's waist as he thrust into her again and again. She had three orgasms, four, five, oh, she finally lost count, but still it was not enough.

"More," she begged through gritted teeth. "Give me more."

He complied, pounding into her until her sex throbbed with the sweetest ache in the entire world.

"Don't stop, don't stop, don't —"

He silenced her with a kiss as he plunged deeper and deeper until she feared his big, hard cock would rip her right in two. Jericho plowed one hand up the back of her neck, threading his thick fingers through her hair. He pulled her head back, exposing her throat. He suckled on her skin, moving kisses down toward her breasts again.

She reached down to caress the shaft of his penis as it slipped in and out of her. She brought up her fingers, dripping with her own juices, and smeared the wetness over her swollen breasts.

Jericho opened his mouth wide over her nipple, taking in as much of her as he could, suckling her as if he wanted to swallow her whole.

Zoey gasped, almost sobbing with the bliss of it all.

He groaned her name and then he just groaned. He kissed her hard, thrusting his tongue in her mouth as his cock thrust up hard inside of her.

She was close. So damn close.

His corded muscles tightened against her, his buttocks stiffened. He was close too. Blood pulsed hot and fast through her veins. Her womb clenched. She looked into his eyes and he looked in hers and time evaporated.

"You keep doing that and I'm gonna come."

"Doing what?"

"You know what you're doing."

"You mean this?" She flexed her inner muscles.

He groaned. "Wench."

She grinned. "You love it."

"Please don't make me come yet. I want you to go first," he said, slowing his rhythm. "What's it going to take?"

She touched the tip of her tongue to her upper lip. "You're doing it."

"Come for me, sweetheart," he crooned, his voice low and guttural. "I want to see your face when you come."

Jericho moved faster then and deeper than she ever thought possible.

In an instant, Zoey felt sensations splintering inside her and the orgasm clutched her. "Jericho!" She moaned out his name and all the air left her body as explosion after explosion rolled through her body.

"Zoey," Jericho whispered. "Zoe-Eyes."

He shoved into her one last plunging thrust and she felt the convulsive throb of his own release let go. "Zoe-Eyes," he whispered again. "Bright as diamonds." He buried his face against her neck and held her tight.

Slowly, in a tangle of hazy lust and sweaty limbs, they sank back to earth, leaving a trail of stars above them in the sky. He zipped up the sleeping bag around them, pulled her into the curve of his body, and there they fell asleep, a couple of spoons nestled perfectly together.

Later, Jericho's rough palms slid over her smooth belly, an erotic contrast that drew a shiver from her. His breath was warm against the nape of her neck, feathering the fine hairs that grew along her hairline. Was he awake or simply shifting over in his sleep?

Should she say something? Why did this feel so awkward? They were best friends. It should have been so easy. But of course that was the problem, wasn't it? Best friends trying to carve out uncharted territory and uncertain if rocky shoals lay just ahead.

His hand moved from her belly to her hipbone. Active. Seeking.

She felt a dull, hard pressure at her lower spine. Oh yeah, he was awake all right, every inch of him.

Last night the sleeping bag had been a safe cocoon, now it tightened like a strait-jacket as it fully dawned on her what they had done. Everything had changed between them and they could never go back to the way things were before.

Unexpected tears burned the backs of her eyelids, but she blinked them away. No crying. This new direction in their relationship might be scary, but it was growth. Growth was good.

Wasn't it?

His palm surfed the curve of her body, sliding up to cup her breast.

Instantly, her nipples hardened. Her nerve endings pulsed, sending pleasure messages rushing up and down her body. His thumb brushed across one straining nipple and it tightened to the size of a raw green pea.

Her breathing quickened, each thready inhalation followed by shallow exhales. If she kept this up, she'd soon grow dizzy. He continued to gently knead her breast, sending insistent pinches of pleasure pushing up from deep inside her.

"Jericho," she whispered on a sigh, and wondered if she was dreaming. She'd imagined this for so long, maybe it wasn't even real.

His mouth branded the back of her neck,

his hot tongue teasing and probing her as if she were some delicious find he'd unearthed. As he moved, the material of the sleeping bag made a slithery synthetic noise that made her think of parachutes opening. She'd gone skydiving once and loved it and this was even more thrilling than that.

Geronimo! Pull the cord. Here I come.

He strummed her skin, playing her like a guitar. Goose bumps sprang up everywhere his fingers touched, ignited brave little fires up and down her body. His palm planed over her belly, his calloused thumb rimming her navel.

Zoey exhaled a great gush of air and arched her spine against him.

He chuckled. "God, you are so responsive."

"I want to see you face-to-face."

His tongue was skimming her outer ear.

"You're driving me crazy." She groaned, wriggled. "Devil."

"She-devil. You've been making me crazy for years. Giving back a little of that torture you've been giving out."

"I never tortured you," she protested.

"Maybe not intentionally, but you tortured me plenty."

They made love again and rode one wave of pleasure into another, cementing the bond they'd formed, growing together, twining around each other. The moon moved across the sky and the night was one long, exquisite dream. She'd never been with a man who could please her in so many different ways. A man who took his time and knew how to please.

When they were too exhausted to make love anymore, but too wired to sleep, they talked and kissed and talked and kissed. She thought about telling him about Clarissa McCleary, but she didn't want to ruin the special moment. Besides, she'd decided she did not want to dig any deeper into the past. Let it stay buried, right? As long as she left it alone, it was nothing but supposition, no one else had to know the secret.

"I really wished you hadn't quit the dig," he bemoaned.

"If I hadn't quit, we wouldn't be here right now."

"But we would have ended up here eventually."

"I couldn't wait, Jericho. I've been waiting for you my whole life."

"Me too," he said, and kissed her forehead. "I just didn't know how much."

She smiled against his chest.

"What are you grinning about?"

"I think I know why I could never get serious about any of the guys I dated."

"Why is that?" His voice rumbled in his chest. She liked the way it resonated against her ear.

"I thought it was because — per my family and their insistence that love will hit you like a bolt from the blue, that when you see your beloved, you'll just *know* — I was waiting for that red-hot lightning to strike."

"And it never did," he said.

"No. It sneaked in steady and quiet."

"That's the way it started for me too."

"It's been growing from the moment I peeked over the fence and saw you digging up Junie Mae's backyard."

"We did become instant friends, but I can't tell you how much I got teased because I was friends with a girl four years younger than I was."

"Pfft on them. We know the truth."

"What's that?"

"That I'm a hell of a lot of fun to be around."

"You can say that twice and not be wrong." He laughed and traced a finger over her cheek.

"I'm a hell of a lot of fun to be around."

"Do you have any idea how beautiful you are?"

"Stop, you're making me blush."

"Your breasts are perfect —"

"Be honest, they're on the small side."

"Pert and firm and fit right in the palm of my hand."

"That won't last. A couple of kids and a few decades and they'll be banging around my kneecaps."

"I'm going to ignore that exaggeration because I know that no matter how many kids you have or how old you get I'm always going to see your breasts they way they are right now."

She pulled back and looked him in the eyes. "When did you get so romantic?"

"The minute you crawled into the bed of this pickup truck with me." His fingers swirled over her nipple.

"Stop, you're making me dizzy. I can't think."

"Thinking is overrated. You've been trying to tell me that for years and I finally get what you mean." He put his mouth to her nipple.

She let out a groan. "Wait, there was something I was trying to tell you but I forgot what it was."

"Must not have been important," he murmured.

"But it was." She squirmed away from his exquisite mouth while she still had the fortitude to do so. "I was trying to tell you why and how I've changed."

"Okay," he said, propping himself up on his elbow and studying her. "I'm listening."

"Where was I?"

"Lightning strikes, love at first sight, etc. . . ."

"Oh yes, the men I used to date. Do you know what I finally realized about them?"

"What's that?"

"It wasn't that there wasn't chemistry or electricity with those guys, because there was."

"I'm not sure I really want to hear this." He covered his ears with his palms.

"All that lightning bolt stuff is nothing more than lust, after all. So yeah, I had some lusty times with some of those guys, but I never wanted to get involved with them and I never mistook a good time in bed for love. You know what I mean."

"I'm pretty certain that I *do not* want to hear this. Do you want me telling you about the intimate details of my relationship with Mallory?"

"Shh." She put a finger to her lips. "Listen a minute, this is really important."

"No intimate details of bedtime with other men?"

"No."

"All right, so what do you want to tell me?"

"I never wanted to be with any of those guys long-term because I always compared them to you. None of them could keep up with me mentally like you do — I'm not bragging that I'm smart. I'm just saying that my mind hops around a lot. But *you* get me. You understand who I am and you like me anyway. You don't try to change me. You accept me, Jericho, and no man has ever done that for me. Maybe my father would have accepted me unconditionally if he hadn't died. I like to believe he would have, but I never had complete acceptance from any man except you." Tears misted her voice and she bit her bottom lip to keep it from trembling.

"Ah hell, Zoe-Eyes." He squeezed her tight. "You know I love you, don't you?"

She nodded.

"I always have and I always will. You've been the one constant in my life. You've been there when my own parents weren't."

"Oh, Jericho." She wanted so badly to tell him she loved him too but the words got clogged up in her throat. She did love him, with all her heart and soul, but she was so afraid to come right out and say the words. So scared that somehow she'd screw this up. She'd never been a long-term girl. Everyone knew it. She hadn't even been able to keep a cat or stick with an archaeological dig.

And how could she truly say she loved him when she was keeping things from him? He trusted her so completely and yet she had this big secret she could not share with him because she'd dug up those artifacts again behind his back after she'd given him her solemn word that she would not. What would he say if he knew she'd excavated those mounds after she promised she would not? How would he react?

Yes, but holding on to this secret was putting a wall between them. How could they ever build a lasting, intimate bond if she couldn't tell him everything?

Self-doubt swept over her in waves. She was overwhelmed with feeling and that's all there was to it, and for a girl who'd spent her life keeping everything light and breezy, it was hard to dig deep and root out those strong emotions.

"You don't have to say it," he whispered. "I know you love me too. I do get you, Zoe-Eyes, and I'd never put expectations or limitations on you. You're free as a bird. My love does not bind you, but it's here for you. Forever. And no matter what happens, I will always, always have your back." With his knuckle, he brushed the tear from her eyes.

Her breath caught on a hiccup.

"Shh, shh, everything is okay," he soothed. "As far as you and I are concerned it's always okay."

Misery nibbled at her. That's because he didn't know what she'd done. How she'd broken her promise and was now basically lying to him.

Say it. Just tell him what he wants to hear.

But it felt like cheating to say those words without being completely honest with him first. She'd spent so long hiding the feelings from herself that she did not know how to say the words.

She squeezed his hand. He squeezed hers back. He was the most wonderful, patient man in the world.

Maybe she couldn't speak the words, but she could show him. She kissed Jericho deeply, passionately, and used her body to tell him exactly what her mouth could not yet say.

I love you, Jericho Chance. I always have and I always will.

Chapter 19

Traits: Any element of human culture, material objects, or human practices.

The sound of a vehicle engine woke them just after dawn.

Bleary-eyed, Zoey unzipped the sleeping bag, crawled to the tailgate, and peeked out over the back of the truck. The wire fence and metal gate the crew had put up at the bottom of Triangle Mount before they started the dig was less than two hundred yards away from where Jericho's pickup was parked. A blue Lincoln Town Car pulled up beside the Cupid's Rest van she'd driven over the previous evening. It was a car she had seen before in the faculty parking lot at Sul Ross.

"Oh, crap." She ducked back down.

"What is it?" Jericho raised his head.

"Dr. Sinton."

At least the rising sun would be in the

director's eyes, making it harder for him to see them scrambling around for their clothes.

Jericho bolted up. "Jeans, jeans, where are my jeans?"

"Here." She passed him a pair of Levi's. "No, wait, those are mine." She grabbed them back, and keeping down on the bed of the pickup, humped like an inchworm to get them pulled up.

"What's he doing up here at this hour?" Jericho finally found his pants underneath the sleeping bag.

"Probably came up here about my resignation letter."

"If that's the case, why come up here? If you resigned, he wouldn't expect to find you at the dig site." Jericho stuffed his feet into his boots.

The car door slammed. A scowling Dr. Sinton got out.

Her stomach soured. This was not good. Not good at all. She buttoned her shirt, fluffed her hair.

Jericho tossed the sleeping bag aside. "My shirt? Where's my shirt?"

"You threw it over the side of the truck last night."

He groaned and he fed his belt through the loops of his jeans.

"It's okay," she said. "I quit the dig, don't panic."

"Even so, this reflects badly on me."

"Dr. Chance," Dr. Sinton called out as he reached the gate. "Might I have a word?"

Jericho leaned over and gave her a big kiss on the cheek.

"Are you nuts? Kissing me in front of him!"

"If I'm going down, I'm going down. It's not going to stop me from showing you how I feel about you," he said, and then clenched his jaw, placed one hand on the side of the truck bed, and vaulted over the side. He landed with a cloud of dust, picked up his shirt and put it on, buttoning it as he strode toward Dr. Sinton.

Battling guilt, anxiety, and fear, Zoey climbed over the tailgate and followed him. She wasn't going to let him face the director alone.

Jericho was just opening the gate for the director when Zoey rushed up to them. "Good morning, Director Sinton," she said cheerfully as if she and Jericho hadn't just spent the night having wild monkey sex in the back of a pickup at a field school dig site.

"Zoey." Dr. Sinton nodded curtly, his face carved in stone.

Uh-oh.

For a moment, they all three stood there not saying a word. Dr. Sinton's gaze played over them.

Jericho moved to put an arm around her shoulder. While it might not have been the wisest move in the book under the circumstances, it made Zoey's heart flutter. He might be in hot water, but he was not ashamed of what they'd done and he wasn't afraid to show it.

"Did you get my e-mail resigning from the dig?" Zoey asked, figuring she might as well take the bull by the horns.

"I did."

"I quit the dig. So being with Jericho isn't breaking any rules."

The director gave her such a hard stare it was all she could do not to back up. That, and there was the fact that Jericho held her firmly at his side. "You were the one hiding in the closet at the lab," he said flatly.

She couldn't lie about that. Mutely, she nodded.

Dr. Sinton arched an eyebrow. He didn't have to say what he was thinking. She'd still been on the dig that night, and while she and Jericho hadn't actually consummated their relationship that day, it was a very fuzzy gray area.

"Director," Jericho said, "I'm assuming you're here about the problems we've been having at the dig. Vandalism, Avery's injury, students quitting amid irrational fears of a curse and —"

"While those are matters of concern," Dr. Sinton interrupted, "that's not why I got out of bed at five in the morning to drive up here."

Jericho straightened his spine, squared his shoulders. He looked like a soldier waiting to be court-martialed. "What is the reason, sir?"

"Marcus Winz-Smith called me at that lovely hour to tell me one of your team has been excavating outside of Triangle Mount in clear violation of the contract we signed. Not only is he shutting down the dig effective immediately, but he's also suing Sul Ross."

Jericho's heart sank. His career was thoroughly screwed and he knew it, but how had Winz-Smith learned Zoey had dug around on those mounds? That was a couple of weeks ago.

Dr. Sinton cocked his head. "Might I speak to you privately, Dr. Chance?"

"Of course, sir."

"I'm going to put on some coffee." Zoey

pointed over her shoulder and started walking backward uphill toward the camp. "You want some?"

"No." Dr. Sinton frowned. "I'm good."

"Jericho?" Zoey's voice was wavery.

"I'm fine. Go ahead, Zoey."

The director waited until she was out of earshot and then he cleared his throat. "Miss McCleary is a student."

"Was," Jericho corrected, knowing good and well he was grasping at straws, splitting hairs, and playing with semantics. "She dropped the course."

"Because of you." Dr. Sinton scratched his soul patch.

Guilt delivered a swift roundhouse kick to his gut. True enough. "She's my best friend. I've known her since I was eight years old."

"All the more reason to keep your dick in your pants." Dr. Sinton glowered.

"I apologize. I should have told you that night in the lab that we were seeing each other. I am her instructor. I was in the wrong. I have no excuse for my behavior."

"You were warned, Chance. You violated the conditions of your probationary employment."

How had he gotten himself into this mess? He wasn't that guy — the one who perpetually tripped himself up — except now it seemed that he was. How *had* this happened?

Zoey, that's how.

Not that he was blaming her. He took responsibility for his own actions. It was just that his need to be with her had superseded everything. The attraction had taken him hostage, kidnapped every rational thought he possessed. Nothing was more important to him than she was, and that included his career.

Damn. He blinked, realizing for the first time just how much she really did mean to him.

"In case you weren't aware of this, Miss McCleary is the one who excavated outside Triangle Mount. Someone saw her there yesterday and informed Winz-Smith about it."

"Yesterday?" No, that couldn't be right. Zoey had excavated the mystery mounds almost two weeks ago. "Are you certain Winz-Smith wasn't misinformed?"

"No, I don't believe so. The witness who saw her there was her fellow student, Catrina Bello. She saw Miss McCleary digging up and removing something from an area near the lake between Triangle Mount and Widow's Peak. I had to ask myself why did Miss Bello feel more comfortable going to

Winz-Smith with Miss McCleary's transgressions instead of you?"

Jericho gulped.

"My arrival here this morning answered that question. Undoubtedly, Miss Bello knew you were having a relationship with Miss McCleary and realized you could not be impartial."

Jericho scowled. Something smelled fishy. Why *had* Catrina gone to Winz-Smith instead of directly to Dr. Sinton? And what had she been doing spying on Zoey in the first place? Things weren't adding up. Especially since he was already uneasy about Catrina.

"This infraction is a clear indication that you do not have the necessary leadership skills for this position. I'm sorry to have to do this, Dr. Chance, but you've given me no options. I'm going to have to ask for your immediate resignation."

Zoey was flipping bacon in the iron skillet when Jericho walked up. She switched off the gas burner on the camp stove and dusted her hands against the seat of her jeans. "How bad is it?"

"The worst."

"You've been fired," she guessed.

"I have."

"Oh, Jericho, I'm so sorry. This is all my fault." She clasped her hands to her face.

"I accept full responsibility for my actions. I knew that loving you was wrong but I chose to do it anyway."

"Well," she laughed nervously, "I wouldn't say *wrong* exactly."

"Can we talk?"

"Um, you want to have breakfast first?"

"I'm not hungry."

Suddenly, neither was she. "What is it?"

He stopped four feet from her, and scratched his head. "I'm perplexed about something."

Uneasiness spread over her like a bad case of chicken pox. "What's that?"

"How was it that Catrina saw you excavating the mounds by the lake yesterday afternoon?"

Fear played her up and down her spine. "Catrina saw me?"

"So you're not going to deny it? You went back to excavate the mounds after you promised me that you would not go back down there?"

"Yes, I did but —"

Jericho held up a silencing palm. "I don't want to hear any excuses, Zoey, you've disappointed me far more than you can know."

His words ripped her heart right out of her chest, threw it on the ground, and stomped on it until nothing was left but tattered, barely stitched-together threads.

"You . . . you don't understand," she stammered.

He crossed his arms over his chest. "You're right about that. I certainly do not understand why you went back to the mounds after you swore to me you would not, especially when you knew that if you did, the school could be sued and I could lose my job. That's not the way friends treat each other, Zoey."

"I'm so sorry. I . . . I didn't think it through."

"You never do," he said so bitterly the sound of his voice burned her ears.

"Please, you have to let me explain."

For one horrible moment, she thought he was not going to let her defend herself, but eventually, he pursed his lips and gave a short, terse nod. Bit by halting bit, she told him where she'd gone after he'd left her the previous day. How she'd found Clarissa's name in the family genealogy and how she'd been drawn back to the mounds by a compulsion she could not resist. How she'd taken the artifacts to the B&B and carefully cleaned them just the way he had taught.

And at last, she told him the terrible truth she had not been able to tell him last night. That the settlement had once been a McCleary stronghold and they'd burned their own settlement down rather than taking the risk of having their dark secret come out.

When she finished, he just stood there staring at her as if he'd never seen her before. It unnerved her and she hugged herself against the chill that seized in the warm summer morning.

"So you knew all this last night," he said stiffly.

She nodded.

"And you didn't trust me enough to tell me that you'd excavated the mounds a second time? You let me go face-to-face with Dr. Sinton completely unaware and unarmed to defend myself?"

"Jericho, I — that's not how I intended it to happen."

"Whether you intended it or not, Zoey, that's exactly what you did."

"I'm sorry."

He shook his head, his eyes full of sorrow. "Sorry is not going to cut it, Zoey. Not this time. Actions have consequences."

"You're turning your back on me?" Her voice quavered. What about all the promises he'd made her last night? That he would always have her back, no matter what? That he put no demands on her, allowed her to be who she was unconditionally. That he would love her forever, no matter what. Had it been nothing more than heat-of-the-moment vows?

But no, that could not be so. He had been her friend for twenty years. He could not abandon her over this. Not after what they'd done together.

Oh no, oh no. She could not accept this feeling. It hurt too much. She tried smiling. That usually worked. Grin. Get him to grin back at her. She gave it a shot.

He did not return her smile.

"It's going to be all right. You'll get another job. I know you will. I'll go talk to Dr. Sinton, make it clear that this was all my doing, that you had nothing to do with this, that —"

"Stop," he said. "Just stop talking."

But she could not. She felt like she was fighting for her life. "I was going to tell you. I came up here to tell you. But no one was here and I just knew in my gut that the mounds were the old McCleary settlement and I had a compulsion I simply couldn't control, no matter how hard I tried I couldn't just leave it lie. That's a big step for me, Jericho. It would have been so easy to just forget about what I'd found, to just pretend —"

"You've never had trouble quitting something in the middle before. Why this? Why now?"

"Don't you see how hanging with this was *positive* growth for me?"

"And yet the results were disastrous. You know what cuts me to the quick?" he asked.

She shook her head, unable to speak, gulped, and ran a hand over her nose. She wasn't crying. She was *not* going to cry. No siree. Not her.

"Do you know what hurts more than you breaking your promise, more than the way you betrayed me by not telling me what you'd done."

She whimpered. Oh God, oh no! He *was* turning his back on her. Panic grabbed her by the throat. She felt as if someone had thrown her inside a tiny dark closet, slammed and locked the door and thrown away the key.

"What really stabbed me in the gut was when I told you that I loved you and you couldn't say it back to me. That's what kills me, Zoey. You couldn't say it back. You claim going back to the mounds was positive growth for you, but that's not the way I see it."

"How do you see it?"

"The same old, same old. You didn't think your actions through. Or worse yet, you thought them through and decided to act impulsively anyway."

"It wasn't like that, I was —"

"What?" he snapped.

"Trying to get to the truth so I could make amends for the past."

"Well, you flopped on that, big-time, didn't you?"

Without another word, he turned and walked back to his pickup truck, climbed in, and sped away, leaving a rooster tail plume of dust in his wake.

Jericho Drove, not even knowing where he was going. The terrain of the Chihuahuan Desert rolled past his window. He'd lost his job, he'd lost his dignity, his reputation, and now, he was on the verge of losing his best friend.

How had he gotten here? He was a rational man, a practical man, a logical man. He believed in collecting data to help him gain insight into how the world worked. He believed in cause and effect and right and wrong. He believed, like Francis Bacon, that knowledge was power. His personal credo was *Cognito ergo sum,* I think, therefore I am. And yet, in this matter, he had not thought at all.

When Zoey had shown up at the camp last night, his body had gotten the better of him and he had blindly, impulsively reacted.

Jericho clenched his hands around the steering wheel. Dammit! Zoey wasn't at fault. He wouldn't fault a parrot for being brightly colored and inquisitive. Nope. All the blame lay at his clay feet for expecting her to be something she was not. He'd known all along what she was like. Why did it surprise him when she simply acted in character?

He should never have taken the job when he learned she was going to be on the dig team. That was his undoing, his own bad decision.

The thing was, when they were just friends, he *hadn't* put any expectations on her. He'd accepted her for exactly who she was, loved her *because* of her quirks and traits and not in spite of them.

The problem cropped up when he'd started thinking of her as more than a friend, and suddenly, he wanted to change her. He knew she was impulsive. Knew she had trouble getting serious. Knew expressing deep emotions was hard for her. Knew she avoided dark topics like what she'd uncovered about the McCleary side of her family. Knew she preferred to skim the surface of life.

Why was he having a problem with her when he loved the fact that she saw the world as full of open doors? Life to Zoey was an adventure. Her mercurial mind cried out for experiences, feasted on associations and patterns, savored time and space. She lived more succinctly in the now than anyone he'd ever met. She had a knack for remembering the good times, while the bad faded from her memory.

Most likely that was why she had not told him about going back to the mounds. Not because she'd been trying to actively hide her actions from him, but because she hadn't wanted to face what she'd discovered about her family. She'd come to him for solace, to give and receive pleasure and a way to soothe her troubled soul.

That was Zoey's way. Always had been, always would be.

He was the one who had let her down, not the other way around. And that was the heart of the issue, the reason that he'd never pursued her before his return to Cupid, the real reason that he'd driven away today.

Jericho did not know if he could keep up with her. Not as a lover anyway. Deep intimacy with Zoey would require everything he had inside him. She needed an upbeat partner who was game for her many activities. Was he nimble enough to keep up with her priorities that could shift at a moment's notice? Could he keep her interested?

Yes! his heart yelled. *Yes, you can. She'll keep up on your toes, but that's one of the things you love most about her.* She brought out his carefree side and tickled his sense of humor. Whenever he was around her, he was . . . well, he was quite simply happier.

C'mon, what was he thinking? He had nothing to offer her. Not now. He was unemployed, and getting fired so soon after getting hired didn't bode well for future employment. It was going to take a lot of work to rebuild his reputation. Not to mention, he had allowed a unique find to be stolen right out from under his nose, and that chapped his hide.

Someone had filed down the rungs on the ladder, not as a prank, not to spook the students into quitting the dig, not even as a threat. Whoever had filed down the rungs and left out the tools could not have accurately predicted that someone would fall on the ice pick, but what they could safely assume was that anyone who fell four feet into the dig pit would be harmed in some way, causing everyone's attention to be drawn to the victim.

A light bulb went off in his head.

The damaged ladder, the strewn tools had been nothing more than a distraction. Someone had wanted his attention diverted so they could steal the medicine bundle. That's what it had all been about.

That Catrina had reported seeing Zoey excavating the valley mounds the previous afternoon meant only one thing. Catrina was on Triangle Mount yesterday when no one else had been around.

There was no doubt in Jericho's mind which culprit had strewn the tools, filed down the ladder rungs, and stolen the metal locker containing the medicine bundle. It had to be Catrina Bello. What he didn't know was why she would do such a thing.

But he sure as hell was going to find out.

Chapter 20

Depression: An area where cultural activity took place.

Devastated by Jericho's reaction, Zoey didn't know what to do. Leave him alone? Go after him? Plead her case with Winz-Smith and beg him to drop the lawsuit? Yeah. There. That one. She'd go to see Winz-Smith and give Jericho time to cool down before she tried again to apologize.

Except getting an audience with Winz-Smith was easier said than done. She had no idea where he was or how to get hold of him, but she knew someone who did.

Tabitha.

And by the time she got to town — Zoey switched on her phone to check the time — Tabitha would be on her way to the tri-weekly meeting of the Letters to Cupid volunteers.

She cleared her possessions out of her

tent, loaded them in the van, and headed to the Cupid Community Center. Her sneakers squeaked against the freshly waxed floor as she walked inside, her heart so heavy it ached every time she took a breath.

The door stood open and she could hear voices from those gathered inside.

In a déjà vu moment, she stood in the hallway, listening once more to her family and friends talking about her. What? Did they talk about her constantly? Or was she simply the most fortuitous eavesdropper ever? And hey, the next time she felt inclined to gossip about somebody when she was at one of the meetings, she was darn well going to get up and close the frigging door.

"I'm so proud of Zoey," Natalie was saying. "She's really thrown herself heart and soul into this archaeological field school."

Obviously, neither the fact that she had quit the field school nor word of what had happened this morning on Triangle Mount had yet made its way to the Cupid grapevine, but it wouldn't be long before everyone knew the truth.

Zoey cringed, bit down on her bottom lip. She would have been better off if she'd never even tried to commit to something in the first place, rather than fail so spectacularly.

"Well," Carol Ann pointed out. "Walker did put her feet to the fire. She has to stick with this dig or permanently lose her trust."

"I think he went a bit too far to make his point," Great-Aunt Delia said. "But it is amazing how Zoey is staying up there on the mountain. I expected her to come flitting through here at least a time or two, restless as always."

"Giving up that kitten seemed to take the wind out of her sails," said Sandra. "You have to admit, the girl does have a tender heart."

Everyone murmured in agreement.

Yeah, and look where a tender heart had gotten her. Missing a kitty that had never been her own and wrecking her friendship with Jericho. Tears sprang to her eyes but she rapidly blinked them away. When had she turned into such a crybaby? She'd never been this sensitive before.

"I'm wondering if her newfound dedication to archaeology has as much to do with my stepgrandson coming home as anything else," Junie Mae mused.

"Jericho and Zoey do make a cute couple." Natalie sighed wistfully. "Jericho is so good for her."

"And her for him," Junie Mae said. "She gets him out of his head."

"What do you think, Lace?" Carol Ann asked. "You were up there with them. Is there something more than friendship going on between Zoey and Jericho?"

"I think they're head over heels for each other," Lace said. "Only they're both too scared to admit it."

"Heaven's sakes, why would anyone be afraid of love?" asked Great-Aunt Delia.

Mignon started humming, "Que Je T'Aime."

"Think about it," Sandra said. "Jericho and Zoey would make the most beautiful babies, with his raven hair, and her big, green, heartbreaker eyes."

"And how many people can say they fell in love with their best friend?" asked Junie Mae. "It has its own special kind of magic."

Here they were so proud of her, so excited about her relationship with Jericho. They had no idea what her newfound dedication had cost her.

Zoey's throat burned and she put a hand to her neck. She was going to disappoint them all over again, just like she always did. She'd quit the dig to be with Jericho and somehow she'd even managed to screw that up. No way could she go in there and face them after hearing this. That's what she did. Let people down.

The bitter realization caught her low in the solar plexus, a roundhouse kick that stabbed, stung, twisted. How foolish of her to think she could escape herself. She was who she was, for better or worse. Except right now, it certainly seemed for the worse.

"You know," Natalie said. "I've never been prouder of my sister than I am right now. She really has come into her own."

Hauling in a deep breath, Zoey spun on her heels and ran away as fast as she could run.

Catrina did not answer any of the texts or voice mails Jericho left for her. Honestly, he hadn't expected her to. He texted the other students and none of them had spoken with her. Avery had already been released from the hospital, but he didn't know where she was either.

Jericho went to the apartment in Alpine that Catrina had listed in the school records as her address. The man who came to the door claimed never to have heard of her.

After that, he drove to his office at Sul Ross. Thankfully, he still had access to it, and he skimmed through his computer enrollment files to discover that Catrina had just recently transferred to the college as a foreign exchange student, and the field school was her first class.

Something wasn't right about all this.

Had she been nothing but a plant all along? Put in the field school to spy or steal artifacts or both. By whom and to what end? It was only a field school dig. No one could have predicted they'd actually find something monumental. Placing a spy or an artifact thief on the dig team didn't make any sense.

His immediate inclination was to talk this over with his best friend, except right now things were pretty rocky between him and Zoey. She'd tested his patience plenty of times and they'd had disagreements over the years, but they'd never had a real fight before. Cement settled in his stomach, solidified.

Go talk to her. Just talk this out.

Yeah. They could work through this. Sure they could. Wouldn't they?

He sat in his pickup truck in the Sul Ross parking lot, blew out a long breath, and tapped on the speed dial icon that had her smiling picture peering up at him from the tiny smart phone screen.

After five rings, it went to voice mail. Not knowing what to say, he hung up.

He waited a few minutes and tried her cell again, lost connection before the call ever went through. Damn piss-poor reception in the mountain passes. He slung his phone across the cab of his pickup truck, doffed his cowboy hat, and jammed a hand through his hair.

Over the years, he'd let very few people get close to him. Grandpa Joe had been one, Zoey the other. Mallory had often accused him of loving his pal Zoey more than he loved her. It wasn't until Mallory cheated on him that Jericho realized she was right. Zoey was the one he turned to when things went bad. The one he called when he had a victory to share. She was his go-to girl, and now all of that was in danger.

What if he'd hurt her beyond repair? He had walked out on her after he'd promised nothing would alter their friendship. What an idiot he'd been. Of course making love to her had altered *everything.*

As he drove past Telescope Road, which led to the astronomy summer camp where he'd been a counselor the summer Zoey had jumped off the Telescope Cliff into Tranquility Pool, he saw the back of a white van with lettering on the side. From this distance, he couldn't make out the emblem on the vehicle but his hopes rushed into his throat. Was it the Cupid's Rest B&B van? He made a U-turn, circling onto the side of the road and kicking up dust as he went after her.

"Zoey, where are you going?" he mumbled, pressing hard on the accelerator and zooming after the van that had already started up the grade to the summer camp.

But she had a good head start and even though he was speeding along far faster than was prudent on the weathered asphalt, he couldn't catch up to her. Ten minutes later, he drove through the gates of Camp Cameron, spied the van parked outside the cantina, and felt an unexpected flutter deep in the center of his chest as if his heart had torn loose inside him and was flapping around like some crazed bird trying to escape a too-small cage.

He hopped out and saw it wasn't Zoey's van at all but a local delivery service bringing in food supplies. His heart snapped back hard against his spine. Dumbass. He adjusted his hat, climbed back in his pickup, and took another route down the mountain that meandered past the peak from which Zoey had dove into Tranquility. He parked, got out, walked to the spot, and looked down.

A horde of laughing and screeching kids splashed about in the water.

He knelt one knee down on that hard dry ground, remembering that moment when

Zoey so fearlessly flung herself over the edge, to the surprised and delighted gasps of the other children. Recalled how helpless and alone he'd felt when he thought for those horrible minutes — the worst of his life — that she'd drown.

The terrifying fire of that moment swept over him again and he felt as lost and helpless now as he had then. She'd done it again. Made a surprising move without him. Left him behind. Just as his parents had when they'd gone off to China and left him with Grandpa Joe and Junie Mae. He'd been crippled by that abandonment, even as he'd tried hard not to show it. Rationally, as an adult, he understood why they'd left him, but that kid, the one who'd tried to dig to the opposite side of the world with his gregarious pigtailed neighbor, still felt as if he'd done something to cause them to leave.

A hard realization hit him. A possibility he'd never considered. For years, he'd kept Zoey at arm's length because he was worried that such a mercurial woman would never be able to commit, when the problem wasn't with her, but with him.

The real question that had been lurking in the back of his mind like the Grim Reaper sharpening his scythe — a question he'd turned a blind eye to because to examine it hurt too much — was that maybe *he* was the one who could not sustain a long-term romantic relationship. He'd let Zoey take the fall for his inadequacy. He was the one who had no role model for a workable family. He was the one who prized his career above relationships.

Zoey might have her flaws, but the woman was fearless. She'd never had a long-term relationship because she'd known none of those other men were right. That's what she'd been trying to tell him. She had faith. She'd just been waiting for him to catch up to what she already knew.

All along, all this time, *he* was the one who was afraid to commit to love.

Since the McCleary side of the family had seriously let her down, Zoey turned to the Greenwood-Fant legend to guide her. She'd been raised to believe in the romantic idea that Cupid could fix your love woes, and she would give anything to have Jericho's friendship.

So she did what many of her relatives had done before her. She made a pilgrimage to the Cupid stalagmite tucked away in a dark cave of the Cupid Caverns.

This time of night the Caverns were

closed, but Zoey, being a Greenwood-Fant, knew where to get a key to the padlocked gate.

She took a pen and paper and drove up to the caverns. By the light of the moon — the same damn moon that had smiled down on her and Jericho the night before — she opened the gate and slipped inside.

Inside, the caverns were a good ten degrees cooler than outside. The wall sconces stayed on all the time, so she didn't really need the flashlight she'd brought with her, but from the time she was small, she'd been trained to bring one with her whenever she went into the caverns, just in case.

The slow, steady drip of stalactites echoed loudly in the silent space — *plop, plop, plop* — straight ahead, a downhill path that diverged in two directions amid the jagged teeth of rock formations. She knew the place by heart, had been up here more times than she could count. Although she'd never been as particularly enamored of the romantic legend as the rest of her family, she had to admit, in the quiet stillness, there was a serene reverence here. Of course, serenity and reverence had never been Zoey's style, but then look where her style had landed her so far. Might as well give this beseeching Cupid thing a shot. She had nothing left to lose.

The left-hand path led to the cave that housed the Cupid stalagmite. Jagged rocks of orange, green, yellow, and brown protruded from every direction — up, down, left, and right. As a kid, she liked to pretend she was a tiny dragon slayer about the size of a peanut and after the dragon had eaten her, all she had to do to slay him was slide down his throat and cut out his heart. When she told Natalie her fantasy, her sister had shuddered and said she was a morbid child, but Jericho had given her pointers on a few other ways she could take down a dragon.

Plaques had been mounted underneath key wall sconces that told stories of the people who had come before. There was Mingus Dill who'd first found the cave and prayed to Cupid to save him from a relentless sheriff's posse, and his prayers had been answered in the form of a lonely widow, Louisa Hendricks, who saved his life by agreeing to marry him. There was the story of her great-grandmother Millie. The story of how Wallis Simpson had once visited the Cupid Caverns and not long after her sojourn King Edward abdicated the throne for her.

A quarter of a mile into the cavern, she entered a smaller cave that housed the

Cupid stalagmite. The path was a cul-de-sac with Cupid in the center. There was only one way in and one way out of this room. The stalagmite towered more than seven feet tall and almost touched the top of the cave's ceiling. The rock formation that looked like Cupid stood on one leg, with the other leg bent at the knee as if he were running, a cocked bow in his arms, an arrow ready to be flung into unwitting hearts. There was a big blob where a face would have been if it were a man-made sculpture.

As she stood staring at it, an old memory that she'd completely forgotten washed over her.

Jericho's sixth-grade science teacher had assigned the homework of visiting the Cupid Caverns to study the rock formations, and Jericho allowed her, a silly second grader, to tag along on his expedition. She recalled standing in this same spot, looking up at Cupid, with her mouth hanging open.

"How'd this get here?" she'd asked.

"Water containing minerals seeps into a cave," he said.

"Huh? That don't make no sense." She shook her head vigorously. "Water can't make a rock."

"Sure it can," he said easily. "The water drips from the ceiling to the floor."

"So? I spill water at home and it doesn't turn into a stalaggy thing."

"Your house isn't a cave and it's not a continual drip. Depending on how much water evaporated and what kind and amounts of minerals were in the water, some are left on the ceiling and some drop to the floor. You can remember which one is which by thinking that stalac*tites* cling *tight* to the ceiling, while stalag*mites might* rise up from the floor. Over time, the stalagmites and stalactites will meet and form a column, just like they did with old Cupid here."

Awed, she studied his face. His eyes were lit with an unusual fire and his voice grew louder. He loved this stuff and she loved that he loved it. Her stomach hurt in a weirdly pleasant way like it did when she ate too much candy.

"You think what they say 'bout this is true?"

"What's that?"

"That if you ask Cupid to help, he'll bring you together with your one true love?"

"Nah." He shook his head. "It's just a stalagmite. How can a stalagmite help you find love?"

She wrinkled her nose. "Yeah, you're right." How come that hurting in her stomach wasn't so pleasant anymore?

A drop of water splashed onto the top of Zoey's head, yanking her back to the present.

"Well, Cupid," she said. "It's time to put your money where your mouth is . . . er, although I guess in your case it isn't. Let's see if this myth is total bullshit or if there's something to this after all."

She sat cross-legged on the path — the cave floor cool against her fanny — turned on her wide-bottomed flashlight, and stood it upright beside her. A yellow glow fell over her lap. From the notebook, she tore out a piece of paper, clicked her roller ball pen, and did what she'd never thought she'd do. Wrote a letter to Cupid herself.

Dear Cupid,

I've gone and ruined everything by falling in love with my best friend. Now, not only have I lost my lover, I've lost the one person in the world that I could tell anything to. But that's not the half of it. I thought I was doing a good thing by searching for something meaningful. People accused me of being frivolous and shallow, so I was determined to earn a little respect, prove I could commit, dig deep, find my roots, and discover who and what I am. Guess what? I did and that's what started all the trouble. The things I have uncovered could destroy people I love. I'm at my wits' end. I don't know how much longer I can hang on. Help!

Spontaneous to a Fault

She glanced down at the letter, saw water drops staining the page. Not tear drops. Oh no siree. She wasn't a crier. The water had to be coming from one of those pesky stalactites dripping down on her.

Swiping a hand under her nose, she looked up at the impressive stalagmite. "What now?"

Her question echoed around the small cave.

What now? What now? What now?

Not sure what she expected, Zoey folded the letter and stuck it into the pocket of her hooded sweatshirt. One thing was for certain; she wasn't going to find an answer to her questions here.

Zoey didn't want to go back to the B&B in case Jericho was spending the night at Junie Mae's house. She wasn't ready to face him yet. She folded down the seat, crawled into the back of the van, and tried to sleep.

No sooner had she closed her eyes than

her cell phone rang.

Jericho!

Eagerly, she checked her phone, only to have her hopes shudder to a halt when she saw Lace's name on the caller ID. For a moment, she considered not answering. Surely by now the grapevine was buzzing with the news of how she'd screwed up the dig and she just didn't want to talk about it.

Nah, she had to answer. No doubt the family was worried about her. As much as she would like to stick her head in the sand and ignore her family, she couldn't do it. "Hello?"

"Zoey," Lace said. "Have you seen Jericho? I've been trying to call him for hours."

"He might be on Triangle Mount," she answered. Obviously, Lace hadn't yet heard about the mess she'd caused. Good. "The reception is for shit up there."

"Why aren't you on Triangle Mount?"

"Long story."

"Is something wrong?"

"What did you need to tell Jericho?" she asked, neither wanting to lie nor get into the details of why she wasn't at the dig site.

The ploy worked. "Both the seeds and petals you found in the medicine bundle are from the Golden Flame agave." Lace breathed. "I'm so excited. This is incredible."

"It's gotta be gratifying to be proven right."

"It's the find of a lifetime. You and Jericho are going to be famous."

"Hey, you too. You're the one who always believed the plant existed. We were originally looking to debunk or confirm the theory the flatiron was a pyramid. We had no idea we'd unearth your holy grail."

"Yes, but without your dig, I would never have been able to prove my theory. But that's not the half of it."

"No?"

"Hold on to your hat, because here's the really exciting part."

"What's that?"

"The Golden Flame is a true centennial plant. I did calculations based on these seeds. I factored in the genetic —"

"Zoom!"

"Gotcha," Lace laughed. "I'll cut to the chase. If my figures are indeed correct any Golden Flame agave plants that might be in existence on foundation land could burst into bloom any day now. Of course, I could be off base on the timeline. Predictions like this certainly aren't foolproof, but all signs point to a summer bloom this year!"

"*If* the agave still exists."

"Even if it doesn't," Lace said, "there's a possibility that I could extract DNA from these botanicals and clone a new agave. Can you imagine? An extinct plant brought back to life? Of course, I wouldn't be around in a hundred years to see those plants bloom, but just to be able to revive a long dead species is any botanist's dream come true."

"That's so exciting. I know you're over the moon. I'll be sure to tell Jericho when I see him."

Lace paused a moment. "Are you okay, Zoey?"

"Sure."

"You don't sound like your usual zippy self."

"I'm fine," she reiterated.

"Is there something going on between you and Jericho? You guys didn't have a falling out, did you?"

"No, no," Zoey lied, desperate to get her cousin off the phone before she broke down and told her everything.

"Because if you want to talk, I'm here to listen."

"Listen, Lace, I've gotta go, but thanks so much for telling me this super exciting news."

"I can't wait to write this find up. I'm *sooo*

glad I didn't take that job at the Smithsonian."

From the background, Zoey heard Lace's husband, Pierce, call to her. "Hey, sexy botanist, take me to bed or lose me forever."

"Sounds like Pierce is ready for some lovin'," Zoey said, relieved to have a good excuse to end the conversation.

Lace giggled.

Giggling? Lace? She couldn't believe this was her serious-minded cousin. Falling in love with Pierce had changed Lace in countless ways, all of them for the better.

"Don't give up," Lace said, and then purred softly, "Oh yeah, do that again, cowboy."

"You talking to me or Pierce?"

Lace giggled again. "I was never very good at multitasking, but don't despair if you're having a few bumps in the road with Jericho. When you redefine any relationship you have to expect some ups and downs."

"We're not —"

"Don't try to deny it," Lace said. "Anyone that sees you two together knows you've slipped from being friends into lovers, and honestly, we're thrilled for you both. We were wondering when the two of you were going to catch up to what everyone else already knew."

"What's that?"

"You guys were meant for each other."

"Zoey," Pierce's voice came on the line.

"Uh-huh?"

"Gotta take my wife to bed now, she'll talk to you tomorrow."

"Good night, Pierce."

"Night," he said.

Lace giggled some more.

Zoey let out a wistful sigh, hung up the phone, and noticed she had ten missed calls, all of them from Jericho.

It took her a good ten minutes to work up the courage to call him back, but when she did, his phone went to voice mail. "Hi, this is Jericho, I'm probably out digging something up somewhere. You know what to do."

A beep sounded.

"Jericho, I . . ." She had no idea what to say. "Never mind."

She switched off her phone and lay back down, thinking about the miserable day and everything her cousin had said. After several restless hours, she fell into a fitful sleep.

A tumble of images assaulted her. The etchings on the tomahawk came to life — a handsome brave, a beautiful young woman, a deadly scorpion with a black stinger on his back, coiled and ready to strike. She whimpered in her sleep, tossed and turned.

In her dream she kissed a frog and it turned into a coyote. She saw Little Wolf and Clarissa as children, holding hands, and at some point their images fractured and turned into Jericho and Zoey.

Then from somewhere in the dream, Great-Great-Uncle August appeared and glowered at them. She turned around and Jericho was Little Wolf again, carrying the medicine bundle under his arm, and she was sick, so very sick, burning up with a high, hot fever.

Sweat drenched her body, but Little Wolf knelt at her side, bathing her face with a cool cloth, and insisted she drink a foul-tasting tea. Was she Clarissa now or still Zoey? She gulped it down just to please him and discovered, to her surprise, that she soon felt much better.

Little Wolf hovered over her, his face full of distress. She reached up to touch him, but he shied from her. That's when she saw the flames licking up from Triangle Mount, rolling fast and quick down the mountain, and in the center of the flames glowed a bright yellow flower in full bloom.

"Run!" Little Wolf cried, and grabbed her hand, although now he was Jericho again.

She clung to him as he dragged her up Widow's Peak. Flames blistered the ground behind him. Thundering hoofbeats shook the earth. They ran and ran and ran until she thought her lungs were going to explode and her feet would break off at the ankles.

"Please," she begged. "Please just let me die."

"We're meant to be together forever."

She and Jericho looked into each other's eyes and time stopped.

Past was present, present past, and her dream world became as real as any other. They stood atop Widow's Peak Mountain, and below they saw Triangle Mount and the valley consumed by fire. Gone, everything they knew and loved was gone.

He put out his palm and took her hand. She clung to him. He was her lifeline.

But their pursuers were upon them. No escape. Someone fired a shot and a bullet whizzed over their heads so close she could hear the projectile whistle as it cut through the thin air, but clearly designed not to hit them.

His dark eyes were solemn and the wind whipped his black hair behind him. "We can let them take us alive, separate us forever, probably torture me —"

"Or we can go together," she finished for him. "I am not afraid to die, as long as you are with me."

"I love you," he whispered. "I always have and I always will."

She opened her mouth to tell him she loved him too. Loved him so much, in fact, that she could not make lips form the words, when Great-Great-Uncle August reappeared, holding up a book that looked a lot like the formulary displayed in the Cupid Museum, but it had black binding instead of brown and he had it turned to the page of his Spanish flu remedy.

She frowned. This formula looked slightly different from the one in the formulary at the Cupid Museum, but the strange little doodle at the top of the page was exactly the same.

The doodle of two side-by-side triangles wasn't there by accident.

The triangle on the right was slightly taller and there was a small dot just below the peak of that triangle. In between the triangles, at the base level was a narrow oval — almost the shape of an almond — and directly above the oval was an arciform that resembled an eyebrow arched over an eye.

At that very same moment, Little Wolf cried, "Jump."

She felt the ground fall away from beneath her feet. Her heart pumped wildly, not from fear, but from love. She was not afraid to die. Not when he was with her and she knew he loved her more than life itself.

They were in freefall together, arms twined around each other. They were going to die, but she felt such an intense feeling of calm and peace she wondered why she had ever been scared at all.

The ground rushed up to meet them, and just as they hit the hard-packed desert earth . . .

Zoey awoke with a startling epiphany.

Chapter 21

Decipher: Crack the code;
figure out something's meaning.

After a sleepless night, Jericho got up at dawn with a plan.

He was going to take this one step at a time. First find Catrina and confront her about stealing the medicine bundle. Once he had that squared away and the medicine bundle recouped and in Dr. Sinton's hands, then he could give his full attention to Zoey.

It was a tough call to make. Everything inside him yearned to straighten things out with Zoey, but he couldn't do that with these distractions hanging over his head. They were going to need a good long time to talk. And another good long time after that to make love, because he had no doubt in his mind that they could fix this.

What if she doesn't want to fix it? She's not returning your calls.

He pushed aside the dark voice. One way or the other, they would straighten it out. If they gave up being lovers, so be it, but he would fight to the death to hang on to their friendship because he valued her more than any other person in his life.

He'd no more than told Junie Mae he didn't have time for breakfast when his cell phone rang. Hope shoved hard against his chest. He yanked his cell from his pocket. "Zoey?"

"No, it's me, Lace, I can't get Zoey to answer my calls or texts this morning. I take it you haven't seen her either? Did she tell you what I told her last night about the Golden Flame agave?"

"I haven't heard from her. What's up?"

Quickly, the botanist gave him the rundown on her findings about the Golden Flame agave.

"It's a miracle because the botanicals you collected are the only things we have left of the medicine bundle."

"What do you mean?" She sounded alarmed. "What happened to the artifact?"

"Someone looted it from the camp."

Lace swore colorfully.

Invisible fingers clamped icily around his spine and his mouth went dry. Something in her tone told him more bad news was on the way. "What's wrong?"

"That's not the half of it. Last night, my lab was broken into. That's why I called so early in the morning. Someone took the botanicals, Jericho, and they were the only things stolen."

Her bones felt loose inside her skin, as if all the cartilage and ligaments had liquefied, leaving her skeleton floating and detached. The sleepy golden light of early morning that had followed her from the caverns burned off into alert yellow as she neared foundation land.

Would Jericho be there breaking up camp? Would others be there as well? Or if Jericho was there, would they be completely alone?

C'mon, please be there; be there. No, can't take this. Please do not be there, or if you are there, let other students be there too.

Yeah, okay, flakey Zoey was of two minds about this. What else was new? Both her body and heart ached for him, but her brain was fogged, scared, confused, and *guilty.* God, was she really ready for this?

The road curved, and up ahead loomed the entrance to Triangle Mount. The fence and gate they'd erected to protect the dig site was gone, pulled up. By Jericho and the crew? By Dr. Sinton or maybe one of Winz-

Smith's employees?

Wow. It *was* officially over.

Her throat tightened and she blinked rapidly. Okay. Over. Some things just weren't meant to last. No big deal. Wave good-bye with a smile and move on. New adventures loomed on the horizon. Right?

There was no sign of Jericho's truck.

She parked and got out of the van; walked to the spot where his pickup had sat the night they made love in it. It seemed eons ago now. She ran her fingers over her lips, remembering the feel of his mouth on hers. The warm earth smelled of him, the salty taste of his skin lay vivid on her tongue. A cawing crow flew overhead. A myriad of footprints, going in both directions, covered the ground.

Loneliness choked her, but she managed to swallow it down. She was glad Jericho wasn't here, she needed to investigate her suspicions, see if there was any validity to the realization that had hit her in her dream before she shared it.

The heated wind blew a dusting of sand over her hiking boots. She went to the back of her van, settled her pink straw cowgirl hat on her head, and retrieved her backpack loaded with rough terrain necessities — water, snacks, sunscreen, lip balm, utility tool, and a map of the land. She locked the vehicle, put the keys in her pocket, pushed her sunglasses on her nose, and headed for the lake.

By the time she reached the lake, she was in a full body sweat, but as tempting as it might be to jump in for a swim, she refused the allure, although she did pause a moment to rehydrate and eye the mounds that hid the dirty McCleary family secret.

Poor Clarissa. Poor Little Wolf. Her heart wrenched. She imagined the star-crossed pair in the winter, late at night, running hand in hand through the snow, desperate to escape Clarissa's cruel clan.

In spite of the sun beating down, she shivered.

To her right lay Widow's Peak looming above the mounds. The mountain did not slope steadily upward as the adjacent, but much shorter flatiron, of Triangle Mount, but consisted of jagged ridges and sharp ravines that staggered unevenly up to the bald pinnacle. She thought about how frightening it would have been to scale the rocks, slick with ice and snow, in the pitch black. Even now it was daunting.

Because August McCleary had dedicated the land as a private nature preserve back in the early 1900s, no one but family ever came up here, and even precious few of them. Now she understood why. It wasn't conservation reasons that had led Great-Great-Uncle August to turn this land into a preserve, but rather concealment of the family's ugly sins.

How many of her family members knew about what had been done to Clarissa and Little Wolf and the Keepers of the Flame? Did her cousin Walker know? Had her grandfather Raymond? She hated to believe that of either of them, but clearly Great-Great-Uncle August *had* known what Zachariah McCleary had done, and surely he hadn't gone to his grave keeping the dark secret.

Zoey consulted the map, and then looked up at the top of Widow's Peak. There was no footpath up this mountain. The southernmost route seemed the easiest, but the spot where she was headed was nearer to the north side. Once upon a time, the easy route would have been a no-brainer, but the last few weeks had taught her the value of hard work. The most arduous path held the most reward. Why had it taken her so long to figure out that easy does was not always the best way to go?

Right. North route it was. This was going to take hours, so she might as well get on it.

She ate a handful of walnuts and dried cherries, drank some more water, and took off.

At noon, she stopped halfway up the mountain for another break. She opened her backpack and took out a different map. When she'd first seen it, she hadn't realized it was actually a map. It had only been upon awakening after her troubled dreams the night before that she'd realized Great-Great-Uncle August's doodle had not been a doodle at all, but a map. Relying on memory, she'd copied the doodle as she recalled it from August's formulary.

Two side-by-side triangles, the one on the right slightly taller than the one on the left. The smaller one was Triangle Mount, the larger one Widow's Peak. The narrow oval was the lake. She could see it clearly from where she now stood looking back down in the valley below, and the lake looked just like a blue almond. And from this vantage point, the two mounds of the old McCleary settlement blended together in a sod arciform curved above the lake like an eyebrow.

The only remaining mystery on the doodle map? What did the dot on Widow's Peak represent? Zoey had a pretty darn good idea what it was. Which was the reason she was up here in the first place.

She ate a PowerBar, wiped melted chocolate on the seat of her pants, and climbed higher. The terrain grew rockier, and several times she slipped and was forced to grab for whatever handhold she could find to keep her upright. Working on Triangle Mount for the past couple of weeks had acclimated her to the higher altitude, so she wasn't short of breath, but she was getting a workout.

By two o'clock she was nearing the peak. At one point, she thought she'd heard someone following her, but it turned out to be a clueless armadillo waddling through the brush behind her. The mesquites had given way to aspen and madrones. From her peripheral vision, she caught a glimpse of something through a clot of madrones. She stopped, backtracked a few feet, and took another look.

It was a cabin.

Hmm. No one had ever told her about a cabin on Widow's Peak Mountain. Then again, no one had ever told her about a McCleary settlement either. What if the dot on the map represented this cabin instead of what she thought it represented? Well, that was a new wrinkle. She took out the doodle map. Yep. The cabin was just about in the location of the dot. She changed directions, stopping her ascent to take a lateral path through the madrones.

A jackrabbit leaped up in front of her. Startled, Zoey gasped, plastered a hand over her chest, and felt her heart gallop. "Jeez Louise, calm the hell down," she growled under her breath.

She picked her way along the ridge. The cabin was constructed on a narrow plateau and she had to pick her way over a tangle of thorny undergrowth to reach it. Brambles tugged at her clothing, clutch at her skin. One thorn cut a long scratch across the back of her hand, brought blood. "Ouch!"

A cloud passed over the sun, temporarily darkening the afternoon and casting the cabin in deep shadows. A blue jay screeched from one of the madrones, just as her face made contact with a spider. She pawed the sticky web from her cheek and spat it from her lips as her pulse did a series of wind sprints.

The cabin was made of untreated cedar, the logs gray and weathered. Stepping stones led up to the door and some of them were littered with raccoon scat. Who would build a cabin way up here on such a precarious slab of rock? Come out the door, take a wrong turn, and you'd be off the side of a cliff.

Cautiously, she proceeded to the door that

was held closed by four horizontal wooden blocks nailed into the door frame. She had to stand up on tiptoes to reach the first block and turn it vertically. She slipped off her backpack to make the endeavor easier. The block was stiff and reluctant to give. She had to jump up and smack with the heel of her palm several times before the wood yielded. The next three blocks were equally stubborn, the wood swollen over the years to hold fast the door. Who would have thought four blocks of wood could be more secure than a padlock?

Finally, she had all four blocks of wood turned vertically and she pulled at the rusty wooden handle. It refused to budge. Frustrated, she planted one foot on the left door frame, the other on the right, and yanked with all her might.

The door blasted open, flinging Zoey onto her back on one of the stepping stones and landing her right on top of the raccoon poop.

Eeew!

Thank God it was dried up. She wrestled out of her T-shirt and tossed it over the porch rail. Good thing she always kept a change of clothes in her backpack. She shimmied out of her jeans and tossed it alongside the T-shirt, dug a fresh T-shirt and cargo shorts from her backpack, and put them on.

There now. She dusted her palms together. Where was she?

The cabin door yawned open. Inside it was dim and musty, dust motes dancing like flakes in an up-ended snow globe on a tiny shaft of light slanting in through a single grimy window.

Tentatively, she stepped over the threshold. The boards creaked ominously beneath her hiking boots. There were several holes in the boards gnawed out by one sort of critter or another throughout the years. It was one small room with a lopsided table sitting in the middle of the floor and one bottomless chair.

That was it.

Blinking, Zoe turned in a circle just in case she was missing something. Well, hell, this was not what she had been expecting to find.

When she'd awakened that morning, her insight had seemed so crystal clear that she hadn't doubted her supposition for a moment, but now, standing here in the midst of a rotted-out cabin, she felt both sheepish and silly. When she'd realized that the doodle was a map, she'd really thought she was on to something. So much for her puzzle-solving skills. Honestly, she'd believed the dot on August McCleary's doodle map represented the location of the yellow flame agave.

Color my face red. Good thing she hadn't told anyone else what she'd suspected.

Now what?

Get yourself back down the mountain before it gets dark, dumbass.

Right. She turned to go, but as she did, she stepped onto one of the holey boards and her boot went right through the floor.

After leaving Triangle Mount, Jericho went to Lace's lab. The cops were there taking her statement and dusting for fingerprints. Since he was already there, Jericho went ahead and told the police officers about the medicine bundle that had been looted from the dig site. That turned into a rigmarole that involved an icy Skype call with Dr. Sinton and took much longer than Jericho anticipated. When the officers asked him whom he suspected could have taken the medicine bundle, he hesitated. He had no proof Catrina had taken it, and all the fingerprints lifted from Lace's lab belonged to either her, Pierce, her assistant, or other close family members, including Zoey.

"So any of the students could have stolen

the artifact," the police officer said.

"Actually, anyone at all could have done so. When we took Avery to the hospital, everyone left the dig site," Jericho admitted. "In retrospect, it was very stupid of me to leave the artifact unattended, but I was so worried about Avery and Braden that it slipped my mind. It was a confusing morning."

"Even Miss McCleary could have taken it," Dr. Sinton said over the computer. "In fact, she quit the dig that same day."

"As did four other students," Jericho reminded him. "Zoey did not take the artifact."

"How can you be so certain?" asked the lead police officer. "We did find her fingerprints in the lab."

"Zoey didn't take the artifact," Lace backed him up. "She would never do something like that."

"The jury is still out on that," Dr. Sinton said.

It took Jericho another two hours to finally track down Catrina, and he found her quite by accident as she was slipping out the back entrance of the Cupid Museum. He slammed on the brakes, did a U-turn, and went after her.

Catrina's eyes widened and she looked

like she was about to take off at a dead sprint, but she was dragging a wheeled suitcase and carrying a shoulder bag. Indecision warred on her face and he could see her mental gears clicking on whether to abandon her possessions for a shot at freedom or not.

Jericho stopped in the middle of the street, and bulleted from his pickup. "Don't move!"

The young woman clutched the wide strap of her shoulder bag with both hands, and froze.

"Hold it right there," he said, striding toward her. "I've got a bone to pick with you."

Catrina's eyes widened. She dropped her bag, spun on her heels, and took off at a dead sprint.

"Seriously?" he called. "You're really going to make me run in cowboy boots?"

Using her bare hands, and getting a painful splinter underneath her fingernail in the process, Zoey pried up the rotten boards trapping her foot. She pulled her foot free and that's when she saw a brown glass bottle stoppered with a cork.

Maybe it was vintage whiskey. Aged hooch? What luck. Right now, she could use a stiff drink.

She picked up the bottle but it was very light. No liquid in it. Evaporated most likely. Bummer. Just her luck.

But as she was about to toss the bottle into a corner, she realized there *was* something inside of it after all and held it up to the light. It was a rolled up piece of paper. Message in a bottle? Maybe not as good as whiskey, but interesting nonetheless. Her hair fell across her face, and she flipped it back over her shoulder. She was going to need something to pry the cork from the end of the bottle.

Taking care to skirt the iffy boards, Zoey eased back outside to retrieve the utility knife from her backpack. The late afternoon sun had brought a cool breeze with it. She slipped on her hooded sweatshirt and as she zipped it up, she heard a crinkle of paper in the pocket. She stuck her hand inside to investigate and pulled out the letter to Cupid she'd written the night before. It reminded her of Jericho. Would they be able to straighten things out between them? Pocketing the letter, she hoped so.

The cork quality had deteriorated over the years so there was no using the corkscrew. She had to dig it out with the knife blade, which seemed to take forever. By the time she freed the scroll of paper, flecks of musky-smelling cork littered her clothing.

The paper was yellowed and brittle. It took a great deal of care to unroll the paper without breaking off pieces of it. The first thing she saw was a date at the top of the page. A hundred years ago to the exact month and year.

Below the date was a chemical symbol much like the one in August McCleary's formulary, but this one was slightly different. Beside the symbol was the drawing of a plant in bloom. It looked just like the plant on the beaded medallion Granny Helen had given Jericho and the one sewn into the medicine bundle.

Zoey sucked in her breath.

This was an illustration of the Golden Flame agave.

Underneath the sketch of the plant was a third drawing that appeared to be a map of Widow's Peak Mountain with X marking a spot not far from the north face of the pinnacle.

Scrawled at the bottom of the page was another date — of the current month and year.

Zoey's mind whirled, playing with patterns, conjuring up *what ifs*, filtering through everything she'd learned and discovered over the past few weeks. Suddenly, she knew without a shred of doubt that this was the *real* formula Great-Great-Uncle August had used to cure the Spanish flu, with the Golden Flame agave as the key ingredient, and that if she followed the map it would lead her to the location of the century plant.

Her cousin Lace had been correct in her calculations. The rare agave did indeed exist, and according to this piece of paper, it could bloom at any moment.

Chapter 22

Rescue archaeology: The swift excavation and collection of artifacts at sites in immediate danger of destruction.

Gobsmacked, Zoey staggered from the cabin. It was four-thirty. Sunset was around nine o'clock. If she tried to find the Golden Flame today, she'd end up stuck on the mountain overnight. No way was she dumb enough to hike down in the dark.

She shouldered her backpack, looked to the peak, and then back at the cabin, then down the mountain she would have to traverse, and then back to the peak again. Hmm, what to do? Too bad her cell phone didn't work out here or she'd call and tell Jericho what she was up to.

Jericho.

Could she still just pick up the phone and call him the way she used to do? Was that lost to her forever?

Zoey gulped. She couldn't think about that now. Feeling like Scarlett letting Rhett go until tomorrow, she raised her chin and squared her shoulders. *You've come this far, might as well commit all the way.*

"Golden Flame, here I come," she sang out and struck out for her goal.

The spot on the map wasn't all that far from the cabin, but it was over especially rugged terrain — the climb was steeper, the rocks craggier, and the vegetation rougher. It was downright chilly too. Wind gusted against her, whipped her hair into her face with stinging lashes. She zipped her sweatshirt all the way up to her neck, pulled up her hoodie, and tied the string.

At some point, she heard more rustling behind her, but she was on too precarious of a rocky perch to look around. What if it was a javelina? How high up in the mountains did javelinas range? She should have paid more attention when people tried to tell her naturey stuff like this. *Please don't let it be a javelina. Please don't let it be a javelina.* Um, what if it was a mountain lion? Or even a wolf?

"Please let it be another armadillo, please let it be another armadillo," she chanted.

To kept from freaking herself out, she started singing Kelly Clarkson's "Stronger," but then belatedly she realized it wasn't just about being tough, but about being tough after a breakup and that made her think of Jericho and damn if she didn't get something in her eyes. Plus her nose was stuffy too. Must be allergic to some damn pollen up here.

Focus. Keep going.

It took almost an hour to reach her destination. An area flanked by thick rows with prickly pear cactus. Zoey glanced toward the sky. "Seriously, it had to be prickly pears?"

Don't be a whiner. It's better than rattlesnakes.

Point taken.

Okay. She rubbed her palms together to warm them. Where was this Golden Flame thingamajig growing? Somewhere in the midst of rocks and prickly pears? The crumbly limestone outcropping she treaded was no more than four feet wide.

Gingerly, she high-stepped her way over the paddle-shaped cacti with three-inch-long thorns sticking out of them. Sharp tips caught her here, there, everywhere as if a tiny Zorro was making his mark on her skin. Okay, seriously, clomping around knee-deep in prickly pears atop an unreliable rock ledge really should qualify as some level of

Dante's Hell. Maybe *Inferno* the prologue?

Keeping her gaze on the ground — both to prevent herself from turning into a human pincushion and to search for the agave — she tramped around the side of another rocky protuberance and then another; it was beginning to look like a rock maze with a prickly pear carpet. She slipped around one more tall slender rock shaped like a shoulder blade and boom!

There it was.

The Golden Flame.

Blooming like a son of a bitch.

Blue-green, spiky, tonguelike blades, which resembled the leaves of most other species of agave, jutted skyward. From the center of the leaves grew a thick butter-colored stalk about the width and sturdiness of a broom handle, rising six feet into the air. On the end of the stalk proliferated a single lemon yellow head that was flush with fuzzy flowers, giving it the appearance of an oversized bottle-brush.

Holy macaroni and Yankee Doodle hooha! She had found it!

Lace would pee herself over this. Zoey wasn't a botanist and she was pretty darn impressed. Speechless, she reached around for her backpack, to pluck out her camera and get a picture of this sucker before the light was gone, when she heard the snap of a twig on the ridge above her.

She froze, her blood running cold; two words branded the inside of her forehead so that she could read them like a movie marquis — "MOUNTAIN LION."

Slowly, she turned her head, terrified that she was going to find a very big cat lounging overhead. When she saw the man, she was almost relieved. Except the pistol in his hand caused a ripple of concern to spread through her stomach. She recognized him. He was Marcus Winz-Smith's bodyguard.

"Hi!" she said inanely, as if she did not see the gun pointed straight at her. "Are you lost?"

"On the contrary," said a voice from behind the back of the freezer-sized bodyguard. "Hallelujah, we're found." Winz-Smith, still managing to look quite dapper in hiking gear instead of his tailored suit, stepped into view.

Huh?

Slowly, Winz-Smith started clapping his hands in that way people do when they're applauding sarcastically. *Clap. Clap. Clap.* The punitive sound echoed down the valley. "Aren't you a smart little thing, Cousin Zoey? They all underestimated you, but not me. I knew you'd find the Golden Flame, but you know what they say." He clucked his tongue. "Curiosity killed the cat."

Zoey wasn't sure what was going on here, but the hairs on the back of her neck were standing out stiff as the thorns on the prickly pear cactus surrounding her.

"Here's what's going to happen," Winz-Smith said. "Adrian —"

"Who's that?"

The bodyguard grunted.

"Don't interrupt," Winz-Smith said. "Adrian here is going to throw down a rope to you and you're going to use it to climb up here with us."

"And if I say no?"

"Then I'll tell Adrian to shoot you."

Obligingly, Adrian aimed the gun directly at her head.

"Rope it is then," she said.

Winz-Smith handed the bodyguard a rope. Adrian looped one end around the trunk of an aspen, tied it securely and tossed the other end down to her. It dangled like a snake in front of her face. Her upper body strength wasn't all that hot, but if she couldn't pull herself up to the ledge where Winz-Smith and Adrian were standing, she'd fall back into a heinous bed of prickly pear and probably get shot to boot for her troubles.

The rope stung her hands, but failure wasn't an option. Winz-Smith and Adrian both were leaning over watching her climb up. Directly behind and straight up above them, the top of Widow's Peak narrowed to a point.

The aspen bent against her weight. They were not thick trees. Good thing she was small. She moved one hand over the other, grasped, tugged, moved the next hand up, grasped and tugged.

"You're getting there," Winz-Smith said. "Don't look down."

"Thanks for the tip."

"Hey, I do what I can."

Her mind galloped. What was he doing here and why was he having his goon aim a firearm at her? Clearly, he was after the Golden Flame, but why did he have to be all gangsta about it?

When she was almost up to the ledge where they were standing, Adrian reached down, grabbed her by the scruff of her hoodie, and lugged her the rest of the way up. He deposited her in front of Winz-Smith, who was now holding the bodyguard's gun, took hold of the rope, and started rappelling down it with the ease of Spider-Man riding a web in spite of the groaning aspen.

"Impressive," she said.

"He used to work for Blackwater. Just FYI," Winz-Smith commented.

"Is that supposed to scare me?"

"You're stupid if it doesn't."

"Alrighty then." Zoey huddled inside her sweatshirt. The wind was a killer up here and she didn't really know what she was supposed to do now. What was the protocol when dealing with a distant cousin who was holding you at gunpoint? Surely small talk was neither expected nor required.

She couldn't resist peering over the edge to see what Adrian was up to. He plowed through the prickly pears like he was walking through cotton balls. He pulled some kind of container from the black flak vest he wore, opened it up, and started pouring liquid all over the Golden Flame. The scent drifted up, assailed her nose.

Gasoline.

The hairs on the nape of her neck were ice picks now, frozen cold and razor-sharp. She spun back around to face Winz-Smith. "He's going to burn the Golden Flame?"

"You are a bright little thing, aren't you?"

She blinked. "Bu-but why? It's got the power to cure the flu!"

"Precisely." Winz-Smith nodded.

"I . . ." She shook her head vigorously. "I

don't understand."

"I'm in the business of manufacturing Flugon. The medication shortens the duration of the flu, but doesn't cure it. Therefore when people get the flu the first thing they do is run to their doctor for a prescription of Flugon. If we cure the flu, then poof . . ." He snapped his fingers. "My empire goes up in smoke as quickly as that plant Adrian is setting fire to."

She hazarded another glance down at Adrian, who was putting flame to gasoline.

A loud *whoosh* ignited. Heat blistered all the way up to where they were standing. Mr. Badass Bodyguard had sidestepped just far enough away to keep from being singed. Clearly, he'd done this before.

Zoey drank in a sense of loss so strong it flooded her entire body. The precious Golden Flame would soon be completely destroyed. The elixir that Little Wolf and Clarissa had died for would be no more.

"How did you know about the Golden Flame?" she asked as her mind scrambled for some way out of this. Behind her was a drop-off, Adrian, a fire, and prickly pear cactus. To the right was another drop-off. Winz-Smith was standing to her left, and straight head of her was the sheer cliff to the top.

"It's the dark family secret." Winz-Smith's grim smile stretched tight across his teeth. "As you found out."

"Who in the family knows?" she exclaimed.

"Not many are privy to the knowledge that Zachariah McCleary stole the Golden Flame from the Keepers of the Flame and allowed them to die from the flu his people brought into their midst. Zach was a heartless son of a bitch, I'll give him that. Usually only the most alpha of the McCleary males are brought in on the secret. In fact, until you, dear cousin, I must say it's been something of a boys' club. Currently, I'm the only living male in possession of this secret. Me and that crazy old Comanche woman in the nursing home that no one listened to in the first place."

"I listened!"

"Yes, you did. To my gain and your detriment, I might add."

Uneasy fear burrowed deep under her skin, and she cast another glance down at Adrian, who stood with his arms folded over his chest watching the plant burn. Tears came to her eyes. She couldn't believe this was happening.

"So Walker doesn't know either?" She coughed against the acrid air. Gray smoke drifted up from Adrian's fire below.

Winz-Smith shook his head. "If Walker had known he wouldn't have been stupid enough to write a book about August, and now he's gone and drummed up movie interest. He caused me one helluva headache. All it would take was for some movie crew to come here and start poking around in the past to dig up trouble. I was wracking my brain trying to think how I could throw a monkey wrench into Walker's movie deal and then, as if by Providence, you and your boyfriend, Dr. Chance, show up practically begging me to let you excavate Triangle Mount. I admit it took me a few minutes to figure out how to use you to my advantage."

"I am confused why you would allow us on Triangle Mount if you know there was a chance we could stumble across the McCleary secret."

He waggled his index finger at her. "If you'd stayed on Triangle Mount per the contract, it wouldn't have been a problem, but you've got the mind of a magpie. Can't live well enough alone, can you? Of course, that's what I was counting on."

"What are you talking about? Why let us on the land in the first place? If you're trying to hide a big secret?"

He smiled that strange smile again. "Because I had no idea where the Golden Flame was. I had both of August McCleary's formularies of course, so I knew it was the essential healing ingredient in the compound; the rest of the formula, the one that's on display in the museum, is nothing but Flugon, give or take a few ingredients. I'd actually soothed myself with the idea that the Golden Flame was indeed extinct and I had nothing to worry about —"

"And then you read Lace's article," she said, remembering the day she'd met him at the museum and he'd had *American Journal of Botany* rolled up and sticking out of his jacket pocket.

"I realized she was right. That the Golden Flame was still around and the reason no other McClearys had come across it besides August was that it was a true century plant and it was due to bloom in my lifetime." He shrugged. "Adrian and I tried to find it on our own. We traversed up and down this mountain and couldn't identify it. Turns out the Golden Flame looks like any other damn agave until it blooms. So I took a gamble. Figured why not let you excavate Triangle Mount. I had the contract. I could control you and shut down the dig if you wandered off the mountain. If you found something, fine. If you didn't that was fine too, it would keep out those nut jobs who think Triangle Mount is a pyramid. Of course, I had to put a spy in your camp. Had to know what was going on."

"Catrina," Zoey said.

"Catrina." He confirmed with a nod of his head.

"You had her pretend there was a man in black on the mountain, playing off the local lore of *el hombre vestido de negro.*"

"Actually, that was Adrian. He makes a pretty good spook, don't you think?"

"He filed the ladder down, scattered out the tools."

"All a part of the ghostly apparitions. You were finding out too much about the Keepers of the Flame. We needed to scare you off at that point. It worked too. A third of your crew quit. Although we didn't mean for that young man to get an ice pick through his foot. Must admit it made the story juicier."

"You stole the medicine bundle," she accused.

"Catrina did the lifting."

"Under your orders."

"She does work for me. She also broke into Lace Bettingfield's lab and stole the seeds she'd extracted from the medicine bundle."

"The botanicals are all gone?" Zoey's heart fell to the ground.

"Indeed. Once Adrian has pulled up those roots and burned them as well, that's the end of the Golden Flame that sweet Clarissa and her lover Little Wolf planted the night before Zachariah chased them off the mountain."

"You got Jericho fired."

"Oh no, no. You can't lay that off on me. *You* violated the contract fair and square. I was holding my breath hoping you'd revert to type so I could use it as an excuse to close the dig when I was ready and you did not let me down, dear cousin."

"I'm not your dear anything," Zoey spat.

"It's a pity I have to dispose of you." He gave her a sorrowful look that lowered her body temperature twenty degrees.

"Wh-wh-what?" she stammered.

"You really didn't think I could let you leave after all this."

"I won't tell anyone, I swear . . . I . . ." All she could think was *I'll never see Jericho again. Never touch his dear face. Never kiss those amazing lips. Never be able to tell him how very much I do love him.*

"I know you won't," he said, "because you aren't going to leave this mountain alive. But just to show you I'm not a completely heartless bastard, I'll give you a head start to the peak. Adrian is just now coming up the rope."

She glanced over her shoulder to see Adrian halfway up the rise. Should she call Winz-Smith's bluff? He might not have the courage to pull the trigger but she had no doubt in her mind that Adrian did. Either way, if she turned and ran she knew she was going to get shot in the back. If she was going to make a move, it had to be now before his bodyguard topped that rise.

"On your mark," Winz-Smith said. "Get set —"

Before he said "go," Zoey rushed him, shoving Winz-Smith as hard as she could. He shrieked like a girl, stumbled, lost his grip on the gun, and teetered on the edge of the ledge.

She didn't wait around to see if he tumbled over or not. Shucking off her backpack as she ran, she took off up the mountain at a dead sprint.

Minutes later she stood quivering atop Widow's Peak on private land, directly across from Mount Livermore, the very spot where her parents had died more than twenty years earlier.

Not so lucky now, huh, McCleary. Looks like

you've used up the last of your nine lives.

In her hand she crushed the crumpled letter she'd written to Cupid the previous evening. Last night, she thought she'd smacked rock bottom; now she fully understood how much farther she had to fall.

Her pulse beat a hot stampede across her eardrums; she was exposed and vulnerable, stiff with fear, tension strained muscles, sweat slicked skin, nicks and scratches oozed blood, lungs flapped with the excruciating pain of trying to draw in air after a dead run up the mountain.

Heat from the setting summer sun warmed her cheeks. Desert wind whipped through the Davis Mountains, blowing sandy topsoil over her face. She licked her dry lips, tasted grit. On three sides of her yawned sheer drop-off. Overhead, a dozen buzzards circled.

Waiting.

Something tickled her cheek, feather-soft and startling as the sweet sensation of an unexpected midnight kiss. She gasped and brushed at her face, her work-roughened fingertips scratching her skin, and for one crazy moment she thought, *Jericho.*

But of course it wasn't Jericho. It was merely the caress of a passing cloud. He was still warm in their bed where she should be, but her impulsiveness had driven her here before she'd had a chance to tell him she loved him as more than just a friend, and now she'd never have that chance.

She put her palm to her lips, kissed it, whispered, "Jericho," and blew the kiss into the gathering mist. "I'll love you throughout all eternity."

From behind her, she heard her pursuers crashing through the aspen and madrone trees, cursing black ugly threats. They were coming for her. This was it, the end of the trail, the end of the world, the end of *her,* and nowhere left to go but down.

The thundering footsteps were nearer now, closing in. Soon, her trackers would emerge from the forest and join her on the skinned, igneous peak.

Her heart took flight, faster than a humming-bird and thudding with jumpy brutality. Panic shuddered her bones. She could not stop trembling no matter how hard she willed it.

Directly below her lay the burned remains of the Golden Flame, all that was left now was a patch of scorched earth. She imagined Little Wolf and Clarissa burying the seeds of the Golden Flame in that spot before they too had made the same futile rush up to the mountaintop. Such a tragedy, but at least they'd been together. She was completely alone.

Oh Jericho, I sure screwed this up.

Teeth chattered. Knees wobbled. Nostrils flared.

Don't just stand there. Do something! Do something!

But what? There was only one solution, only one clear way out. Zoey gathered her courage, took her last deep breath, and jumped.

Chapter 23

Absolute dating: A dating method that attempts to determine an object's exact age in calendar years or in years before present.

"Hurry, hurry," Jericho urged the helicopter pilot who'd agreed to fly him to the top of Widow's Peak.

"I'm not going to be able to land up there, you understand," the pilot said. "That mountain's too craggy, and besides, it's on private land."

"Just go, man!" After he'd found Catrina, he'd taken her to the Cupid police. She'd admitted taking the medicine bundle, but it had taken hours of interrogation before she confessed her full role as Marcus Winz-Smith's spy in the camp. The police had backed off a bit then. Winz-Smith wielded a lot of power, and all they had was the word of a pretty foreign exchange student against a pharmaceutical CEO and native son.

Frustrated and still unable to reach Zoey, Jericho had become more and more concerned. He went back to Triangle Mount and found the Cupid's Rest van parked there. He'd known instantly something was wrong. He didn't have the time to search for her on foot so he'd asked Lace to call the family and get them out searching foundation land while he arranged for a helicopter search of the area.

"It's almost sunset," the pilot said. "I don't like to be out in the dark."

"Fly, dammit!" A hundred horrible scenarios beat against his brain, but he brushed them off, determined not to borrow trouble. He had to stay calm and effective, for Zoey's sake.

The pilot zoomed over Triangle Mount dotted with search and rescue teams composed mainly of Zoey's family. She was a lucky woman to have so many people who loved her. Then again, who wouldn't love her? She was the most genuinely warm and open person he'd ever known.

The pilot buzzed closer to Widow's Peak. Jericho spied two men out in the open. One was Winz-Smith, the other his bodyguard, and they both held weapons.

And at the very top of the peak stood

Zoey, but only for a brief second. One minute she was there, the next she was gone.

Stunned, Jericho could only stare.

"She jumped!" the pilot cried. "She jumped off the mountain!"

Every muscle in Jericho's body turned to stone. He could not believe what his eyes had just seen. "No!" he said adamantly. "No!"

"Those guys had guns!" The pilot gasped. "They were chasing her. I'm radioing law enforcement."

"She's okay," Jericho said. "Zoey is *not* gone."

"Man, are you blind? She jumped off the fucking cliff to get away from those sons of bitches."

He reminded himself of the time when she was fourteen and jumped off Telescope Cliff and into Tranquility Pool. He'd been so scared then, but he wasn't scared now. She had to be okay. He could not — would not — lose her. If something happened to her, he'd purposely hunt down Winz-Smith and tear his limbs from his body with his bare hands.

The pilot zoomed over the heads of Winz-Smith and his bodyguard who were now sliding down the hill for the cover of madrones and flew past the peak where Zoey had jumped.

"Omigod," the pilot yelled.

"What is it?" Frantically, Jericho peered out his window trying to see what the pilot was talking about. What he saw turned his organs to liquid.

There, in the golden glow from the setting sun, was Zoey, hanging on to a thin rope attached to a bent aspen, and dangling over a steep drop-off. She was alive, but for how long?

"Can you land up here?"

"I've never done it before —"

"If we don't try something, she's going to die."

"Yeah, okay, let's do it. I'll see if I can set her down, but the wind from the blades could shake her loose."

"Just get me close enough to where I can jump out."

"What if you break a leg?" Sweat poured down the pilot's face.

"I won't," Jericho said grimly and opened the door.

The pilot nodded and angled the helicopter as close as he could to the top of Widow's Peak. It was a good five-foot drop. "This is the best I'm going to do. Already that aspen she's dangling from is shaking like a toothpick."

Jericho coiled his muscles, readied himself for the jump. "Here I go," he yelled, and pushed himself through the door. He landed in a crouched position on top of the rock, let the shock of impact jar up his knees and into his hip, but he had no concern for his own pain. All he could think about was Zoey. He had to save her. She was barely clinging to life.

The chopper spun away, leaving him to race as fast as he could to the edge of the cliff. He splayed out on his belly. Zoey was just out of arm's reach.

"Jericho!" she cried, her face turned up to his.

"Zoe-Eyes, whatever you do, don't let go," he gasped, trying to figure how he was going to get down the four feet of the sheer rock face to the narrow ledge where the weary aspen was bent almost completely over. He could jump, but if he landed wrong, he could knock her loose; he could turn, go down the mountain a bit, and find a place to come at this from a different angle, but there wasn't enough time.

"Jericho," she whimpered.

"I'm here."

"I don't know if I can hold on."

"Of course you can hold on," he said. "You're the toughest woman I know."

He had to jump down. There was simply no other way. If she let go of that rope before he got to her, he was just going to go into the abyss right after her.

Bracing himself, he dropped one leg over, then the other, and hit with an impact that made the first one seem like a game of hopscotch in comparison. His teeth jammed together and he bit his tongue. His knees buckled, but he shook it off. He'd made it. Granted, he was standing on about a two-foot chunk of crumbly rock, but at least he was beside the aspen. He went down on his belly again, ignoring the sharp stones and prickly thorns. He slapped one hand around her first wrist, one hand around the second.

"I gotcha, babe."

"Jericho," she said, looking so deeply into his eyes he knew she was seeing straight into his scared-stiff soul. "I love you."

"You sure you're not just saying that 'cause I'm going to keep you from breaking every bone in that pretty little body of yours?"

"Well," she said, keeping her sense of humor in spite of everything. "There is that, but no, I loved you long before this."

"You say that now," he said, hauling her up and over the rock. He heard her wince, felt the pain twist up her muscles. "But will you still love me tomorrow?"

He toppled backward into the side of the mountain. Zoey tumbled atop him. They lay against each other, breathing heavily, both knowing it was nothing short of a miracle that they were breathing at all.

"Jericho Hezekiah Chance, I'll love you to the end of time."

Getting down from the mountain took some doing, and it was after midnight by the time they limped into the emergency room at Cupid General Hospital, surrounded by an army of family and friends. They were a mess, both of them, covered in dirt and grime, bearing bloody scratches and scrapes and rope burns.

But they were alive and together and it felt glorious.

Jericho caught a glimpse of his reflection in the glass doors. His hair stuck out in a hundred directions and Zoey reached up to pluck grass from the dark strands in the possessive way of a lover. She was his lover, after all. She had every right to groom him. He paid her back in kind, dusting grass off the seat of her pants.

A nurse came in to separate them in different examining rooms, but they refused to be parted and she finally gave up. Jericho recognized her as the nurse Zoey had tried to fix him up with at Walker's autographing party.

The nurse sank her hands on her hips. "The least you can do is get on separate gurneys."

They agreed but as the nurse took the blood pressure in his left arm, Jericho reached out across the space between the gurneys to take Zoey's hand. He never wanted to let her go ever again. He could not believe how close he'd come to losing her. The idea of it made him sick all over.

"I need to take your temperature," the nurse said. "You're shivering."

"I'm fine," he said brusquely. "Look after her."

"She's got a nurse of her own," his nurse said. "Now hold still."

For the first time, he noticed Zoey did have a nurse buzzing around her. He'd been so busy looking at her he hadn't seen anything else.

After what seemed an eternity, the nurses left them alone, still holding hands. Zoey ran an abraded thumb over his knuckles swathed with a dozen cuts.

"You saved my life," she whispered.

"Correction. You saved mine."

"How do you figure?"

"If you'd jumped off that cliff without a plan, I would have died right along with you."

"It was a damn thin one, but the only plan I had. It was either jump and try to reach the rope Winz-Smith's bodyguard had tied to that aspen in order to rappel down and burn the Golden Flame, or let them fill me full of lead."

"I still can't believe your cousin was willing to kill you."

"All for money," she said. "He couldn't afford to let me go and risk exposing the McCleary family's ugly secret, and he couldn't let people find out about the Golden Flame. If the agave could be cultivated and used to cure the influenza virus, Flugon would be worthless."

"It's all over for the bastard now."

A long moment passed between them when they said nothing, just held hands.

"I'm sorry," she apologized, "that I couldn't tell you that I loved you when you needed to hear it. Don't think it was because I wasn't sure of my feelings for you. On that score I've never been more certain of anything in my life. It's that I was unsure of my feelings about *me.*"

"Meaning?"

"I didn't know if I could be the kind of

woman you deserved."

"I lied when I said I didn't have any expectations, because I do have expectations of you, Zoey McCleary. I expect you to want to be with me the way I want to be with you."

"I do, Jericho, I do!"

The door opened and Dr. Sinton walked in. Zoey tightened her grip on Jericho's hand. Jericho's gut tightened. What did the man want?

"I'm glad to see that you two survived the ordeal you've been through," the director said. "I just wanted to say I'm sorry I jumped the gun and fired you, Jericho, and I hope you'll consider taking your job back. No probation this time."

"I'll consider it," Jericho said. Not sure what he wanted to do about his career. Right now, just being here with Zoey was enough.

"And Zoey." The director turned to her. "I don't accept your resignation from the dig. There's a lot more work to be done out there."

"Oh," she said. "Okay."

"Heal quickly," Dr. Sinton said. "We've got a lot to talk about when you're up and about."

As soon as he left, Zoey's cousin, Deputy

Calvin Greenwood, came into the room to take their full statements. When they were done, he shut off his tablet computer. "We've arrested Winz-Smith and his bodyguard. They've both lawyered up. Admitted nothing. About what you'd expect. But Catrina did confirm she destroyed the medicine bundle at Winz-Smith's behest. I'm sorry, but the artifact is gone."

"We still have the tomahawk," Zoey told Jericho. "That's something."

"Yeah, but any evidence of the Golden Flame is gone."

"Maybe there's another plant out there somewhere. Just imagine if we really could wipe out influenza."

"It's still a possibility," Lace said from the doorway. "While my lab was broken into and the botanicals stolen, the thieves didn't realize I had samples under the microscope. There's enough there to clone."

"That would be amazing," Zoey said. "You're going to be famous."

"We're all going to be famous," Lace said. "This is a find of a lifetime."

Jericho turned his head and looked straight into Zoey's eyes. "Yes, she is," he said. "Yes, she is."

A week later, Zoey and Jericho made plans

to meet back up at the dig site. Their injuries were minor and they were recovering quickly. Dr. Sinton had sent out a crew to set up the camp. The old dig team had been reassembled and everyone, except for Catrina, who'd been sent back to Portugal, was returning after the upcoming Fourth of July holiday.

Instead of picking her up, Jericho had told her to meet him on Triangle Mount at ten A.M. on the Fourth of July. She arrived, but did not see his pickup there. Restlessly, she walked up to the dig site.

"Hello, Zoe-Eyes." Jericho stood in the middle of the dig, a plethora of archaeological tools at the ready and a large cardboard box beside him. An irascible cowlick had escaped from under his battered straw cowboy hat and flopped devilishly over his forehead. The sleeves of his cream-colored shirt were rolled up and waterproof markers stuck out of the left front pocket. He was a devastating contrast of scholar and adventurer.

She couldn't breathe. She wanted to run to him, throw her arms around his neck, hang on tight for dear life, and never let go, but she'd learned her lesson about curbing her impulsiveness. No more simply reacting. First, she'd fully think things through before she made a move.

He took her breath, just as surely as if their pairing had been one of those love-at-first-sight lightning strikes her family loved to romanticize, except what they had was so much better. They knew each other inside and out. They'd started from a strong base of friendship and it had bloomed into the best kind of passionate love.

Jericho looked at her with certain eyes, a lifetime of love in those dark depths. The sun glistened off his raven hair and high, proud cheekbones.

All these years she'd feared being deprived or trapped in pain. Maybe it came from losing her parents or watching her sister, Natalie, go through so much struggle and pain to come back from the debilitating injuries she'd suffered in the plane crash. Maybe it was because her family had pampered and spoiled her and she'd grown too accustomed to that velvet royal treatment.

Her very human desire to be happy had deteriorated into frenetic escapism — through repeatedly changing careers and dating guy after guy after guy, getting serious about none, and flitting from one interest to the next, never settling on any one thing for long. She was always anticipating what she was going to do next instead of enjoying what she had in her hand. Her impulsive pleasure seeking had brought upon her the very thing she'd feared — pain and unhappiness.

Until archaeology.

Until Jericho.

Until she finally accepted what her heart had known all along. Digging down deep, looking for those roots had made her focused and profound, and for one blissful night, with Jericho, she'd skipped through the stars, drunk from the Milky Way, slid down the moon into the utmost pleasure of all.

"Walker decided not to take my trust money away," she said. "Considering everything we've gone through, he said he understood why I quit. And hey, I'm back again."

"Anything new on the movie front? I imagine Walker was worried that when word got out about what Winz-Smith had done, it would ruin the movie deal."

"It didn't ruin it at all." Zoey smiled. "It's set to go full steam ahead. Great-Great-Uncle August came out smelling like a rose. Seems he felt so terribly guilty over what our ancestors did that he dedicated his life to trying to eradicate influenza, but he ran out of Golden Flame shortly after the Spanish flu outbreak in 1918. That's why he hid the map to where the Golden Flame was so that someone like Marcus couldn't find it and misuse or destroy the plant."

"Score one for Great-Great-Uncle August."

"So all the blood that runs through my veins isn't bad."

"Nothing about you is bad, Zoey," he said. "You can't help it if you had an unsavory relative."

"Zachariah was more than unsavory. He was mean and cruel."

Jericho pulled an envelope from his back pocket. "I got the results back."

Her heart flopped into her throat. While they were at the hospital, Jericho had asked if he could have his DNA tested so they could compare it to the hair he'd found on the tomahawk in hopes it could show if Granny Helen was right and he did descend from the Keepers of the Flame.

"It might not be a historic hair," he said. "In fact, it could have been my own. Wouldn't that be a laugh?"

"You didn't open it already?"

"No," he said. "I wanted to wait for you."

She climbed down the ladder into the pit with him. "I'm here. Open it."

He blew out his breath, slipped his finger underneath the sealed envelope. He stood there reading it for so long that Zoey thought she was going to explode.

"Well?"

"There's a lot of stuff here about markers and haplotypes and alleles. Since we don't know Little Wolf's surname and can't provide a genealogical paper trail, it can't be considered fully conclusive, but my DNA matches the markers twenty-four out of twenty-five."

"Which means?"

He raised his head, stared into her eyes. "I'm most likely related to Little Wolf, if that's his hair we found on the tomahawk."

"And I know I'm related to Clarissa."

"Two related sets of friends who became lovers."

"Except we did not die on that mountain."

He came toward her. "No, we did not."

"I feel like they're living on through us."

"They are."

"I think Little Wolf and Clarissa would approve."

"I know they would." He swept her into his arms and kissed her.

She kissed him back with everything she had in her.

He broke the kiss after a long moment. "Before we get too carried away," he said, "I've got something for you."

"A surprise? For me?" She giggled, feeling light as a schoolgirl.

"Uh-huh."

"What is it?"

"Close your eyes."

She closed her eyes. Heard a rustling noise and a soft mewling. Her eyes flew open as Jericho put a Siamese kitten in her hand. "Eggy?"

"Not Eggy," he said. "Eggy Two. I got him at the animal shelter."

"Oh Jericho! He's beautiful." She wrapped an arm around Jericho's neck and kissed him again.

"You've proven beyond a shadow of a doubt you can stick with whatever you set your mind to."

"I set my mind to sticking with you. And Eggy Two and archaeology and —"

"It's okay. You don't have to convince me. I was there. I saw how you kept digging to unearth the truth." He wrapped his arm around her.

The kitten snuggled in the curve of her neck and began to purr. Jericho kissed the top of her head, and Zoey's heart filled to bursting.

"You know," he whispered, "friends do make the very best of lovers."

And as she gazed into the eyes of her

beloved, Zoey McCleary knew that for her, it was absolutely true.

The employees of Thorndike Press hope you have enjoyed this Large Print book. All our Thorndike, Wheeler, and Kennebec Large Print titles are designed for easy reading, and all our books are made to last. Other Thorndike Press Large Print books are available at your library, through selected bookstores, or directly from us.

For information about titles, please call:

(800) 223-1244

or visit our Web site at:

http://gale.cengage.com/thorndike

To share your comments, please write:

Publisher
Thorndike Press
10 Water St., Suite 310
Waterville, ME 04901